Children's Literature

Volume 24

Volume 24

Annual of
The Modern Language Association
Division on Children's Literature
and The Children's Literature
Association

Yale University Press

New Haven and London

1996

Children's Literature

The editors gratefully acknowledge support from Hollins College.

Editorial correspondence should be addressed to The Editors, *Children's Literature*, Department of English, Hollins College, Roanoke, Virginia 24020

Manuscripts submitted should conform to the style in this issue. An original on non-erasable bond with two copies, a self-addressed envelope, and return postage are requested. Yale University Press does not accept dot-matrix printouts, and it requires double-spacing throughout text and notes. Unjustified margins are required. Writers of accepted manuscripts should be prepared to submit final versions of their essays on computer disk in XyWrite, Nota Bene, or WordPerfect.

Volumes 1–7 of *Children's Literature* can be obtained directly from John C. Wandell, The Children's Literature Foundation, P.O. Box 370, Windham Center, Conn. 06280. Volumes 8–23 can be obtained from Yale University Press, P.O. Box 209040, New Haven, Conn. 06520-9040, or from Yale University Press, 23 Pond Street, Hampstead, London NW3 2PN, England.

Set in Baskerville type by Tseng Information Systems, Inc., Durham, N.C.
Printed in the United States of America by Vail-Ballou Press, Binghamton, N.Y.

Library of Congress catalog card number: 79-66588
ISBN: 0-300-06628-7 (cloth), 0-300-06629-5 (paper); ISSN: 0092-8208

A catalogue record for this book is available from the British Library.

The paper in this book meets the guidelines for permanence and durability of the Committee on Production Guidelines for Book Longevity of the Council on Library Resources.

10   9   8   7   6   5   4   3   2   1

Contents

From the Editor

In this volume two essays on illustrators—the Bewick brothers and Chris Van Allsburg—frame a group of related essays, all but one of which deal with American children's books. Because Hilary Thompson in her essay on the Bewicks discusses the significance of a frame—or its absence—in their woodcuts, it seemed appropriate to use the two essays on illustration as a framing device. Although they are separated, they speak to each other in interesting ways. Thompson argues for both Bewicks' influence on modern conceptions of childhood and the picture book, Joseph Stanton for Van Allsburg's appropriation of surrealistic and "strangely-enough" conventions. But if John Bewick pioneered the integration of text and image that we take for granted in the modern picture book, the unframed vignettes of Thomas Bewick appear to have anticipated Van Allsburg's mysterious illustrations in their ability to encourage the free play of the child reader's imagination.

The redundantly framed woodcuts of John Bewick present a constricted world comparable to that of the dollhouse, as described by Frances Armstrong. Yet as Armstrong goes on to show, the dollhouse can indeed provide a "ludic space," where girls, and even boys, can exercise their imaginations, if not their bodies, as freely as the children portrayed in the vignettes of Thomas Bewick. And some dollhouse scenes, whether deliberately or inadvertently staged, rival Van Allsburg's in their incongruous, subversive, and surreal elements. Armstrong's illuminating, and often humorous, discussion of the way dollhouses inculcate domestic ideology or subvert it, constrain girls or liberate and empower them, introduces many issues in the essays that follow, as well as in Lois Kuznets's *When Toys Come Alive*, reviewed in this volume.

Carolyn Sigler's essay on the American writer Anna Matlack Richards's 1895 version of Lewis Carroll's *Alice* provides a bridge from the British focus of Thompson and Armstrong to the American essays. Just as Armstrong concludes her essay with the description of an Edwardian work that deserves to be much better known, so Sigler makes a strong case for the significance of Richards's *A New Alice*. Like many of the discussions and works discussed in this volume, *A*

New Alice, even more than its prototype, offers a trenchant critique of educational theory and practice, including the then-new kindergarten movement. And by providing *her* Alice, based on her own daughter, with a maternal guide to Wonderland, Richards grants her a freedom that, ironically, Carroll's Alice, who is often forced into the role of mother, never achieves. Just as the dollhouse as stage can confer authorship and authority on the girls who play with it, so the boundaries of the domestic sphere prove elastic and actually become a source of power for Richards's Alice Lee.

Armstrong ends with a discussion of a turn-of-the-century story that could serve as a model for gender relations. In "Professor Green," Diana and her male cousin make of their dollhouse a miniature utopia. Whether Louisa May Alcott's *Little Women* provides such a utopia has been a matter of much recent critical debate. (See, for example, the book reviews in this volume; and recall that Meg refers to her home as a baby-house, the Victorian term for dollhouse.) Musicologist Colleen Reardon, by examining the neglected motif of music in the novel, concludes that both women and men, primarily the musician Laurie, must sacrifice their individuality in order to conform to prescribed gender roles. She does, however, view Jo's marriage more favorably than many commentators, for Professor Bhaer's musicality, and his acceptance of Jo's lack of it, indicate his comparative freedom as an immigrant from such cultural constraints.

With Holly Keller's "Juvenile Antislavery Narrative and Notions of Childhood," we turn from matters of gender to matters of race and to a more drastic form of confinement than the Acts of Enclosure protested by Thomas Bewick or the dollhouse on which Ibsen's Nora slams the door. In this essay Keller introduces us to a neglected body of writing for children and challenges several assumptions about it. Her essay, like those of Anita Clair Fellman and Hamida Bosmajian, also relates to contemporary controversies over history standards in the schools and the role of ideology in American education. Fellman's essay, and the other two on Laura Ingalls Wilder's (and Rose Wilder Lane's) Little House series, examine the values that mother and daughter convey, both consciously and subtextually. Fellman demonstrates how Wilder and Lane shaped Wilder's experience to conform to the prevailing myth of the American frontier. She concludes that the series should be studied as an embodiment of the myth, as part of the history of its construction, rather than as unvarnished truth. Suzanne Rahn's essay, which focuses on a single work in the series, supports the validity of Fellman's thesis but also complicates it, for Rahn sees Wilder and Lane, despite their emphasis on the independent individual, celebrating community as well. Claudia Mills, like Fellman, deals with the entire series but focuses on the moral development of the protagonist, Laura. Taking into account Fellman's thesis, Mills sees Laura, under her parents' tutelage, developing moral autonomy but also what Carol Gilligan has called an ethic of care. Like Rahn, she discerns in the Little House books strands of both individualism and community, but for her the two are inextricably bound up with each other rather than separable as text and subtext.

Finally, Hamida Bosmajian's essay also deals with a renowned series of historical novels. Whereas Wilder and Lane were writing in the 1930s and 1940s about Wilder's childhood in the nineteenth century, Mildred Taylor writes about these two decades from the perspective of the late twentieth century. Like Wilder and Lane, Taylor is concerned with both American and family values, as well as the relationship between the two. (In fact, a fascinating course in American studies, American literature, or social studies could be based on these two series at the middle school, high school, or college level.) Cassie Logan's father, like Laura's, encourages his children "not to depend on anybody else," but the Logans inhabit a world where efforts at self-respecting independence are viewed as defiance and more apt to be punished than rewarded. Thus Cassie cannot, like Laura, uncritically accept such documents as the Declaration of Independence, and her grounds for questioning the authority of her government and its laws are very different from those of Laura's Pa. Holly Keller explains how antislavery writers frequently contrasted the privileges of the white child with the deprivations of the black. In Laura, for all her family's hardships, and Cassie, for all her family's strengths, we see the same contrast.

The essays on American children's literature in this volume provide a tribute to its power to celebrate, perpetuate, interrogate, subvert, expose, and even openly defy cherished myths and deeply entrenched ideological assumptions. Every reader of this volume will be able to relate its contents to contemporary debates over the past, present, and future of our society. As the end of our century—and millennium—rapidly approaches, it is not too early to begin thinking about topics for a special issue in the year 2000. As always, we welcome your suggestions.

Elizabeth Lennox Keyser

Articles

Enclosure and Childhood in the Wood Engravings of Thomas and John Bewick

Hilary Thompson

In the second half of the eighteenth century, two artists, Thomas and John Bewick, became illustrators for a commercial genre of children's books. Although they were brothers, the demands of this market led them in very different directions. The elder, Thomas, worked, stubbornly, in Newcastle upon Tyne, achieving international fame as a wood engraver of children's books and natural histories. The younger, John, headed for London, where he illustrated for John Newbery's successors, the publishers of early children's books.[1] The second died tragically young without achieving his full potential.

The political and social attitudes of the brothers Bewick (particularly regarding the parliamentary Acts of Enclosure at the onset of the Agricultural Revolution),[2] together with their choices of books to illustrate, translate into a revealing contrast in styles of illustration;[3] their joint work foreshadows both the romantic depiction of children as creatures living close to nature and the modern picture book in which image and text are integrated.

One of the techniques that contributes to the elder Bewick's influence on the romanticizing of childhood is, quite simply, the presence (or absence) of a frame, or enclosure, around his wood engravings. Although both brothers created unframed illustrations, Thomas invented and perfected the form of illustration known as the vignette,

I wish to thank Sylvia Gardner at the Opie Collection of the Bodleian Library, the librarians at the Brotherton Library (University of Leeds), the Newcastle Public Library (Pease Collection), the University of New Brunswick Education Resource Center, and the Osborne Collection at the Toronto Public Library for their help and encouragement.
Children's Literature 24, ed. Francelia Butler, R. H. W. Dillard, and Elizabeth Lennox Keyser (Yale University Press, © 1996 Hollins College).

which, always unframed, follows many stories and fables that he illustrated. To examine the import of the choice of frame for the content
of the illustrations is my focus here. For when, and when not, to use
the vignette or the frame is a matter that depends on the depiction
of childhood in the material being illustrated; this, in turn, both reveals and then generates contemporary attitudes toward children and
children's books.

At the same time, the brothers' attitudes to landscape influence
the choice of frame. The changing face of England, from expanses of
common land to framed fields (the patchwork-quilt aerial view with
which we are familiar) was being effected as these illustrators worked.
And, while Thomas was a countryman, John had opted for city life.[4]
Thomas held, and expressed in his unabridged *Memoir* (edited by Iain
Bain), strong opinions on the politics of Enclosure. John was involved
in his work in illustrating for the contemporary children's book market and has left no written commentaries on his political opinions.

Enclosure and the Rural Idyll

Time, place, and socioeconomic factors coincided with talent and
skill to establish the position of the Bewicks in children's literature;
the political situation shaped an artistic response. Yet some editors
and collectors of Thomas Bewick's work, such as Montague Weekley
(1955) and Thomas Hugo (1866), are unsympathetic to his outspoken
political statements in the *Memoir* and edit them out, feeling that they
detract from the matter at hand, namely, the life of the artist.[5] On
the contrary, Edmund Blunden, in his edition of the *Memoir* (1961),
recognizes a valid expression of political opinions from "within the
social tradition of the Yeoman" (Blunden, introduction, pages un-
numbered). The yeoman class of freeholders of land like Bewick's
father, who had afforded Bewick the funds to become an indentured
engraver and thus to gain the status of an artisan, was under much
pressure from the parliamentary Acts of Enclosure against which Bewick writes at some length.[6]

This artist's concern for the changing landscape gives rise to nostalgia for a way of life symbolized by the hard-working but independent
peasantry.[7] Naturally, given his views, Bewick's engravings feed into
the myth of an eighteenth-century domestic rural idyll. His vignettes,
in particular, depict childhood memories of the farm at Cherryburn
and his journeys along the rolling hillsides of the Tyne River valley

from 1767 onward. Bewick's life and some of his illustrations, particularly those accompanying *History of Quadrupeds, History of British Birds,*
and *Fables of Aesop,* typify the rural images of early to mid-eighteenth-
century England that were to prove so persistent in the work of later
poets and historians.[8]

Bewick's strongly held political opinion shaped the conventions as
well as the content of his art, for the best of his illustrations are unframed vignettes depicting his free-ranging childhood experiences
of the unenclosed countryside. Both Bewicks reflect the eighteenth-
century concern for and interest in collections of folklore. John Bewick illustrated both Ritson's collection *Pieces of Ancient Popular Poetry*
and his stories of *Robin Hood,* and Thomas Bewick worked on Bishop
Percy's "The Hermit of Warkworth."

Both Bewicks created engravings for Oliver Goldsmith's "The Deserted Village." In this poem Goldsmith describes the suffering of
rural England caused by the Acts of Enclosure. John Bewick's illustration "The Sad Historian" depicts the "wretched matron" of the
village (37). Like an eighteenth-century bag lady, she is a "widowed,
solitary thing" wrapped in rags. Standing before the plain on which
the ruined village sits, she surveys the "plashy spring" and tests the
ground before her with her cane (36). With similar uncertainty the
displaced people of the countryside faced their future.

Later, in his illustrations for the *Fables of Aesop* (1818), dedicated
to the "Youth of the British Isles," Thomas Bewick's tailpiece for the
fable of "The Mole and Her Dam" (whose moral decries ostentation,
vanity, and affectation) returns gratuitously to the results of the Acts
of Enclosure (fig. 1). This vignette depicts two boys standing outside
a fence and gazing at a cracked tablet set among the trees (fig. 1).
On the tablet we read Goldsmith's lines from "The Deserted Village,"
which reinforce the sense of injustice:

> Ill the land, to hastening ills a prey,
> Where wealth accumulates, and men decay:
> Princes and lords may flourish, or may fade;
> A breath can make them, as a breath has made;
> But a bold peasantry, their country's pride,
> When once destroy'd, can never be supplied.   (32)

The sense of the injustice of the Acts of Enclosure, captured so poi-
gnantly in "The Deserted Village," still concerns Bewick in 1818 and
is woven into the theme of loss expressed by a number of his other

Figure 1. From Thomas Bewick, *Fables of Aesop,* 32.

vignettes in *Fables of Aesop.* This particular sense of the loss of a rural way of life is precipitated by the parliamentary Acts of Enclosure, but it reinforces the general human tendency to mourn the passing of a nonspecific golden age. Frequently such a loss is identified with lack of freedom and the passing of childhood.

Frame and the Enclosure of Childhood

Thomas Bewick set his brother, and his imitators, an example in his life, in his subject matter of natural history, and in his vignette engravings. He talks of his illustrations for children in his memoir: "The extreme interest I had always felt in the hope of administering to the pleasures and amusement of youth, and judging from the feelings I had experienced myself that they would be affected in the same way as I had been, this whetted me up and stimulated me to proceed. In this, my only reward besides, was the great pleasure I felt in imitating nature. That I would ever do any thing to attract the notice of the world, in the manner that has been done, was the farthest thing in my thoughts" (124). His depictions of childhood in the vignettes of the *History of Quadrupeds* (the headpieces being illustrations of the animals) show children at play (fig. 2), free to explore the qualities of

Figure 2. From Thomas Bewick, *History of Quadrupeds* (1800 ed.), 401 (*top*), 21.

mud, of fields and woods, and in proximity with animals. Like many of the framed woodcuts in the broadsides and chapbooks he read as a child, these vignettes have no direct connection with the text in which they appear. They appeal to the child-reader's sense of enjoyment of the image and the adult's nostalgia for lost innocence and lost freedom.

Thus, *Children's Pastimes* (1975), a collection of new prints taken from the original blocks of Thomas Bewick vignettes that had been used as tailpieces in *History of Quadrupeds* and the *History of British Birds* (vols. 1 and 2), draws its seven characteristic tailpieces from among the many tailpieces based on Bewick's childhood memories. These children fly kites, ride rocking horses and go-carts, play with animals, sail boats, and pretend to be soldiers. All of the above texts and *Fables of Aesop* use unframed vignettes as tailpieces.

John Bewick also created some tailpieces. Most of the material he illustrated, however, consisted of didactic texts for the London market: "He was almost entirely employed by the publishers and booksellers in London, in designing and cutting an endless variety of blocks for them" (Bain 100). Examples of the moral texts are *The Oracles, Proverbs Exemplified, False Alarms, or the Mishievous Doctrine of Ghosts,* and *The History of Little Jack.* In such texts only framed images were engendered on the blocks, as if to reflect the enclosing and confining of children within a strict moral and educational framework. Elsewhere, in similar texts that he also illustrated, such as Le Grand's *Looking Glass for the Mind,* humorous or decorative vignettes as tailpieces accompany the framed headpieces for each moral tale. Such playfulness alleviates the previous sense of confinement.

The framed headpieces designed and executed by John Bewick appear in the moralizing texts published by the Newberys, Stockdale, Trusler, and Harrison. These texts speak to benevolent adult purchasers of books of instruction. They reflect rational moralist encouragement of reason and moral judgment, an attitude to literature that emanates from Rousseau and Pestalozzi: "The wisest of his [Rousseau's] disciples were not long in discovering that the story [*Emile*] was meant only by way of illustration, and that before they could apply the principles it illustrated they must work out methods appropriate to their own conditions. . . . Pestalozzi, through whom Rousseau's ideas passed into the life and work of the ordinary schools of Europe, based his new methods on the work of the good mother in the home, and analysed learning into its elements for the better instruction of children" (Boyd 1–2). *The Oracles,* illustrated by John Bewick, provides benevolent parents with a cypher for their teachings (fig. 3). Mr. and Mrs. Wilson tell their children that "after much trouble and expence, we have procured these SPEAKING FIGURES to be made, and which we have agreed to call your ORACLES" (41). These figures are hung in a room and surrounded by silk curtains that can be drawn up and let down "by means of silk lines and tassels" (40); the children consult the figures for advice and moral guidance with regard to correct behavior. The Oracles (their parents?) communicate to the children through mouth trumpets.

The illustration and text show images of children controlled by strings and enclosed by clothing, curtains, walls, and then frames. No fewer than four physical frames—the white circular space, the black circular line, the square frame, and the decorative outer frame—com-

Figure 3. From *The Oracles*, 41.

bine with the internal framing devices to express control over the action of the children who consult the Oracles. Like the puppets, the children live in a limiting environment, physically and educationally.

In spite of the limitations placed on the children, the Oracles are visually interesting. The appeal of the image is enhanced further by awkward attempts to integrate it within the text for both educational and aesthetic purposes. Here John Bewick, who also illustrated Dr. Trusler's eighteenth-century version of *Orbis Pictus*, anticipates the modern picture book. As Perry Nodelman suggests, "Most accounts of their [picture books] educational value derive from two contradictory ideas about the purpose of illustration, both of which are implied by the definition of the word 'illustration' offered by *The American Heritage Dictionary:* 'Visual matter used to clarify or to decorate a text.' Because pictures can provide information that completes the meaning of the words, their purpose is clarification—as it was in *Orbis Pictus*" (3). For purposes of clarification and integration, the presence of decorative illustration within the text is explained in *The Oracles* in a manner not usual in other didactic texts (fables, proverbs, and moral stories) nor deemed necessary by Thomas Bewick in didactic works he illustrated, such as *Moral Instruction, Fables of Aesop,* and

Choice Emblems. The illustrations in *The Oracles* are not headpieces or
tailpieces but part of the text, encouraging the reader to understand
the function of an illustration within a text. There are a number of explanations about the presence of the illustration similar to this clumsy
effort: "As it is difficult to convey a proper idea of them by words, I
have, by the kindness of my friends, been enabled to procure a very
masterly drawing of them" (*The Oracles* 40). This is, however, an early
example of the effort to integrate image and text both to clarify and
to encourage children to appreciate the beauty of the illustration. Referring to later developments in the art of the picturebook, William
Moebius comments that "from Edmund Evans on, the making of the
picturebook was seen more and more to require an integral relationship between picture and word" (142).[9] Walter Crane condescends to
comment (perhaps reacting to John Ruskin's overenthusiasm to the
work of Thomas Bewick) on Bewick that he had "no regard whatever
to the design of the page as a whole" (Ruzicka 4). Yet John Bewick,
whom he overlooks, together with Elizabeth Newbery, who published
The Oracles, is aware of the importance of the placement of an illustration on the page, despite the limitations of the material he is illustrating.

Eighteenth-century publishers and booksellers of John Bewick's
work diversified, creating reading cards out of illustrations as a marketing ploy to sell more books and to get more use out of the excellent woodblocks produced by John Bewick. Mr. J. Harrison, who
employed John Bewick to create seventy cuts for *Harrison's New Nursery Picture Book* (fig. 4), also created ninety-six spelling cards from
similar blocks "for Children that are learning to read, to play with"
(Opie Collection, Bodleian, from an advertisement quoted by Peter
Opie in a handwritten note to an album).

These cuts first appear in the rational moralist, updated version
of *Orbis Pictus:* namely, Dr. Trusler's *The Progress of Man and Society.*
Other engravings executed by John Bewick and contained in this
same album are "more than two hundred cuts taken from sheets of
Harrison's *Amusing Prints,* some of the earliest sheets of small pictures produced specially for children to cut out and paste in albums"
(handwritten note by Peter Opie). Again the children are depicted
in confinement: most of the images of children in Trusler show them
within rooms or walled gardens. They are often accompanied by
an adult guide or are depicted in approved play situations such as
"Child-ish Sports," "Boy-ish Sports," "Child-ish A-muse-ments," "Girl-

Figure 4. From *Harrison's New Nursery Picture Book,* n.p.

ish Amuse-ments," "Boys un-der In-struc-ti-on." The children pursue oratory, dancing (decorously), fencing (in the prescribed manner), riding and driving, swimming and skating. These activities are prescribed for health, while disobedience and risk taking cause injury ("Un-skil-ful Ri-ders" and "Child-ren in Dan-ger"), freakishness ("De-form-i-ties"), and insanity ("Man Void of Rea-son").[10] Among the hundred or so illustrations for his book, Trusler used only four vignettes by John Bewick. All of the cards and prints are in frames, both circular and square (as in fig. 4). Of course the frames would facilitate a child's cutting around the pictures and pasting them into an album. They are, after all, being used for educational, as well as aesthetic, purposes.

Enclosure and the Modern Picture Book

Such images and their diverse uses create an intertextual phenomenon similar to that found in illustrated series books today (Moebius 147). Furthermore, although the written texts illustrated by John Bewick demand that the illustrations use images of children behaving in an exemplary or admonitory manner, the illustrations interpret narrative.[11] Although Brian Alderson in his history of the English picture-book tradition acknowledges the significance of Thomas Bewick for his "attractive habit of incorporating into them [texts] what

Figure 5. From Berquin, *Looking Glass for the Mind,* 102 (*top*), 128.

Figure 6. From Berquin, *Looking Glass for the Mind,* 8.

he called 'tale pieces' " (35), he mentions John Bewick only in passing. John Bewick's illustrations, however, are used to illustrate stories like those found in the *Looking Glass for the Mind.* Nodelman emphasizes the different processes used in viewing images in narrative books like this one and in *Orbis Pictus:* "Those picture books that have practical purposes, such as alphabet books and word books, require their viewers to focus on the names of the objects their pictures convey; picture books that tell stories force viewers to search the pictures for information that might add to or change the meanings of the accompanying texts" (18). The title of Berquin's *Looking Glass for the Mind* implies that the illustrations will mirror for the reader or viewer images of correct mental attitudes and, hence, physical and social behavior. These illustrations appear as headpieces preceding short moral stories (fig. 5).

The exemplary children in the framed illustrations learn from the adults around them in formal gardens and well-appointed rooms. They are contained safely within the lines and frames of ordered living. Poor children and those in error appear in disorderly country settings. In figure 6, nature is a threat to civilization rather than a playground, as it usually is in the work of Thomas Bewick. Here Anabella, six, has persuaded her reluctant mother to allow her to

accompany her to market and has gotten lost. She is saved and returned to her mother by an old woman who looks like a witch but is
really very kind. The possible dangers inherent in this situation are
observed in the illustration, where Anabella is outside the walls of a
safe contained place. Being lost and alone and facing potential danger is the result of disobedience.

Enclosure and Freedom: Views of Childhood

The picture of childhood that emerges from these related texts and
images is one of decorum, order, control, and obedience to one's
guide.[12] Disobedience and headstrong behavior are punished by circumstances that lead to disorder, harm, and unhappiness. The settings of the action, together with the frames and containers around
and within the illustrations, add to this picture of a calm and happy,
but enclosed and controlled, childhood. Such images contrast with
those found in Thomas Bewick's work, especially in his popular
vignettes.

Thomas Bewick was much appreciated by his contemporaries. John
Ruskin praised him highly; Wordsworth extolled him in verse and
used his early (one-line frame) engravings to illustrate a version of
"We Are Seven."[13] Most memorably, Charlotte Brontë (who wrote a
poem in praise of Bewick)[14] begins *Jane Eyre* with a reader-viewer response to the vignettes in the *History of British Birds*. The words and
images of the introductory pages impress young Jane's active imagination so that they "connect[ed] themselves with the succeeding
vignettes" (2). She explores the image of "solitary churchyard . . .
girdled by a broken wall," cataloguing the objects appearing therein
and deducing from the "low horizon" and "newly-risen crescent" that
"this [was] the magical 'hour of eventide.' " She interprets the images
of "two ships becalmed on a torpid sea," a "fiend pinning down the
thief's pack," and a "horned thing seated aloof on a rock." For her,
"each picture [tells] a story; mysterious often to my undeveloped
understanding and imperfect feelings; yet ever profoundly interesting" (2). Indeed in 1829 and 1830 Charlotte Brontë copied and re-
created vignettes from Volume 2 of Thomas Bewick's *History of British
Birds,* from *Water Birds* and the *Fables of Aesop,* and from volume 1 of
History of British Birds (Campbell). Her reaction to potential danger
and unframed, untamed nature is that of the romantic, extolling freedom. And Jane Eyre's paintings take this point of view to an extreme,

their subjects and method almost slavishly imitating the vignettes described earlier.

Bewick is most revered for his creation of the vignettes,[15] whose narrative propensity Iain Bain and Brian Alderson have noted and on whose use of narrative closure I have commented elsewhere (Thompson). Each vignette holds a story for readers and viewers to decode. Many of these stories tell of childhood's pleasures and vicissitudes and are unrelated to the texts in which they appear. It is as if Bewick, like Brontë and Nodelman, is aware that children read images differently than do adults. Preliterate people, and those exploring early literacy, have reactions similar to those of Jane Eyre. They see narratives within sections of the illustration. Quoting McLuhan, Nodelman observes that

> "literacy gives people the power to focus a little way in front of an image so that we take in the whole image or picture at a glance. Non-literate people have no such acquired habit, and do not look at objects in our way. Rather they scan objects and images as we do the printed page, segment by segment. Thus they have no detached point of view" (37). Anyone who has watched young preliterate children with little experience of books scan pictures in just this way, and consequently focus their attention on what are meant to be insignificant details, will appreciate the extent to which pictorial perception depends on their very basic learned experience. (7)

It is my observation that many children continue to interpret aspects of images, to make up stories about decorations that may only be forms of marginalia, as they play with meaning and absorb literacy skills.

Perhaps Thomas Bewick acknowledges that not all children will take the trouble to follow the clues in the framed headpieces of his *Histories* and relate them to the description of the animal or bird that follows in the text. Instead children may invent stories of their own from the images they see, stories unconnected to the overt teaching of natural history. Thus Bewick creates "talepieces" and in them includes many pictures of wild countryside, domestic animals, childhood play, adult lessons, and tribulations.[16]

In these unframed, unenclosed pictures, children are shown sailing boats, riding on tombstones, flying kites, and playing shuttlecock (fig. 7). Frequently the vignettes tell a story about what might hap-

Figure 7. From Thomas Bewick, *Commemoration,* 18; children flying kites (*top*) and playing shuttlecock.

pen next or leave room for a child to draw moral implications from the scene. But the morals are seldom overt, as they are in the framed "preceptory" prints (fig. 5).

Bewick has no illusions about the nature of children. He shows boys beating a cat and a dog that are pulling a cart into water; or being encouraged by a gross-faced tanner who stands laughing as the

It is not so ugly as a purse-proud, ignorant, wicked man.

Figure 8. From Thomas Bewick, *Fables of Aesop,* 290.

youngsters chase a dog with a can tied to its tail. He depicts a child practicing to become a hunter, a potential destroyer of nature, surrounded by pictures of hounds and horses, riding his rocking horse with a whip in his hand. Nevertheless, in some vignettes kind children lead a blind man. They may lead him into danger because they cannot read, but they are not intentionally malicious. Instead they provide a moral for sluggish and backward readers that they should be more engaged with their lessons and teachers.

The intertextuality of all of these images in his *Histories,* in smaller chapbooks for Davison (a publisher in Alnwick, Northumberland), in *Fables of Aesop,* and in *The Hive of Ancient and Modern Literature*[17] implies that in Thomas Bewick's vision of childhood children are free to learn from their mistakes and to explore the natural world around them without the controlling strictures of the rational moralists and outside the enclosed space of house and walled or formal garden. Nature itself, as Wordsworth was to state explicitly, is the teacher.

As we have seen, teaching and morality are not absent in Thomas Bewick's work: it is direct and unmistakable (see also fig. 8). Indeed, that the puritanical use of demons in shadows and trees behind drunks and thieves should inspire the romantic and gothic imagination of Jane Eyre is strangely ironic. The mysterious level she adds to her interpretation is very much of her own romantic inclination, not his. His natural inclination is toward a nonconformist Christian morality; yet its artistic representation allows freedom for the imagination to act beyond the simple moral. Consider, for example, the vignette in figure 8. Here the fat warty toad is ready to spring: his front feet pressed down, his back feet spread out. His weight will be a problem for lift-off, but so too will earthly monetary concerns weigh down the wicked miser who would rise up to heaven. The holographic script engraved below the image breaks the sensation (and possible boredom) of reading printed text in a book. And it makes the reader-viewer connect the moral to the image by, literally, providing space for the eye to rise and fall as he or she examines the significances between the two. Both the eye and the mind have room to move. Charles Rosen and Henri Zerner have described this use of space as "a kind of visual pun" when referring to the vignette in the *Fables of Aesop* of the dog baying at the moon (87).

Thomas Bewick's influence on the image of childhood was far more important than that of his brother, whose similar images were circumscribed by the material he was asked to illustrate. Thomas's place in art and literature is, however, complicated by the response he calls forth from influential readers: "that the passionate admiration of certain writers—Wordsworth in particular—reflects not only their regard for his work but also their sense of the disparity between his accomplishment and his artistic culture; his status was not that of an artist but of an inspired artisan, an artistic bon sauvage" (Rosen and Zerner 92). Thus both Thomas's life and his images of childhood in his unframed vignettes set within a rural environment, showing children with animals rather than with adults, appeal to Wordsworth while also being closer to the teachings of Rousseau than to the admonitory texts of the rational moralists: "The child is not a man. This principle, which might have seemed self-evident, is one of Rousseau's cardinal principles, and his main point of attack on education, as he believed it to be practised at that time, is that it treats the child as if he were an adult. He is, on the contrary, closer to the animal and should be allowed to live as his animal nature demands. He is equipped with the means of self-preservation and the rest lies dormant within him to mature at a later date" (Boas, 30). Wordsworth's (and Rousseau's) attitude toward childhood as a time when we are close to nature corresponds to Bewick's depictions of childhood. Bewick's images illustrate the chapbook of Wordsworth's poem "We Are Seven," published in York by James Kendrew.[18] He uses an early wood engraving from the "History of Little Red Riding Hood" (1777). As

Figure 9. Thomas Bewick's illustration for Wordsworth's "We Are Seven" (*top*), n.p.; and his earlier illustration for "History of Little Red Riding Hood," in *A New Year's Gift for Little Masters and Misses,* n.p.

we can see, the engraving relies on Bewick's image but is not a reproduction of the original block (fig. 9).

The obvious finesse with a graver, producing clear lines of detail and depth, or the lowering of the block, is not evident in the illustration of Wordsworth's poem. The position of the child and the objects in the scene (tree, cottage, and rock) are the same. The debt to Bewick is obvious. Yet, instead of depicting a girl dutifully delivering her mother's gift to her grandmother (with strict instructions to avoid the dangers lurking in the wood), the text of Wordsworth's poem refers to "little cottage girl" reveling in the wildness of her surroundings. Her hair, clothes, and eyes have a rustic beauty. Only the drooping cape in the original tells of the fairy tale. The details of Bewick's beloved countryside, the bark of the tree, the thick foliage, the cottage on the slope of the hill, have more to do with Wordsworth's poem and his view of childhood than the text of Perrault's story. The depiction of a child as one who is free to move over fields and through forests shows her to be accustomed to country walks and hillsides. The union of these realistic rural images and Wordsworth's ideal of the child reaffirms the influence of Thomas Bewick and his concept of childhood. As Rosen and Zerner suggest, it also owes much to his later creation of the wood-engraved vignette (Rosen and Zerner 81–84).

By creating the vignette, Bewick throws away the frame, rejecting the containment and control of a child. He develops a form of illustration whose center is the activity of rural people internally framed by the countryside they freely inhabit. I would suggest, therefore, that both the Bewicks' concern about the Acts of Enclosure affects their depictions of childhood. Thomas Bewick chooses to specialize in unframed mid-eighteenth-century rural images containing children, whom he depicts as free, playful, and sometimes cruel individuals, coming to terms with reality. Ironically, in doing this, Bewick has been espoused by those who romanticize childhood. Thus, his influence on our appreciation for the art of illustration is immeasurable.

John Bewick, on the other hand, had little choice of the texts he had to illustrate. He found himself in the center of a flourishing trade in children's books with engraved blocks. The didactic and rational moralist texts required his use of framed, confined, controlled images. His choice of frames was echoed in the images of an urban, Rousseauesque eighteenth-century childhood. His images of enclosure depict protection and education by adults. Ironically, his integration of image and text anticipates the narrative art of the picture book with its appreciation of illustration for both educational and aesthetic purposes. The conclusions to the personal stories of the Bewick brothers and their influence have the same ending: a significant place in the history of children's book illustration.

Notes

1. John Bewick illustrated for both Carnan and Elizabeth Newbery. Samuel Pickering tells us that "after Newbery's death in 1767, his relatives opened separate publishing houses." From 1768 to 1780 rival Newberys operated two establishments: one owned by John Newbery's stepson (Carnan) and son Francis, the other by his nephew, also named Francis Newbery. On the retirement of the former and the death of the latter, in 1780, the publishing company was controlled by the latter's widow, Elizabeth (Pickering 91 and n.).

2. Common land worked by peasants had been "enclosed" by fences, walls, and hawthorn hedges for centuries. By 1700 half the arable land in England was in private hands and similarly landscaped. This could be achieved by private agreement or, particularly if common land was affected, by an act of Parliament. In the eighteenth century such parliamentary enactments increased from 64 in 1740–49 to 472 in 1770–79 to 574 in 1800–1809 (Porter 209).

3. Thomas Bewick, partner of Ralph Beilby for twenty years (following his apprenticeship, a walking tour of Scotland, and a short commercial stint in London) and then owner of his own wood-engraving studio until his death, had considerable choice of works to illustrate. John Bewick probably had less choice, because illness forced him to leave London as he was beginning his career; he eventually returned to London and died there.

4. Fourteen-year-old Thomas Bewick (1753–1828) began his career as a wood engraver of cuts for children's books at exactly the right time and place for success. In 1767, when Bewick was apprenticed to an engraver, Ralph Beilby of Newcastle upon Tyne, Thomas Saint was printing many children's books for William Charnley. Beilby worked in metal, and Bewick, who was the only apprentice indentured to Beilby at that time, was given the responsibility of engraving on wood. He began to engrave on the end grain of boxwood, a skill that he revived by using metal engraving tools. In her article "The Beilby and Bewick Workshop," Margaret Gill examines the day books, ledgers, and workbooks of the Beilby establishment. She discovers that the Thomas Saint account included many children's books engraved by Bewick.

At this point in children's book publishing, Newcastle upon Tyne was "probably the next largest centre to London for the production of chapbooks and broadsides, and they were here from the early eighteenth until well into the second half of the nineteenth centuries" (Cunningham 8). Cunningham also refers to London, York, Birmingham, and Newcastle upon Tyne as "the principal places in England for printing chapbooks" (8). As a child, Thomas Bewick was an avid consumer of such cheap literature. Robert Robinson, writing after his discussions with Bewick's daughters, describes Thomas's youthful reading: "Chap books, broadsides, and ballads adorned with rude woodcuts, supplied by hawkers, or bought when at Newcastle on market-days, sufficed to amuse both old and young through the long winter nights" (3). Furthermore, in *Bewick to Dovaston: Letters, 1824–1828*, we read of the development of this trade "which is said to have been larger than that of any city except London" (10). However, this did not prevent John Bewick (1760–1795), also an apprentice, from leaving Newcastle for London once his indentures were cancelled following completion of his five-year apprenticeship. Thomas had taught him well, but personal (though not irreconcilable) difficulties caused their separation. In London John illustrated children's books for the Newberys and for Carnon.

5. The Reverend Hugo regrets that "chapters on religious and political matters were not omitted" from the *Memoir* (Hugo xiii). This is understandable considering Bewick's attitudes to the established church.

6. Bewick was so discomforted by the English political situation in the late eighteenth century and so in agreement with the moral and social values of the American

colonies that he considered emigrating (Weekley 8). He praises the breakaway colonies as "the wisest and greatest Republic & nation the World ever saw—which," he says, "when its immense territory is filled with an enlightened population & its government like a Rock founded on the Liberties & the Rights of man" will have a great future (Bain 95). It is useful to remember that William Cobbett (1766–1835) admired Bewick's work and that Bewick read Cobbett's *Weekly Political Register* (Weekley 11). In fact, Weekley tells us that "Bewick grew up in the English puritan tradition of the small farmer and skilled artisan class with the political views of a left-wing whig" (2).

7. Thomas Bewick's condemnation of enclosure is a view interestingly shared by John and Barbara Hammond in their classic three-volume study of labor. New introductions to these works examine the authors' biases toward and sympathies for the idyll of the golden age of rural England before the Industrial Revolution. The Hammonds are particularly strong in the condemnation of the Acts of Enclosure for destroying the English country way of life. Their biases may well have been reinforced by the image, in the literature of their nineteenth-century childhood, in nursery rhymes, and in anthologies of Mother Goose stories, of a rural golden age in the eighteenth century—a myth given visible shape in the illustrations of the Bewicks.

8. In *The Village Labourer,* and when describing the English village before enclosure (here before 1774), the Hammonds speak of the yeomen as "freeholders, some of whom might be large proprietors, and many small" (2). The Bewicks' father was one of those small proprietors, running a colliery and a farm that he rented and on which his sons were expected to work. In the mid-eighteenth century, collieries in Northumberland were operated by a few men with buckets, shovels, baskets, and a donkey; they were not the industrial mines of later years.

9. It is interesting to note that Edmund Evans owed much to the influence and work of the Bewicks, for he "had been apprenticed to Ebenezer Landells (a favorite pupil of Bewick)" before he established "his own engraving and colour-printing firm" (Maloney 21).

10. This concern with physical health can be attributed to John Locke: "Following Locke's lead, Newbery began *A Little Pretty Pocket-Book* with a discussion of 'the Nurture of Children' " (Pickering 139).

11. There are many books that call for such images in John Bewick's engravings. They include *The Children's Miscellany, The History of the Family at Smiledale, The Adventures of a Silver Penny, The History of Tommy Playlove, Youthful Portraits, The Fables of the Late Mr. Gay, Tales for Youth, The Blossoms of Morality, The Life of a Fly,* and Mary Pilkington's *A Mirror for the Female Sex* (containing some cuts by John Bewick). Add to these titles those already mentioned in this article and the intertextual picture of childhood is even further extended.

12. Owing to the pressure of work, John Bewick, or his publisher, would reuse ideas and engravings. William Dodd's *The Beauties of History,* for instance, contains seventy or more cuts previously used in A. Berquin's *Looking-Glass of the Mind.* Berquin's text also reuses the form and composition, though not the exact cut of "Girl-ish A-musement" from Trusler's *Progress of Man and Society* to illustrate "Caroline; or a Lesson to Cure Vanity" (202). Such repetitions of images reinforce the intertextual picture of childhood in these rational moralist books.

13. Wordsworth's *Lyrical Ballads* includes this verse: "O now that the genius of Bewick were mine, / And the skill which he learned on the banks of the Tyne! / Then the Muses might deal with me just as they chose, / For I'd take my last leave both of verse and of prose" (Quoted by Rayner 7).

14. Charlotte Brontë's handwritten "Lines on the Celebrated Bewick," dated November 1832, four years after his death, bring together his art, his depiction of nature through the English countryside, and the nostalgic feelings about childhood that he evoked: "But now the eye bedimmed by tears may gaze / On the fair lines his gifted

pencil drew, / The tongue unfalt'ring speak its need of praise / When we behold those scenes to nature true— / True to the common Nature that we see / In England's sunny fields, her hills, and vales, / On the wild bosom of her storm-dark sea, / Still heaving to the wind that o'er it wails. . . . . 'A change comes o'er the spirit of our dream,' / Woods wave around in crested majesty, / We almost feel the joyous sunshine's beam / And hear the breath of the sweet south go by. / Our childhood's days return again in thought, / We wander in a land of love and light" (T.L.S., Jan. 4, 1907).

15. This appreciation of Bewick's work appears in critical commentaries from John Ruskin and Charlotte Brontë to John Rayner and Iain Bain.

16. Bewick puns "tailpieces" with his "talepieces," knowing the narrative propensity of his vignettes (Bain, *The Workshop*, 75).

17. This text was illustrated by Thomas Bewick and his apprentice, Luke Clenell. Clenell created the headpieces, and Bewick engraved the tailpieces. They are images of children riding hobby horses, skipping, whipping tops, rolling a hoop, skating, crossing a river on stilts, flying a kite, and playing shuttlecock, leapfrog, and blindman's bluff (fig. 7).

18. Speculation exists about the relationship of Archdeacon Wrangham's library, established for the people of the East Riding of Yorkshire in 1808, and Kendrew's press, bookshop, and publication of "We Are Seven" (Summerfield 27–28).

Works Cited

Alderson, Brian. *Sing a Song for Sixpence.* The English Picture-Book Tradition and Randolph Caldecott. Cambridge: Cambridge University Press, 1986.

Bain, Iain. *A Memoir of Thomas Bewick.* London: Oxford University Press, 1979.

———. *The Workshop of Thomas Bewick.* Newcastle: Bewick Birthplace Trust, 1989.

Berquin, Arnaud. *Looking Glass for the Mind.* 75 cuts in wood by J. Bewick. 1792. Reprint. London: J. Harris, 1806.

Bewick, Thomas. *Bewick to Dovaston: Letters, 1824–28.* London: Nattali and Maurice, 1968.

———. *Children's Pastimes.* Newcastle: D. Esslemont, 1975.

———. *Commemoration.* Newcastle: D. Esslemont, 1978.

———. *Fables of Aesop.* Newcastle: E. Walker, 1818, 1823.

———. *The Hermit of Warkworth.* A Northumberland Ballad in Three Fits by Dr. Percy. Alnwick: Catnatch, 1807.

———. *History of British Birds,* vol. 1. Newcastle: S. Hodgson, 1797.

———. *History of British Birds,* vol. 2. Newcastle: E. Walker, 1804.

———. "History of Little Red Riding Hood." In *A New Year's Gift for Little Masters and Mistresses.* 1777. Reprint. Toronto: Osborne Collection of Children's Books, 1981.

———. *History of Quadrupeds.* Newcastle: S. Hodgson, 1790.

———. *The Hive of Ancient and Modern Literature.* 4th ed. Newcastle: S. Hodgson, 1812.

Blunden, Edmund. *A Memoir of Thomas Bewick.* London: Centaur, 1961.

Boas, George. *The Cult of Childhood.* London: The Warburg Institute, University of London, 1966.

Brontë, Charlotte. *Jane Eyre.* With wood engravings by Fritz Eichenberg. New York: Random, 1943.

———. "Lines on the Celebrated Bewick," *Times Literary Supplement,* Jan. 4, 1907.

Campbell, Colin. "Every Picture Tells a Story," *Cherryborn Times,* Spring 1994, 3–7.

Cunningham, John. *Amusing Prose Chapbooks.* London, 1889.

Day, Thomas. *The Children's Miscellany: In Which Is Included the History of Little Jack.* Ill. by John Bewick. London: J. Stockdale, 1790.

Dodd, William. *The Beauties of History.* London: Vernon and Hood, 1976.

Gill, Margaret. "The Beilby and Bewick Workshop." In *Bewick and After.* Ed. P. C. G. Isaac. Newcastle, 1990.

Goldsmith, Oliver, and T. Parnell. *Poems.* Ill. by John and Thomas Bewick and apprentices. London: W. Bulmer, 1795.

Hammond, John L., and Barbara Hammond. *The Skilled Labourer.* Ed. John Rule. 1919. Reprint. London: Longman, 1979.

———. *The Town Labourer.* Ed. John Lovell. 1917. Reprint. London: Longman, 1978.

———. *The Village Labourer.* Ed. G. E. Mingay. 1911. Reprint. London: Longman, 1978.

Harrison's New Nursery Picture Book. London: J. Harrison, ca. 1972.

Hugo, The Rev. Thomas. *The Bewick Collector.* London, 1866.

Johnson, Richard. *False Alarms or the Mischievous Doctrine of Ghosts.* Ill. by John Bewick. London: E. Newbery, 1796.

Maloney, Margaret Crawford, ed. *English Illustrated Books for Children.* London: Bodley Head, 1981.

Moebius, William. "Introduction to Picturebook Codes," *Word and Image* 2, no. 2 (Apr.–June 1986): 141–58.

Nodelman, Perry. *Words about Pictures.* Athens: University of Georgia Press, 1988.

The Oracles. Ill. by John Bewick. London: E. Newbery, 1792.

Pickering, Samuel. *John Locke and Children's Books in Eighteenth-Century England.* Knoxville: University of Tennessee Press, 1985.

Porter, Roy. *English Society in the Eighteenth Century.* London: Penguin, 1990.

Rayner, John. *Wood Engravings by Thomas Bewick.* London: Penguin, 1947.

Ritson, John, ed. *Pieces of Popular Poetry.* Ill. by John Bewick. London: T. and J. Egerton, 1791.

———. *Robin Hood.* London: T. Egerton and J. Johnson, 1795.

Robinson, Robert. *Thomas Bewick: His Life and Times.* Newcastle: R. Robinson, 1887.

Roscoe, Sydney. *John Newbery and His Successors, 1740–1814.* Great Britain: Five Owls Press, 1973.

Rosen, Charles, and Henri Zerner. *Romanticism and Realism.* New York: Viking, 1984.

Ruzicka, Rudolph. *Thomas Bewick Engraver.* New York: Typophiles, 1943.

Sander, David. *Wood Engraving.* New York: Viking, 1978.

Summerfield, Geoffrey. *Fantasy and Reason: Children's Literature in the Eighteenth Century.* London: Methuen, 1984.

Thomson, Francis. *Newcastle Chapbooks.* Newcastle: Oriel Press, 1969.

Thompson, Hilary. "Narrative Closure in the Vignettes of John and Thomas Bewick." *Word and Image,* 10, no. 4 (Oct.–Dec. 1994): 395–408.

Weekley, Montague. *Thomas Bewick.* London: Oxford University Press, 1953.

The Dollhouse as Ludic Space, 1690–1920

Frances Armstrong

"The modern girl . . . is tired of living in a doll's house," says the first editor of *The Girl's Realm;* earlier generations were brought up under the rule of "Don't," but for the girl of 1899, the rule is "Do" (The Editor 216). The dollhouse metaphor evidently needed no explanation; it had been twenty years since the heroine of Henrik Ibsen's *A Doll's House* had startled audiences by walking away from a belittling domestic life. Yet one of the things a modern girl could do, according to an article only five pages earlier, was help make a dollhouse for her younger sisters. Might she not have wondered whether she was encouraging those sisters to perpetuate an ideal she had already rejected? Or was Ibsen's title by then a dead metaphor—perhaps a metaphor that had never had much connection with small girls at play?

Taking as an initial hypothesis the idea that by 1899 there were two distinct meanings attached to dollhouses—as metaphorical places of imprisonment for women and as actual structures used in play—I set out to trace the textual history of dollhouses. Precursors of Ibsen's metaphorical dollhouse are easily found in a series of references in Dickens's later novels. Bella Wilfer wanted to be worthier than a doll in a dollhouse (*Our Mutual Friend* 746); Esther Summerson, given a miniature version of Bleak House on her marriage, soon expanded what she saw as "quite a rustic cottage of doll's rooms; but such a lovely place" (*Bleak House* 912); she was preceded by the unhappy example of David Copperfield's wife, Dora, who was unable to stop behaving like a doll, and by Little Em'ly, who chose disgrace rather than live in a "little house . . . as neat and complete as a doll's parlour" (*David Copperfield* 501). In Dickens's earlier novels, however, dollhouse living is delightful, particularly in *The Old Curiosity Shop* and *Martin Chuzzlewit*. To the best of my knowledge, the pejorative

Illustrations are reproduced by permission of the Osborne Collection of Early Children's Books, Toronto Public Library. I wish to thank the librarians, especially Dana Tenny, for their patient help and advice. I am grateful also to the Canadian Social Sciences and Humanities Research Council for financial support.
Children's Literature 24, ed. Francelia Butler, R. H. W. Dillard, and Elizabeth Lennox Keyser (Yale University Press, © 1996 Hollins College).

metaphor of the dollhouse (or baby-house) as a place of restriction is rare in any texts before *David Copperfield*—though likening women to dolls goes back much further.[1]

The dollhouse metaphor as developed by Dickens and Ibsen, then, seems to have had a short history in comparison with the history of the dollhouse itself. Miniaturized domestic settings are found in Egyptian tombs dating from about 2000 B.C.; dollhouses in their current Western form go back to the mid-sixteenth century. But the hypothesis of two distinct sets of meanings is too simple: neither dollhouses themselves nor textual references to them can be divided neatly into adult and child categories. It is true that adults have used dollhouses for their own purposes (as I am doing in this essay), but the purposes may be playful as well as analytic or didactic; it is also true that children's dollhouse play may carry its own conscious or intended metaphorical meanings, but these are rather different from those of Ibsen and Dickens. Although early dollhouses were valuable artifacts supplied and controlled by adults, it seems quite clear that most girls were able to regard dollhouses as their own ludic spaces, places dedicated to their own play, rather than as sites for training in compliance. Showing flexibility and individuality, they interspersed reassuring enactment of routine with humorous or subversive innovation and readily improvised both narratives and accessories.

I have taken 1690 as the starting date for this essay because the first written evidence in English of children playing with dollhouses comes from the baby-house given to Ann Sharp, who was born in 1691. The evidence is believed to be in her own hand, name tags that have remained pinned to the dolls in the house ever since (Greene, *English Dolls' Houses* 87). Although many baby-houses were made in the decades that followed, for children as well as for adult collectors, the first detailed textual references to children playing with them seem to come from the 1780s, when literature for or about children became more prevalent.[2] To make things more difficult, the term *baby-house* during this period often means merely an arrangement of large dolls' furniture on a shelf or in a box. During the nineteenth century baby-houses assume the standard form, an array of rooms vertically contained in some kind of box with a roof; by 1850 they are likely to be smaller and simpler and to be called dolls' houses or doll's houses in England and dollhouses in North America.

Although certain chronological trends in the textual history of dollhouses can be traced, particularly in overtly didactic stories for children, variations in actual dollhouse play resist schematization. This may be because of universal patterns of child development, but another important factor is the private familial nature of early doll-house play. Until about 1850, baby-houses were usually large family heirlooms, and how a girl played with them may have been influenced more by family tradition than by games played by her contemporaries. Even after dollhouses began to be mass-produced, they usually remained at home, and the dolls at home within them, each miniature household living its individualized and often idiosyncratic existence. Larger dolls could be carried on visits, and larger-scale dolls' tea parties followed current fashions in clothing, food, and manners, but dollhouses were too big and too detailed to be adapted to the latest trends.

The choice of 1920 as a final date is not meant to suggest that by then the influence of Ibsen's metaphor had entirely disappeared. The meanings of dollhouses continue to multiply; since about 1965, adult interest in miniature domestic settings has been very strong, and so much recent children's fiction has had a dollhouse setting that a single essay on the subject would be seriously reductive. I have stopped at 1920 because of a number of significant changes at about that time. After World War I had shaken notions of privacy and insularity (to put it mildly), the whimsical stories of A. A. Milne and Kenneth Grahame became popular with adults, offering miniaturized domesticity that centered on boys and male animals rather than on girls and dolls. The much-publicized dollhouse built for Queen Mary in the early 1920s was a national project that cut across the family-centred tradition of the dollhouse, arousing interest in undertakings on a similarly ambitious scale by Sir Nevile Wilkinson, Colleen Moore, and Mrs. James Ward Thorne (Eaton; Greene; Jacobs). Queen Mary's Dolls' House can be seen as the end point of the dollhouse's shift from insular family tradition into public domain, a process that had begun in about 1850. It would not be facetious to suggest that the Queen's Dolls' House had a (small) impact on the whole field of English literature, since nearly two hundred authors, from Arthur Conan Doyle and Joseph Conrad to Edith Wharton and Vita Sackville-West, contributed texts to its miniature library, many specially composed and handwritten in tiny format for the purpose (Benson and Weaver; Stewart-Wilson). Ten years later, American writers made similar contributions to the library of Colleen Moore's miniature castle, among them Sinclair Lewis, F. Scott Fitzgerald, Willa Cather, Edgar Rice Burroughs, and John Steinbeck (*Colleen Moore's Fairy Castle*).

Evidence about dollhouse play between 1690 and 1920 is difficult to find. Material evidence—the few old dollhouses and their furnishings that have survived—can be revealing, although (as with all toys) the survivors are often the failures, playthings that were not enjoyed to the point of extinction. Direct textual evidence is scarce: few diaries or letters written by girls have survived, and some of those were subject to adult scrutiny at the time of writing. My references here include only two texts written by children themselves, one a thank-you letter to Queen Victoria and the other a letter written to a children's magazine. (The name tags Ann Sharp attached to her dollhouse dolls in the 1690s can hardly be called texts but are perhaps more reliable as evidence than the kind of letters mentioned.) Books of practical or moral instruction are also important for their influence rather than as reflections of fact; these works (mostly written before 1850) seldom attempt to describe the details of dollhouse play.[3] Autobiographical reminiscences are obviously not always accurate, but they do have significance in that a mother's or grandmother's memories of childhood play, no matter how altered in the telling, may have a strong influence on the games of the next generation of that particular family, especially during the period when an old family dollhouse rather than a television-advertised novelty was the center of play. In large families, siblings might set up traditions within a single generation. In the later nineteenth century, when cheaper or homemade dollhouses were more common than the heirloom kind, magazine articles helped to establish a tradition of play, often describing dollhouses and their owners of earlier generations from memory or from research.

Because games of dollhouse play are themselves fictions, it is hard to draw a firm line between autobiographical accounts and declared fiction. The magazine articles I have just mentioned, for instance, include many accounts of the dolls and dollhouses of Queen Victoria and her children and grandchildren, so Frances Hodgson Burnett can credibly introduce one such grandchild as a character in *Racketty-Packetty House*. The dollhouse in Beatrix Potter's *Tale of Two Bad Mice* is known to be based on the one made by her fiancé Norman Warne for his niece (Judy Taylor 115). When several members of one family are writers, their stories may overlap in ways that confirm elements of factual accuracy: Margaret Gatty and her daughter Juliana Horatia Ewing, in *Aunt Sally's Life* and *The Land of Lost Toys*, respectively, write about toys that have passed through several generations; "Aunt Sally" and Ewing's "the Dowager" appear to be the same doll. Many such stories are framed ambiguously so that they can be read as fact or as fiction.

I have used the incongruously formal term *ludic space* in my title partly to draw attention to the perception that the study of girls' culture ought to be dressed in academic respectability if it is not to appear ludicrous. But *ludic space* does convey more than its literal meaning of "play area": the term implies a space specifically designated for play, often by adults who intend that children play nowhere else.[4] Even modern researchers have noted that girls tend to occupy smaller play spaces than boys do (Thorne 83); during the eighteenth and nineteenth centuries, when women were encouraged to stay within the sphere of home, a dollhouse could be a means of discouraging girls from appropriating any other space:

> Go take up your doll, to your baby-house go,
> And there your attention much better bestow!
>
> (Kilner 68)

This particular dismissal comes from a boy whose sister is playing with the top he had lost; although an adjudicating father finds his daughter in the right, the boy's words have a memorable ring and must have been uttered by many brothers. In doing so, however, they were also excluding themselves from the baby-house, because young Edward's poem goes on to mock the idea of a boy dressing dolls, pouring their tea, and putting them to bed. An almost fearful avoidance of public association with dollhouses is nearly universal among boys in every period, but many boys did enjoy dollhouses and played with them in the privacy of the family.[5]

A problem of demarcated ludic spaces is that a child given a special place to play will often be subject to authority in that area: even if not confined to it as to a prison, she may be watched while she plays there. The panopticonlike structure of a dollhouse also lays the dolls themselves open to surveillance.[6] One might indeed argue that a dollhouse is not so much a ludic space as a glamorized storage area, since almost all dollhouses keep children firmly outside, seldom allowing more than one hand to intrude with any degree of comfort.[7] But it has the advantage of permanence: large and heavy, with fragile furnishings that have to be kept, according to a frequent admonition, "neat and complete," it is not likely to be moved around or tidied away. One of the more practical requirements for imaginative play that involves concrete objects such as miniatures is a place relatively free of interference, where a complicated game can be set up and left in place for a reasonably long time. As Edith Nesbit pointed out, any "scene of magnificence" needs a large safe space: "It is better for the child's mind that the cherished doll should safely be baby for ever, than that it should be Francis the First and get walked on" (Nesbit 62).

Because of its permanence and intrinsic value, however, the traditional dollhouse is a place controlled by adults in a way that other popular ludic spaces—treehouses, clubhouses, attics, "desert islands" —are not. Dollhouses differ from these other spaces also in that they are nominally places where dolls, not children, live. In this essay, I first look at the dollhouse as a ludic space under some degree of adult control; next, I try to find out how dollhouses were used when girls were left to their own devices; finally, I consider examples of dollhouses viewed through the eyes of their doll inhabitants. To some extent, these divisions are chronological: texts before 1850 tend to feature adult supervision, and the most detailed doll's eye views come from texts written after 1880. As these examples will show, girls have used the ludic space of the dollhouse for a number of curious purposes, but they certainly do not seem to have been uncritically perpetuating repressive domestic ideals.

A Space under Adult Control

Historians of the dollhouse, though they have little textual evidence to guide them, agree that early detailed miniature domestic scenes belonged to the adult domain. Some of these models come from the early Egyptian tombs mentioned, and some from elaborate displays in locked cabinets (with or without outside architectural detail) of sixteenth- and seventeenth-century Europe; the Egyptian examples are usually explained as providing the deceased with furnishings for the afterlife, and the European examples as displaying familial wealth. Miniature displays seem to have entered English and America culture a little later, at the end of the seventeenth century, and to have been already ceded to children. Adults still held on to some control, though, partly because these early models were elaborate and expensive and partly—and consequently—because they feared that owning such valuable toys might tempt children to pride and vanity. Early textual references therefore tend to have a strong didactic note.

Dollhouses could be used to instruct girls in the details of household duties, but this custom was apparently more common in Europe than in England, the large detailed rooms known as "Nuremberg kitchens" being the best-known examples (Greene, Jacobs). On occasion collections of miniature rooms and houses were put together for historical purposes, as a careful record of domestic life (Eaton; Jacobs). It is moral instruction, though, that predominates in the earliest references to English dollhouses. Until about 1850, most fictional texts present baby-houses as fraught with opportunities for sinful thoughts and behavior and as likely to evoke pride, envy, and selfishness in particular. At their most positive, these texts stress the value of tidiness, but writers seem more inclined to repress than to encourage girls' dollhouse play. After 1850 adult control is likely to take the indirect form of suggesting ways of making and furnishing dollhouses.

One reason for the early stress on pride and vanity may be that many adults felt the appeal of an elaborate dollhouse as strongly as children did. Miniatures attract the imagination by offering a possessible condensation that preserves whatever is most valued in the original; dollhouses are playful exercises in ingenuity that fascinate and amuse because they carry miniaturization to a useless and mildly comic extreme (e.g., Bachelard 150; Millhauser 130, 135). Although such treasures may arouse envy, there is a balancing advantage: the high level of visual satisfaction means that ownership of a dollhouse does not always need to be contested. Sharing can be relatively painless, especially because the delicate perfection of the best-made miniatures may encourage admirers to look without touching. On the other hand, the same fragility means that even the gentlest touching can destroy—in Dickens's apparently autobiographical "A Christmas Tree," the narrator remembers "visiting" a dollhouse and swallowing a teaspoon while enjoying a miniature cup of tea (290).

The earliest children's story about dollhouse play that I know of is "The Baby-House," a very short story in Eleanor Fenn's *Cobwebs to Catch Flies* (1783).[8] A small illustration shows a single-room house perhaps two feet high, which is being completely ignored by two girls holding a doll the same size as the house. The girls dress the doll and discuss its clothes, paying due tribute to mamma's neat stitching, and conclude with a decision to give money to a poor child rather than buy a doll's gown.

In Mary Mister's *The Adventures of a Doll* (1816), we are told that the wealthy and cruel Miss Rachel Harper loved "to display all the riches of her baby-house" (11), but Mister does not display them to us. The equally nasty Miss Amelia Fry notices some little girls improvising a playhouse on the beach, and "could not but feel, that they had more joy with their simple shells and broken china, than she had ever had in her magnificent baby-house" (107). No details are given about either of the grand baby-houses.

When Mary Martha Sherwood introduces a baby-house into *The Fairchild Family* (1818), she realizes that some of her readers may not know what a baby-house is and goes on to describe one: "It is a small house, fit for dolls, with doors and windows, and chimney outside; and inside there is generally a parlour and a kitchen, and a bedroom, with chairs, tables, couches . . . beds, carpets, and everything small, just as there is in a real house for people to live in" (1: 93). This baby-house belongs to Miss Augusta Noble, and when Lucy and Emily Fairchild see it they are "very much pleased." Later their mother tells them that such toys encourage sinful ambition; with her notorious relentlessness, Sherwood later drives home her moral point by having the baby-house owner suffer a fiery death as a result of pride (1: 102, 152).

In "A New Year's Gift," a poem by Adelaide O'Keefe (1804), Rose and her sister Emma play with their new baby-house for nearly a whole day (Taylor, Taylor, and O'Keefe 87–89). They eagerly examine their gift, feed the dolls, and put them to bed; they even light the candles without mishap. But sinful behavior soon destroys this ludic space. After a small disagreement, disasters mount up: toys are broken, mother reprimands the sisters, Rose collapses with measles, and Emma becomes a penitent nurse. New Year's Day ends with Rose struggling for breath and the baby-house quite forgotten.

Anna Laetitia Barbauld's poem "The Baby-House" (1824) seems calculated to diminish any sense that a girl's dollhouse is a place entirely her own. "Dear Agatha," congratulated on her "mansion in itself complete," is reminded that it is "fitted to give guests a treat." The speaker imagines what she calls "ourselves" turned into elves and visiting the house at night after Agatha has gone to bed and then goes on to a more outright appropriation:

> But think not, Agatha, you own
> That toy, a Baby-house, alone.   (1: 287)

A baby-house, she says, has adult parallels: a pyramid, Versailles, and other ostentatious buildings. The parallels are unconvincing: the link is that such structures are displays of "pomp and folly," but the differences in scale and in the power to endure make the message unclear. Why a pyramid should be thought of as "a Baby-house to lodge the dead" is not explained, and like many portentous but puzzling phrases, it might remain hauntingly in a child's imagination. The poem ends with these lines:

> Then do not, Agatha, repine
> That cheaper Baby-house is thine.   (1: 289)

Cheaper than a pyramid or Versailles, Barbauld means, but if she wants Agatha to value her baby-house for its simplicity, she does not make the point clear. "Cheaper" takes the shine off a new gift, which may be just what Barbauld wanted, in order to keep Agatha off the path of pride that leads to pomp and folly. (Of course, if Agatha had indeed been repining aloud at having been given a cheaper baby-house than she had hoped for, she no doubt deserved this dispiriting poem.)

By about 1820 the tone begins to lighten up, and instead of warning about pride, fiction writers suggest ways of sharing one's treasures. In *Little Polly's Doll's House,* a picture book published in the mid-nineteenth century, Polly is taken to a large toyshop to choose a present for her fourth birthday. Her mother suggests a dollhouse. Polly is happy with the choice, though she had wanted a doll; it is her brother George who gets not one but four "handsome dressed figures" (dolls, in fact). Polly is able to enjoy showing her visiting cousins the "won-ders of her fai-ry pa-lace," and George's figures cause much amusement.

Elizabeth Prentiss adopts a similar tone in *Little Susy's Six Birthdays* (1854). As in her other books about Susy, the strongly didactic element is tempered by a close and sympathetic observation of stages of child development; by the time Susy gets a dollhouse for her fifth birthday, she has been carefully guided through four previous birthdays. (There is no celebration on her first birthday; for her second, she and her mother have a party with the dolls' tea set; Robbie and

Figure 1. Father looks with modest pride at his handiwork, but perhaps someone should keep an eye on little Robbie. From Prentiss, *Little Susy's Six Birthdays*. Osborne Collection of Early Children's Books, Toronto Public Library.

the dolls join them on her third birthday, and Father, two cousins, and a friend attend the fourth.) The baby-house has been made by her father, with contributions from mother, nurse, and aunt; the illustration shows an impressive edifice (fig. 1). Susy involves her small brother Robbie in a dollhouse game but is interrupted by nurse, who wants to dress him in his first pair of trousers. Interest centers around the dollhouse, not as an object of admiration but as a source of fun for all the household.

In these stories, Ibsen's metaphor of the prisonlike dollhouse hardly applies; most of the dolls and children are harmlessly, if aimlessly, enjoying themselves. A form of adult participation that might have been more constricting was the setting up of two standards for dollhouses: neatness and completeness. The tidy and satisfying coupling of *neat* and *complete* exemplifies its own meaning. This theme becomes a favorite literary tag throughout the nineteenth century, turning up in poetry, fiction, and nonfiction.

The New Year's gift given to Rose and Emma in O'Keefe's poem, for instance, is

> A baby-house quite neat
> With kitchen, parlours, dining room,
> And chambers all complete.
>
> (Taylor, Taylor, and O'Keefe 87)

The sisters' quarrel begins when Rose ventures to question completeness and endanger neatness by deciding to move some chairs to a room where they will match the carpet better.

Two decades after this, the real-life five-year-old Anne Evans was given a baby-house that had been made for her godmother's great-grandmother; on her seventh birthday, she received this rhyming note from (it is assumed) her father:

> I'm really very glad I'm able
> To give my little girl a table,
> Since that will make her house complete
> If she will only keep it neat;
> And when her seventh birthday's past
> I hope she'll tidy grow at last,
> And all her faults both great and small
> She'll study to correct them all.
>
> (Greene, *English Dolls' Houses* 160)

The rather daunting expectations apparently did not turn Anne against her baby-house; she gave it back to her godmother's family when she grew up but retrieved it with delight in her mid-sixties. She saved the poem, too; it remained in the storage drawer below the dollhouse for another century and a half. The insistence on neatness and completeness presumably became part of the family tradition that, I am arguing, was an important element in earlier dollhouse history.

Although moral prescriptives are less direct in the later nineteenth century, they still endorse neatness, often by associating girls with order and boys with mess. In Katharine Pyle's account (1889) of a dollhouse made in the early 1800s, a brother and sister use two shelves of a linen closet as a playhouse; but because boys are "not so careful and orderly in their ways as little girls," the neatness is short-lived, and the shelves fill up with "bits of stick fit for whittling," an old dog collar, string, fishing line, and "many other odds and ends" (Pyle 448). Seeing that her daughter is worried by this mess, a sympathetic mother orders a proper dollhouse to be made and decorates it herself. One suspects that the untidy brother either reformed or was excluded, because the dollhouse survived in good condition, to be described seventy-five years later.

Articles such as Pyle's made known to a later, and growing, audience the standards of earlier dollhouse play. Frances Hodgson Burnett contributed to the process through her fictional *Racketty-Packetty House* (1907): in the early nineteenth century the house of that name belonged to its current owner's grandmother, who kept it "very neat," having been "a good housekeeper even when she was seven years old" (10). Cynthia, the present owner, allows Racketty-Packetty House to fall into disarray and is given a new dollhouse, pointedly named Tidy Castle. Although when Cynthia sees Tidy Castle she is ashamed of Racketty-Packetty House, she ignores it rather than tidying it up. Burnett, writing in the twentieth century, is not particularly concerned with neatness; Racketty-Packetty House is a far more interesting place than Tidy Castle, and a visiting princess finds it most attractive. Cynthia gives the princess Racketty-Packetty House, which is subsequently "made gorgeous."[9]

It is tempting to see the dollhouse as no more than a place where girls were required to practice the kind of domesticity and conformity expected of women of the time. But the requirement of neatness should not be judged too hastily as an adult imposition; as the twentieth-century architectural critic John Summerson suggests, small playhouses for children should have "neatness and serenity within, contrasting with wildness and confusion without" (2). "Complete" could sound as negative as "neat," if taken to mean that the house is finished; completeness of that kind is stultifying in a toy and likely to evoke no emotions stronger than formal gratitude and short-lived admiration. But completeness in a dollhouse can also be a satisfying fullness, combined with a sense of wonder that every detail of a real house has been replicated in miniature. Although the replication is never really perfect, surprise and delight at the maker's ingenuity override any notice of what may be missing.

Some autobiographical accounts cast doubt on the attractions of tidiness for children, however. Milly Acland and her siblings, who devised many imaginative games during the 1880s, found their large old dollhouse delightful in theory but disappointing in reality, perhaps because of the adult supervision deemed necessary:

> One of us would say: "Hurrah, it's a real wet day. Let's play the whole morning with the dolls' house." There had to be a definite decision, because the windowed front of the house was kept locked, and a grown-up had to come and unlock it and latch it back against the wall and tell us to mind and not go breaking the glass. Then, somehow, when we had straightened up the fallen bits of furniture, and tidied up the beds, and had a roll-call of the doll inhabitants, we failed to develop any really amusing game. (Acland 60)

On the other hand, the expected virtues might themselves trigger amusing games. Against the rigid decorum of a dollhouse, incongruities stand out sharply, so that mere looking can lead to subversive thoughts. As a child, Emma Evans, eight years younger than her sister Anne, was rarely allowed to play with Anne's dollhouse, but in old age she still remembered the "almost sisterly resemblance" between the dollhouse's cook and its mistress, Lady Delany (Greene, *English Dolls' Houses* 158). Such incongruities may be deliberately introduced: because a dollhouse offers accessibility and privacy, even a heavily supervised child may commit acts of innovation or transgression while ostensibly dusting and tidying. Accessories can be hidden, inverted, misplaced, or stolen. Frances Hodgson Burnett, who fitted up a cupboard as a dollhouse for her adult enjoyment, admitted that the occasional visitor might be a "good housekeeper, in which case she usually drops down on her knees before the Toy Cupboard, sticks her little head inside and has a housecleaning, from which she emerges glowing and triumphant." [10] But others had a more mischievous spirit and liked "to turn things upside down, putting the footman into bed with measles in the nursery, and giving balls in the kitchen at which the grandpapa seems expected to dance with the cook" (Burnett, "My Toy Cupboard" 4).

The intriguing oddities that survive in some old dollhouses suggest that many children responded to the rigidity and apparent discomfort of dollhouse dolls in their formal settings as an invitation to move the dolls around and give them more exciting lives. In one of the earliest baby-houses known to have been played with by a child, the one given to Ann Sharp in the 1690s, a small boy and a monkey are alone in an adult's dressing room (Gwynfryn 709; Greene, *Family Dolls' Houses* 88). In another house, a doll was hidden for a hundred years under a mattress (Greene, *Family Dolls' Houses* 101). More curious still is the female doll discovered in a dollhouse belonging to the Shelley family: the doll's painted hair was permanently decorated with a yellow comb, but she was dressed in men's trousers and an apron and was lying in a four-poster bed (Greene, *Family Dolls' Houses* 124). The dollhouse can make vulnerable the very ideal of domesticity it purports to represent.

A Space under Girls' Control

What did girls do with dollhouses when left to their own devices? Almost certainly, the most popular activity was the acting out of daily domestic routine.[11] To outside observers—like Dickens and Ibsen, perhaps—the uneventful and repetitive nature of such play may make dollhouses seem like prisons, and girls unwitting accomplices in glamorizing a boring existence for women. But such a conclusion oversimplifies dollhouse play. A girl may indeed be identifying with the mother doll as she puts her through her daily routine, but she is not necessarily internalizing the desirability of boredom. She may be wondering how she herself will one day cope with the multitude of housewifely duties; or identifying with a child doll and enjoying the security of a miniaturized daily routine perhaps because she fears, or already knows, that her real home is less secure. The routine may be a background against which she is setting some new disturbing factor, like sickness, birth, or death, perhaps shifting identification from one doll to another as the play proceeds. She could be viewing the trivialities of daily routine from a distanced, perhaps even satirical, angle or perhaps focusing not on human activities themselves but on the challenge to craftsmanship of replicating them in miniature.

Although a child's interest in the enactment of daily routine may vary, the general attraction of this activity seems to be remarkably consistent in children of all periods and places. The following description of a young French duchess at play in 1630 has a timeless quality: "The dolls were undressed and put to bed every evening; they were dressed again the next day; they were made to eat; they were made to take their medicine. One day she wished to make them bathe, and had the great sorrow of being forbidden."[12] Even such a short passage suggests that a number of interests are being served. Meals and bedtime occur with a regularity that may be reassuring in this case, since the scene is meant to be a lying-in room, and a baby has just been born. Depending on the duchess's personal experience, the medicine may have been administered in the spirit of punishment or as a welcome source of relief. The sorrow at being forbidden to bathe the dolls perhaps reflects the quashing of an ingenious plan to incorporate a little water play.

The children's author Alice Corkran said of her dolls that "events in their home were the faithful mirror of what happened in ours" (Corkran 41). Rather than boring repetition, such exact mirroring could be a kind of journal keeping and could also challenge one's miniaturizing skills. An anonymous account of 1888[13] gives a detailed example of this kind of activity: the girl concerned always got her dolls out of bed in the morning, dressed them, and gave them breakfast before settling them down to their school lessons with the little schoolbooks she had made specially for them. They remained there until her own lessons were finished; later the dolls "took a walk along the front of the bookcase or on the mantelpiece." Dinner was followed by more lessons, tea, and baths, after which "mamma" came to wish the small ones goodnight. The older daughters and their parents then enjoyed an evening of music and cards. Papa locked up the house, and all went to bed. In this case, a similar regularity prevailed in the girl's home, and her mother commended her "for doing the duty of this toy house." It is clear, however, that the mother did not adopt a controlling role. She did add encouragement by making accessories such as a full deck of little playing cards.

Such accounts show striking similarities across time and place. In this kind of play, social class is the greatest source of difference, because dollhouse games require leisure and space as well as materials. There are, of course, accounts from many places and periods of dolls and dollhouses improvised from sticks, rags, and stones, but historians of play seldom mention that the word *baby-house* could apparently be used, even by well-to-do children, to refer to a very simple arrangement of furniture with no enclosing walls. In Eleanor Fenn's *Juvenile Correspondence* (1783) the fictional six-year-old Miss Mary Gentle says, in a letter from boarding school: "I have set my bureau on a window-seat—and that is our baby-house" (24). Seventy years later, Elizabeth Prentiss tells how Little Susy spends part of her second birthday making "a pretty baby-house in one corner of the room" and then decides she can make a better one; "she pulled it down, threw her toys all about the floor, and began again" (Prentiss 22–23). Some of these improvised baby-houses may have had little of the visual appeal of the expensive detailed model, but it seems that even sticks and stones were quite adequate for imaginative play.

At the other extreme, rich children who were not oversupervised in their play reportedly enjoyed games of domestic ritual as much as poorer children did. Royal children seem to have taken particular delight in games of domestic routine. Princess Charlotte of Belgium, writing in 1848 to thank Queen Victoria for the gift of a dollhouse, says that "every morning I dress my doll and give her a good breakfast; and the day after her arrival she gave a great rout at which all my dolls were invited. Sometimes she plays at drafts on her pretty little draft-board and every evening I undress her and put her to bed." [14] Even within this exclusive group, reasons for enjoying routine games may have varied: some princesses may have longed to live ordinary lives, whereas some (like the one who became Queen Victoria) did in fact live very simply.

Routs like the one mentioned by Princess Charlotte, and parties of any kind, were a frequent occurrence, because they gave one a chance to use the tiny dishes and utensils that were a great source of pleasure to so many (including such fictional characters as Gulliver and Dickens's Barkis [*Gulliver's Travels* 78; *David Copperfield* 507]). Parties provided variety within routine, lessening any possible sense of imprisonment or boredom: new clothes and visiting dolls opened up imaginative possibilities without disrupting security for those who valued ritual and repetition.

The potential for drama contained within routine might be suggested by setting the dollhouse like a stage, with action frozen at a particular moment. Girls who had not thought of this themselves might take a hint from *Edith and Milly's Housekeeping*, where Milly prepares a dinner party in careful detail before her friend Edith arrives.

A slight crisis has been caused by the late departure of afternoon visitors, who had tiresomely called too close to dinnertime; the evening's guests are now about to arrive, and the pheasants are being basted in the kitchen.

Although many children find real parties uncomfortable because of the high standards of dress and behavior required, the small scale of a dollhouse party paradoxically allows perfection to coexist with incongruity, so that mistakes bring laughter, not chaos. Delighted that such tiny knives and forks and plates could be made at all, players hardly notice discrepancies or omissions. If they do, the prevailing sense of play makes these part of the fun. Memories of dollhouse play often imply that lapses of decorum were greatly enjoyed: Alice Corkran, for instance, records that arranging a dollhouse dinner party was a "supreme delight," but the details she remembers are details of disaster, caused by the "delicious sense of hurry-scurry": the housemaid's broom left by the dining room table, or a frying pan reposing on the drawing-room sofa (Corkran 41). I would distinguish between these "lapses" and deliberate attempts at subversion: a supervising adult, one imagines, might be amused to see the frying pan in the wrong place but disturbed to encounter the hostess embracing the footman. Even on serious occasions such as weddings or funerals, unexpected incongruities can provide welcome relief to all but the most compulsive-obsessive personalities, without seriously disrupting the mood.

The small scale of the dollhouse diminishes the risk of disaster, but it also creates distance, limiting the degree of identification between child and doll. This is not a major problem, because most girls also own large dolls and identify more closely with them; the distancing is more likely to be an advantage, preventing any Nora-like feeling of being trapped in a little domain. Fictional and factual accounts suggest that girls sometimes simply disregarded their relative hugeness and joined in dollhouse activities: Edith and Milly entertain the dollhouse guests by singing to them, without assigning themselves a physical location. The illustrations to that story take liberties with proportion, so that the girls almost blend into the dolls' activities and the line between small and large house becomes pleasantly blurred: "And now it was evening—the lamp was lighted, and the kettle sang on the hearth. Milly sat on her little stool by the fire." (*Edith*, n.p.).

Illustrations tend to open up the dollhouse rather than emphasize its prisonlike quality, often showing pieces of furniture unceremoni-

Figure 2. The original illustration by Oscar Pletsch in *Aunt Judy's Magazine,* upon which this one is based, shows the same proportioning of doll, house, and furnishings, with Jemima similarly draped over the roof. Richard Andre's illustration to Juliana Horatia Ewing's "House Building and Repairs," in *Dolls Housekeeping* (London: SPCK, 1884). Osborne Collection of Early Children's Books, Toronto Public Library.

ously placed on the floor in front of the house, with play apparently continuing as if still contained by miniature walls (fig. 2). Sometimes the dolls and furniture remained in the dollhouse while the children acted out the roles themselves; sometimes large-scale dolls and their furniture were used, the dollhouse acting merely as backdrop. For children who put a high value on realism, the difference in scale could then be explained as a matter of artistic perspective.

Girls could choose the distance and perspective appropriate for each occasion, as one girl did when "playing at 'Death.'" She had experienced no deaths in her own family, but her mother had often commented on the drawn blinds that signified a house of mourning. So every week the child spent her Saturday penny on a small doll, which she immediately put to bed in her dollhouse. Rather than nursing the invalid or enacting a death-bed scene, she busied herself making blinds for the dollhouse windows and then wheeled her large doll in its carriage past the dollhouse, remarking that someone must have died. Unceremoniously she buried the small doll in the garden, removed the blinds from the windows, and took the large doll past the dollhouse again, commenting that the funeral must have taken place. "I was no longer a little girl with her doll, but a mother with her child, dignified, knowledgeable and full of concern" (McCrea 56). In this case the dollhouse becomes the home of strangers, where death can be safely contained; the girl playing mother is left glowing with satisfaction, having reassured the doll—and herself—by means of a ritual that placed death adequately for the moment.

"I had no pre-occupation with death, no secret fear of dying," this narrator maintains from the perspective of old age, and she may be right; but dollhouse play does give opportunities to act out anxieties. The small scale allows control[15] and a degree of privacy: modern therapists often give child clients the opportunity to play with dollhouse settings, in the hopes that hidden fears and preoccupations will come to the surface. No doubt children of earlier centuries also used dollhouse play to express their unconscious feelings, but the greater the privacy and the deeper the feelings, the less likely such play is to have been recorded in writing or even remembered. Only traces, like the doll under the mattress, remain. As a writer of 1870 said about the dolls in Ann Sharp's baby-house, still bearing the name tags pinned on them in about 1697, "It is quite tantalizing to see her little people all standing there as she is said to have placed them nearly two hundred years ago, and never to know what she meant by it all" (Gwynfryn 708).

We do have one very convincing account of how a child used dollhouse play to cope with emotional stress, in this case the recent sudden death of both her sisters. "Fannie H. H. (aged 9½ years)," writing to a children's magazine in 1889, describes how she and her sisters had enjoyed playing with their dollhouses and how after they died she was afraid that she could not bear to play with her own dollhouse any more.[16] Following an aunt's suggestion, however, she ingeniously combined all three dollhouses into a school, with thirteen dormitories and five pianos. Fannie found relief not by acting out a painful event but by thinking creatively and refashioning; the tone of the letter suggests that she is pleased and proud with the results and ready to start acting out new kinds of narrative.

Strangely, perhaps, even the most extreme stress seldom seems to

There's a sad hole in the floor, but Bill says the wood
is as rotten as rotten can be:
Which was why he made such a mess of the side with
                                    trying to put real glass
                                    in the window, through
                                    which one can see

Bill says he
believes that

the shortest plan would be to make a new Doll's
house with proper rooms, in the regular way.

Figure 3. Illustrations by Richard Andre, from Juliana Horatia Ewing, *Dolls Housekeeping* (London: SPCK, 1884). Osborne Collection of Early Children's Books, Toronto Public Library.

end in the willful destruction of a dollhouse. There are many grue-some accounts of dolls being viciously mutilated by both girls and boys, but dollhouses themselves seem to have been safe as ludic spaces, even in the absence of adult control. Overenthusiastic reno-vation could be dangerous (fig. 3), as could the accidental or experi-mental misuse of miniature candles and lamps. But there seems to have been an awareness that the satisfaction of destroying an entire dollhouse would not outweigh the severity of the punishment that would follow. One angry boy went so far as to break a dollhouse win-dow, but he then removed the "King" and "Queen" inhabitants and burned them in the fireplace rather than setting the dollhouse on fire. The incident was considered significant enough to be mentioned in a family account a century later (Greene, *Family Dolls' Houses* 37).

A Place for Dolls

Dickens's Bella Wilfer, hoping to be "something so much worthier than the doll in the doll's house" (*Our Mutual Friend* 746), accurately narrows down the problem that made Ibsen's Nora leave home. Bella's objection is not primarily to dollhouses in themselves or even to being treated like a doll; it is a *dollhouse* doll that she sees as less than worthy. Dollhouse dolls are generally at the negative extreme of the doll spectrum, because children find them less satisfactory playthings than most other dolls and often regard them as little more than part of the dollhouse furnishings. Although large dolls are likely to be "friends" who share an intimate individualized relationship with a girl, dollhouse dolls are part of a social entity and are made to interact with one another rather than with a girl. They are kept, literally, at arm's length. This means that even if a child recognizes their lives as restricted, she does not necessarily internalize their woes; she may, indeed, be parodying their behavior.

The dismal life that some dollhouse dolls lead may be caused by problems that are specific to the dollhouse. The constrictions of some cheap or poorly designed dollhouses make it difficult for a child to move dolls around. Even a distant observer could see problems: as R. C. Lehmann put it, writing as "little Queenie" in *Punch* (1901), a dollhouse is "devided into four compartments, like a rabit hutch. . . . There is no trace of any hall, or even passidge. There are no doors, so if a droin-room doll should find herself in the kitchen or nursery by any chance, there she has got to remane until some cumpationat hand releases her to her propper sphere!" ([Lehmann] 268).

Dollhouse furnishings were often much more successfully miniaturized than houses but tended to show up dolls' inadequacies by contrast. Surrounded by realistically detailed small accessories, dolls appear awkward, unstable, and inflexible. As E. F. Benson put it, "The only voluntary and self-impelled movement a Doll can make is to fall down" (Benson and Weaver 163). It was often the male dolls, lacking the support of a long skirt, who were "decidedly shaky" (Gwynfryn 708), a tendency that was sometimes taken to indicate moral laxity. In fiction the stasis is sometimes made comic, as when a doll is kept perpetually ironing because she tends to fall over when assigned to other tasks ("Aunt Laura" 7) or when John the footman is "stuck to the carpet for the present" (*Edith* n.p.).

Action was further hampered by the stiffness of the dolls, their relatively heavy clothing obstructing joints that were intended to be flexible. Dollhouse dolls were notorious for their inability to sit properly: "They have a tendency to sprawl in their gorgeous drawing-rooms in the most ungainly fashion, and if you try to straighten their backs you have to bring their chins to their knees" (Corkran 47). Ernest Shepard and his brother, having gained possession of their sister's old dollhouse, found an alternative: modeling wax fixed the dolls firmly into their chairs, so that "the wretched creatures . . . were condemned to sit at rigid attention instead of sliding off on to the floor (Shepard 167).[17] A sophisticated, but perhaps unintentional, solution is found in a room from the eighteenth-century "Mon Plaisir" collection: as Faith Eaton remarks, the five dolls in this room—and even the lady in a portrait on the wall—seem to be leaning back in order to gaze at the elaborately painted ceiling (Eaton 38–39). Unrealistic as stiffly posed dolls might be, they were often amusing, and even falling down and sliding off chairs are *actions* that can come as pleasant surprises to children who are well aware that dolls cannot move on their own.

Dollhouse dolls tended to lack individuality: the prettier wax or china dolls were likely to be the ladies of the house, and the coarser wooden dolls became servants. Black dolls almost always seemed to be called Dinah and to be relegated to the kitchen. At another extreme, some doll households were so heterogeneous as to make realistic play almost impossible: one fictional group included "a Zouave, a Nun, a Red Riding Hood, [and] a Highlander," with an even wider range of personalities turning up for parties (Aunt Laura 17–18). Such mixtures of characters offer new possibilities for interaction and comic incongruities, and as I have already suggested, stereotyped dolls could also be a source of amusement if they were reassigned an incongruous status. Alice Corkran remembers that when too many guests had been invited to a dinner party, one might "relieve the pressure at table" by demoting some dolls to "take service with the cook" (Corkran 41). In the Graham Montgomery dollhouse, "Mr. Bligh" was discovered after spending several years at the back of a drawer; his wife having found a new husband, he settled for the role of gardener, which included a "splendid set of gardener's implements" (Latham 57).

What from one point of view is a healthy breaking down of stereotypes could, of course, be seen as heedless disregard for a doll's individuality. The same might be said of gender change: when a male doll's legs got broken (a frequent occurrence), he might be turned into a female, with the defective legs hidden under a skirt. As dollhouse historian Ann Sizer has remarked, male dolls tend to get mis-laid or maimed (Sizer 35); in Ann Sharp's dollhouse, for instance, Sir William Johnson is "lost to posterity," surviving only through a slip of paper bearing his name (Gwynfryn 712). The disappearance of male dolls could also reflect antagonism toward men or simply a child's desire to mirror more accurately the daytime household as she knew it, with its preponderance of women.

From the girl's point of view, this facile refashioning of miniature people, including class or gender transformation, might have been a sign of empowerment; from the doll's point of view, such a change might have been a reminder of its helplessness. From the point of view of an observing adult in the later nineteenth century, the pas-sivity of a dollhouse doll made it a good metaphor for the compli-ant housewife. Were girls aware of this implication and made to feel guilty as perpetuators of the housewifely stereotype?

Children's literature before 1920 seldom views dollhouses through dolls' eyes. Many stories of this period featuring dolls as heroines give them extremely exciting lives, but the action takes place not only outside the dollhouse but outside any kind of house—for example, on city streets, in gypsy camps, or in garbage dumps or rivers. These stories constitute a subgenre of children's literature, one that might be called the dolls' picaresque: dolls are moved passively through a series of misfortunes and a series of owners, reminding one of Daniel Defoe's Moll Flanders or of Robinson Crusoe before he settled down on his island.[18]

One story that includes both picaresque elements and a few refer-ences to dollhouse life is Julia Charlotte Maitland's *The Doll and Her Friends* (1858). "Lady Seraphina" is one of the earliest fictional dolls small enough to fit into even the smaller dollhouses that had by 1858 become the norm. She is more fortunate than true picaresque hero-ines in that she moves only from maker to toystore to Rose's home, where she lives for many years in her own dollhouse before being sent to the home of a servant's niece. Her house is only an adapted packing case, as Hablot Browne's illustration shows (though Browne makes the doll too big; fig. 4); she likes it because it is a place of her own, where she does not feel like "an insignificant pigmy in the vast abodes of the colossal race of man" (31). The doll remains fond of her house and looks longingly toward it while being hanged by cruel cousin Geoffrey (52)—Browne's illustration softens this humiliating

THE DOLL'S PARTY.   Page 42.

Figure 4. The illustrator correctly makes the dollhouse very simple but follows conven-
tion rather than the text in showing dolls that are far too large for the house, furniture that has been moved outside, and a doll lying on the roof. Illustration by Hablot
Browne, from Julia Charlotte Maitland's *The Doll and Her Friends* (London: Griffith and
Farran, 1858). Osborne Collection of Early Children's Books, Toronto Public Library.

incident (fig. 5). Home for Lady Seraphina, as for the girls and boys in most children's stories, signifies a place of safe return after adventuring, not a prison from which one needs to escape.

Maitland takes pains to adopt a doll's point of view, and early on Lady Seraphina learns to distinguish between herself and human beings. The careful distinctions she draws prevent readers from making easy analogies between dollhouse dolls and housewife. Dolls, she admits, are dependents, even slaves, and their mental and moral qualities "exist rather in the minds of our admirers than in our own persons"; although dolls may influence "housewifery, neatness, and industry," they do so silently and unconsciously (Maitland 1–2). Like other fictional dolls of this period,[19] Lady Seraphina makes it clear that her purpose is to be "of use" and that she feels no pain, thus implicitly exonerating children from guilt when they choose to transform (or mutilate) her. To a doll, there is no such thing as *abuse*. The text as a whole does not licence wanton destruction, however; Geoffrey learns from a long discussion with his older cousin Margaret that dolls' owners can feel pain (57).

A thoughtful reader of Maitland's story would be able to understand Ibsen's metaphor without seeing it as a negative comment on dolls or dollhouses; but she might get a very different message from James Mason's *The Doll's Letters to Her Mistress,* published serially in the *Girl's Own Paper* of 1881. The "Baroness" is an unpleasantly supercilious doll who has learned to read and write while listening to her mistress's lessons and who now boasts about her own superiority in spelling. On one level, she seems a welcome example of a doll with a mind: she has a sense of her cultural history—she knows that the fairies have disappeared and fears that dolls will follow them—and she responds with animation to a boy's challenge that she is capable of more than saying "Mamma" and "Papa." Unfortunately, while writing the history of her ancestors she overturns her candle and suffers lurid, fiery death in the burning dollhouse. If that were the whole story, it would read as a warning—direct or ironic—against female learning, or at the least against burning the midnight oil; but this interpretation would not fit with the emphasis on the Baroness's aristocratic pride or with the fact that her mistress's house nearly burns down too. It would also not explain the long central section of the book in which the doll sends her owner on a futile hunt for treasure in order to teach her the shallowness of material wealth, a moral to which the author returns in the final sentences. Mason's intention is unclear, but one

THE DOLL IN TROUBLE.   Page 52.

Figure 5. Browne focuses attention on naughty Geoffrey and makes Lady Seraphina too large and too cheerful. According to the doll's own account, a muddy string has been tied tightly round her neck, and she looks longingly at her dollhouse home. From Julia Charlotte Maitland's *The Doll and Her Friends* (London: Griffith and Farran, 1858). Osborne Collection of Early Children's Books, Toronto Public Library.

suspects that because the story would have been read when Ibsen's play was attracting great attention, many readers would have taken the Baroness as a warning against unconventional dollhouse behavior in general and against female intellectual pretensions in particular.

Racketty-Packetty House, written a quarter of a century later, has a more relaxed tone. Going up in flames with one's dollhouse is a threat here too, but the dolls face it with equanimity—"they never sat up all night with Trouble" (48)—partly because they believe that burning is not painful to dolls made of wood. Those dolls who enjoy the boring life of Tidy Castle are not condemned, but Lady Patsy chooses to break her leg in order "to get a change" (62). For the dolls of the old house, nothing is more important than having fun. These characters are distinctly dolls and cannot easily be put to metaphorical use.

Lucinda and Jane, the mindless dolls in Beatrix Potter's *Tale of Two Bad Mice,* are clear examples of the kind of dollhouse doll no girl would want to emulate. They are defined entirely by what they do *not* do; the readers' sympathies are with the mouse intruders, who detect and destroy what is most irritatingly unreal, the plaster food, and then create a cosy household with the furniture they steal. When Hunca Munca sets up a daily routine of housecleaning as compensation for the theft, the impassive dolls are unlikely to be grateful. The real beneficiary of the housecleaning will surely be the owner of the dollhouse, who perhaps now will be able to spend more time enjoying the skipping rope and badminton rackets always pictured alongside it.

To my mind, the most interesting account of dollhouse life is found in "Professor Green" (1906), a short story by Ada Wallas that is clearly written for what *Girl's Realm* called the "modern girl." Soon after Ibsen's *Doll's House* was first performed, Ada Wallas (then Radford) was a student at Newnham College, Cambridge; by 1906 she was married to Professor Graham Wallas and had a small daughter, who went on to an academic career at Newnham herself. The story features a real-life professor and his daughter; her dollhouse in turn is the home of the miniature Professor Green.

The first part of the story, set within the dollhouse, suggests that life there need not be intellectually constricting: Professor Green, his wife, and their friends have an intelligent discussion about dolls' cultural history, comparing the New and the Old in Doll's House Land. (The Old food is solid but inedible, like fish glued to a plate, whereas the New consists of "biscuits and sugar and hot messes" [Wallas 124–25]; the Old fires, no more than red tinsel, were replaced by New fires laid like real ones, though they were not lit.) As in Maitland's story, the subject matter reminds one that these are dolls, not symbols. Wallas (who later wrote *Before the Bluestockings,* a study of early feminists) makes her points subtly, often by reversal: instead of an imprisoned housewife doll, she gives us Professor Green, who in fact has escaped *to* the sanctity of the dollhouse, after a previous owner had put him in charge of her Noah's Ark. He now spends his time peacefully writing a history of the universe: "No smaller subject would have comforted him; in its largeness he found comfort" (Wallas 123). The comic contrast of subject matter and physical size is enhanced by a family joke: Wallas's husband, Graham, was the author of such works as *The Art of Thought, Human Nature in Politics,* and *The Great Society.* Wallas's story, like James Mason's, brings intellectual activity into the dollhouse, but without the penalty Mason imposes; the Greens, like Lady Seraphina, the Racketty-Packetty dolls, and the Bad Mice, enjoy the coziness of home without feeling trapped by its littleness. Except for Mason's, all these stories could be reassuring to girls who might have picked up negative connotations of dollhouse life from adult literature.

For readers of the 1899 *Girl's Realm* editorial who were worried about the political correctness of dollhouse play, Ada Wallas's story offers answers. The early adult concern that dollhouses encouraged pride had already faded by this time, as mass-produced and home-made miniatures became the norm; in the second part of "Professor Green," where the point of view shifts from doll's to child's level, making one's own accessories for the dollhouse is most of the fun. Neatness and completeness are not adult-imposed demands here but, rather, ways of making life more pleasant for the dolls. Professor Green is happy that Diana, his present owner, does not incessantly houseclean, but he is pleased too when she notices that he could do with his own waste basket. Diana does not find dollhouse play confining: she builds an outdoor house for a china gardener and his wife and brings the indoor family on visits; she expresses her special interest, reading, by making books for the dolls and works through a personal problem of shyness toward her father by modeling Professor Green on him.

The security of Diana's dollhouse as a ludic space of her own is challenged by the arrival of cousin Richard, stereotyped in advance by Diana as a destructive boy; Richard, in fact, admires the dollhouse as much as she does and secretly begins to make just the right accessories and additions himself, including that always-desirable feature, a staircase. The story ends with the discovery that Richard and Diana have been working toward the same goal.

No one would want to escape from this dollhouse; Richard and Diana observe the dolls and respond to their needs. Family traditions are perpetuated and new activities introduced. Diana had pretended to have no interest in dollhouses because she believed that boys only attack what one cares about; she is liberated from her fear, and Richard earns his place as a contributor to the household. Unfortunately, though perhaps appropriately, this story that offers so attractive a model of dollhouse play for the "modern girl" has not become well known outside the Wallas family tradition; the only copy I have encountered so far was given to the Newnham College Library by Wallas's daughter. It deserves a wider audience.

Notes

1. Bathsua Makin, writing in 1673, refers to women "dressing and trimming themselves like *Bartholomew*-babies" (*Essay* 30). Mary, Lady Chudleigh spoke in 1701 of women appearing to be "made, like puppets, to divert mankind" (Lonsdale 2). Rousseau commented in the 1750s that a girl would in due time "be her own doll" (*Emile* 331). Women throughout the eighteenth century were often likened to "babies," a word interchangeable with "dolls."

2. Gulliver's Brobdingnagian "little nurse," Glumdalclitch, is a borderline example; *Gulliver's Travels* certainly did much to stir up popular interest in miniaturization.

3. The best-known comments are those of Maria and R. L. Edgeworth, who objected to ready-made dollhouses on the grounds that there was nothing children could do with them (*Practical Education* 1: 4–5).

4. Juliet Mitchell, discussing the carnivalesque, points out that the carnival is not an alternative to the law but "is set up by the law precisely as its own ludic space" (quoted in Eagleton, *Feminist Literary Theory* 102).

5. According to modern research, playing house and playing with dolls were more popular among boys in the nineteenth century than in recent years; see Brian Sutton-Smith and B. G. Rosenberg, "Sixty Years of Historical Change in the Game Preferences of American Children" (Herron and Sutton-Smith 37). "Dingley Hall," now in London's Bethnal Green Museum, is a well-known example of a huge dollhouse elaborately furnished by Lawrence and Isaac Currie as young boys in the 1870s. Building a dollhouse for one's sister was, of course, a socially acceptable activity that could easily slide into play.

6. For details of Jeremy Bentham's plan to structure institutions as Panopticons under constant surveillance, see Bentham 1: 498–503, and 4: 37–78.

7. Until the mid-nineteenth century, dollhouse rooms were big enough to allow a child to climb inside, though at the expense of any miniature furnishings. Frances Power Cobbe mentions enjoying this kind of retreat (Cobbe 17).

8. I have not been able to examine the 1783 edition; the 1800 and 1815 editions have the same text, though some illustrations differ.

9. The princess is supposedly a granddaughter of Queen Victoria, and Racketty-

Packetty House reminds her of the house Victoria had as a child. This story further confuses any attempt to separate fiction from nonfiction; Victoria's dollhouse—a very plain one—had been on public display (as it still is today), and children's magazines ran many articles about the playthings of Victoria's descendants and those of other royal children from all over Europe.

10. The image of the child with her head in the cupboard is reminiscent of Burnett's account of how as a child she pretended that the sitting room cupboard was a temple in Central America, where "strange pigmy remnants of the Aztec royal race" were kept and worshipped as gods; she would kneel on the floor with her head in the cupboard (*The One* 66–67). This game was inspired by a pamphlet she had seen advertising an exhibition that included two Aztec dwarfs. I am reminded of Enoch Emery and his "tabernacle-like cabinet" in Flannery O'Connor's *Wise Blood* (New York: Harcourt, Brace, 1952).

11. In making this estimation, I assume that such games, because of their conventional and repetitive nature, are likely to be underemphasized in memoirs and in fiction.

12. Account of Tallemant des Reaux; quoted in Jacobs, 91.

13. From *The Young Lady's Book* (Routledge, 1888); reprinted in *International Dolls' House News* (Autumn 1974): 10.

14. Letter from Princess Charlotte of Belgium to Queen Victoria, July 18, 1848 (Benson and Esher 2: 220).

15. Dorothy and Jerome Singer cite a study by Diana Franklin showing that children who often played fantasy games with blocks tended to see positive happenings as being caused by their own efforts rather than by outside forces. "This 'illusion of control' of happy events may well emerge from the way in which fantasy play provides the child with opportunities to practice manipulation and power over a miniaturized world" (147–48).

16. Letter from "Fannie H. H." in *Harper's Bazaar for Children* 1889; quoted in *International Dolls' House News* (Winter 1983): 21.

17. The two boys had been forbidden to play with modeling wax because of the damage it caused to carpets; presumably they were not concerned about damaging the dolls' clothes.

18. The dolls' picaresque, and other aspects of dolls' helplessness in the face of abuse, are discussed more fully in my forthcoming *Pocket Companions*.

19. Margaret Gatty's "Aunt Sally" is a striking and, I believe, parodic example.

Works Cited

Acland, Eleanor. *Good-bye for the Present: The Story of Two Childhoods*. London: Hodder, 1935.

Aunt Laura [Barrow, Frances Elizabeth]. *The Dolls' Surprise Party*. New York: Breed, Butler, 1863.

Bachelard, Gaston. *The Poetics of Space*. Trans. Maria Jolas. 1958; Boston: Beacon, 1969.

Barbauld, Anna Laetitia. *Works*. London: Longman, 1824.

Benson, A.C., and Viscount Esher, eds. *Letters of Queen Victoria: A Selection from Her Majesty's Correspondence between the Years 1837 and 1861*. 3 vols. London: Murray, 1908.

Benson, A.C., and Sir Lawrence Weaver. *The Book of the Queen's Doll's House*. London: Methuen, 1924.

Bentham, Jeremy. *The Works of Jeremy Bentham*, ed. John Bowring. 11 vols. 1838–43. Reprint. New York: Russell, 1962.

Burnett, Frances Hodgson. *The One I Knew the Best of All*. 1893. Reprint. New York: Scribner's, 1903.

————. *Racketty-Packetty House.* London: Warne, 1907.

————. "My Toy Cupboard." *Ladies' Home Journal* 32, no. 4 (1915): 11.

Cobbe, Frances Power. *Life of Frances Power Cobbe by Herself.* 2 vols. Boston: Houghton, Mifflin, 1894.

Colleen Moore's Fairy Castle. Milwaukee: Ideals, 1981.

Corkran, Alice. "In Doll-House Land." *The Girl's Realm* 2 (1900): 41–50.

"Cousin Josie." "Our Baby-House." *Demorest's Young America* (Jan. 1867): 276–77.

Cousins, Martha. "A Doll Sky-Scraper." *Youth's Companion,* Oct. 18, 1906, 501.

Dickens, Charles. *Bleak House.* 1853. Reprint. Harmondsworth: Penguin, 1971.

————. "The Christmas Tree." *Household Words* 2 (Dec. 21, 1850): 289–95.

————. *David Copperfield.* 1849–50. Reprint. London: Penguin, 1966.

————. *Our Mutual Friend.* 1864–65. Reprint. London: Penguin, 1971.

Eaton, Faith. *The Miniature House.* London: Weidenfeld, 1990.

Edgeworth, Maria, and R. L. Edgeworth. *Practical Education.* 2 vols. London, 1815.

Edith and Milly's Housekeeping. London: Frederick Warne, [1865].

The Editor. "Chat with the Girl of the Period." *Girl's Realm* 1 (1899).

Ewing, Juliana Horatia. *Dolls Housekeeping.* London: Society for the Propagation of Christian Knowledge, 1884.

————. "The Land of Lost Toys." In *The Brownies and Other Stories.* 1870. Reprint. London: Dent, 1954. Pp. 151–83.

Fenn, Lady Eleanor. *Cobwebs to Catch Flies.* 1783. Reprint. London: Marshall, ca. 1800.

————. *Juvenile Correspondence.* London: Marshall, 1783.

Gatty, Margaret. *Aunt Sally's Life.* London: Bell and Daldy, 1865.

Greene, Vivien. *English Dolls' Houses.* 1955. 2d ed. New York: Scribner's, 1979.

————. *Family Dolls' Houses.* London: Bell, 1973.

Gwynfryn [Miss Jones]. "A Doll-House of Queen Anne's Reign." *Aunt Judy's Magazine* (July–Dec. 1870): 705–15.

Herron, R. E., and Brian Sutton-Smith, eds. *Child's Play.* New York: Wiley, 1971.

Ibsen, Henrik. *A Doll's House.* Trans. James Walter MacFarlane. 1879. Reprint. Oxford: Oxford University Press, 1961.

Jacobs, Flora Gill. *A History of Dolls' Houses.* 1953. Rev. ed. New York: Scribner's, 1965.

Jefferies, Richard. *Bevis.* 1882. Oxford: Oxford University Press, 1989.

Kilner, Mary Ann. *Memoirs of a Peg-Top.* York: Wilson, 1784.

Latham, Jean. *Dolls' Houses: A Personal Choice.* London: Black, 1969.

[Lehmann, R.C.]. "Art in the Dolls' House." *Punch* (April 3, 10, 17, 24, 1901): 250, 268, 286, 304.

Little Polly's Doll's House. London: Routledge, [1856].

Lonsdale, Roger, ed. *Eighteenth-Century Women Poets.* Oxford: Oxford University Press, 1990.

McCrea, Lilian. *First Loves.* Cromford, Eng.: Scarthin, 1985.

Maitland, Julia Charlotte. *The Doll and Her Friends: Or, Memoirs of the Lady Seraphina.* London: Griffith, 1858.

[Makin, Bathsua.] *An Essay to Revive the Antient Education of Gentlewomen.* 1673. Reprint. Los Angeles: University of California Press, 1980.

Marks, Mary A. M. "Our Dolls' House." *Little Folks.* 1896. Reprint. *International Dolls' House News* (Autumn 1971): 13–14.

Mason, James. "The Doll's Letters to Her Mistress." *Girl's Own Paper* (1881): 604–05, 693–94, 764–66.

Millhauser, Steven. "The Fascination of the Miniature." *Grand Street* 2, no. 4 (1983): 128–35.

Mister, Mary. *The Adventures of a Doll.* London, 1816.

Mitchell, Juliet. "Femininity, Narrative and Psychoanalysis." In *Women: The Longest Revo-*

lution. London: Virago, 1984. Reprinted in Mary Eagleton, *Feminist Literary Theory.* Oxford: Blackwell, 1986.

Nesbit, Edith. *Wings and the Child.* London: Hodder, 1913.

Pollock, Alice. *Portrait of My Victorian Youth.* London: Johnson, 1971.

Potter, Beatrix. *The Tale of Two Bad Mice.* 1904. Reprint. London: Warne, n.d.

Prentiss, Elizabeth. *Little Susy's Six Birthdays.* London: Sampson, Low, 1854.

Pyle, Katharine. "The Story of a Doll-House." *St. Nicholas* 16 (1889): 448–51.

Rousseau, Jean-Jacques. *Emile.* Trans. Barbara Foxley. 1757–60. Reprint. London: Dent, 1911.

Shepard, Ernest Howard. *Drawn from Memory.* 1957. Reprint. Harmondsworth: Penguin, 1975.

Sherwood, Mary Martha. *The History of the Fairchild Family: Or, The Child's Manual.* 1818. Reprint. London: Hatchard, 1853.

Singer, Dorothy G., and Jerome L. Singer. *The House of Make-Believe: Children's Play and the Developing Imagination.* Cambridge: Harvard University Press, 1990.

Sitwell, Osbert. *Two Generations.* London: Macmillan, 1940.

Sizer, Ann. "Dolls' Houses in Literature from Edwardian to 1930." *International Dolls' House News* 21, no. 1 (1992): 35–37.

Stewart-Wilson, Mary. *Queen Mary's Dolls' House.* New York: Abbeville, 1988.

Summerson, John. *Heavenly Mansions and Other Essays on Architecture.* New York: Norton, 1963.

Swift, Jonathan. *Gulliver's Travels.* 1735. Reprint. New York: Modern Library, 1958.

Taylor, Ann, Jane Taylor, and Adelaide O'Keefe. *Original Poems for Infant Minds.* 2 vols. London, 1804.

Taylor, Judy. *Letters to Children from Beatrix Potter.* London: Warne, 1992.

Thorne, Barrie. *Gender Play: Girls and Boys in School.* Buckingham: Open University Press, 1993.

Wallas, Mrs. Graham [Ada]. *Before the Bluestockings.* London: Allen and Unwin, 1929.

———. "Professor Green." In *The Land of Play.* London: Arnold, 1906. Pp. 121–209.

The Young Lady's Book. Routledge, 1888.

Brave New Alice: Anna Matlack Richards's Maternal Wonderland

Carolyn Sigler

Alice's Adventures in Wonderland (1865) and *Through the Looking-Glass* (1871) are among the most enduring and successful Victorian works for children. At the end of the nineteenth century a poll by the *Pall Mall Gazette* to determine the twenty best books for ten-year-olds ranked *Alice's Adventures in Wonderland* first and *Through the Looking-Glass* eleventh (Avery 131). Now Lewis Carroll's Alice books have become an accepted part of both the children's and adult literary canons, appearing in countless classic paperback editions for both audiences and on virtually every Victorian bibliography of "great books." It is little wonder, then, that Carroll's popular and canonical successes have generated almost two hundred parodies, sequels, and imitations, including some, such as Anna Matlack Richards's *A New Alice in the Old Wonderland* (1895), that I believe construct radical revisions of the original Alice adventures. Richards's work, I shall argue, deserves special consideration in the Alice-imitation canon, because it indicates to the modern reader some of the ways that nineteenth-century American women read, responded to, and resisted the construction of femininity in the original Alice books.

To understand Richards's work more fully, it is important to place it in the context of the numerous works inspired by Carroll that proliferated in the late nineteenth and early twentieth centuries. Many of the best parodies, like Hector Hugh Munro's *The Westminster Alice* (1902) and Edward Hope's *Alice in the Delighted States* (1928), use the liberating nonsense of the Alice books for political and social satire; sequels, such as Hartley Georget's *A Few More Chapters of Alice Through the Looking-Glass* (1875) and John Rae's *Another Alice Book, Please!* (1917), continue or expand upon Alice's adventures. A majority of the works that modeled themselves after *Alice in Wonderland* and *Through the Looking-Glass,* however, could best be described as imitations: dream fantasies adhering to a similar plot structure (that of the journey) and using poems, songs, nonsense language, and famil-

Children's Literature 24, ed. Francelia Butler, R. H. W. Dillard, and Elizabeth Lennox Keyser (Yale University Press, © 1996 Hollins College).

iar characters from nursery rhymes and games.[1] Many of these Alice imitations are didactic in nature, transforming Carroll's nonsensical Wonderland and Looking-Glass worlds into a place where lessons and morals are communicated directly rather than obliquely—"if only you can find [them]," as the Duchess wryly observes in *Alice in Wonderland*. Carroll was very interested in the many imitations that followed the publication of his two Alice books, and he notes in his diary entry for September 11, 1891, the acquisition of several of them for "the collection I intend making of the books of the *Alice* type" (*Diaries* 2:486).

Yet not all of the Alice imitations are merely didactic or, for that matter, merely imitations. Among the most radical revisions of the Alice myth were those written by women writers in the last three decades of the nineteenth century. These include Jean Ingelow's *Mopsa the Fairy* (1869), Christina Rossetti's powerful *Speaking Likenesses* (1874), Alice Corkran's *Mrs. Wishing-To-Be* (1883), Maggie Browne's *Wanted—A King; or How Merle Set the Nursery Rhymes to Right* (1890), and Richards's *A New Alice*, all of which pose feminized (if not directly feminist) alternatives to Carroll's oppressive and autocratic vision of Wonderland. Indeed, as Nina Auerbach and U. C. Knopflmacher point out in *Forbidden Journeys*, female fantasy writers "*had* to speak gently (like Lewis Carroll's Duchess) even when they were most enraged" (6, italics added). Ingelow's *Mopsa the Fairy* both complicates and resists the conventional morality and sentimentality of Carroll, Charles Kingsley, and many other Victorian fantasy writers.[2] Rossetti's *Speaking Likenesses* offers up a dark antidote to what Auerbach and Knopflmacher characterize as the "cheerfulness demanded of good women" (317). Browne's *Wanted—A King* is, by contrast, exuberant and energetic in its subversion. Her protagonist, Merle, successfully rids the fantasyland, Endom, of a dictatorial ruler and restores the rightful king. Merle is encouraged by the Rhyme Fairy to be a defiant and resistant heroine:

> "If you would banish Gunter Grim,
> Have not the slightest fear of him.
>
> . . . .
>
> Defy, Deride, Desist, Deny,
> Heed not a growl, or scowl, or sigh."   (86–88)

Among the many Victorian Alice imitations, sequels, and revisions, however, Anna Richards's *A New Alice in the Old Wonderland* seems particularly radical in its intent and effect. Indeed, Richards's *New Alice* is less an imitation of Carroll's *Alice in Wonderland* than a challenge to it. An anonymous reviewer in *The Dial* of December 1, 1895, describes Richards's *New Alice* as a "hazardous experiment," for unlike other imitators who modified the formula of the magical land and child adventurer by adding different characters and settings, Richards retained the Wonderland and Looking-Glass settings of Carroll's Alice books; she also used many of the original characters and situations, all to fulfill the desire of Alice Lee—Richards's protagonist as well as her daughter, who is fictionalized in the text—to have her own adventure in the real Wonderland rather than an imitation. It is precisely because Richards remains close to Carroll's works that she is able to refute him on his own turf, using the characters, settings, and themes of the original text to question and subvert the violence and oppression that characterize the Alice books' darker, yet ultimately more conventional, ideologies of education, the status of women and girls, and adult-child relationships—particularly those of mothers and daughters.

Little is known about Anna Matlack Richards; indeed, her novel is occasionally misattributed to her daughter, Anna M. Richards, Jr., who furnished the Tenniel-like drawings for the book. What information is available concerns mostly her relationship with her husband, William Trost Richards, a successful pre-Raphaelite painter who devoted himself to painting nature studies, particularly seascapes, and who was a follower and acquaintance of John Ruskin's.[3] At the time of her marriage to Richards, in 1856, Anna Matlack, the daughter of a Quaker physician, was already well known as a poet and playwright. She and William traveled abroad, during which time he painted and exhibited his work, and finally settled in Newport, Rhode Island. They eventually had eight children. Anna published *Dramatic Sonnets* in 1881 and *Letter and Spirit* in 1891, which William Morton Payne, a reviewer for *The Dial,* called "exquisite," comparing Richards's verse favorably to that of Matthew Arnold, particularly in what Payne characterized as a "modern" longing for faith. In the 1890s Richards published comic poems for children in the popular children's magazines *Harper's Young People* and *The St. Nicholas Magazine* and in 1895, five years before her death, released *A New Alice in the Old Wonderland,* an expanded version of the stories she had invented for her young children, to whom the novel is dedicated, about their favorite storybook world. In the 1890s Carroll was involved in a flurry of efforts to reinterpret and repackage his Alice books, including the release of the first published edition of *The Nursery Alice* in 1890 and the marketing of such products as an Alice postage-stamp case (1890) and an Alice biscuit tin (1892). The release of Richards's *New Alice* thus came at a time of renewed public awareness of Carroll's *Alice* and apparently met with success, for a second edition was released in 1896.[4] The differences, however, between Carroll's and Richards's Alices (and, indeed, Carroll's own attempts to reinterpret his original work in revisions such as *The Nursery Alice*) point to changes in domestic ideology over the thirty years between the 1865 release of Carroll's *Alice in Wonderland* and the 1895 release of Richards's *A New Alice in the Old Wonderland*.

Carroll's 1865 Alice is in many ways an abandoned child who must suddenly confront the frightening prospect of having to make her own way in a world she cannot, despite all her efforts, understand. Unsure even of her own identity, she longs for reassurance and rescue: " '[O]h dear!' cried Alice, with a sudden burst of tears. . . . 'I am so *very* tired of being all alone here!' " (*Wonderland* 16–17). Carroll's Alice tries to cope with the nightmare in which she finds herself through the prescribed codes of Victorian femininity: by being deferential and demure and displaying her repertoire of ornamental accomplishments such as polite manners and recitation.

Above all, Alice survives by repressing her feelings. She attempts to contain her annoyance at the caterpillar, "swallowing down her anger as well as she could" (36), and her fear of the Duchess, whom Alice politely begs to " '*please* mind what you're doing' " as the Duchess tosses her baby into "the shower of saucepan, plates, and dishes" flung by the furious cook (48). Carroll depicts adulthood as an autocracy of fools, in which meaningless didacticism is wielded as a weapon, rules of behavior and decorum are hypocritical and contradictory, and the threat of punishment always looms: " 'Give your evidence,' " says the King of Hearts to the Hatter, " 'and don't be nervous or I'll have you executed on the spot' " (*Wonderland* 99). Carroll's heroine learns to cope with, and ultimately adapt to, the bewildering, illogical, and randomly violent world of adults, ironically satirized by Carroll as enormous infants who must be alternately comforted, admonished, and feared by the resolute Alice, who is both child and mother figure.

Indeed, in the absence of either her mother or an acceptable substitute, the child Alice often assumes the parental role in both the Wonderland and Looking-Glass adventures, passing out the prizes after the Caucus Race, taking care of the abandoned pig-baby, tolerantly humoring Tweedledee and Tweedledum's "battle," and gently tucking the helpless White Queen's unruly hair back into its pins. Yet, although she is expected to assume the role of an adult, Alice has no adult authority. She is the one who must adapt and conform to the needs of those around her; the Red Queen's promise to Alice that "in the Eighth Square we shall be Queens together, and its all feasting and fun!" remains unfulfilled (*Looking-Glass* 128). Thus, despite the apparently liberating satirical edge of the Alice books, they are in many respects very conservative in their treatment of gender. A Victorian Angel-in-Wonderland, Alice has no more power as a mother figure than as a girl to transform the world she inhabits.

Richards follows the dream framework of Carroll's *Alice in Wonderland* and *Through the Looking-Glass* yet adapts it to her own purposes. The novel opens with a conversation between Alice Lee, a young American girl, and her mother. The girl longs for adventure, and her mother encourages her love of "pretending." Thinking back to her many pretend adventures, Alice Lee's "thoughts wandered into the Wonderland of the Alice books, with their little world of people so much more real than the ones in the ordinary Wonder books" (14), and she remembers when she used to rub the looking-glass over the mantelpiece "to see whether it ever showed any sign of melting" (15). That evening a parcel arrives for Alice Lee that turns out to be a box containing a slice of wedding cake "sent by a cousin of hers from a distant city, whose wedding her father and mother had attended the week before" (16). Advised to place the cake under her pillow to make her dreams come true, Alice Lee begins to feel that "this was almost an adventure in its way" (16).

That night, unable to sleep, Alice Lee succumbs to temptation and nibbles on the piece of cake. Suddenly she realizes that the patch of moonlight across from her bed has become a door, and eagerly opening it, she enters a garden and heads off boldly in search of adventure: "She was perfectly sure . . . that she was in Wonderland, and she thought the best plan would be to keep along the road, where something interesting would be the most sure to turn up." (30)

Readers familiar with Carroll's books—like Richards's young adventurer, Alice Lee, who "almost know[s] them by heart" (19–20)—find themselves quickly and "delightfully at home" (33) in Richards's *A New Alice in the Old Wonderland*. The author reminds us that she is taking us back to "that very same Wonderland, of course" through Alice Lee, who declares with a touch of solemn irony that "all the

other books about some other kind [of Wonderland] were perfect
nonsense" (Richards 14). In this new vision of "that very same Wonderland" the mad tea party continues, the Cheshire cat grins on, and
the Frog Footman still stands at his post outside the Duchess's house,
which remains "delightfully . . . full of pepper" (32). At the same
time, Richards reconstructs Carroll's "old Wonderland" through the
pervasive, nurturing voice of Alice Lee's mother, who watches over
Alice Lee while she sleeps and provides the impetus for her dream.
This maternal presence is further intensified through the voice of the
narrator, who is the story's mother-author-storyteller, and the novel's
fictional mother. Carroll's Alice does not directly mention her mother
or father in *Alice in Wonderland* or *Through the Looking-Glass* (though
her older sister is present in the frame to Alice's Wonderland adventures); however, she does infrequently and indirectly refer to them,
usually in allusions to incidents of conflict or transgression. At the
beginning of chapter 12 in *Alice in Wonderland* ("Alice's Evidence"),
for example, the tipped-over jury box reminds Alice "very much of a
globe of gold-fish she had accidentally upset the week before" (92).
In *Through the Looking-Glass,* after escaping through the mirror, Alice
gleefully exclaims that she'll be both warmer and *safer* in the looking-
glass room because "'there'll be no one here to scold me away from
the fire. Oh what fun it'll be, when they see me through the glass in
here, and ca'n't [*sic*] get at me'" (112). The few oblique allusions to
Alice's parents or governess in the Alice books therefore make them
sound disapproving and dictatorial, little different from the often
peevish and authoritarian adult characters in the Wonderland and
Looking-Glass worlds. Maternal characters, such as the Duchess and
the Red and White Queens, are portrayed as aggressively violent or
helplessly feeble.

In Richards's *New Alice,* however, the powerful symbolic presence
of Alice Lee's mother is pervasive, and Alice Lee thinks of and in-
vokes her frequently as a source of power.[5] When events at the Mad
Hatter's tea party threaten to get out of hand, Alice Lee restores
order by reading the assembled party recipes from "her mother's
'Cookery Book,'" which mysteriously appears on the table. The lists
of dishes and ingredients reduce the quarrelsome creatures to tears
of longing (75), in an ironic reversal of Alice's own "pool of tears" in
the old Wonderland. "Reading about all those good things has been
too much for 'em," the March Hare tells Alice Lee reproachfully.
Such episodes suggest the larger influence of nineteenth-century do-

mestic ideology, which argued that the world could be transformed by maternal values; certainly motherhood was already, as early the 1852 publication of *Uncle Tom's Cabin,* a "highly politicized concept" (Ammons 160). According to Gillian Brown: "The domestic values celebrated by *Uncle Tom's Cabin* and popular domestic novels represent an alternative, moral, feminine organization of life which could radically reform . . . society" (507). These radicalized maternal values inform Richards's *New Alice,* providing a bridge between the mid-century view of women's influence represented by Alice Lee's mother, and the late-century view of women's power represented by Alice Lee.

References to maternal nurturance abound in the domestic fantasy world created by the voice of Alice Lee's mother: the Cheshire Cat is now a mother with a litter of kittens to fuss over, "the sweetest little cherubs" (40; figs. 1 and 2). A smiling Humpty Dumpty assures a concerned Alice Lee that he has hard-boiled himself to avoid future calamities (89). In her mother's re-creation of Wonderland Alice Lee discovers that family connections and loyalties (particularly those among women—symbolized by an older cousin's gift of a piece of her wedding cake at the beginning of the book) are more important than conflict. When the Cheshire Cat generously admits to Alice Lee that the Duchess's pig-child is perhaps "a very *little* handsomer" than her own children, she adds, "it's all in the family, besides, so it don't count" (40).[6] Indeed, the impetus of the plot concerns Alice Lee's journey to and attendance at the children's performance at the Royal Kindergarten, aided and encouraged by the children's proud mothers.

The subversive impulse of Anna Richards's *A New Alice in the Old Wonderland,* however, lies not merely in her matriarchal re-creation of Wonderland but in her transformation of Carroll's anxiously polite Alice into the courageous "new Alice," Alice Lee, who does not fall into but consciously searches out new adventure. Unlike many Alice imitations, it is Alice Lee herself—rather than Wonderland—who is markedly different in Richards's fantasy, "set[ting] off on her journey, quite sure that she was going to have some real adventures . . . not at all concerned, as the other Alice had been, by remembering that she was too big" (30–31). Alice Lee is a daring, even defiant female hero: she laughs at the peevish Hatter and Hare, and when chased by the Duchess's cook (who terrorizes Alice with a pair of fire irons and a shower of saucepans in the original), Alice Lee finds the incident "rather fun than otherwise" (44). Richards has given her new

Figure 1. Alice appeals to the Cheshire Cat for directions. From Carroll, *Alice's Adventures in Wonderland.*

Alice the qualities of the turn-of-the-century "New Woman," who represented the extension of the private domestic sphere into public, political action such as the woman's suffrage and educational reform movements.[7] As William Chafe argues: "By the late nineteenth century . . . middle and upper-class white women had so thoroughly expanded and empowered their separate 'sphere' that it had become more an instrument for political influence than a barrier to freedom" (Chafe 5).[8] "New Alices," like their adult New Women counterparts, embody "courage and daring, not submissiveness and dependence" (Honig 12), using the very language of domesticity to challenge its constraints.

Certainly, in accounting for the differences in domestic ideology, the thirty years that separate these two Alice novels must be kept in mind: the greater power of the female characters, the emancipa-

Figure 2. Alice Lee and the maternal Cheshire Cat. From Richards, *A New Alice*.

tory rhetoric of the narrative, the fictive transformation of the domestic mother figure through her daughter into a transcendent New Woman. Alice Lee's emancipation from the restrictions of the past is further made possible by her and her mother's thorough knowledge of the old Alice's adventures, enabling Alice Lee always to maintain power over her circumstances. She resolves not to eat or drink anything in Wonderland, as Alice's physical changes "seemed to her the only unpleasant part of the other Alice's adventures" (52), and, familiar with Queen's blustering ways, she is "not very much concerned about her head" when the Queen of Hearts interjects her usual threats into their conversation (270). The last chapter of the novel finds Alice Lee not only wearing a crown, as Carroll's Alice does at the end of *Through the Looking-Glass*, but also brandishing power and authority in the image of a sword. On the one hand, Alice's Looking-Glass journey ends in frustration, with illustrations depicting Alice dejectedly propping up the two other dozing Queens (197) or attempting in vain to enter the door marked "QUEEN ALICE" after being told by an anonymous creature, "No admittance till the week after next!" (198; fig. 3). On the other hand, the parallel "Queen

Figure 3. Queen Alice. From Carroll, *Alice's Adventures in Wonderland*.

Alice" illustration in Richards's *New Alice* depicts Alice Lee proudly guarding the gate to the Red Castle—herself in charge of refusing others admittance—looking in the illustration like a young Joan of Arc (fig. 4): "I never heard of anybody else in the whole world having such a glorious adventure," she declares as she stands guard over the castle entrance (298).

Richards discursively empowers her fantasy hero Alice Lee by having the voice of her mother initiate and control her adventures. In fact, much of Alice Lee's new power in the old Wonderland is due to the narrative authority of her mother, who promises Alice Lee that "if I happen to come across any adventure I will be sure to let you have it" (12). Alice Lee's mother presides over her fantasy, sitting and watching "close by" throughout her daughter's dream (308). Her influence is demonstrated throughout the book in Alice Lee's power over the Wonderland creatures, which replicates the maternal authority demonstrated by Alice Lee's mother in the novel's framing scenes. Anna Richards's maternally inspired brave "new Alice" is an extension, and ultimately a transformation, of the nineteenth-century middle-class ideology of motherhood as a powerful moral force that Ruth H. Bloch characterizes as the ideal of the "Moral

Figure 4. Queen Alice Lee. From Richards, *A New Alice.*

Mother" (105). Nancy Chodorow and Susan Contratto describe this ideal as the mythic "fantasy of the perfect mother" in which "women's maternal potential . . . enables fully-embodied power" and in which "the child who evokes this arrangement must also be all-powerful" (60). Indeed, although Carroll's Alice is forced to conform and adapt through the assumption of a proto-maternal role, her resulting lack of power may be due to her lack of a mother. Although in fantasy the absence of mother can mean a kind of freedom, an experience that Alice herself celebrates at the beginning of *Through the Looking-Glass,* such motherless fictional daughters, as Cathy Davidson points out, are also "unguided, uneducated, [and] unprotected" (120).

Female relationships and female power dominate Alice Lee's adventures in Wonderland; even the talisman that enables Alice Lee's transition from one world to the other is bound up in Victorian female ritual. Alice Lee nibbles on the piece of wedding cake sent to her by her female cousin, which she has placed under her pillow because she has been assured that it "will make you dream exactly the thing you want to" (17). The matriarchal power provided by the domestic sphere that frames Alice Lee's fantasy adventure endows both her and her mother with the ability to play imaginatively with the conventions and boundaries of that sphere, as Alice Lee tries out different roles and relationships on the course of her journey, embodying the "mobile, magic woman," described by Nina Auerbach at the beginning of *Woman and the Demon*, "who breaks the boundaries of family within which her society restricts her" (1).

Women's increasing control over issues of education, child rearing, and literature for children informs much of the satiric force of *New Alice* against conventional models of public education, which Richards depicts through a series of pompous and pedantic male professors. Richards's parody of Carroll—who uses both Alice books to satirize conventional educational moralizing as well as the pointless tradition of recitation—provides a vehicle for further insights from a woman's perspective. Richards attacks rigidly traditional classroom techniques, such as recitations and memorization, as well as contemporary educational fads, such as those recommended by Friedrich Froebel's kindergarten handbooks, which seemed to do little more than dress up old conventions. The discussion of schooling in *New Alice* is the satirical inversion of that in *Alice in Wonderland* (in which the Mock Turtle does most of the talking); indeed, some of the more oppressive moments in Carroll's Alice novels occur when the characters suddenly assume a role of authority, as when the Mock Turtle and Gryphon insist that Alice recite for them:

> "I should like to hear her try and repeat something now. Tell her to begin." [The Mock Turtle] looked at the Gryphon as if he thought it had some kind of authority over Alice.
>
> "Stand up and repeat ' 'Tis the voice of the sluggard,' " said the Gryphon.
>
> "How the creatures order one about and make one repeat lessons!" thought Alice. "I might just as well be at school at once." (82)

Alice's recitation of course sounds "very queer indeed" as she recites the parodic " 'Tis the voice of the Lobster" instead of the well-known

Figure 5. The Mock Turtle describes his education. From Carroll, *Alice's Adventures in Wonderland.*

Watts poem (82); the parody turns darker, however, as the Gryphon insists that Alice continue: "Alice did not dare to disobey, though she felt sure it would all come wrong, and she went on in a trembling voice" (83; fig. 5). In the *New Alice* version of this scene, Alice Lee instead tells the Mock Turtle about *her* education (fig. 6), including a reading (of Poe's "The Raven") that she attended with her mother: "But what is a '*reading*'?" the Mock Turtle asks Alice Lee. "Oh, nothing much," replies Alice. "Somebody just reads and reads, and the people all sit round and wait till he is done" (222).

Richards's satire is a reflection of a number of nineteenth-century educational controversies. By the end of the nineteenth century, American reformers such as Mary Lyon, Catherine Ward Beecher, and Kate Douglas Wiggins (who wrote *Children's Rights: A Book of Nursery Logic* [1892], and the sentimental *Rebecca of Sunnybrook Farm* [1903]) had "asserted not only women's control over family child care but also their right to control education, Sunday Schools, and

Figure 6. Alice discusses education with the Mock Turtle. From Richards, *A New Alice*.

other institutions for children, institutions that could become powerful agencies for the transmission of feminine ideals to future generations" (Boylan 157–58). Richards's claim of cultural authority in such
issues as education and child nurturing is demonstrated in her parodies of both recent innovations such as public kindergartens (which
had become fashionable in America in the 1870s) and older educational conventions like recitations and object lessons, in which children were supposed to use simple objects such as balls and cups to
deduce scientific concepts. Richards satirizes this still-popular notion
in Alice Lee's discussion with the Mock Turtle after she notices a
collection of "odd-looking things" behind the teacher's desk at the
kindergarten (227; fig. 7):

> "Those are *objects,* you know," said the Mock Turtle.
> *"Objects!"* repeated Alice.
> "Yes, for object-lessons. Don't you know what object lessons
> are?"

Figure 7. The object lesson. From Richards, *A New Alice.*

Alice had heard of them, and had, indeed, taken many such lessons herself, without knowing them under any particular name. She could learn nothing from these objects, however. (228)

Richards also expresses satiric contempt for Friedrich Froebel's concept of the kindergarten (or nursery) school, which usurped the mother's care of young children. Alice Lee is intrigued by the Royal Wonderland kindergarten (which she imagines as an ongoing party); Richards cautions us, however, that Alice Lee's mother disapproves of parents who, daunted by educational theorists, "shunted their offspring along to the new kindergartens." Clearly, Alice Lee's mother is a believer in the nineteenth-century ideal of "fireside education" (Hardyment 148). Richards assures us that Alice Lee's mother "so earnestly believed that love of home was the first, and throughout the most important, factor in the right development of little children, that she could not approve of Kindergartens" (197). Early kindergarten pedagogy was also designed to further the assimilation of working class immigrants, and Richards's resistance to kindergartens is clearly a response against their political agenda to control and indoctrinate immigrant children who were depicted as having been socially neglected, " 'left fallow,' and treated like 'wasting weeds,' " (Rothman 100).

Richards's satire of the kindergarten movement thus seems most directed at these repressive aspects of its pedagogy—which ironically echo the conservative ideology of Carroll's Alice—through which, in the words of Richard Watson Gilder, the editor of *Century* magazine, "children are brought into a new social order" and are taught "a new and highly valuable respect for law and order" (132). As one educator asserted: "The kindergarten . . . should train the child in social habits, he should know when to subordinate himself for the good of the whole. . . . He should be trained in habits of obedience, attention, concentration, orderliness and the like" (Garland 60–61). Froebel's theories were implemented through carefully sequenced games and tasks: "The kindergarten children in their daily games would march —and learn that their marching was part of an allegiance to country. They would set out to make a clock or draw a calendar and learn that 'the clock helps us to be good' " (Rothman 100). At the Wonderland kindergarten performance in Richards's *New Alice,* the pupils satirize Froebel's kindergarten agenda through a verse they have memorized and repeat endlessly, accompanying each line with the appropriate action:

> "We hop, hop, hop,
> Then we stop, stop, stop,
> Then we flop."

Their male teacher explains to the astonished Alice Lee that his pupils thus "are . . . taught what it is to *hop,* and to *stop,* and to *flop,* the same theory being applied to other branches of life. By this plan, at once instructive and amusing, they learn things without knowing them, which is the aim of all true education." (247)

Richards rejects classroom conformity in favor of the domestic codes of heroism, love, and maternal insight—codes passed on not through the passive process of memorization but through the dynamic process of individual empowerment that characterized the late nineteenth- and early twentieth-century discourse about the New Woman, who liberated the powerful moral mother of Richards's generation from the confines of the strictly domestic sphere and in so doing further "challenged gender relations and the distribution of power" (Smith-Rosenberg 245). Alice Lee is literally (to paraphrase Judith Kegan Gardiner) "her author's daughter," a new generation of female hero who controls, rather than submits to, her fantasy. Created out of the same millennial vision that informed her earlier sonnet sequence *Letter and Spirit,* Richards's new Alice, Alice Lee, is a New Woman in training, anticipating through dreams, fantasy, and play a new age of possibilities that Richards saw dawning at the end of the nineteenth century.

It is also important to remember, however, that this new age, like her fictive daughter-hero, was still young. Richards's often parodic use of Carroll's Alice books allowed her to assume an even greater degree of cultural authority by invoking a familiar text that had already achieved the literary status of a classic and that had recently been propagated in new editions, material products, and earlier imitations and parodies. Richards is indebted as well to the emancipatory qualities of nonsense and play that the old Alice brought to children's literature. Yet, her revisions and amendments in *A New Alice in the Old Wonderland*—which remains one of the most readable and engaging of the many Alice imitations and parodies—also suggest the resistant and subversive ways that Anna Richards may have "read" the original *Alice* books to her children, enabling modern readers to trace one nineteenth-century woman's attempts to challenge rather than sentimentalize the conservative ideologies of age and gender that haunt the dreams of Lewis Carroll's Alice.

Notes

1. For a detailed and useful list of criteria for describing an Alice imitation, see Sanjay Sircar's "Other Alices and Alternative Wonderlands: An Exercise in Literary History," *Jabberwocky* 13:2 (1984), 23–48.

2. See Jan Susina's "Educating Alice: The Lessons of *Wonderland*" for a discussion of the ways that Carroll's Alice books, despite their emphasis on nonsense, can be seen not as a "radical departure" from nineteenth-century instructional children's literature but as "part of the well-established British tradition of didacticism for children" (3).

3. Indeed, Ruskin's friendship with the Liddell family and his fondness for Alice Liddell, whom he tutored in drawing for a time, provides an interesting link between both the real and fictionalized Alices.

4. Reception presents one of the most difficult problems in doing research on writers like Richards, a largely ignored author writing in a disregarded genre. I have discovered few reviews of Richards's work, though these are all positive. The second edition does suggest that the first edition of *A New Alice* was successful.

5. Nina Auerbach and U. C. Knopflmacher point out in their introduction to *Forbidden Journeys: Fairy Tales and Fantasies by Victorian Women Writers* (a collection that includes Rossetti's *Speaking Likenesses,* Ingelow's *Mopsa the Fairy* and two shorter Alice

imitations by Julianna Ewing and Frances Hodgson Burnett) that in Victorian fantasies by women, like Richards's, older women were more often helpful rather than obstructive characters (15).

6. Richards is clearly influenced in her style and rhetoric by the sentimental tradition of nineteenth-century domestic fiction, which includes such authors as Stowe, Susan Warner, and Maria Cummins. In *Sensational Designs: The Cultural Work of American Fiction, 1760–1860,* Jane Tompkins argues that "the popular domestic novel of the nineteenth century represents a monumental effort to reorganize culture from the woman's point of view: that this body of work is remarkable for its complexity, ambition, and resourcefulness; and that, in certain cases, it offers a critique of American society far more devastating than any delivered by better-known critics" (124).

7. "If the urban bourgeois matron of the 1860s and 1870s alarmed," Carroll Smith-Rosenberg writes, "her daughter frightened" (176). The term "New Woman," coined by Henry James, described a new class of young, independent, often unconventional American women. As a social and political concept, the New Woman represented a number of late-nineteenth century middle-class social and educational trends, including later marriages and a rise in the numbers of single women after the Civil War, the founding of female colleges and professional schools, and the growing numbers of women in the workplace: "In short, the New Women, rejecting conventional female roles and asserting their right to a career, to a public voice, to visible power, laid claim to the rights and privileges customarily accorded bourgeois men. They were, at the same time, the daughters of the new bourgeois matrons" (Smith-Rosenberg 176).

8. Summarizing the findings of a number of women's history scholars, Chafe concludes "that women used their distinctive sphere to achieve a degree of influence perhaps never seen before or since. Gender, Baker says, 'rather than other social or economic distinctions, [represented] the most salient political division' in nineteenth-century America. Politics, as traditionally defined, was a man's world. Women remained outside of man's political sphere. Yet as they immersed themselves in 'feminine' activities of welfare and nurture on the local level, they soon became involved in issues that were public in nature. When these issues, in turn, became central to a whole era of political decision making, women's political culture gradually assumed ascendancy over man's. As a result, Suzanne Lebstock concludes, the years 1880 to 1920 comprised 'a great age for women in politics' " (9–10).

Works Cited

Ammons, Elizabeth. "Stowe's Dream of the Mother-Savior: *Uncle Tom's Cabin* and American Women Writers before the 1920s." In *New Essays on* Uncle Tom's Cabin, ed. Eric Sundquist. London: Cambridge University Press, 1986. Pp. 155–95.

Auerbach, Nina. *The Woman and the Demon: The Life of a Victorian Myth.* Cambridge: Harvard University Press, 1982.

Auerbach, Nina, and U. C. Knopflmacher. *Forbidden Journeys: Fairy Tales and Fantasies by Victorian Women Writers.* Chicago: University of Chicago Press, 1992.

Avery, Gillian. *Nineteenth-Century Children: Heroes and Heroines in English Children's Stories, 1780–1900.* London: Hodder and Stoughton, 1965.

Bloch, Ruth H. "American Feminine Ideals in Transition: The Rise of the Moral Mother, 1785–1815." *Feminist Studies* 4, no. 2 (June 1978): 101–26.

Boylan, Anne M. "Growing Up Female in America, 1800–1860." In *American Childhood: A Research Guide and Historical Handbook,* ed. Joseph M. Hawes and N. Ray Hiner. Westport, Conn.: Greenwood, 1985. Pp. 153–84.

Brown, Gillian. "Domestic Politics in *Uncle Tom's Cabin.*" *American Quarterly* 36, no. 4 (Fall 1984): 503–23.

Browne, Maggie. *Wanted—A King, or How Merle Set the Nursery Rhymes to Rights.* 1890. Reprint. London: Duckworth, 1910.

Carroll, Lewis. [Charles Lutwidge Dodgson]. *Alice in Wonderland and Through the Looking-Glass.* 2d ed. Ed. Donald J. Gray. New York: Norton, 1992.

———. *The Diaries of Lewis Carroll.* Ed. Roger Lancelyn Green. 2 vols. London: Cassell, 1953.

Chafe, William H. *The Paradox of Change: American Women in the Twentieth Century.* New York: Oxford University Press, 1991.

Chodorow, Nancy, and Susan Contratto. "The Fantasy of the Perfect Mother." In *Rethinking the Family: Some Feminist Questions.* Ed. Barrie Thorne with Marilyn Yalom. New York: Longman, 1982. Pp. 54–75.

Davidson, Cathy. "Mothers and Daughters in the Fiction of the New Republic." In *The Lost Tradition: Mothers and Daughters in Literature.* Ed. Cathy Davidson and E. M. Broner. New York: Ungar, 1980. Pp. 115–27.

Gardiner, Judith Kegan. "The Heroine as Her Author's Daughter." In *Feminist Criticism: Essays on Theory, Poetry and Prose.* Ed. Cheryl L. Brown and Karen Olson. Metuchen, N.J.: Scarecrow, 1978. Pp. 244–53.

Garland, Mary J. "The Kindergarten." *Kindergarten* 16 (January 1904): 58–69.

Gilder, Richard Watson. "The Kindergarten: An Uplifting Influence on the Home and the District." *Kindergarten* 16 (November 1903): 129–40.

Hardyment, Christina. *Dream Babies: Child Care from Locke to Spock.* London: Jonathan Cape, 1983.

Honig, Edith Lazaros. *Breaking the Angelic Image: Woman Power in Victorian Children's Fantasy.* New York: Greenwood, 1988.

Payne, William Morton. Review of Anna Matlack Richards's *Letter and Spirit. The Dial* 12 (Aug. 1891): 111.

Review of *A New Alice in the Old Wonderland. The Dial* 19 (Dec. 1, 1895): 340.

Richards, Anna Matlack, Sr. *A New Alice in the Old Wonderland.* Illus. by Anna M. Richards, Jr. Philadelphia: Lippincott, 1895.

Rodgers, Daniel T. "Socializing Middle-Class Children: Institutions, Fables, and Work Values in Nineteenth-Century America." *Growing Up in America: Children in Historical Perspective.* Ed. N. Ray Hiner and Joseph M. Hawes. Urbana: University of Illinois Press, 1985. Pp. 118–132.

Rothman, Sheila M. *Woman's Proper Place: A History of Changing Ideals and Practices, 1870 to the Present.* New York: Basic, 1978.

Smith-Rosenberg, Carroll. *Disorderly Conduct: Visions of Gender in Victorian America.* New York: Knopf, 1985.

Susina, Jan. "Educating Alice: The Lessons of *Wonderland.*" *Jabberwocky* 18, nos. 1, 2 (Winter/Spring 1989): 3–9.

Tompkins, Jane. *Sensational Designs: The Cultural Work of American Fiction, 1790–1860.* New York: Oxford University Press, 1985.

Music as Leitmotif in Louisa May Alcott's Little Women

Colleen Reardon

Early in the first chapter of *Little Women,* Louisa May Alcott furnishes a detailed physical portrait of Meg, Jo, Beth, and Amy, purportedly leaving the readers to discover for themselves the character of each. As Nina Auerbach has pointed out, this mystery is "no mystery at all," for Alcott has etched their personalities into their features (59). At the end of the same chapter, Alcott paints another picture of the four sisters. This image is more difficult to read, because the author has encoded the description in musical terms: "No one but Beth could get much music out of the old piano; but she had a way of softly touching the yellow keys and making a pleasant accompaniment to the simple songs they sang. Meg had a voice like a flute, and she and her mother led the little choir. Amy chirped like a cricket, and Jo wandered through the airs at her own sweet will, always coming out at the wrong place with a croak or a quaver that spoilt the most pensive tune" (20–21).

In the following chapters, the reader is introduced to Laurie, the rich boy next door, who is a talented pianist. Accounts of musical performances involving Laurie and the March family appear throughout the book. The incorporation of such scenes does more than add mere color and vivacity to the story. Read carefully, Alcott's discussions of musical ability, or lack thereof, the characters' willingness or unwillingness to perform music, and the occasions when music making occurs offer a rich subtext, full of meaning for the interpretation of the novel and of clues to the emotional journey her characters undertake. It is this subtext that I wish to explore.

Anne Phillips has demonstrated most convincingly that writers of children's books use collaborative music making to "affirm community" (145). The idea that group musical performance could represent a unified community (including its smallest unit, the family) was dear to Alcott and figured in several of her novels, including *Eight Cousins*

I wish to thank Professor James Heldman and Lyn Straka, both of whom read earlier drafts of this essay and offered many valuable suggestions.
Children's Literature 24, ed. Francelia Butler, R. H. W. Dillard, and Elizabeth Lennox Keyser (Yale University Press, © 1996 Hollins College).

and *Little Men* (Phillips 146, 150; Alcott 458). Alcott exploits the metaphor with great skill in *Little Women,* strategically placing scenes that depict ensemble performance. In the first pages, Alcott seizes upon the March family's traditional evening sing-along as a means of establishing the close relationship among the sisters and their mother. The health of this community of mother and daughters is indicated by its appealing musical diversity: Beth the pianist accompanies Marmee and Meg, the "flutes," Amy, the "cricket," and Jo, the "croaker" (Phillips 150). The quality of the performance is clearly not an issue; what counts is the participation of all members of the family. When Amy burns up Jo's book in chapter 8, for example, the resulting family discord is revealed in the lack of cohesion at singing time: Beth can only play, Jo will not sing, Amy dissolves in tears, and Meg and Marmee alone cannot find the right harmony (Alcott 74). Nor does the family sing-along that takes place the evening before Mrs. March is to depart for Washington to be with her gravely ill husband go well. The sisters' inability to perform as a group (all except Beth break down in tears) reflects their fears about the possible loss of their father, who, though far away, is a vital member of the family group (Alcott 148).

Mr. March does not die, of course; nonetheless, it is his illness that precipitates the disintegration of the March family community to which the reader was introduced initially. Beth will die (she develops her eventually fatal malady during her mother's absence), and the other March girls will marry (John Brooke asks for Meg's hand in marriage after accompanying Mrs. March to her husband's bedside in Washington). It is significant that Alcott includes no ensemble singing in her descriptions of the March sisters' weddings. It is not until the last chapter of the book, when the living March sisters, their husbands, and their children gather to celebrate Marmee's sixtieth birthday, that choral singing signals the establishment of a new, larger clan with Jo as its matriarch. Here, Friedrich Bhaer and Jo's boys serenade the extended family with a song for which Jo herself provided the words and Laurie the music (Alcott 422).

The only other scene of group performance in *Little Women* takes place at the picnic Laurie arranges at "Camp Laurence." The social tensions that arise between the English guests and their American hosts are so successfully handled and diffused by all involved that the day ends with the entire party "singing at the tops of their voices" as they row home (Alcott 124).

Although Alcott utilizes the idea of collective music making to represent the harmonious blending of diverse personalities in a larger community, only a few of the many passages featuring music in *Little Women* fit this category. Indeed, the author frequently alludes to a character's individual musical ability and his or her personal relationship to music; such references emerge even in passages describing a group performance. As with so much in this richly textured novel, these traits can be interpreted in a number of ways. The one that I shall suggest below depends on our understanding the practice of music as a gendered activity.

In Victorian England, as Nicholas Temperley has observed, the British male viewed music as "something to be provided for one's entertainment by lesser breeds, among which Italians and ladies were certainly included" (16). However provocative the statement, it is one to which numerous documents and literary works from the period clearly attest. The English, perhaps more than other Europeans, regarded music as a suspicious activity for men, an attitude fostered by centuries of philosophical writing on the subject. Linda Phyllis Austern has shown that Puritan religious writers continually described the "sweet, deceptive allure of music . . . as feminine or having a feminizing effect, weakening the intellect by leading to pure physical pleasure—making one more like a woman" (350). Such concepts about music were transplanted to the American colonies with the English Puritan settlers. Temperley's observation thus applies equally well to the nineteenth-century American male. Prevailing social attitudes did not, of course, prevent men from pursuing musical careers, either in England or in the United States; in both countries, most professional musicians were male. Nonetheless, the art of music making was viewed as an accomplishment for a woman, an asset that could enhance her value on the marriage market. It was not expected that a skilled woman musician would pursue a career (although some certainly did) but rather that she would be able to provide entertainment in the home for her future husband and children (Burgan 51–53; Pendle 98).

Recently, Julia Eklund Koza has offered convincing proofs of the powerful association of music with the "feminine sphere" in America during the decades immediately preceding and following the Civil War. By examining the articles and fictional stories from *Godey's Lady's Book*, the immensely popular monthly magazine for women published between 1830 and 1898, she has identified recurring themes related to the practice of music. She observes, for example, that numerous heroines of the fictional stories printed in the magazine were gifted with musical skills, which were often characterized as particularly feminine because they made use of women's perceived sensitivity and capacity for emotional expression (104–05). The heroes in those stories were rarely, if ever, musicians. One heroine's description of her ideal man is especially revealing, for she expressly states that she does not want "any waltzing butterfly, celebrated for the cultivation of his antennae, fluttering to opera music through the perfumed airs of conservatories"; no indeed, her hero was "a man, manly in all his attributes" (105). Musicality and manhood were thus clearly perceived as incompatible (Burgan 59–60). Koza notes that these narratives reflected typical attitudes of the time. As illustration she offers the story of a male editor on the magazine's staff who wrote music under a pen name, fearing that if his avocation were discovered, his chances for success in his business pursuits would be impaired (105).

The implication that the practice of music, and indeed music itself, was deleterious to manhood is perhaps nowhere more evident that in the reminiscences of the American composer Charles Ives, born in 1874. He confessed that although he loved music, he went into business because he was ashamed of his talent, "an entirely wrong attitude, but it was strong—most boys in American country towns, I think, felt the same" (Ives 130). Throughout his life, Ives was terrified of being considered the practitioner of an unmanly art. He went so far as to launch diatribes against Haydn, Mozart, Mendelssohn, Chopin, Gounod, Massenet, Tchaikovsky, and Wagner for writing music he defined as "sop" because its sole purpose, in his eyes, was to "massage the mind and ear, bring bodily ease to the soft, and please the ladies" (Ives 41, 134–35). Preoccupied with asserting his masculinity, Ives was constantly revising his scores to include increasing amounts of dissonance (Solomon 465–66). Those critics who did not appreciate his music were "lily-pads" whose minds and ears were not "hard" enough for the task (Ives 41, 63, 94, 132). The fear that his choice of career could somehow reflect negatively on his manhood is reflected in a phrase that occurs often in his *Memos*, sometimes in the form of a statement and sometimes in the form of a question: "Hasn't music always been too much an emasculated art?" (30, 41, 74, 101, 131, 134).[1]

We have every reason to suppose that Alcott was keenly aware of such attitudes and that she understood, either consciously or subconsciously, that in nineteenth-century America, musical talent represented the feminine. In *Little Women,* many of the scenes involving music making or participation in musical activities serve to define the characters' involvement in the feminine sphere.

The most domestic of Alcott's little women is the shy Beth. When, at the end of chapter 1, each sister defines her burden, the first two words out of Beth's mouth are "dishes and dusters" (Alcott 20). Nonetheless, until her death, Beth is the sister most closely connected to the traditional (and unrewarded) feminine occupation of housework. It is no accident that the "housewifely creature" who helps Hannah keep home "neat and comfortable for the workers [!]" (Alcott 44) is the musician in the family and that her chosen instrument, the piano, is the one most closely associated with the woman's realm of hearth and home (Burgan 51–52).[2] Unlike many string or wind instruments, which required the player to adopt "unattractive" positions to produce a proper tone, the piano allowed a woman to play with graceful movements and thereby maintain the elegance and decorum expected of her (Koza 109–11; Pendle 117–18). A piano was also one of the most versatile of instruments: it afforded a woman a variety of ways to fulfill her mission of providing entertainment for the family. She could, for example, play, sing, and accompany herself or accompany others who wished to sing, play, or even dance. So strong was the affiliation between the piano and women's domestic realm in post–Civil War America that it was common to find pianos sold in the same showroom as sewing machines. One company went so far as to create a combination sewing machine-melodeon so that a woman could "play at tones or at stitches as she felt inclined" (Loesser 561–62).[3]

Beth's devotion to music and her talent as a pianist thus serve as manifestations of her complete involvement in the feminine sphere. She cannot imagine a life in which she is not the domestic helpmate. Recent critics of Alcott's *Little Women* are nearly unanimous in the opinion that the self-sacrificing Beth represents "femininity" at its most self-destructive (Fetterley 379–80; Gaard 14; Keyser 65; Murphy 571). Her nearly absolute subjugation of her own desires to those of others is evident even in her music. The passage from chapter 1, which presents her accompanying the family sing-along, is representative. As a soloist, she is timid, often choosing her father's favorite tunes rather than those she likes (Alcott 148; Bassil 193). She desperately wants to go to the Laurence home to play the piano but hesitates for fear of disturbing someone. When she at last enters the mansion, her musical performances are controlled by Mr. Laurence, who leaves on the piano the kind of simple, pretty music thought suitable for young women (Burgan 56–57) and then eavesdrops on Beth. It is significant that when the self-effacing Beth consents to play for Mr. Laurence, she does so at twilight or in the evening "before the lamps are lighted," that is, at an hour of day when one imagines that she can hardly be seen (Alcott 112, 134).

Beth is a composer as well as a performer, but she appears afraid of exercising her powers in that area. In a crucial scene from chapter 7, Mrs. March castigates Amy for the conceited display of her gifts, noting that talent is more appealing when presented with great modesty. Laurie heartily agrees and narrates the story of a young girl with exceptional musical gifts who composed lovely pieces when alone but would never admit to having any skill whatsoever. When Beth expresses the desire to know the girl, Laurie tells her that she does know her; the young girl is Beth herself (Alcott 69–70). After such an unnerving discovery, Beth refuses to play for Laurie, and Alcott does not mention further independent creativity on her part. Apparently, she can be moved to compose only when her labor serves others. When her father returns from Washington, for example, she goes to the piano and sings a song she composed for him because he liked the verses so. Alcott notes that the text of the song, which is a paean to self-diminution ("He that is down need fear no fall") is, in fact, particularly fitting for Beth (198).

Second to Beth in musical ability is her oldest sister, Meg.[4] In the evening singing scene from chapter 1, her voice is characterized as flutelike; subsequent descriptions reinforce her talent as a vocalist. In the sisters' Christmas production of Jo's drama, "The Witch's Curse," Meg, playing the part of Hagar, performs a song that demonstrates her gifts for both lyrical and dramatic expression: the audience considers her singing the best part of the performance (Alcott 28). So talented is she that when she spends a fortnight at the home of the rich Moffat family, she is asked to sing at an evening ball. Meg thus closely resembles her mother, whose habit of serenading the family with merry voice prompted Judith Fetterley to observe, "It is not enough that little women be content with their condition; they must be positively cheery at the prospect" (372). Seen in this light, Meg's blithe singing symbolizes her cheerful acceptance of the narrow domestic life awaiting her, first in her "baby house" and then later "on the shelf." Her most discordant actions are to withdraw from both husband and housework and to devote herself exclusively to her babies. John finds relief by running over to visit another married couple, where the house is neat and the "piano in tune" (Alcott 339). When Meg finally becomes uncomfortable with this situation, she asks her husband to take her to a concert to put her "in tune" (Alcott 346). Although the metaphor might seem a trope on the idea of collaborative music making as an affirmation of community, Meg is asking to be a passive listener rather than a participant in the larger community. Alcott's imagery tells the reader that Meg herself is dissonant and, like a jangling piano, must be put back in tune with the entire range of domesticity expected of her.

Alcott's most compelling characters are, of course, Jo and Laurie, and as more than one critic has suggested, these characters are "androgynous doubles, symbolic twins" (Crowley 392; Estes and Lant 106; Keyser 66). Whereas Jo has definite masculine traits (she is eternally disappointed over not being a boy; she crops her hair and shortens her name to be more masculine; she continually refers to herself as a man), Laurie is given suggestively female characteristics: the nickname "Dora," delicate physical features, and a propensity for shyness (Showalter 56). The feminine side of his personality emerges most forcefully in his devotion to music.[5] It is this overt manifestation of femininity that creates such tension between Laurie and his grandfather (Keyser 66). When Jo first hears Laurie play, for instance, she immediately notes Mr. Laurence's displeasure. Mrs. March later informs Jo that Mr. Laurence's dislike of Laurie's playing is perhaps a reflection of his antipathy toward Laurie's Italian mother, a musician. She adds that he doubtless fears that his grandson, too, may want to be a musician.

Here, it seems, is the crux of the problem, for Mr. Laurence clearly loves music himself. He makes friends with Beth by telling stories of the great singers and fine instruments he has heard, and when Beth comes over to play on the grand piano, he opens his study door to hear her. More important, he also had a granddaughter whose musical talent he at least did not discourage, for he carefully preserved her cabinet piano after her death. Mr. Laurence's displeasure is a manifestation of a deeper fear that emerges when he cuts off Jo's compliments on Laurie's performance. Although he grudgingly admits that his grandson's playing is not bad, he hopes that the young man will do well in "more important things"—that is, in endeavors more appropriate to the masculine world (Alcott 57). The older man's apprehension is justified. Laurie's revelation of his "castle in the air" in chapter 13 shows a complete disdain for proper masculine occupations and concerns: he desires to live in Germany, to be a famous musician, and never to bother with either money or business (Alcott 130). Mr. Laurence appears to deflect his apprehensions about his grandson's "femininity" onto himself. In chapter 6, he admits to John Brooke that he has been coddling the boy as if he were his grandmother (Alcott 59).

Laurie's talent and devotion to music stand in stark contrast to Jo's utter lack of ability. She is the least musical of the March family, threatening to spoil the family sing-along in chapter 1 with "croaks and quavers." Likewise, her singing in "The Witch's Curse" is, in general, marked by great passion (gruff tones and shouts) rather than vocal technique (Alcott 26). Like Mr. Laurence and most of the male characters in the novel except Laurie, Jo can appreciate music, but she is not a polished performer.

The manner in which Laurie and Jo relate to music serves to highlight how each defies societal norms for his or her gender. Jo would like nothing better than to work, to make money, and to support herself; she wants independence rather than the dependence offered in the domestic sphere represented by music. Laurie, on the other hand, could not care less about business or money; he simply wants to play the piano. Unfortunately, in Alcott's world, there is no room for an adult Laurie or Jo with such ideas (Crowley 393–96). Both must change to adapt to the reality of circumscribed gender roles. And if many critics have noted that Jo is forced to acquiesce to the demands of little womanhood, few have seen that Laurie too, far from being able to shape his own destiny, must conform to the demands of American manhood, in which there is no place for his feminine side.[6] Their adaptations are reflected through musical metaphors.

Laurie is actually given a chance to make his castle in the air a reality. In book 2 (*Good Wives*), his grandfather takes him to Europe to forget his heartache over Jo; while there, he does indeed have his fill of music. Alcott, however, gives both Laurie's grief and his musical aspirations short shrift. He is not allowed to show his heartsore state openly. When he meets Amy at Nice, she rebukes him for his indolence and urges him to "wake up and be a man" (Alcott 357). His attempts at writing a requiem and then an opera are described with comical disdain. Laurie is essentially too lazy to fight what his grandfather and, by extension, his culture expects of him. He "becomes a man" by relinquishing any hopes for a musical career and closes off his youth by proposing to Amy. Indeed, instead of practicing music himself, he assiduously cultivates his wife's skills in that area. When Laurie and Amy write home about their engagement, for example, the letter is described as a "duet." The duet is, however, remarkably one-sided. The reader hears only Amy's voice, for Alcott does not include Laurie's contributions to the letter (Alcott 378–80). Even more significant is the evening singing scene at the March home upon the young couple's return. Laurie asks Amy to play something on the piano so that her family can hear how much she has improved under his tutelage. She demurs, choosing instead to sing Beth's songs with "tender music in her voice" (Alcott 391). The chirping cricket of chapter 1 has thus been transformed into a singer by her husband, whom she addresses as "my lord." And Laurie, whom many readers prefer to remember as a passionate, musical youth, allows himself to become manly in all his attributes—that is, he gives up his piano and metamorphoses into a thoroughly dull merchant of Indian teas.[7]

Laurie's musical ambitions, which never completely die, later find an outlet in patronage. In *Little Men,* he plays Maecenas to the musically talented orphan Nat: he finds him a home at Jo's Plumfield school, provides him with music, takes him to concerts and even composes music for him to play (Alcott 436–37, 462, 651). It is to be noted that Alcott makes Nat a violinist rather than a pianist; the violin was considered a more "masculine" instrument than the piano and, therefore, more appropriate for a boy (Koza 107).[8] The lingering association of music and the feminine is, however, clear in Alcott's description of Nat. Jo thinks him "weak" (not at all a "manly boy"), and her husband, Friedrich Bhaer, finds him "as docile and affectionate as a girl"; he actually refers to Nat as his "daughter" when speaking of him to Jo (Alcott 465).

As Laurie must come to terms with what society expects of him as a man, Jo must come to terms with what society requires of her as a woman. Her concessions to cultural expectations are apparent in her decisions to burn the gothic stories of which Friedrich disapproves and to take on, at least temporarily, Beth's role as "angel in the house." Such concessions are signaled by her increasing involvement with music. In chapter 19 of *Good Wives,* for example, Jo learns to hum her dead sister's songs (Alcott 376). Nonetheless, Jo's refusal to surrender unconditionally to the demands of the feminine sphere is reflected in her continuing lack of musicality. Nothing, for instance, could be further from Amy's lyrically romantic duet with her silent future husband than Jo's blunderingly comical performance with her future spouse, Friedrich, on his first introduction to the March family. When Jo suggests that Friedrich sing, he asks her to sing with him because they make a good duo. Alcott dryly notes that although Jo "had no more idea of music than a grasshopper," she consents and proceeds to warble away, out of time and out of tune. Jo's lack of ability does not matter, however, and soon she subsides into a hum, leaving Friedrich's mellow voice to carry the performance (Alcott 392).

That scene has much to tell us both about Jo and about her husband-to-be. Alcott has Friedrich perform "Mignon's song," that is, a piece sung from a female protagonist's point of view. In fact, he possesses a powerful feminine side to balance the patriarchal features many critics have seen in him (Bassil 192; Fetterley 382; Keyser 72–73; Murphy 578). Alcott can allow this quality in Friedrich precisely because he is German and therefore not bound by American codes of behavior for his gender (Showalter 61). For instance, he loves children and interacts with them differently from any other male characters in the book. John Brooke disciplines his son; Mr. March teaches his grandson; but Friedrich gets down on all fours and plays elephant with his nephews and their friends (Alcott 296–97). Later, in *Jo's Boys,* he prefers to hug his sons rather than settle for the cold "American" slap on the shoulder (Showalter 61). He can also sing without compromising his manhood, and in his singing, he declares openly his passion and affection for Jo (Showalter 60–62). He is, in other words, a man unafraid of emotional expression and the domestic sphere. Furthermore, although he wants Jo to sing with him, he is essentially unconcerned about her lack of musicality; he does not aspire to teach her to be a musician, as Laurie does with Amy. From this, we can infer that he accepts at least some of Jo's "masculine" qualities. Jo chooses to marry Friedrich not out of desperation but because he alone offers her the chance to earn her living and work alongside him as an equal (Auerbach 70; MacLeod 109; Murphy 568–69, 571, 579).

This is not to dismiss the sacrifice that Jo makes by marrying. Alcott has taken pains to paint Friedrich as affectionate and more involved in the feminine sphere than any other male in the novel; the sexual attraction between Jo and Friedrich is also strong. Nonetheless, in order to fulfill her personal needs, Jo lays aside her literary ambitions. Although Alcott wanted to make Jo a spinster, she perhaps performed a greater service by pointing up the thorny problems inherent in a woman's search for both domestic happiness and professional fulfillment, problems we still grapple with today (MacDonald 13).

Although Alcott can and does use collective musical performances to "affirm community" in *Little Women*, music is more commonly exploited to represent the feminine sphere as Alcott and the culture of her time defined it. Each sister's acceptance of or entry into that domain is depicted through scenes of musical performance. Laurie, the so-called fifth sister, must, conversely, take the opposite path on his journey; his attainment of manhood is symbolically represented through the silencing of his musical voice. The musical leitmotif in *Little Women* tells us much about gender roles in American culture and about the limited choices facing not only nineteenth-century American women but also nineteenth-century American men.

Notes

1. For more on Ives's character and music, see Solomon. I should note here that Ives admired both Bronson and Louisa May Alcott. The third movement of his *Second Pianoforte Sonata; Concord, Mass., 1840–60* is subtitled "The Alcotts." For the composer's remarks on the work, see his *Essays before a Sonata* (New York: Norton, 1961).

2. See, e.g., Phillips's discussion of the importance of the piano as the "center of the house" in a series of books by Lovelace (Phillips 147, 149–50).

3. The melodeon was a small reed organ also called a cottage or parlor organ. During the nineteenth century, it "vied with the piano for popularity" as an instrument for domestic use; see Barbara Owen, "Reed Organ," *The New Grove Dictionary of Musical Instruments*, ed. Stanley Sadie, 3:219. This was undoubtedly the type of organ acquired by the Ingalls family in Laura Ingalls Wilder's *Little House* books; see Phillips (153).

4. Hollander asserts that Meg is completely untalented, a view with which I take exception (30).

5. I disagree with Clark's suggestions that Laurie lacks a "whole-hearted commitment to music" and that he is not as talented musically as Amy is artistically (95 n7). Laurie's desire to be a musician despite his grandfather's opposition is painfully clear throughout *Little Women*. Of his accomplishment, there is no doubt, for at the age of twenty or so, he is able to play—apparently from memory—one of the more difficult Beethoven sonatas, the Sonata op. 13 "Pathétique" (Alcott 320).

6. Estes and Lant, e.g., maintain that Laurie can "actively alter reality in accordance with his own will" (106). Clark, on the other hand, notes that Laurie "submerges his own yearning for musical achievement" (95 n7).

7. Murphy is one of the few critics to have noticed Laurie's transformation (578). For different interpretations of Laurie's growth into adulthood, see Dalke (573–75) and Hollander (34–35).

8. It is notable, for instance, that in the Wilders' *Little House* books, Pa plays the fiddle, but his daughters Laura and Mary learn to play a keyboard instrument, the organ (Phillips 147, 149, 153). Similarly, in the Plumfield band described in *Little Men*, the males play traditionally masculine instruments (Nat, the violin; Friedrich, the bass viol; Franz, the flute), whereas Jo plays the piano (Alcott 458).

Works Cited

Alcott, Louisa May. *Little Women, Good Wives, Little Men.* London: Octopus, 1978.

Auerbach, Nina. *Communities of Women: An Idea in Fiction.* Cambridge: Harvard University Press, 1978.

Austern, Linda Phyllis. " 'Alluring the Auditorie to Effeminacie': Music and the Idea of the Feminine in Early Modern England." *Music and Letters* 74 (1993): 343–54.

Bassil, Veronica. "The Artist at Home: The Domestication of Louisa May Alcott." *Studies in American Fiction* 15 (1987): 187–97.

Burgan, Mary. "Heroines at the Piano: Women and Music in Nineteenth-Century Fiction." *Victorian Studies* 30 (1986): 51–76.

Clark, Beverly Lyon. "A Portrait of the Artist as a Little Woman." *Children's Literature* 17 (1989): 81–97.

Crowley, John W. "*Little Women* and the Boy-Book." *New England Quarterly* 58 (1985): 384–99.

Dalke, Anne. " 'The House-Band': The Education of Men in *Little Women*." *College English* 47 (1985): 571–78.

Estes, Angela M., and Kathleen Margaret Lant. "Dismembering the Text: The Horror of Louisa May Alcott's *Little Women*." *Children's Literature* 17 (1989): 98–123.

Fetterley, Judith. "*Little Women:* Alcott's Civil War." *Feminist Studies* 5 (1979): 369–83.

Gaard, Greta. " 'Self-Denial Was All the Fashion': Repressing Anger in *Little Women*." *Papers on Language and Literature* 27 (1991): 3–19.

Hollander, Anne. "Reflections on *Little Women*." *Children's Literature* 9 (1981): 28–39.

Ives, Charles E. *Memos.* Ed. John Kirkpatrick. New York: Norton, 1972.

Keyser, Elizabeth Lennox. *Whispers in the Dark: The Fiction of Louisa May Alcott.* Knoxville: University of Tennessee Press, 1993.

Koza, Julia Eklund. "Music and the Feminine Sphere: Images of Women as Musicians in *Godey's Lady's Book,* 1830–1877." *Musical Quarterly* 75 (1991): 103–29.

Loesser, Arthur. *Men, Women and Pianos: A Social History.* New York: Simon and Schuster, 1954.

MacDonald, Ruth K. "Louisa May Alcott's Little Women: Who Is Still Reading Miss Alcott and Why." *Touchstones: Reflections on the Best in Children's Literature,* 3 vols. West Lafayette, Ind.: Children's Literature Association, 1985. Vol. 1, pp. 13–20.

MacLeod, Anne Scott. "The *Caddie Woodlawn* Syndrome: American Girlhood in the Nineteenth Century." *A Century of Childhood, 1820–1920.* Rochester: The Margaret Woodbury Strong Museum, 1984. Pp. 97–119.

Murphy, Ann B. "The Borders of Ethical, Erotic, and Artistic Possibilities in *Little Women*." *Signs* 15 (1990): 562–85.

Pendle, Karin, ed. *Women and Music: A History.* Bloomington: Indiana University Press, 1991.

Phillips, Anne. " 'Home Itself Put into Song': Music as Metaphorical Community." *The Lion and the Unicorn: A Critical Journal of Children's Literature* 16 (1992): 145–57.

Showalter, Elaine. *Sister's Choice: Tradition and Change in American Women's Writing.* Oxford: Clarendon Press, 1991.

Solomon, Maynard. "Charles Ives: Some Questions of Veracity." *Journal of the American Musicological Society* 40 (1987): 441–70.

Temperley, Nicholas. "The Lost Chord." *Victorian Studies* 30 (1986): 7–23.

Juvenile Antislavery Narrative and Notions of Childhood

Holly Keller

> *I tell you this: unless you turn round and become like children you will never enter the kingdom of heaven. . . . Whoever receives one such child receives me.*
>
> Matthew 18: 3–5

> *Oh! May each blossom catch the sacred fire,*
> *And youthful minds to virtue's throne aspire!*
> Phillis Wheatley, "To the Rev. Dr. Thomas Amory
on Reading His Sermons on Daily Devotion"

The early years of the nineteenth century produced many changes in the texture of white middle-class family life in America. The child ascended to a position of ideological prominence, and new positive definitions of his or her character replaced earlier negative views. The status of mothers changed as full-time motherhood was acknowledged to be necessary for the nurturing of the newly important child (Zelizer 9), and a separate literature for children was born of the concern with the role children would play in the nation's future (Crandall 3; MacLeod, *A Moral Tale* 9; Brodhead 85).

Concern about unethical business practices, social inequality, poverty, war, and alcohol was also part of the social fabric of those years, as was the knotty problem of slavery. Although parental guidance, school instruction, and the new children's literature clearly invoked youth's commitment to honesty, hard work, care of the poor, pacifism, and temperance, the articulation of the issues surrounding slavery was more complex. Whereas poverty or alcoholism might be seen as the result of individual human weakness and, therefore, remediable by personal effort, abolition really meant reform of the nation's whole social and economic structure. Yet it was in connection with abolition that nineteenth-century children played their most interesting roles as both symbols and agents of reform.

Children's Literature 24, ed. Francelia Butler, R. H. W. Dillard, and Elizabeth Lennox Keyser (Yale University Press, © 1996 Hollins College).

Because of the alarming imperative of abolition, schoolbooks, as well as most popular fiction written for children, dealt very gently with the matter of slavery. Nevertheless, Anne MacLeod's claim that "slavery was all but invisible in juvenile fiction" (*American Childhood* 92) seems overstated. In combination with publications of the antislavery societies, which were not always as timid as MacLeod suggests in her earlier book, *A Moral Tale*, scores of pamphlets and books were written for children on the subject of slavery and abolition between 1825 and 1870. As a response to the failure of established institutions to attack slavery aggressively and promote abolition, this literature was fairly radical. If judged by the dominant standards of correct behavior for children, it was also quite subversive. The authors of these texts often urged their child readers to speak out against slavery and in favor of abolition in their homes. This prompting was a clear challenge to the moral authority of adults and an obvious infringement of the popularly held belief that children should not correct an adult "no matter how helpfully" (*American Childhood* 91). Children were also urged to take positive action by aiding fugitive slaves (American Anti-Slavery Society, no. 4, p. 17; *Louisa in Her New Home*), by boycotting products made by slaves and by contributing money to the cause (Richardson; American Anti-Slavery Society, no. 4, p. 8). Most important, these stories challenged the idea that the American republic was a nearly perfected nation that needed to be protected and defended, not criticized and restructured.

In these juvenile texts the child took on the symbolic role of teacher and redeemer. Just as Jesus set a child in the midst of the Apostles when he sensed that they thought themselves too wise, so abolitionists believed that the natural innocence of childhood might work to counter the arrogance of nineteenth-century society. In *The Child and the Republic*, Bernard Wishy writes that the image of the child redeemer did not appear until the 1870s (85), but it was everywhere apparent in this literature very early in the century. John L. Crandall, who looks closely at the juvenile antislavery literature, and primarily at the periodicals, locates its cessation around 1850 (17). The absorption of abolitionists into mainstream politics and the perceived need to restore national consensus did result in the dissolution of the antislavery societies and the termination of the publication of some children's texts. But many titles were issued by other publishers after 1850, and *Uncle Tom's Cabin*, which appeared in 1852, provided a model for many subsequent children's tales (see Aunt Mary, *The*

Edinburgh Doll and Other Tales for Children, 1865; Richardson, *Little Laura: The Kentucky Abolitionist,* 1859; and *Gracie: The Child Emancipator,* 1865). Even after the Emancipation Proclamation, books were written for children that addressed the need to treat freed slaves fairly (see Kellogg, *The Young Deliverers of Pleasant Cove,* 1871; MacCabe, *The Slave and the Hostage,* 1871; and Kellogg, *John Godsoe's Legacy,* 1873).

At the same time that white middle-class children were being schooled in the practical arts of making their way in a competitive and materialistic society, a sentimental and idealized child was being invented in the literature. The fictive child—innocent, virtuous, and instinctively color-blind—provided a foil for the grim realities of pre-war society and a measure of hope for the nation's future. "Your little child," says Augustine St. Clare in *Uncle Tom's Cabin,* "is your only true democrat" (273). A comment in a story in *The Slave's Friend* spoke to the belief in the natural neutrality of childhood:

> If it [prejudice against color] were natural children would be as shy of colored people as grown up white people usually are. A runaway slave called at a house just as a little child . . . was going to bed. The sweet little boy went round to give a kiss to his parents, and then to all the rest in the room. He did not pass the black man, but went up and kissed him. Now this fact shows that the dear child had no prejudice against colored people. Does it not? All children act so. (no. 4, p. 16)

The burden of expectations for the behavior of the real child never weighed as heavily as that placed upon the symbolic younster (far too many child heroines wept and died for the cause), but considerable confidence was invested in the redemptive capabilities of the young. Addressing her child readers in *The Negro Boy's Tale: A Poem* in 1825, Amelia Opie said it simply: "You will make the world what we of the present generation wish it to be, but are not able to make it ourselves" (preface). The rationale for this confidence, in fact for the whole body of juvenile abolitionist literature, is well expressed by Elizabeth Jones in *The Young Abolitionist* (1848). She relates the following argument used by a white mother who is attempting to convince her husband of the wisdom of telling children about the true horrors of slavery: "Benevolent enterprises have received great advantage from the moral influence of children. . . . They are effective preachers of righteousness; and their freedom from guile, and clearness of vision, render them powerful agents for good when properly instructed" (21). A little song in a book called *The Juvenile Companion* sums up the role of the idealized white child:

> Oh, teach him this should be his aim
>> To cheer the aching heart,
> To strive where thickest darkness reigns
>> Some radiance to impart.
> To spread a peaceful quiet calm
>> Where dwells the noise of strife,
> Thus doing good and blessing all
>> To spend the whole of life. (50)

Similar qualities were attributed to idealized black children, who could also serve as potent moral agents. In *The Generous Planter* (1837), a free black mother (Lucy) and her two children are living a life of hard work and stoic deprivation in the North in order to save enough money to purchase the father (Ben), who is still enslaved. The children go to a neighboring boarding house to get scraps of leftover food and to pick up the laundry by which their mother is earning money. One day they encounter a man at the boarding house to whom they explain their undertaking, and the man silently follows them home. Standing in their kitchen doorway unnoticed, he hears them tell their mother about the kind man who inquired about their welfare. The man, of course, turns out to be the father's master, and the "proud, the wealthy, the hospitable, the humane planter, as he had been called, when he compared himself to these poor slaves, felt himself sunk to the very depths of littleness" (20). Whereupon he declares Ben to be free. When he returns home to his plantation, he immediately frees all his slaves, through which he is truly saved: "The universal rejoicing among them [the freed slaves] at the intelligence, was far beyond what he had expected, and it showed him how entirely mistaken he had been in supposing with many others, that they were, in general, contented with their lot, because he had never heard from them any expression of a desire for liberty" (20). Thus, the author of this story (who, like many abolitionist authors, wrote anonymously) challenges one of the most pervasive arguments in the proslavery liturgy. Arguments supporting the notion of the slaves' contentment with their lot often appeared in the literature for children of the 1820s and 1830s to document the efficacy of religious instruction relating to the notion of Christian brotherhood (see Ambrose Serle,

The Happy Negro [1823–25?] and Mrs. John Farrar, *The Adventures of Congo in Search of His Master* [1824–34?]). Perhaps even more important, the author elevates the black children of the story to a higher position of moral authority than that of the white Christian adult.

A variety of factors contributed to the creation of this symbolic youngster. In addition to the abandonment of the eighteenth-century religious doctrine that had declared children to be inherently sinful, some other changes were taking place in the society at large. As long as the economy of the South continued to be agricultural, the economic value of the black child continued to appreciate. But as the economy of the North became increasingly industrialized, the economic value of the white child decreased. No longer an asset on the family balance sheet, the white child began to take on a sentimental value that was enhanced by his association with moral and social reform (Wishy 48; Zelizer 6).

Notions of child rearing and discipline were also changing. Moral instruction, applied with generous doses of love, was replacing the rod and the strap, and new emphasis was placed on developing the child's reason and conscience (Brodhead). The glaring contrast that could now be drawn between the disciplinary treatment of free white and enslaved black children became a major issue in the appeal to the juvenile abolitionist. Harriet Beecher Stowe draws attention to this transition throughout *Uncle Tom's Cabin,* most obviously when Ophelia fails in her attempt to control Topsy by physical punishment and Eva succeeds through love and reason. Pairs of black and white children troop across the pages of juvenile antislavery texts, not only to emphasize the innocence and vulnerability of the black child but to comment upon the obligation of white children to those whose lives the system has jeopardized. Here again Stowe epitomizes the abolitionist writer's technique: "There stood the two children representatives of the two extremes of society. The fair, high-bred child, with her golden head, her deep eyes, her spiritual, noble brow, and prince-like movements; and her black, keen, subtle, cringing, yet acute neighbor. They stood the representatives of their races. The Saxon, born of ages of cultivation, command, education, physical and moral eminence; the Afric, born of ages of oppression, submission, ignorance, toil and vice" (*Uncle Tom's Cabin* 361).

Antislavery literature written specifically for children began as a very tentative self-examination. Focusing on the institution of slavery primarily as a violation of Christian morality, early writing appealed initially to that same morality to right the wrong. By the 1830s, however, criticism of the hypocrisy with which Christian doctrine was being applied was included, and the failure of the adult community to address the issue of abolition forthrightly was also condemned. In the introduction to her book of stories, *The Liberty Cap* (1846), Eliza Follen, a well-known antislavery activist, wrote: "We pretend to be a Christian nation, to believe the religion of Him who told us to do as we would be done by, who said that the substance of religion was to love God with all our heart and our neighbor as ourselves, and that our neighbor was the poor, and the suffering, and the oppressed. . . . I say we pretend to believe this" (6).

A story in the same book, entitled "Picnic at Dedham," has a young boy say to his mother: "I think that if the men don't all do something about slavery soon, we boys had better see what we can do, for it is all too wicked" (17). In an anonymous book called *The Envoy* (1840), a little girl observes the obvious distress of a bird and its babies in a cage. The father bird has been removed to a different cage, but the little girl does not understand the source of the mother's anguish as it appears that she still has everything she needs to be comfortable. The child's father explains that the mother bird misses its mate, and that, in any case, it would rather not be in a cage at all. Later the adults are heard to express exasperation with a discontented slave, whose husband has been sent to another plantation for several months, and the child points out the parallel. "Goodnight, mother, goodnight, father," she says coyly as she leaves the room. "Do as you would be done by" (53). The same point is made by Jonathan Walker in *A Picture of Slavery for Youth* (1847). Walker relates the story of his own imprisonment for attempting to transport seven escaped slaves from Florida to Nassau. In chains for eight and a half months, he tells his child readers that it was "all because I did 'unto others as I would they should do unto me' if I were in their condition" (27).

The issues of slavery were sometimes approached through a fictionalized narrative that was based loosely on factual incidents retold from the point of view of the symbolic child. Anna Richardson's *Little Laura: The Kentucky Abolitionist* concerns a man who published an abolitionist newspaper and whose print shop was burned by angry slaveholders. Laura, the printer's daughter, preaches from her deathbed to some children who had shunned her because of her family's sentiments, and the children are soon moved "with righteousness" to see the error of their ways. In addition to appealing to child readers to

follow Laura's spiritual lead, the author asks them to send money to
her father so that he can continue his work.

That most of the stories of slavery had child protagonists made the
issue all the more poignant to the child reader. Slavery was presented
not only as an assault on Christian morality and democratic ideals
but as an attack on the very sanctity of childhood. Speaking to that
issue, Eliza Follen wrote a poem entitled "Lines on Hearing of the
Terror of the Children of the Slaves at the Thought of Being Sold":

> When children play the livelong day
>   Like birds and butterflies,
> As free and gay sport life away
>   And know not cares or sighs,
> Then all the air seems fresh and fair,
>   Around, below, above,
> Life's flowers are there, and everywhere
>   Is innocence and love.
> When children pray and fear all day
>   A blight must be at hand;
> Then joys decay, and birds of prey
>   Are hovering o'er the land.
> When young hearts weep as they go to sleep,
>   Then all the world is sad,
> The flesh must creep and woes are deep
>   When children are not glad.   (22)

"Resolve that your voice shall be ever heard, and your influence
felt, in behalf of justice and of mercy, whether the cause be popular
or unpopular," wrote John C. Abbott in his book for boys entitled *The
School Boy* (1839). Like most educators of the day, Mr. Abbott would
probably not have included abolition on his list of worthy causes, but
as members of another powerless group, whose primary concerns
were also security, home, family, and freedom, children could easily
be rallied to support the antislavery crusade.

Because of the conservatism of all but the most progressive
nineteenth-century schools, most antislavery, and surely all abolitionist, texts for children were read outside the classroom. "Abolitionism,"
Merle Curti notes, "was the communism of its day" (131), and no
teacher or principal wished to appear subversive by confronting such
problematic issues as slavery's travesty of the Declaration of Indepen-

dence (Elson 87). Although most schoolbooks condemned slavery as a moral wrong, criticism tended to focus on the international slave trade. Because the slave trade had been legally abolished in America in 1807, other countries were targeted, as were African chiefs occasionally for their participation. Harriet Beecher Stowe comments on the popularity of this practice: "Who does not know how our great men are outdoing themselves, in declaiming against the foreign slave trade. . . . Trading negroes from Africa, dear reader, is so horrid! It is not to be thought of! But trading them from Kentucky,—that's quite another thing!" (*Uncle Tom's Cabin* 213).

The accepted mode of teaching American history certainly did not promote notions of radical social reform. The history of the republic was presented to school children as "providing a special moral lesson, revealing the march of a unique people toward fulfilling the idea of liberty under God's constant guidance and aid" (Curti 58). With that sort of burden, a critical evaluation of the nation's shortcomings, let alone possible remedies for them, could hardly be expected. The parental instruction most children received at home reenforced the school's position by emphasizing obedience and compliance.

The process by which books were selected for use in northern schools also inhibited the examination of controversial social issues. School boards, then as now, were highly politicized and often consisted of successful businessmen who had strong reasons to look upon social upheaval with disfavor. Some undoubtedly had economic interests connected to the South. Those books that were chosen frequently oversimplified important issues like slavery in order to avoid the dilemma posed by the more obvious moral inconsistencies. Northern schoolbooks expressed passion on such subjects as religion, patriotism, and honesty, but not about abolition. When northern textbooks were used in the South, those pages that did refer to matters of slavery were often pinned or sealed together (Elson 8). Under these conditions, political activism was not a likely by-product of public education.

Even an educational reformer like Horace Mann, who certainly made the connection between moral education and social reform, skirted the issue of abolitionism in the schools. Although Mann was an outspoken opponent of slavery, he criticized Samuel May, whom he had appointed head of a normal school, for taking students to an abolitionist meeting. When Mann learned that May intended to give a lecture on abolition, he wrote to him: "I have further plans for obtaining more aid [for the schools], but the moment it is known or supposed that the cause is to be perverted to, or connected with, any of the exciting party questions of the day, I shall never get another cent" (quoted in Curti 72–73). If children were to apply their energies to the problematic realities beyond the classroom, leadership had to come from some other quarter. Speaking of her character George and his struggle to escape bondage, Stowe comments: "If it had been only a Hungarian youth, now bravely defending in some mountain fastness the retreat of fugitives escaping from Austria into America, this would have been sublime heroism; but as it was a youth of African descent, defending the retreat of fugitives through America into Canada, of course we are too well instructed and patriotic to see any heroism in it; and if any of our readers do, they must do it on their own private responsibility" (*Uncle Tom's Cabin* 299).

The antislavery texts that were provided for children by abolitionist societies, some religious groups, well-known abolitionists, and anonymous or unknown sympathetic authors addressed that responsibility. Making use of the moral and religious arguments with which the children were all too familiar, they also relied heavily on the kinds of sentimental arguments that predominated in adult literature of the time. Emphasizing sympathy for slave children and encouraging an empathetic identification with them, these texts contained bitter invective against slaveholders, kidnappers, and traders. Although the victimization of black children was graphically depicted, every opportunity was taken to demonstrate their courage, pride, and struggle for survival. Most important, by providing specific recommendations for constructive action, these texts empowered the white child as an agent of reform. Even very young children were considered candidates for instruction. *The Anti-Slavery Alphabet,* presented at the antislavery fair in Philadelphia (1847), began with "A" for abolitionist and ended with "Z" for the zealous man who would plead for the cause of the slaves.

The need to compensate for the shortcomings of the schools on the subject of slavery was implied in a fictional conversation in *The Young Abolitionist.* After a mother has just finished telling her son about the fine character of a man named "Mr. Wright," the child asks: "Does he [Mr. Wright] answer all the questions children ask him? If he does, I wish we could have him for our teacher. I don't think Mr. Gardener [his teacher] loves children very much. He don't like to answer questions. The other day when Jennie was reading her Bible, she asked him what it meant to 'hide the outcast.' . . . He told her she asked quite too many questions" (Jones 21). In *The Anti-Slavery Picknick*, (1842), a collection of essays, speeches, and poems for children by noted abolitionists and antislavery sympathizers, the editor, John Collins, attacks the accepted practice of teaching that mankind is divided into separate races defined by different physical, mental, and emotional capabilities (3). But to counter any suspicion of disloyalty, abolitionism and patriotism were emphatically equated, as in this passage from *The Slave's Friend:* "Abolitionists love their country, and they love the union of the states. Slavery threatens to break the Union. Emancipation will prevent it. . . . Who then love their country best?" (no. 2, p. 163). Having the right "feelings," however, was not enough. An article in *Youth's Cabinet,* a weekly newspaper for children, gave the following caution: "Does every child, as he thinks of the unhappy slave, drop a tear? If so, it is well; but he must do something more than feel. He must ACT" (quoted in *The Slave's Friend,* no. 4, p. 17). A poem suggested a course of action:

> LISTEN, little children, all,
> Listen to our earnest call:
> You are very young 'tis true,
> But there's much that you can do.
> Even you can plead with men
> That they buy not slaves again,
> And that those they have may be
> Quickly set at liberty.
> They may harken what *you* say,
> Though from *us* they turn away.
> Sometimes, when from school you walk,
> You can with your playmates talk,
> Tell them of the slave child's fate,
> Motherless and desolate.
> And you can refuse to take,
> Candy, sweetmeat, pie or cake,
> Saying "no" unless 'tis free—
> The slave shall not work for me.
>
> (*The Slave's Friend,* no. 4, p. 1)

Many poems and stories were written to persuade children that their efforts would not be in vain, but the obstacles to their power to effect change were also noted. Amelia Opie's *The Negro Boy's Tale,* which touched on many of the aspects of the children's campaign, also acknowledged its potential limitations. The poem begins with a recitation by a slave boy named Zambo, who recounts his brutal separation from his mother and his wish to return to her and his home. He is talking to a little girl named Anna, who is sailing from Jamaica to England with her father, because he knows that

> . . . sorrow's plaintive sound,
> Could always gain her ready ear;—
> [and that] to soothe the slave's distress,
> Was gentle Anna's greatest joy;

After establishing the unspoiled virtue of the child, the poet has Zambo raise the question of religious hypocrisy:

> Dey say we should to oders do
> Vat I would have dem do to me;—
> But if dey preach and practice too,
> A Negro slave me should not be.

The color issue is also addressed:

> Missa, dey say dat our black skin,
> Be ugly, ugly, to de sight;
> But surely if dey look within,
> Missa, de Negroe's heart be white.

Finally, comes the failure of ideology:

> O Missa's God! dat country bless!
> (Here Anna's colour went and came);
> But saints might share the pure distress,
> For Anna blushed at other's shame.

Zambo implores Anna to take him with her to England, but

> I cannot grant thy suit, she cries;
> But I my father's knees will clasp,
> Nor will I, till he hears me, rise.

Anna's father, however, refuses to listen, and the ship sails off, leaving Zambo on the shore at the mercy of his master. In a last desperate effort, Zambo runs into the sea and tries to catch the ship. Finally the father is moved to relent. He tries to rescue the boy, but it is too late, and the poem concludes with the sad thought that Zambo's death was perhaps more fortunate than his life:

> Anna, I mourn thy virtuous woe;
> I mourn thy father's keen remorse;
> But from my eyes no tears would flow,
> At the sight of Zambo's silent corpse.

The vulnerability of the black child to the immorality and hypocrisy of the white world was given additional force in stories that recounted the mistreatment of black children who, like Harry in *Uncle Tom's Cabin*, were to all appearances white. Even more frightening were tales of the enslavement of truly white children. For example, a story in *Juvenile Miscellany* (1834) tells of a white girl, symbolically named Mary, who is kidnapped by a slave trader, disguised as a mulatto, and sold into slavery.

Although not written specifically as a juvenile text, *Uncle Tom's Cabin* is perhaps the ultimate celebration of the role of the child in the abolitionist movement. It was certainly the author's intention that the book be read by (or to) children, and unknown numbers of children did in fact read it (Fiske 357). In many ways it was a summation of the methods and arguments developed in adult and juvenile antislavery texts before 1850 (Crandall 15; Kraditor 242; *The Slave's Friend*, no. 11, pp. 1–12). Real-life incidents such as the suicide of slaves by drowning and escape across the Ohio River would have been well known to child readers. The highly emotional style of the story, the simplicity and familiarity of the tale, and its many child heroes and heroines undoubtedly gave it a natural appeal to children. Almost as though she were addressing the parents of mid-nineteenth-century children, Eva makes the case for youthful readership: "You want me to live so happy, and never to have any pain,—never suffer anything,—not even hear a sad story, when other poor creatures have nothing but pain and sorrow, all their lives: it seems selfish. I ought to know such things, I ought to feel about them!" (403).

Eva, who is probably the best-known symbolic child in nineteenth-century literature, first appeared on Christmas day in the original serialized version of the novel. She is the paradigmatic child teacher and redeemer. Topsy's conversion by Eva on her deathbed, and the redemptive aspects of that scene, form the emotional apex of the story. The scene is witnessed by Eva's father, St. Clare, and the drama, en-

acted by child performers, is revealed to the audience of sinful adults
within the book and without. The truth of Eva's moral superiority is
unquestioned, as is Topsy's damning statement of the failure of Christian charity and its devastating consequence: "There can't nobody
love niggers, and niggers can't do nothin'" (409). When Topsy finally
breaks down and cries, acknowledging that Eva has "reclaimed" her,
the children have done their work. Even Eva's Aunt Ophelia, the
quintessential expression of the limitations of northern sentiment,
wishes to learn Eva's Christ-like compassion. "It wouldn't be the first
time a little child has been used to instruct an old disciple," concludes St. Clare (411).

"Each of you can become angels," the child savior says before she
dies, and it is clear that her intended audience is larger than the one
immediately surrounding her. In the concluding installment of the
serial publication, Stowe addressed children directly:

> The author of *Uncle Tom's Cabin* must now take leave of a wide
> circle of friends. . . . In particular the dear children who have
> followed her story have her warmest love. Dear children, you will
> soon be men and women, and I hope you will learn from this
> story always to remember to pity the poor and oppressed. . . .
> Never, if you can help it, let a colored child be shut out from
> school or treated with neglect and contempt on account of his
> color. Remember the sweet example of little Eva and try to feel
> the same regard for all she did. Then, when you grow up, I hope
> the foolish and unchristian prejudice against people merely on
> account of their complexion will be done away with. Farewell,
> dear children, until we meet again. (Quoted in Stern 564)

The year following the publication of the book Stowe did write a special juvenile version entitled *Pictures and Stories from Uncle Tom's Cabin*,
which did not endure. The adapted text was quite simplified and not
nearly as strong a statement as many earlier texts for children. What
remained, however, was the image of the morally superior child. The
story ends with Eva chastising her mother for criticizing Topsy's gift
of flowers:

> I'm going fast, where there will be
> No difference, but in sins forgiven.
> And, mother, it might chance that we
> Would bring poor Topsy flowers in heaven.   (26)

When the child readers of the articles, pamphlets, and books that courageously addressed the issues of slavery and abolition gave their lives for the Union cause, the symbolic child and the real child became one. Both North and South had been guilty before God, Stowe wrote, and the remedies were prayer, honest self-appraisal, and resistance to authority when necessary—all appropriate tasks for the young.

Works Cited

Abbott, John C. *The School Boy*. Boston: Crocker and Brewster, 1839.
American Anti-Slavery Society. *The Slave's Friend* 3, nos. 2, 4, 11 (1839).
The Anti-Slavery Alphabet. Philadelphia: Mathew and Thompson, 1847.
Aunt Mary. *The Edinburgh Doll and Other Tales for Children*. Boston: John P. Jewett, 1854.
Brodhead, Richard H. *Cultures of Letters*. Chicago: University of Chicago Press, 1993.
Collins, John A., ed. *The Anti-Slavery Picknick*. Boston: H. W. Williams, 1842.
Crandall, John C. "Patriotism and Humanitarian Reform in Children's Literature, 1825–1860," *American Quarterly* 21 (1969): 3–22.
Curti, Merle. *The Social Ideas of American Educators*. Totowa, N.J.: Littlefield, Adams, 1966.
Elson, Ruth Miller. *Guardians of Tradition: American Schoolbooks of the Nineteenth Century*. Lincoln: University of Nebraska Press, 1964.
The Envoy. Pawtucket, R.I.: The Juvenile Emancipation Society, 1840.
Farrar, Mrs. John. *The Adventures of Congo in Search of His Master*. Boston: Munroe and Francis, [1824–34?].
Fiske, John. *A History of the United States for Schools*. Boston: Houghton Mifflin, 1894.
Follen, Eliza. *The Liberty Cap*. Boston: Leonard and Bowles, 1846.
The Generous Planter, and His Carpenter, Ben. Worcester, Mass.: Henry J. Howland, 1837.
Jones, Elizabeth. *The Young Abolitionist*. Boston: The Anti-Slavery Office, 1848.
The Juvenile Companion. New Garden, Ohio: Battin and Miller, 1850.
Juvenile Miscellany, 6, 3d ser., 2, (May–June 1834): 186–202.
Kellogg, Elijah. *The Young Deliverers of Pleasant Cove*. Boston: Lee and Shepard, 1871.
———. *John Godsoe's Legacy*. Boston: Lee and Shepard, 1873.
Kraditor, Aileen S. *Means and Ends in American Abolitionism*. New York: Vintage, 1967.
Louisa in Her New Home. Philadelphia: Pennsylvania Anti-Slavery Society, 1854.
MacCabe, William B. *The Slave and the Hostage*. Philadelphia: H. MacGrath, 1871.
MacLeod, Ann Scott. *A Moral Tale: Children's Fiction and American Culture, 1820–1860*. Hamden, Conn.: Archon, 1967.
———. *American Childhood: Essays on Children's Literature of the Nineteenth and Twentieth Centuries*. Athens: University of Georgia Press, 1994.
Opie, Amelia. *The Negro Boy's Tale: A Poem*. New York: Samuel Woods and Sons, ca. 1825.
Richardson, Anna H. *Little Laura: The Kentucky Abolitionist*. Newcastle: Thomas Pigg, 1859.
Serle, Ambrose. *The Happy Negro*. New York: The Religious Tract Society, [1823–25?].
Stern, Philip Van Doren, ed. *The Annotated Uncle Tom's Cabin*. New York: Paul S. Erikson, 1968.
Stowe, Harriet Beecher. *Pictures and Stories from Uncle Tom's Cabin*. Boston: John P. Jewett, 1853.
———. *Uncle Tom's Cabin*. New York: Penguin, 1986.
Walker, Jonathan. *A Picture of Slavery for Youth*. Boston: J. Walker and W. R. Bliss, 1847.

Wheatley, Phillis. "To the Rev. Dr. Thomas Amory on Reading His Sermons on Daily Devotion, in Which Duty Is Recommended and Assisted." In *The Collected Works of Phillis Wheatley*, ed. John C. Shields. New York: Oxford University Press, 1988. P. 90.

Wishy, Bernard. *The Child and the Republic.* Philadelphia: University of Pennsylvania Press, 1968.

Zelizer, Viviana A. *Pricing the Priceless Child: The Changing Social Value of Children.* New York: Basic, 1985.

"Don't Expect to Depend on Anybody Else": The Frontier as Portrayed in the Little House Books

Anita Clair Fellman

Over the years we have heard much about the authenticity and truth of the Little House books. The citations from reviews, literary criticism, and testimonials from readers are endless: "Honest books that any child knows he can believe" (Eddins 2); "The stories are really true; they are peopled with real live human beings" (Stromdahl 114); "A moving and authentic re-creation of American frontier life" (*New Yorker* 115). We have read about Wilder's "power of exact recall" (Lewis 1344) and have heard teachers say again and again that children are thrilled with the fact that the stories are true and are baffled that the books are to be found in the fiction section of the library.[1] One scholar, working in the 1950s, concluded that all the details in the book were consistent with what was then known about pioneer life, and more recent critics have gauged the stories to be "a symbolic portrayal of the qualities which led to the settlement of the American West" and a "realistic portrayal of frontier life" (Cooper; Stott 288–89). Accordingly, the books, despite their classification as novels, have been widely acclaimed choices for use in elementary-school social studies units on frontier life. Thousands of teachers from all parts of the country use the Wilder books in an array of activities meant to illuminate the American past.

If the Little House books teach us about frontier life, the question becomes, what frontier life are we talking about? What interpretation of our past are we inculcating in our children through an uncritical acceptance of the books as history? "Frontier" as both historical phenomenon and guiding American mythology is not a self-evident concept. Over the past century it has come to be a key embodiment of American struggles to define our national identity and to shape appropriate government policy. Because of its centrality to these fundamental undertakings, interpretations of the content and meaning of the frontier have long been contested.

The notion that it was the frontiering experience—more than

Children's Literature 24, ed. Francelia Butler, R. H. W. Dillard, and Elizabeth Lennox Keyser (Yale University Press, © 1996 Hollins College).

European inheritance, Puritan tradition, the impact of the Founding Fathers, ethnic mixture, or climate of the country—that gave
America its distinctive character had long been in the air when historian Frederick Jackson Turner introduced his famous interpretation in an address at the World Columbian Exposition in Chicago in
1893. Turner, whose birth preceded that of Laura Ingalls by just six
years and whose Wisconsin birthplace was only about 150 miles from
hers, argued that the frontier was the dominant influence in shaping
American civilization. The ability to push ever westward, away from
settled areas in quest of cheap land hacked out of the wilderness,
created the distinctive features of the national character: Americans
were restless, innovative, individualistic, pragmatic, buoyant, and willing to take risks. The presence of the frontier was also the major
determinant of the democratic character of American political institutions (Turner 37).

Turner's formulation, coming at a worrisome time, when the frontier appeared to be closing, struck a chord both in and out of academic life. Not only did a whole generation of American historians
go to school on Turner, but Theodore Roosevelt and Woodrow Wilson took up his idea, and as Gerald Nash puts it, "within a few years
writers, artists and musicians joined them until it quickly entered into
national consciousness and myth" (Nash 3–4). The frontier itself became mythologized almost as soon as it had a history. Richard Slotkin
argues that "myths are stories, drawn from history, that have acquired
through usage over many generations a symbolizing function that is
central to the cultural functioning of the society that produces them"
(Slotkin 16). In this sense Turner and his followers, by assigning such
overarching importance to the frontier in American history, contributed to its mythologizing. The mythic frontier and the historic frontier influenced each other (and indeed continue to do so) in an endless series of loops; history provided characters and situations that
became the stuff of myth, and historical figures interpreted their personal experiences through the lens of the mythologized frontier. "As
people accept and assimilate myth," Richard White suggests, "they
act on the myths and the myths have become the basis for actions
that shape history" (White 616).

For years after Turner speculated that the frontier experience defined the American character, written history, political rhetoric, and
popular culture overlapped in their understanding of what made
America. Popular historians conveyed Turner's message in simplified

form to audiences beyond the classroom and outside the historical profession. Some politicians saw the demise of the frontier as requiring conservation of wilderness areas or an increased role for the state to compensate for the disappearance of the safety valve of free land; others, contrarily, thought that the role of government was irrelevant to the new frontiers in trade or technology that would challenge America. The conquering of the West was the source of much of American popular culture, from Buffalo Bill's Wild West Shows to western novels and films.

By the 1920s, however, consensus on Turner's thesis among historians began to break down.[2] Although his influence in the classroom remained strong, detractors in every decade found new angles from which to undermine his vision. For instance, recent historians point out that the conventional focus on the West as frontier takes the typical settler to be an easterner of European origin, erases the land's original inhabitants, both human and nonhuman, homogenizes the new settlers, is indifferent to the wanton destruction of the environment, is blind to gender, overstates the ability of the West to serve as a safety valve for the underemployed of the eastern cities, and underestimates the formative role that the metropolis, federal government, and capital have played in the development of the area that continues to this day to be an economic hinterland (Limerick, Milner, and Rankin; Limerick; White; Slotkin 32–47). To the degree that such historians continue to view the frontier as an important force in American history, they have recast the original formulations and placed the concept of frontier in a global context.

These changes in perspective have put many historians at odds with even the basic outlines of the mythic frontier and with notions of American exceptionalism.[3] Such notions survive, nonetheless, and even flourish in political rhetoric and popular culture; indeed they are surely more influential than anything historians have told us in recent times about American national identity. "In the end," Slotkin says, "myths become part of the language, as a deeply encoded set of metaphors that may contain all of the 'lessons' we have learned from our history, and all of the essential elements of our world view" (16). But if, as so often happens, the tendency of myth is to distill and simplify and deny history (in the sense of refusing to acknowledge that the past is different from the present), then the lessons it teaches us may mislead rather than inform (White 616).

The divorce between frontier history and frontier myth robs us of the potentiality of a more fruitful collaboration between the two. History loses the power of myth to engage and move us, and myth remains oblivious to history's insistence that "any lessons the past teaches are those about processes and change; we cannot derive uniformly valid rules about our present situation from the past" (White 616). Slotkin suggests that the way around overdependence on a constricting myth of the frontier is through "demystifying" the myth and the mythmaking process, which "involves the rehistoricizing of the mythic subject and a historical account of its making" (20). I believe that the same warnings and the same resolution can be applied to the Little House books, which should be examined for the role that their creators played in fitting them into a mythic tradition.

Laura Ingalls Wilder's books, ostensibly a record of the actions and values of her pioneer family, are part of the frontier myth; I would even argue that they are a key means by which the myth gets perpetuated generation after generation, as children read them in school, borrow them from the library, or perhaps get the boxed set for Christmas or a birthday. The myth selects out portions from the vast array of pioneer experiences and projects them as the entire picture. In its focus on the individualism inherent in the settlers' values, for instance, the myth ignores the struggles to form community in regions with the ceaseless coming and going of populations. In its emphasis on self-sufficiency and on the bounty of the land, it leaves out the shaping role of government, the close economic ties of the West to the industrial order, and the dependence of many settlers upon wage labor.

The Little House books do this as well. Out of the fullness of the Ingalls's lives, Laura Ingalls Wilder and Rose Wilder Lane,[4] her daughter and collaborator, selected elements that convey a certain portrait of their family.[5] Their vision of the frontier was created by memory, by their gender, by the dynamics of the relationship between them as mother and daughter, by their politics, by their livelihoods, by the "frontier longings" that they shared with many of their contemporaries in the 1920s and 1930s, and by their awareness, as literate Americans, of the frontier thesis.

Although the myth tells us that a novice sat down at the age of almost sixty-five to write with instinctive artistry the story of her childhood, Wilder actually had spent fifteen years (1911–25) writing for the *Missouri Ruralist* and other regional papers and, with Lane's help, had published several articles in *McCall's* and *Country Gentleman*.

Although her daughter was unsuccessful in rousing her to devote much attention to writing for national periodicals, in 1925 Wilder began researching family stories with the idea of writing some pioneer anecdotes. Her mother's death in 1924 clearly spurred her to this effort, but she may have been inspired as well by the flood of writings on the frontier that appeared in the 1920s and by Lane's keen free-lancer's eye for what was current in publishing. David Wrobel surmises that "the image of the frontier . . . provided a kind of solace for some in the uncertain postwar years" (98). Unlike writings on the frontier that had appeared in the Progressive Era, the "longing[s] for wilderness and pioneer virtues" that permeated writing on the frontier in the 1920s "were less frequently accompanied by concerns over the dangers of excessive individualism in a postfrontier world than they had been in those earlier decades" (99). Sometime in the late 1920s Wilder at last began writing an adult-level autobiography, which she called "Pioneer Girl." Lane, acting on her mother's behalf, was never able to find a publisher for the autobiography, partly because the market for such writings was well saturated, but the two women used the manuscript as the source for the Little House books during the 1930s and early 1940s.

Numerous scholars have pointed out recently that men's and women's writings on the frontier differ and that our perception of the frontier as a place of conquest, escape to freedom, lawlessness, individualism, and concern for autonomy emerges from males' imagined notions of the West (Kolodny; Armitage and Jameson; Graulich; Thacker 78–80). Women's imagined Wests, though sharing aspects of the dominant visions, also embrace, in tension with them, "the making of the garden, the building of the home (town, city), the clearing of the land—the sustaining of the human community" (Elsbree 32). Wilder's West, possibly even more than most female accounts, embodies the tension between the two visions. Her depiction of the frontier does not include a romanticization of violence but does portray some lawlessness as a natural consequence of laws and policies that were inappropriate and foolish. Certainly it is Wilder's father, Charles Ingalls, who is portrayed as the parent with the urge to strike out ever further west and her mother, Caroline Ingalls, as the one who wants to settle down somewhere with access to a church and a school for her girls. Nonetheless, it is Laura, the daughter who shares her father's vision, with whom we are invited to identify and whose long process of socialization into acceptance of feminine values we witness with ambivalence. Furthermore, Caroline Ingalls's attachments to extended family, friends, and community are downplayed; her immediate family forms virtually her entire world, and her commitment to self-sufficiency matches that of her husband. While Laura is being trained for female social roles, she is also being tutored in moral autonomy as the basis for her freedom and independence, regardless of circumstance (Mills, this vol.).

At some point in her life Wilder became aware of the frontier thesis of American development, or at least had absorbed its major tenets. In 1937 when she and Lane were midway in the Little House series, she was invited to speak at a book fair in Detroit. Her talk is filled with language expressive of Turner's formulation of stages of frontier development, of the progression from barbaric to civilized: "I began to think what a wonderful childhood I had had. How I had seen the whole frontier, the woods, the Indian country of the great plains, the frontier towns, the building of railroads in wild, unsettled country, homesteading and farmers coming in to take possession. I realized that I had seen and lived it all—all the successive phases of the frontier, first the frontiersman, then the pioneer, then the farmers, and the towns. Then I understood that in my own life I represented a whole period of American History" (Anderson, *A Little House Sampler* 217). Wilder goes on to describe western Minnesota as "too civilized for Pa," who decided that they should push west to an unsettled part of Dakota Territory. The wording of this talk suggests that Wilder was not simply telling her family's story, but as a matter of course filtered her narrative through a lens, the frontier thesis, that she shared with her contemporaries. In other words, she was a historical actor interpreting her experiences through the mythological frontier.

In addition to the influences of her gender and the context in which she produced her manuscript, Wilder's emotional makeup and her turbulent relationship with her daughter, Rose, helped dictate her view of frontier values. I have discussed the implications of their mother-daughter relationship and their livelihoods for their political ideology elsewhere (Fellman). Here let me say briefly that the two women remained central in each other's emotional lives until the younger woman was well into middle age. Wilder was a much less expressive person than Lane, but each sought affirmation from the other in ways that the other could not provide, and each concluded that overdependence upon another person was futile and self-defeating. Their preoccupations with autonomy rather than attachment colored their views on emotional and material self-sufficiency and on the dangers of dependence upon government.

Although artistic goals clearly shaped the two women's work on the Little House books, Wilder and Lane also had political aims in mind. Mother and daughter, writing in the midst of the Great Depression, were profoundly anti–New Deal. They were opposed to the expanding role of government, feeling that individuals were capable of overcoming hardships on their own and that when government intervened in people's lives, it did so in crude, blundering ways that did more harm than good, as with the farm programs that paid farmers to plow their crops under. In 1936, as grasshoppers descended on the Wilders' Missouri farm, Wilder wrote to her daughter that they were doing what they could to kill them but were futilely battling a judgment of God: "We as a nation would insult Him by wantonly destroying his bounty. Now we'll take the scarcity and like it" (Wilder Papers, folder 19, microfilm roll 2).

As the 1930s progressed, Lane became more and more of a political individualist, maintaining that society was only a meaningless abstraction. She believed that the remarkable energy that had transformed the young United States, and was increasingly affecting the world, stemmed from Americans' rejection of authority and their acceptance of the responsibility that comes from individuals standing on their own two feet, dependent upon no one. Her political ideas, which later contributed to the resurgence of libertarianism in the United States, are most fully expressed in *The Discovery of Freedom,* published in 1943, the same year that *These Happy Golden Years,* the last of the original eight Little House books, appeared. She had been working out her ideas in the 1930s, however, in articles published in *The Saturday Evening Post* and other magazines, as well as in her best-selling novel *Free Land* (1938). Among the many examples of her intellectual influence is the career of the late Roger Lea MacBride, her "adopted" grandson, who ran for president on the Libertarian Party ticket in 1976.

There is strong evidence from their correspondence that Wilder was in agreement with many of Lane's ideas. Wilder left the Democratic Party and opposed Roosevelt, and she frequently commented to Lane that the two of them regarded the events of the day in the same way. She was also filled with unaccustomed praise for *The Discovery of Freedom.* Wilder was less well read and not as politically sophisticated as her daughter, but in crucial ways she had tutored her daughter in the belief in the emotional self-sufficiency that was a corollary to the economic self-sufficiency that Lane advocated. Together, as the two women thought through their family history, deciding what from "Pioneer Girl" to incorporate, what to delete, and what to elaborate in the Little House books, they melded their anti–New Deal politics with the meaning they made of the Ingalls and Wilder family experiences. Thus, part of the artistry of the books is based on a self-conscious, particular vision of frontier life.

A number of sources support this assertion. One is the text of "Pioneer Girl." This work of nonfiction is much less adorned than are the children's books, and one can see not only where Wilder and Lane have changed the facts of the Ingalls's lives between it and the Little House series but also how they have enhanced certain aspects to present a consistent picture of family self-sufficiency and ingenuity. The information in "Pioneer Girl" has been supplemented by Wilder's biographers (Zochert; Anderson). Another source is the Little House books themselves, with their artful juxtaposition of challenge, deferred gratification, and family good feeling. A final source is correspondence between Wilder and Lane about the writing of the books. Ironically, as the overall purpose of what they were creating became clear to them, Wilder began to urge her publisher to stress that the stories were true; indeed, she told her book-fair audience in Detroit that in every story in the series "all the circumstances, each incident are true" (Raymond to Wilder, Dec. 22, 1936, Correspondence, Laura Ingalls Wilder Series; Anderson, *A Little House Sampler* 220). Lane both instructed her mother on the distinction between overarching truthfulness and mere accuracy of detail and insisted to others that the Little House books "are the truth and only the truth" (Lane to Wilder, Jan. 21, 1938; Mortensen, "Idea Inventory").

The series starts with a book, *Little House in the Big Woods*, which I think of as a Protestant Garden of Eden, with the family meeting virtually all its needs through their labor and the skill of their own hands, in combination with the bounty of the woods and land. In many respects, however, the third book in the series, *Little House on the Prairie*, offers the most idyllic version of what Wilder and Lane concluded the Ingalls family to have been seeking. This was a life with no immediate neighbors, supported both by hunting and trapping and by the cultivation of fertile, treeless land. *Little House on the Prairie* is the book based least on the actual memories of Wilder herself, who was only four years old when the Ingallses gave up their Kansas homestead. It is largely the product of remembered family stories, of research that Wilder and Lane conducted into life on the prairies of Kansas and Missouri in the late 1860s, and of their imaginative re-creation of what the good frontier life would have been like. To them this involved a prairie so expansive and bountiful that there is room for Charles Ingalls the farmer as well as Charles Ingalls the hunter and trapper; a home made of materials acquired from nature and processed by Charles Ingalls, with the help of Caroline Ingalls and the fair exchange of labor with other settlers, and the mutual, vol-untary helpfulness of good (if distant) neighbors. "We're going to do well, here, Caroline," they have Pa say. "This is a great country. This is a country I'll be contented to stay in the rest of my life" (74).

Recall that the ending of this idyll in *Little House on the Prairie* comes not from bad weather destroying crops or a decline in crop prices or the fleeing of game before the plow but from the government's failure to keep its promise to white settlers to remove Native Americans to make way for whites. In the novel, despite Laura's and Pa's attraction to the unsettled life of the Indians, Pa refuses to stay long enough to have federal troops remove him forcibly from the land he feels he has made his by the sweat of his brow. Known facts about their so-journ in Kansas suggest another picture. Charles Ingalls spent at least part of his time in the area working as a carpenter; the government had come to a deal with the Osage Indians, permitting white settlers to stay; and the Ingallses left because the man who had bought their farm in Wisconsin reneged on the deal and refused to pay the remain-der of what he owed them, compelling them to return to Wisconsin to reclaim the property in the Big Woods (Mortensen, "Idea Inven-tory" 861; Anderson, *Laura Ingalls Wilder* 41). These are crucial dis-tinctions: in the novel it is governmental blundering and unreliability that destroys the setting that might have allowed the Ingallses to pros-per from the beginning, curing Pa's wanderlust, and eliminating the need for their further, never very successful migrations. Whenever government is introduced in the books, it is always in the context of foolish rules, misleading promises, incompetence, and consequential disorder. Think of the brawl, in *By the Shores of Silver Lake,* when Pa files for his homestead claim (236), or of the need, in *The Long Winter* (99–100), of a youthful but competent Almanzo to lie about his age to file his claim. Both of these scenes were made up for the novels.

In Lane's philosophy minimal government was best. If left on their own, unburdened by unnecessary rules or unfairly distributed privileges, individuals' struggle for survival in a hostile universe would release unlimited reserves of energy and initiative. These were the traits of the pioneer whose restlessness and risk taking were responsible for settling the American frontier and for the technological and material progress that was helping to transform the world for the better. These were also the qualities of the Ingallses as Wilder and Lane interpreted their family history. "My parents possessed the spirit of the frontier to a marked degree," Laura Ingalls Wilder once commented (Anderson, *Laura Ingalls Wilder* 31). The westering impulse, toward the unknown, characterized the pioneer, and so any essentially truthful story of a pioneer family would, in their eyes, focus on the movement west. Consequently Wilder and Lane left out those times when the family backtrailed, returning east, sometimes to the very places they had abandoned earlier. Hence the Little House series has the Ingallses go on to Minnesota from Kansas rather than return to Wisconsin. It leaves out their stay on the eastern Minnesota farm of relatives before they spent a year in Burr Oak, Iowa, as innkeepers. Their commitment to the westering impulse also led them to put the most optimistic face possible on the family's chronically marginal existence, because to acknowledge the defeat of the Ingallses' efforts was to deny the feasibility of the settling of the northern plains frontier by valiant pioneers acting on their own.

Throughout the series, Wilder and Lane accentuate the family's isolation in comparison to the real-life situation of the Ingallses. They do this partly for artistic reasons; focusing on one family is more riveting than cluttering up the story line with numerous others who will soon pass out of the heroine's life. Nonetheless, there were undoubtedly other purposes as well. The family appears more self-sufficient, more dependent upon its own internal resources, material and emotional, if its contacts with other family members or neighbors are minimized. For instance, according to the first version of "Pioneer Girl," when the Ingallses were living in Wisconsin, they often saw a family that had two children, with whom Mary and Laura were close (20). Contrast this to *Little House in the Big Woods,* in which Laura and Mary see relatives and neighbors infrequently. The site that Pa chooses for their homestead in *Little House on the Prairie* is forty miles from Independence, Kansas; in actuality their property was thirteen miles from town, not just around the corner for people dependent upon horses but markedly less isolated than forty miles away.

Before the Ingalls family left Wisconsin for the second time to go to western Minnesota, they spent a winter living with relatives who also uprooted, moving into eastern Minnesota. This is but one of numerous instances in which the novels leave out shared living arrangements. The surveyor's house in *By the Shores of Silver Lake* has come to symbolize the family's ability to be happy under the most isolated of conditions. In fact, a man asked to board with them during that winter they spent in the house, and Charles Ingalls agreed, concluding that it "might be wise to have another man there in case of trouble" ("Pioneer Girl" 82). During *The Long Winter*, we see the family struggling valiantly against the elements, passing innumerable days on their own through the hard work of survival and the pleasures of togetherness. Wilder's correspondence with Lane about this manuscript makes clear that a young couple lived with them in the house in town that winter and that their baby was born upstairs. She did not want to introduce them into the story, partly because she considered them unsuitable characters for a children's book: the woman was already pregnant when they got married, and they turned out to be unpleasant freeloaders. More crucial, however, was Wilder's desire not to detract from the sense of the family's isolation, which she stressed was to be one of the themes of that volume (Mar. 7, 1938, Correspondence, Laura Ingalls Wilder Series). The moral desirability of solitude is illustrated by an exchange between Laura and Ma in *The Long Winter*. When Laura bemoans the social isolation caused by a blizzard, her shocked mother replies, "I hope you don't expect to depend on anybody else, Laura. . . . A body can't do that" (127).

The other theme of *The Long Winter* is Ma's and Pa's ingenuity in providing for the family as their supplies diminish. It had come to be one of Lane's cherished beliefs, shared by her mother, that if left to their own devices, individuals would find a way of making do. In the novels this skill comes to have emotional connotations. In each of the volumes, Pa's and Ma's inventiveness is closely associated with feelings of well-being and security on the part of the children. The family gets enormous pleasure from Ma's use of some of the crop-destroying blackbirds in a pie in *Little Town on the Prairie* and of green pumpkin to create a mock apple pie in *The Long Winter*. In many of the volumes she manages to create satisfying Christmas presents from odds and ends. Throughout the series, Pa's imaginative employment of his violin playing to march or sing them out of fear or lethargy is a motif that connotes security.

At the beginning of *The Long Winter*, Pa tells Laura that, as the Declaration of Independence asserts, humans were created free by God and hence have to take care of themselves. Subsequently we see Pa's ingenuity in twisting hay to burn for fuel once the coal runs out. We see Ma figuring out how to grind seed wheat in the coffee mill to make flour. Nowhere is it mentioned, as it is in "Pioneer Girl," that everyone in town burned hay and ground seed wheat (102–03). The family's struggle in *The Long Winter* is largely solitary, save for a few instances: Pa's cleverness in discerning where Almanzo and Royal Wilder have hidden their seed wheat and his insistence upon paying for a pailful rather than accepting a neighborly donation; and Almanzo's and Cap Garland's adventuresome trek out of town to buy seed wheat for the townspeople. These acts compare favorably to the men of DeSmet's fruitless communal effort, undermined by the predictable incompetence of one of the group, to go hunting for antelope during a lull between blizzards. The individual efforts in the novel are in contrast to Wilder's earlier description in "Pioneer Girl," in which she notes that the townspeople resorted to rationing food among themselves that winter based on the number of people in each family (107). There is no rationing mentioned in *The Long Winter,* and as a matter of fact, Lane made a public show of refusing a World War II ration card just a few short years after that book was published.

The insistence on the family going it on their own is a theme throughout the series. The only consistent exceptions are the Christmas barrels from well-established church congregations out east, to which the family looks forward. These gifts, examples of private, voluntary philanthropy that do not undermine the family's self-sufficiency, are the kind of welfare that Wilder and Lane could accept. On the other hand, there are many examples of Pa and Ma chafing under even a day's indebtedness to another individual for the necessities of life. They both dislike being unable to replace immediately the nails borrowed from Mr. Edwards to put on the roof in *Little House on the Prairie* (124–25). Laura and Mary in *On the Banks of Plum Creek* know better than to let the storekeeper give them a slate pencil on a few days' credit (155–56). In that same volume, when Laura and Mary are invited to a party at Nellie Oleson's house in town Ma even insists that this show of hospitality be returned very soon. Laura's party in the country provides what may be children's single most favorite scene in the series, for it is then that Laura maneuvers the hateful Nellie into getting bloodsuckers all over her legs and feet as she flees from the snapping crab. "Pioneer Girl" indicates that such delicious retribution did happen, not once in the context of a party held to redress the debt of hospitality but, rather, often in the routine visits of Nellie and her brother to the Ingalls house to play.

So too must the Ingalls girls pull their own weight as training for life's exigencies, as needed labor around the household, and as repayment for all that Pa and Ma have spent on them. Suzanne Rahn points out that in *Little Town on the Prairie* the family's newly acquired tiny kitten that determinedly catches a mouse almost its own size is a parallel to the youthful Laura going out to earn her keep doing hand sewing in a dry goods store (Rahn, this vol.).

Wilder and Lane were very adept in this and other examples at working their ideological points seamlessly into the fabric of the story so as to be invisible. Sometimes this involved elaborating what had been a bare-bones description in "Pioneer Girl," and other times it meant altering the facts slightly or even considerably. The reading of the Declaration of Independence is mentioned matter-of-factly in "Pioneer Girl" as part of the common nineteenth-century Fourth of July ritual. In *Little Town on the Prairie* the reading becomes a moment of epiphany for Laura: "Americans won't obey any king on earth. Americans are free. That means they have to obey their own consciences. No king bosses Pa; he has to boss himself. Why (she thought) when I'm a little older, Pa and Ma will stop telling me what to do, and there isn't anyone else who has a right to give me orders. I will have to make myself be good" (76).

In the same volume there is another noteworthy scene often mentioned by children as one of their favorites. By accident Laura finds hidden in a bureau drawer a book of poems that she immediately realizes is to be a Christmas present for her from her parents. In the transition from "Pioneer Girl" to *Little Town on the Prairie*, the poems change from those of Sir Walter Scott to those of Alfred, Lord Tennyson. Wilder and Lane almost certainly made the alteration so that when Laura receives the book at last, she can read one specific poem, "The Lotus Eaters," and respond with disgust to the sailors who give themselves up to sloth when they reach the land where it always seems to be afternoon. The irate Laura concludes: "They seemed to think they were entitled to live in that magic land and lie around complaining" (235). This summed up Wilder's and Lane's view of how Americans were becoming infantalized by the New Deal, robbed of their ability to deal with adversity, and stripped of the individual initiative and enterprise that were the true hallmarks of the American experiment.

Laura Ingalls Wilder's frontier, then, is not a simple depiction of the way things "really were" in her childhood but a collaborative creation born of memory, wish fulfillment, artistry, and ideology. In no way does this fact undermine the artistic accomplishment of the books, nor need it diminish our enjoyment of them. The complexity of Wilder's motives in writing makes her no different from other fine writers. It is our own motives as readers that we must question in our eagerness to attribute to the books a rendering of the American past that is both absolutely historical and timeless. The existence of a pervasive mythology about the frontier is as much a part of American history as are the facts of a Homestead Act or the building of a transcontinental railroad; all are formative in their importance and open to constant reinterpretation. The problem arises when we dehistoricize these events or phenomena, seeking to draw lessons from them that can be applied in sweeping fashion to the present, as do many readers and interpreters of the Little House books—and indeed as Wilder herself did.[6] Wilder's books, in addition to their literary value, are a superb example of the mythology of the American frontier and are worthy of study as such. We do not need to claim more for them as historical documents to continue to give them an honored place in American literature.

Notes

1. Some of my information about teachers' use of the Little House books in the classroom and their students' responses to the books comes from data supplied by more than fifty teachers in response to an inquiry I placed in an instruction magazine in 1992.

2. Nash's *Creating the West* is the best source for historians' responses to the Turner thesis over the course of this century.

3. Weber and Slatta illustrate current historiography, with its acknowledgment that several nations shared the American frontier and that uniquely American cultural forms have their counterparts elsewhere in the hemisphere.

4. The story of the collaboration between the two women (which has been known since the late 1970s but largely ignored) is told with different emphases by Moore, Anderson, Fellman, Holtz, and Miller.

5. My interpretation of Wilder's process of selection differs somewhat from that of Segel, who maintains that a "challenging of certain fundamental assumptions which have characterized the American ideal" (65) influences how Wilder presents Laura and her family. She sees in Laura's "actively questioning, selective response to the expectations of her culture" (65) a critique of repressive gentility, racism toward Indians,

and an acknowledgment of the social and environmental costs of the settlement of the wilderness. I do not find evidence that such a critique was intended.

6. A composite letter (n.d.) from Wilder sent to young fans by Harper and Brothers said: "The 'Little House' Books are stories of long ago. Today our way of living and our schools are much different. . . . But the real things haven't changed; they can never change. It is still best to be honest and truthful; to make the most of what we have; to be happy with simple pleasures and to be cheerful and have courage when things go wrong" (Anderson, *Laura Ingalls Wilder* 239).

Works Cited

Anderson, William. *Laura Ingalls Wilder: A Biography.* New York: Harper Collins, 1992.
————. "Laura Ingalls Wilder and Rose Wilder Lane: The Continuing Collaboration." *South Dakota History* 16, no. 2 (1986): 89–143.
————. "The Literary Apprenticeship of Laura Ingalls Wilder." *South Dakota History* 13, no. 4 (1983): 285–331.
Anderson, William, ed. *A Little House Sampler: Laura Ingalls Wilder and Rose Wilder Lane.* New York: Harper and Row, 1989.
Armitage, Susan, and Elizabeth Jameson, eds. *The Women's West.* Norman: University of Oklahoma Press, 1987.
Cooper, Bernice. "The Authenticity of the Historical Background of the 'Little House' Books." *Elementary English* 40 (1963): 696–702.
Eddins, Doris. "A Teacher's Tribute to Laura Ingalls Wilder." Insert in *National Elementary Principal* 46 (1967): 1–23.
Elsbree, Langdon. "Our Pursuit of Loneliness: An Alternative to This Paradigm." In *The Frontier Experience and the American Dream: Essays on American Literature,* ed. David Mogen, Mark Busby, and Paul Bryant. College Station: Texas A&M University Press, 1989. Pp. 31–49.
Fellman, Anita Clair. "Laura Ingalls Wilder and Rose Wilder Lane: The Politics of a Mother-Daughter Relationship." *Signs: Journal of Women in Culture and Society* 15, no. 3 (1990): 535–561.
Graulich, Melody. " 'Oh Beautiful for Spacious Guys': An Essay on the 'Legitimate Inclinations of the Sexes.' " In *The Frontier Experience and the American Dream: Essays on American Literature,* ed. David Mogen, Mark Busby, and Paul Bryant. College Station: Texas A&M University Press, 1989. Pp. 186–201.
Holtz, William. *The Ghost in the Little House: A Life of Rose Wilder Lane.* Columbia: University of Missouri Press, 1993.
Kolodny, Annette. *The Land before Her: Fantasy and Experience of the American Frontiers, 1630–1860.* Chapel Hill: University of North Carolina Press, 1984.
Lane, Rose Wilder. *The Discovery of Freedom: Man's Struggle Against Authority.* New York: John Day, 1943.
————. *Free Land.* New York: Longmans, Green, 1938.
Lewis, Naomi. "Laura Ingalls Wilder." In *Twentieth-Century Children's Writers,* ed. D. L. Kirkpatrick. New York: St. Martin's, 1978. Pp. 1341–44.
Limerick, Patricia Nelson. *The Legacy of Conquest: The Unbroken Past of the American West.* New York: Norton, 1987.
Limerick, Patricia Nelson, Clyde A. Milner II, and Charles E. Rankin, eds. *Trails: Toward a New Western History.* Lawrence: University Press of Kansas, 1991.
Miller, John E. *Laura Ingalls Wilder's Little Town: Where History and Literature Meet.* Lawrence: University Press of Kansas, 1993.
Mogen, David, Mark Busby, and Paul Bryant, eds. *The Frontier Experience and the Ameri-*

can Dream: Essays on American Literature. College Station: Texas A&M University Press, 1989.

Moore, Rosa Ann. "The Little House Books: Rose-Colored Classics." *Children's Literature* 7 (1978): 7–16.

———. "Laura Ingalls Wilder and Rose Wilder Lane: The Chemistry of Collaboration." *Children's Literature in Education* 11, no. 3 (1980): 101–09.

Mortensen, Louise Hovde. "The Ingalls of Kansas." *Elementary English* 40 (1963): 859–61.

———. "Idea Inventory." *Elementary English* 41, no. 4 (1964): 428–29.

Nash, Gerald. *Creating the West: Historical Interpretations, 1890–1990.* Albuquerque: University of New Mexico Press, 1991.

Review of *Little Town on the Prairie. The New Yorker,* Dec. 6, 1941, 115.

Segel, Elizabeth. "Laura Ingalls Wilder's America: An Unflinching Assessment." *Children's Literature in Education* 8 (1977): 63–70.

Slatta, Richard W. *Cowboys of the Americas.* New Haven: Yale University Press, 1990.

Slotkin, Richard. *The Fatal Environment: The Myth of the Frontier in the Age of Industrialization, 1800–1890.* New York: Atheneum, 1985.

Stott, Jon C. *Children's Literature from A to Z: A Guide for Parents and Teachers.* New York: McGraw-Hill, 1984.

Stromdahl, Judith E. "A Lasting Contribution." *Top of the News* 21 (1965): 111–21.

Thacker, Robert. *The Great Prairie Fact and Literary Imagination.* Albuquerque: University of New Mexico Press, 1989.

Turner, Frederick Jackson. "The Significance of the Frontier in American History." In *The Frontier in American History.* New York: Holt, 1921. Pp. 1–38.

Weber, David J. *The Spanish Frontier in North America.* New Haven: Yale University Press, 1992.

White, Richard. *"It's Your Misfortune and None of My Own": A History of the American West.* Norman: University of Oklahoma Press, 1991.

Wilder, Laura Ingalls. Correspondence, Laura Ingalls Wilder Series, Rose Wilder Lane Papers. Herbert Hoover Presidential Library, West Branch, Iowa.

Wilder Papers. Joint Collection, University of Missouri Western Historical Manuscript Collection and State Historical Society of Missouri, Columbia, Mo.

———. *By the Shores of Silver Lake.* 1939. Reprint. New York: Harper, 1971.

———. *Little House in the Big Woods.* 1932. Reprint. New York: Harper, 1971.

———. *Little House on the Prairie.* 1935. Reprint. New York: Harper, 1971.

———. *Little Town on the Prairie.* 1941. Reprint. New York: Harper, 1971.

———. *The Long Winter.* 1940. Reprint. New York: Harper, 1971.

———. *These Happy Golden Years.* 1943. Reprint. New York: Harper, 1971.

———. *On the Banks of Plum Creek.* 1937. Reprint. New York: Harper, 1971.

———. "Pioneer Girl," typescript, 1926–30. Laura Ingalls Wilder Series, Lane Papers.

Wrobel, David M. *The End of American Exceptionalism: Frontier Anxiety from the Old West to the New Deal.* Lawrence: University Press of Kansas, 1993.

Zochert, Donald. *Laura: The Life of Laura Ingalls Wilder.* New York: Avon, 1976.

What Really Happens in the Little Town on the Prairie

Suzanne Rahn

> *On the wall between the doors of the new bedrooms, Ma hung the
> wooden bracket that Pa had carved for her Christmas present, long ago
> in the Big Woods of Wisconsin. Every little flower and leaf, the small
> vine on the edge of the little shelf, and the larger vines climbing to the
> large star at the top, were still as perfect as when he had carved them
> with his jackknife. Older still, older than Laura could remember, Ma's
> china shepherdess stood pink and white and smiling on the shelf.*
>
> Little Town on the Prairie 18

Forthright tone, transparent style, episodic narrative, and details
we can touch and taste create the illusion of untrained honesty in
the Little House books—the sense that we are simply living Laura Ingalls Wilder's life. As we read through the series, Laura's memories
become ours as well. It always comes as something of a shock when
we uncover the craft, purpose, and design that transformed Wilder's
life into art.[1] *Little Town on the Prairie*, published in 1941, is a prime
example of this transformation. Here, in contrast to the strongly
focused structure of the preceding volume in the series, *The Long
Winter*, Wilder appears merely to be highlighting the most interesting
and amusing incidents of two years in Laura's early teens. Yet by the
end of the book, both Laura and her Little Town have grown up, and
what "grown up" means in America has been carefully defined. For
where *The Long Winter* is essentially about being human—surviving
the winter as a human being rather than an animal[2]—*Little Town* is
specifically about being an American. In linking Laura's maturation
with that of her country, however, Wilder may have revealed more
than she intended. Beneath the thematic structure of *Little Town*, two
very different concepts of history are at war.

As the book begins, late in the spring of 1881, Pa asks Laura
whether she would like to take a job in town. Before Laura answers
him, Wilder flashes back to the end of the Long Winter and spends
three chapters describing the happy spring on the claim. Her pur-

Children's Literature 24, ed. Francelia Butler, R. H. W. Dillard, and Elizabeth Lennox
Keyser (Yale University Press, © 1996 Hollins College).

pose is clear: to show how much pleasure Laura is sacrificing when she agrees to go to work sewing shirts for Mrs. White. For already, at fourteen, Laura is trying to shoulder her share of family responsibility. She wants her teacher's certificate not because she wants to teach, but to help send Mary to a college for the blind and to begin repaying her parents "for all that it had cost to provide for her since she was a baby" (48).

At first glance, "The Necessary Cat," interpolated into the flashback, seems more like a diversion than a necessity. The story of the kitten that Pa pays an outrageous fifty cents for, who kills her first mouse while she is still a baby, has a natural appeal for young readers. But why should the episode occur here, where it interrupts and prolongs the already interrupting flashback—unless "here" simply happens to be where it occurred in real life?

In fact, "The Necessary Cat" typifies how Wilder designed her books, with less concern for plot development than for thematic structure. For the kitten is clearly placed just at this point to underline the significance of Laura's job in town. Like Laura, the kitten assumes the adult responsibilities of mouse hunting at an unusually young age. Perhaps she, too, feels obliged to repay Ma and Pa that fifty cents as soon as possible! It isn't easy for her; the squirming, biting mouse is "nearly as big as the wobbling little kitten," but the kitten will not let go (32). When Ma orders Laura to the rescue, Laura protests, "Oh, I hate to, Ma! She's hanging on. It's her fight" (33). Clearly, Laura herself identifies with the kitten, projecting onto it her own desire for independence and self-respect. And the kitten wins: "All by herself, the kitten had killed it; her first mouse" (33). Laura, too, hangs on that summer, till she has earned her first pay and her unpleasant job is over.

For Wilder, however, full American adulthood does not mean success at this kind of job—mindless assembly-line labor under close supervision—but the ability to "boss oneself" as a farmer does and make one's own decisions. Laura realizes this herself on the Fourth of July, when "The Declaration and the song ['My Country, 'tis of Thee'] came together in her mind, and she thought: God is America's king."

> She thought: Americans won't obey any king on earth. Americans are free. That means they have to obey their own consciences. No king bosses Pa; he has to boss himself. Why (she thought), when I am a little older, Pa and Ma will stop telling me

what to do, and there isn't anyone else who has a right to give me orders. I will have to make myself be good. (76)

Little Town on the Prairie chronicles Laura's progress toward this self-directed goodness, and her occasional setbacks.[3] She stays home and gets the fall housecleaning done while Ma and Pa are taking Mary to college, but succumbs to her dislike for Nellie Oleson and Miss Wilder at school, jeopardizing the education that she needs to qualify as a teacher. That same winter she enjoys an active social life for the first time and "almost [forgets] about improving her opportunity at school" (252). Indignant with the lazy sailors in Tennyson's "The Lotus Eaters" (235), she fails to recognize that she too is lotus-eating. When her final grades are not as high as they might be, however, she makes herself study hard all summer long. And the following winter, she recites "the whole of American history" (274) up to 1825 before the entire community at the School Exhibition. Her performance, the climax of the book, earns her a teaching certificate at fifteen. Having publically demonstrated her self-discipline, she is ready to begin teaching it to the next generation. "An education is worth striving for," she tells her pupils in *These Happy Golden Years*, "and if you can not have much help in getting one, you can each help yourself to an education if you try" (86).

Wilder gives special emphasis to Laura's performance at the Exhibition by summarizing the recitation in some detail. The summary also creates a kind of parallel between this scene and the Fourth of July chapter, in which an unidentified man gives an impromptu oration before reading the Declaration of Independence: here too, Wilder interrupts her narrative to report much of what he says word for word. Both Laura's recitation and the Fourth of July oration deal with American history, and both interpret that history in substantially the same way, though the Fourth of July speaker puts things more crudely and directly:

"There wasn't many Americans at that time, but they wouldn't stand for any monarch tyrannizing over them. They had to fight the British regulars and their hired Hessians and the murdering scalping redskinned savages that those fine gold-laced aristocrats turned loose on our settlements and paid for murdering and burning and scalping women and children. A few barefoot Americans had to fight the whole of them and lick 'em, and they did fight them and they did lick them. Yes sir! We licked the

British in 1776 and we licked 'em again in 1812, and we backed all the monarchies of Europe out of Mexico and off this continent less than twenty years ago." (72–73)

As a result, he concludes, we are " 'every man Jack of us a free and independent citizen of God's country, the only country on earth where a man is free and independent.' " (73)

Laura's version of American history is less class conscious and less emotional, but rests on essentially the same assumptions:

> She told of the new vision of freedom and equality in the New World, she told of the old oppressions of Europe and of the war against tyranny and despotism, of the war for the independence of the thirteen new States. . . . Then, taking up the pointer, she pointed to George Washington. . . . She told of his unanimous election as the First President, the Father of his Country, and of the laws passed by the First Congress and the Second, and the opening of the Northwest Territory. Then, after John Adams, came Jefferson, who wrote the Declaration of Independence, established religious freedom and private property in Virginia, and founded the University of Virginia, and bought for the new country all the land between the Mississippi and California. (291–92)

Like the Fourth of July speaker, Laura sees the Revolution as a moral conflict between opposites: Old World versus New World, oppression and tyranny versus freedom and equality. In succeeding conflicts, the younger, less powerful, yet morally superior America continues to be victorious. Although no historian would now claim that America "won" the War of 1812, the Fourth of July speaker says that "we licked 'em again in 1812," while Laura calls it "the victory that finally won independence." The Monroe Doctrine translates into another victory for the young underdog: "Then came Monroe, who dared to tell all the older, stronger nations and their tyrants never again to invade the New World." Jackson's blatant seizure of Florida becomes, "Andrew Jackson went down from Tennessee and fought the Spanish and took Florida, then the honest United States paid Spain for it" (292–93).

What Laura's version leaves out is equally noteworthy. Because American history after 1825 is "Ida's part" (293), Laura does not have to shoehorn the Mexican War into her moral design, let alone the Civil War or Reconstruction. But she does not mention slavery either—nor even conflicts with the Indians. Unlike the Fourth of July speaker, who calls the Indians "murdering savages," Laura shows no hostility toward them; she simply erases them out of existence. The colonial settlements, the opening of the Northwest Territory, Jefferson's Louisiana Purchase—all seem to have taken place in a totally uninhabited landscape. French and Spanish settlements after the initial era of exploration have also been erased; so has foreign trade (except with Mexico), even French aid to the American Revolution. In Laura's history, European countries exist only to be fought and to purchase land from.

There is no need to invoke Wilder's personal views or the highly charged patriotism of 1941 to explain the version of history presented in *Little Town on the Prairie;* one can find a similar, though much lengthier, version in most American history textbooks of the last hundred years. Such texts, according to Frances FitzGerald, "have portrayed the English colonies as standing quite alone at the edge of a vast—indeed, continental—wilderness" (132–33). Indians were gradually all but eliminated from history textbooks by the 1950s, and foreign relations in these same pre-1960s textbooks were confined to "wars and territorial acquisitions" (136). Laura's version adheres to the officially approved tradition of a righteous and isolated America, which tended to modify or omit whatever did not fit this picture. Even today, readers of *Little Town*—critics included—do not look twice at what Laura says at the Exhibition, simply because there is still nothing unusual about it.

Equally commonplace is the implied definition of history itself—a chronicle of the great deeds of great men. Columbus discovers America, Washington leads the colonies to independence, Jefferson writes the Declaration, Monroe dares to confront the "older, stronger nations," Jackson fights the Spanish and takes Florida. The events of history are explorations, wars, treaties, declarations, the making of laws, and the buying of large tracts of land. The one, odd acknowledgment of ordinary people and their problems is the "hard times" of 1820: "All the banks failed, all business stopped, all the people were out of work and starving" (293). Here, we may suspect, Wilder draws a silent parallel with the Depression of the 1930s, suggesting that America has survived such hard times before. And without help from the WPA, either. As Anita Clair Fellman has shown, both Wilder and her daughter viewed the New Deal with increasing alarm, particularly its farm relief programs (Fellman, "Laura" 551). Franklin D. Roosevelt was one great man whose deeds Wilder did not at all approve of.

Laura's performance at the School Exhibition represents her achievement of adulthood—the self-disciplined, independent adulthood of an American. At the beginning of *Little Town on the Prairie*, she is a kitten fighting her first mouse; by the end, she can be paired symbolically with her native country—in her youth, her struggle for independence, her moral strength, her desire to stand alone among the "older, stronger" nations and ask no help from anyone, even in "hard times." The history she recites justifies not only America but herself. This, we may assume, is what Wilder meant to show.

We know from a speech she gave in 1937 that Wilder did come to see her own life as an exemplum of American history. "I realized that I had seen and lived it all—all the successive phases of the frontier, first the frontiersman, then the pioneer, then the farmers, and the towns. Then I understood that in my own life I represented a whole period of American History" (quoted in Anderson 217). For what most of us mean by "history" is not simply all the events of the past but the significant events—those that determine what is to come, and deserve to be recorded as written history. Wilder, Fellman explains, had absorbed the "frontier thesis" of Frederick Jackson Turner, who viewed the frontier as the principal force shaping American character and civilization (Fellman, this vol.). His thesis enabled Wilder to see her life and the formation of her character as a demonstration of this shaping force. She closes her account of Laura's recitation, "Then the first wagon wheels rolled into Kansas" (293), as though suggesting how Laura's story joins the great mainstream.

Yet there is more than one concept of history—and more than one reading of *Little Town on the Prairie*. Within the past two decades, women's historians, New Historians, and historians of ethnic minorities have begun to formulate new definitions of history, taking adequate account for the first time of those who were not great, or not men, and especially of women as community builders and shapers of civilization. From this perspective, the growing up of the Little Town, and of Laura Ingalls, traces a pattern very different from that of Wilder's carefully constructed thematic structure.

In *The Long Winter*, Wilder had stressed the isolation of the Little Town's separate households in their battle for survival against a hostile nature. Fellman points out that the book says much less than Wilder's original manuscript about "communal techniques" the townspeople used to survive, and suggests that this de-emphasis of community strengthens the message of self-sufficiency (Fellman, "Laura" 558). "I hope you don't expect to depend on anybody else, Laura," says Ma. "A body can't do that" (123). But even between blizzards, the town barely exists as a community. The men gather at the store to exchange news and play checkers; they organize a hunt when a herd of antelope chances within range, though the hunt fails, and we know Pa would have done better on his own. There is a school for the children—a nucleus around which the community will grow. For the women, there is nothing. As far as the reader knows, Ma does not see anyone outside her family all winter long.[4]

One year later, instead of becoming more and more independent of one another, the households are joining and connecting in new ways. The town holds its first communal celebration on the Fourth of July. The event is still heavily masculine—even Laura finds it rough and noisy—and Ma stays at home. But soon men and women meet to organize a church (27), and the women form a Ladies' Aid Society; the Society sponsors a dime sociable, and the church a series of revival meetings. Men, women, and children meet at the schoolhouse to create a literary society, whose first activity is an all-town spelling match. Later entertainments are attended even by homesteaders from far out of town—charades, musical evenings, a debate, a minstrel show. The stores begin to stock items such as name cards, which promote social interaction for its own sake. Even Thanksgiving becomes a community celebration rather than the private family holiday Laura has always known. The town that once served only as a way station for immigrants and a place to buy and sell the bare necessities now has the elements of religion, society, and culture. And its group activities are no longer restricted to men or children only, but summon both sexes and all ages to feast, worship, learn, and play together.

As for Laura, she has been undergoing a similar metamorphosis. In *The Long Winter,* Wilder had stressed her shyness and aversion to both town and school. "She didn't like town; she didn't want to go to school" (66), or "all night, it seemed, she knew that the town was close around her and that she must go to school in the morning. She was heavy with dread when she woke" (72). At the beginning of *Little Town,* Laura still prefers the natural peace and beauty of the isolated claim. Her summer job in town is a disagreeable ordeal, and the town itself seems "like a sore on the beautiful, wild prairie" (49), dirty,

foul-smelling, and ugly. That fall, her difficulties at school with Nellie
Oleson and Miss Wilder—for which her own strong family loyalties
are largely responsible—outweigh the pleasures of friendship with
Mary Power and Ida Brown.

Yet these difficulties also show Laura the limitations of virtuous isolation. When she promises Pa to make no trouble in school, yet ceases
to discourage other troublemakers, the poorly disciplined classroom
dissolves into chaos. "Laura was appalled at what she had started, by
only two smiles at naughtiness" (170). Too late, she realizes that she
herself will suffer if the educational community breaks down and she
cannot study or earn her certificate. As a member of the community, she shares responsibility for its harmony; simply refraining from
wrongdoing is not enough.

Although the classroom returns to normal under a better teacher,
Laura has been subtly but permanently reoriented toward her peer
group. Now she wants name cards, because the other girls are getting
them. She exchanges autographs with her friends, becomes interested
in her clothes and hairstyle, and makes her first unconscious moves
in the mating game when she accepts a buggy ride from Almanzo
Wilder. The polite conversation she manages to maintain while ex-
changing name cards with him would have been entirely beyond her
capacity a few months ago.

Meanwhile, rather than lecturing her on self-sufficiency, Ma and Pa
have been prompt to encourage her budding social life. Ma gives her
the autograph album, and she and Pa treat Laura to a set of name
cards. "You are a good girl, Laura," Ma reassures her when she hesitates at the unnecessary expense, "and we want you to have the pleasures of other girls of your age" (196). They let her go to parties and
cut her bangs in a stylish "lunatic fringe" (203) and spend money to
buy "beautiful brown velvet" for a new hat (256). They are not unnatu-
rally startled—"But she's only fifteen!" says Ma (280)—when Almanzo
walks her home from the revival meeting, but they don't object; nor
do they object to her going sleighriding alone with him (297).

Wilder sets up a conflict between duty and pleasure as soon as
Laura begins to enjoy school, so that she can show Laura developing
the self-discipline an American adult is supposed to have. But the
lesson is undermined by Ma and Pa's reasonable attitude—that Laura
should experience "the pleasures of other girls" of her age—and by
our own realization that Laura is gaining as much in long-overdue
social development as she loses in study time. We read that Laura
"thought rebelliously that she wouldn't see Ida and Mary Power and

Minnie and the boys again, all summer long. She promised herself that she would study really hard, next summer" (262). Later, Wilder makes it sound like a punishment for "self-indulgence" when "it seemed to Laura that she did nothing but study that whole summer long" (267). But one could argue that Laura simply sets her own priorities, and that hindsight shows her instinctive choice to have been the right one. If she does not want to teach school the rest of her life (and she doesn't), she had better become a social creature, and learn how to talk to young men.

In effect, *Little Town on the Prairie*—I believe, unconsciously—undermines its own thematic structure.[5] What Wilder wants to show is that America and its people should be "free and independent," that what they need most is the self-discipline to become truly self-sufficient. What she actually shows—based on what actually happened when she was a teenager—is individual farmers and storekeepers bonding into a community. An isolated young girl becoming thoroughly socialized. And a chapter of American history in which there are no "great men" —only men, women, and children, all essential to the creation of a frontier outpost of Western civilization—a little town on the prairie.

What really happens in *Little Town on the Prairie* is worth noticing, these cracks of self-contradiction running through the plaster of a series that has become an icon of conservative political and family values in America—for the cracks hint at subsurface strains. But even more worth noticing is what *Little Town* shows us about history. *Little Town* sets two definitions, old and new, side by side: what Laura has been taught about America and its history, and what she experiences herself without realizing her own experience. The one, shaped to articulate meaning with perfect clarity. The other, a silent, shapeless, private stream of happening whose meaning we have to seek out ourselves. We can see them both now, after fifty years.

Notes

1. Much has been written about the "collaboration" of Laura Ingalls Wilder and her daughter, Rose Wilder Lane, in the writing of the Little House books. For the purposes of this analysis, I shall be writing of Wilder as the author of the books. Certainly, the political beliefs that underlie the conscious structuring of *Little Town on the Prairie* were shared by mother and daughter, as Fellman has shown in "Laura Ingalls Wilder and Rose Wilder Lane: The Politics of a Mother-Daughter Relationship." Throughout my analysis, "Laura" will be used to denote the character, "Wilder" to denote the author.

2. In the first chapter of *The Long Winter*, Pa points out to Laura how the extra-thick walls of a muskrat's house predict a hard winter ahead:

"'Pa, how can the muskrats know?' she asked. 'I don't know how they know,' Pa said. 'But they do. God tells them, somehow, I suppose.' 'Then why doesn't God tell us?' Laura wanted to know. 'Because,' said Pa, 'we're not animals. We're humans, and, like it says in the Declaration of Independence, God created us free. That means we got to take care of ourselves'" (12). Unlike the muskrats, whose instincts enable them to survive the winter, human beings must rely on their human resources, not simply to stay alive but to stay human. Most of *The Long Winter* is a working out of this concept.

3. For a detailed analysis of Laura's moral growth through the entire series, see Claudia Mills's "From Obedience to Autonomy: Moral Growth in the Little House Books" (this vol.).

4. In fact, as Fellman points out in "Don't Expect to Depend on Anybody Else" (this vol.), the Ingallses actually shared their home with another couple during the Long Winter; this is "one of numerous instances in which the novels leave out shared living arrangements" (page 111). She also notes in "Laura Ingalls Wilder and Rose Wilder Lane" that in Wilder's original "Pioneer Girl" manuscript, a neighboring brother and sister stayed with Laura and her sisters and took care of them while Ma and Pa accompanied Mary to college (557)—in which case, of course, this episode could scarcely demonstrate Laura's progress toward self-sufficiency as it does in *Little Town*.

5. In "Laura Ingalls Wilder's America: An Unflinching Assessment," Elizabeth Segel has suggested that Wilder consciously showed Laura struggling with "certain of the moral assumptions that underlie her family's way of life—in particular, the settler's assumption of his right to the land" (66). It seems unlikely, however, that Wilder would consciously criticize the principle of self-sufficiency that she is known to have held strongly during the writing of *Little Town on the Prairie*.

Works Cited

Anderson, William, ed. *A Little House Sampler: Laura Ingalls Wilder and Rose Wilder Lane.* New York: Harper and Row, 1989.

Fellman, Anita Clair. "Laura Ingalls Wilder and Rose Wilder Lane: The Politics of a Mother-Daughter Relationship." *Signs* 15, no. 3 (1990): 535–61.

FitzGerald, Frances. *America Revised: History Schoolbooks in the Twentieth Century.* Boston: Little, Brown, 1979.

Segel, Elizabeth. "Laura Ingalls Wilder's America: An Unflinching Assessment." *Children's Literature in Education* 8, no. 2 (1977): 63–70.

Wilder, Laura Ingalls. *Little Town on the Prairie.* 1941. Reprint. New York: Harper and Row, 1953.

———. *The Long Winter.* New York: Harper and Brothers, 1940.

———. *These Happy Golden Years.* 1943. Reprint. New York: Harper and Brothers, 1953.

From Obedience to Autonomy:
Moral Growth in the Little House Books

Claudia Mills

Children's fiction, like much fiction for adults, frequently takes as its subject the moral growth of its protagonist. The Little House books of Laura Ingalls Wilder trace Laura's growth in moral awareness and moral development from early childhood through her first employment, her courtship by Almanzo, and her marriage. Laura's moral maturation is rich and multilayered, but at the heart of the Little House books, and shaping their progression as one multivolumed novel, is the theme of obedience giving way to autonomy, literally moral self-rule.

Laura's moral development throughout the seven books of the original series is hardly unusual or idiosyncratic. Indeed, her growth closely follows the pattern laid out in Jean Piaget's ground-breaking *The Moral Judgment of the Child,* in which deference to rules laid down by others gives way to a growing respect for moral rules as self-legislated: "Autonomy follows upon heteronomy; the rule of a game appears to the child no longer as an external law, sacred in so far as it has been laid down by adults; but as the outcome of a free decision and worthy of respect in the measure that it has enlisted mutual consent" (65). Laurence Kohlberg could easily map Laura's growth onto his six stages of moral development: she grows from stage-one heteronomous morality, where she follows externally imposed rules to avoid externally imposed sanctions, to stage-six morality, where she recognizes that moral rules are binding on her because she legislates them for herself. Although I shall argue that Laura's moral development, as presented by Wilder, follows the Piaget-Kohlberg pattern quite remarkably, it also reflects some facets of moral development that are distinctively female, as articulated by Carol Gilligan. Laura develops her moral personality in close connection with her family

An earlier version of this article was presented at the Twenty-First International Conference of the Children's Literature Association, Springfield, Missouri, June 4, 1994. For numerous helpful comments I am indebted to Anita Clair Fellman, Elizabeth Keyser, and the readers who reviewed the manuscript for *Children's Literature.*
Children's Literature 24, ed. Francelia Butler, R. H. W. Dillard, and Elizabeth Lennox Keyser (Yale University Press, © 1996 Hollins College).

and community; the ethic that emerges from her maturation is an ethic of care as much as or more than an ethic of justice.

What is most striking about the vision of moral development in the Little House books is how fully and vividly it is realized and how it is shaped to mirror the American political context. For Laura Ingalls Wilder and her collaborator daughter, Rose Wilder Lane, the individual's moral growth from obedience to autonomy parallels the American polity's growth from subjection to democracy. It is in Wilder's explicit drawing of this parallel that the Piaget-Kohlberg model of moral development most clearly shows its dominance over Gilligan's alternative model, though elements of the latter are clearly present. (Anita Clair Fellman explains Wilder and Lane's attraction to a robustly liberal ethic of rights and noninterference as a possible artifact of the difficulties that arose from their dangerous overdependence on each other in their mother-daughter relationship ["Laura Ingalls Wilder" 540–41].) In any case, at key points in the series, Laura's moral growth toward freedom and independence is linked to the ongoing struggle of Americans to achieve those same values in the political realm.

Although Fellman (this vol.) rightly notes the stress on the highly individualistic moral and political values of freedom and independence, I am concerned with a different point. Whatever values an individual finally adopts as her own—whether those tending toward selfishness or selflessness on the moral spectrum or those stressing an ethic of justice or an ethic of care—most of us think it important that such values emerge at the end of a rich and complex process of moral maturation rather than being adopted in unthinking conformity to existing moral conventions. Likewise, whatever policies one would like to see a democratic government enact—regardless of where they fall on the political spectrum—most would agree on the implementation of such policies through democratic decision making rather than through authoritarian control. Thus, whatever one makes of the particular values Laura ultimately chooses as her own—and I would argue that these center at least as much on unselfish care of others as on self-interested pursuit of her own projects—readers should welcome her emerging ability to make such choices on her own.

I turn now to an analysis of Laura's moral development over the course of the seven volumes in the series. The central moral value in *Little House in the Big Woods* is unquestioning obedience to adult authority. Disobedience in itself, even without a view toward its consequences, is to be punished severely. Here Laura's childhood is hardly atypical for an American child of the nineteenth century. The importance of blind obedience to adult authority provides the moral for many a children's tale of this period. In Jacob Abbott's "The Reason Why," for example, Rollo's teacher explains to her pupils that they may ask their parents "the reason why" to obtain information about the workings of the world but advises them to give unswerving obedience to their parents' commands. Several of Pa's freestanding narratives in the book warn against disobedience. Most notably, in "The Story of Pa and the Voice in the Woods," young Pa disobeys his father and tarries in the woods instead of promptly bringing the cattle home to stable. Although he has already received a bad scare from a menacing screech owl, Grandpa gives him a good thrashing anyway, "so that I would remember to mind him after that." Grandpa tells Pa, "There's a good reason for what I tell you to do . . . and if you'll do as you're told, no harm will come to you" (58). But the reason suggested is only for young Pa to avoid being scared by screech owls, which was unlikely to have been Grandpa's original reason for his instructions. Thus, Pa's chief fault has really been disobedience pure and simple.

Later, when Ma and Laura encounter a bear, mistaking it for their cow, Ma orders Laura to walk back to the house. When they are safe inside, she tells her, "You were a good girl, Laura, to do exactly as I told you, and to do it quickly, without asking why" (106). Although the possible consequences of disobedience are more clear and compelling in this case, the stress remains on prompt and unquestioning obedience.

In the most memorable incident of the book, Laura's rivalry with Mary culminates in her slapping Mary for boasting that "golden hair is lots prettier than brown." Pa whips Laura with a strap, less for the actual offense of striking Mary than for disobeying his prior command.

> "You remember," Pa said, "I told you girls you must never strike each other."
> Laura began, "But Mary said—"
> "That makes no difference," said Pa. "It is what I say that you must mind" (183).

The moral world of *Big Woods* revolves around a literal, legalistic concern with moral rules. The girls work out strict, rule-bound codes for sharing cookies with Baby Carrie, dolls with guests, and even the grated carrots used to color the churned butter. Laura is so focused on a literal interpretation of moral rules that when Pa refers to her cousin Charlie as a "little liar" for repeatedly faking a cry for help, although she is horrified by Charlie's disobedience of his elders, Laura does not understand "how Charley could be a liar, when he had not said a word" (211). Moral rules are straightforward and simple, and obedience to them is to be automatic and absolute.

In *Little House on the Prairie*, obedience remains the moral corner-stone, but the consequences of disobedience are more openly stressed: the girls must mind Pa or Ma not so much because of their parental authority but because of the terrible and life-threatening consequences that could result from disobedience. It is superior wisdom, beyond sheer parental status and brute physical force, that gives one authority to legislate for one's children.

When Pa loses control of the horses in the family's treacherous crossing of a fast-rising creek, "quick as a flash," Laura and Mary obey Ma's sharp command, "Lie down, girls!" (21). Laura later reflects on what could have been the tragic consequences of their disobedience at that point: "If Laura and Mary had been naughty and bothered [Ma], then they would all have been lost" (24). The same incident, however, contains a hint of Pa's fallibility: Laura begs for Jack, the bulldog, to ride across the river in the wagon with the family; when Jack is feared drowned in the crossing, Pa reproaches himself for his decision to let Jack cross by himself.

In a dramatic incident later in the book, Indians come to the house while Pa is away. Before leaving, Pa tells Laura and Mary not to turn Jack loose; but when the Indians enter the house, posing a possible threat to Ma and Baby Carrie, Laura debates disobeying Pa in the light of the altered circumstances.

> "I'm going to let Jack loose," Laura whispered hoarsely. "Jack will kill them."
> "Pa said not to," Mary answered. . . .
> "He didn't know Indians would come," Laura said.
> "He said not to let Jack loose." Mary was almost crying (136).

When Pa returns, he is horrified to hear that Laura even considered disobedience; he explains that if the girls had let Jack loose, they would have provoked trouble with the Indians; the threat of massacre at the close of the book indicates the seriousness of the danger. Repeatedly, Pa stresses the value of obedience: " 'After this,' he said, in a terrible voice, 'you girls remember always to do as you're told. Don't you even think of disobeying me. Do you hear? . . . You girls remember this: you do as you're told, no matter what happens. . . . Do as you're told . . . and no harm will come to you'" (146). Obedience is necessitated by the extreme risks of the pioneer way of life.

Again, moral rules here are for the most part to be interpreted with straightforward literalness, even by adults. Both Ma and Pa think it a moral disgrace to be beholden to their neighbor Mr. Edwards for the loan of a few nails, and Pa makes a special trip to Independence, forty miles away, to repay his debt. But for the first time in the series, Laura encounters a moral conflict between her parents, when Pa decides, over Ma's objections, to risk his life going down the unfinished well to rescue Mr. Scott, who has been overcome with the bends. For the first time, not all moral questions have simple answers. And the larger setting of the novel also suggests difficult moral questions, when the Ingalls family is forced from their homestead to make good on the U.S. government's promise to the Indians, raising the issue of the justice or injustice of American governmental policies toward Native Americans, an issue that Elizabeth Segel has addressed elsewhere. Moreover, that the government is characterized in the novel as blundering in the implementation of these policies indirectly raises the question of whether, if obedience of ruled to ruler is justified by the latter's superior wisdom, an inept government has any justified claim to the allegiance of its citizens.

On the Banks of Plum Creek can be read as a complex exploration of the costs and challenges of obedience and disobedience. It is the last Little House book to treat Laura completely as a child, but even here she is growing toward eventual moral autonomy. The novel is structured around a series of instances of Laura's disobedience to her elders' instructions, culminating in her ultimate freedom from those instructions and responsibility for making her own moral choices.

In the first incident, Laura goes too deep into the river on a family swim. When Pa ducks her for punishment, Laura responds by begging him to do it again. Physical means of punishing Laura have become ineffective. Later, Laura heads back to the swimming hole alone and stops only because she is frightened by a badger in her path. She could keep the incident secret but is tormented by a guilty conscience for breaking a promise to her parents, namely, not to go to the swimming hole. Laura tells herself that "breaking a promise was as bad as telling a lie" (33), showing that she now recognizes that one *can* lie without saying a word. Her punishment is one tailored by Pa to Laura's fault: if she did wrong by breaking her parents' trust, she must be treated as one who can no longer be trusted and must be watched for a long, tedious day by Ma. The third incident of disobedience is treated in a purely playful way: Laura (with Mary) persists in sliding down the haystack despite Pa's command not to. She justifies her behavior by invoking the letter rather than the spirit of Pa's command: "We did not slide, Pa. . . . But we did roll down it" (60). Here Laura is relying on a literal, legalistic interpretation of moral rules, as she did in *Big Woods,* but she now does so tongue in cheek, playing on such literalness to her own advantage. Elsewhere in the book, Laura shows a literal adherence to the moral value of not taking something belonging to another, when she feels the shame of being beholden for a slate pencil and uses her Christmas penny to purchase one; Laura also explores the limits of a literal interpretation of such rules, however, when she and Ma decide that reclaiming her beloved doll Charlotte from little Anna, who has abandoned Charlotte in a mud puddle, is not a case of stealing. Here for the first time Laura participates with a parent in a discussion over the scope and authority of moral rules.

In the fourth incident, Laura goes outside while Ma and Pa are away, disobeying Mary's instructions to stay in the dugout and so refusing Mary's attempt at surrogate authority over her; while outside, she discovers cattle in the family's hay and succeeds in driving them out. When Pa and Ma return home, "Pa said they had done exactly the right thing. He said, 'We knew we could depend on you to take care of everything. Didn't we, Caroline?' " (77–78). It is implicitly conveyed that taking care of everything involves some scope for Laura's independent judgment; taking care of everything involves more than a mechanical adherence to others' rules. In the next incident, Laura almost drowns playing on the footbridge after a flooding rain; here she has violated no specific rule laid down by Ma—she is merely "sure Ma would not let her go to play in the creek" (101). No punishment for this is forthcoming; Laura is old enough now to accept the consequences of her actions without any parental intervention. Ma tells her, "Well, Laura, you have been very naughty, and I think you knew it all the time. But I can't punish you. I can't even scold you. You came near being drowned" (105). Never again in the Little House books is Laura punished by Ma and Pa. In the final episode of disobedience, toward the very end of the book, Laura manages to bring in the entire woodpile before an approaching blizzard, following a discussion with Mary about disobeying Ma's instructions that they must stay in the house during a storm; this discussion closely parallels the discussion in *Prairie* on turning Jack loose. This time, however, Laura has done the right thing: "They knew they were forgiven for disobeying, because they had been wise to bring in wood, though perhaps not quite so much wood. Sometime soon they would be old enough not to make any mistakes, and then they could always decide what to do. They would not have to obey Pa and Ma any more" (291). Thus the six episodes of disobedience culminate in Laura's freedom from punishment from Ma and Pa and in her freedom from literal obedience to their commands. Laura must learn how to rule herself.

A gap of several years takes place between *Plum Creek* and *On the Shores of Silver Lake;* Laura is now an adolescent, witnessing the full complexities of adult moral codes. In this book, Laura faces her chief moral drama not as participant but as spectator, observing the various nuances of adult moral behavior as her world widens beyond the isolation of her little house to full-fledged membership in a larger community.

Early in the novel, Laura and her cousin Lena are horrified to hear of a neighboring thirteen-year-old girl who has just gotten married. Although Lena mourns the girl's loss of fun, Laura regrets her premature assumption of an adult's responsibility, remarking, "I don't want to be so responsible. I'd rather let Ma be responsible for a long time yet" (50). The rest of the novel explores what such responsibility, in moral terms, entails for the adults who face it, in a world no longer marked by simple and unambiguous moral values.

As *Plum Creek* was structured around a series of incidents of Laura's disobedience of moral rules, *Silver Lake* is structured around a series of portraits of the moral complexity of the rules themselves. What is stealing? What is lying? The answers for Laura and her family are no longer simple. And the portraits of human character are now more multidimensional and complex, with fewer clear lines drawn between heroes and villains. Most of the moral rules held up to scrutiny in the novel are also legal rules, thereby suggesting as well that individual citizens must play an active role in interpreting and enforcing the laws by which they are governed.

What is stealing? When Laura's Uncle Hi and Aunt Docia leave their position with the railroad, taking wagons full of company goods with them, Ma worries that Pa, as a representative of the company, should have stopped them. Pa replies, "Oh, come, Caroline! It wasn't stealing. Hi hasn't got away with any more than's due him for his work here and at the camp on the Sioux. The company cheated him there, and he's got even here. That's all there is to it" (131). It isn't stealing to take back what another has wrongfully taken from you.

What is lying? Midway through the book Pa uses his official-looking company stationery to forge sheriff's documents in order to help his friend Mr. Boast collect a bad debt. Although Pa and Mr. Boast treat the incident basically as a joke, the same point is made: moral and legal rules may be bent in the service of securing justice. Once others bend moral rules, we may have to bend them ourselves to see that, in the end, justice is done.

Even the moral status of murder comes into question, when Pa endorses vigilante justice following a settler's murder by a claim jumper: "Hanging's too good for him. If we'd only known in time!" (257). Thus, even the gravest moral commandments are not exceptionless, not in a world where others break them first. And moral virtues are also qualified in the rough-and-ready world of the West. Pa wants to show the traditional virtues of generosity and hospitality to travelers seeking shelter on their way West; Ma replies that if they open their home to strangers, they must charge them for it, and by doing so, the family raises money for Mary's college education.

Two of the most dramatic story lines in *Silver Lake* feature case studies of moral complexity. The first treats the character of the half-breed Big Jerry—a gambler, rabble-rouser, and horse thief but a kindhearted man, nonetheless, who twice intervenes to save Pa from a threat to his life. One learns that basic moral goodness can be compatible with a flagrant flouting of moral rules. In the second, a mob of railway workers storms Pa's office on payday, clamoring for wages they claim were wrongly withheld. With the help of Big Jerry, Pa manages to send the mob away, but the paymaster at another office gives in to the mob's fury. When Ma and Pa discuss the incident, Laura joins in, expressing her own moral condemnation of what she views as the paymaster's cowardice. The conversation that follows explores the complexity of the moral choice faced, asking what degree of risk one must accept to carry out one's moral duties.

The novel closes with the Ingalls family settled on their homestead claim. There Laura's little sister Grace is feared lost in the Big Slough; as Ma and Pa frantically search for her, Laura debates what she and Carrie should do.

"Ma told you to stay with Mary," said Laura. "So you'd better stay."

"She told you to look!" Carrie screamed. "Go look! Go look! Grace! Grace!"

"Shut up! Let me think!" Laura screeched. (277)

Laura ends up looking for Grace and eventually finds her; she searches not because Ma has told her to do so but because she has decided she should. Laura has now faced the need for moral choice amid both the natural and human perils of the West; in doing so she has learned that each moral agent must make a final choice alone. It is important to note, however, that this ultimate moral independence need not mean that moral choices are made in isolation. That each of us bears final responsibility for our choices does not mean that these cannot be informed by the values held by our families, friends, church, and community, just as Laura's are. Nor is Laura's moral maturation framed exclusively in terms of an ethic of rights and justice. Instead, her maturation is most notably one toward an ethic of care. The earlier books in the series were marked by Laura's often bitter rivalry with Mary; the girls are locked in perpetual competition, over everything from whose hair color is prettier to who is more generous in sharing beads with Carrie. But now Laura is willing to place Mary's needs above her own; she thinks to herself that she "would be glad to work hard and go without anything she wanted herself, so that Mary could go to college" (219). Selfishness has given way to unselfishness, self-interest to self-sacrifice.

The Long Winter explicitly defends the idea that full human development—particularly in the American context—involves moral independence, and it plays out this theme by dramatizing a moral choice made by a member of Laura's own generation, her future husband, Almanzo. According to the central message of *The Long Winter,* human beings cannot flourish and achieve fulfillment by rote obedience to the commands of others—whether legal, moral, or even divine. Human beings, alone in all creation, must make their own choices and live with the consequences of them.

In chapter 1, Pa sets the theme for the book by explaining to Laura why God, who tells muskrats to build thick-walled houses in anticipation of the hard winter to come, does not give human beings the same information. The reason, Pa says, is because "we're not animals.

We're humans, and, like it says in the Declaration of Independence, God created us free. That means we got to take care of ourselves." Although muskrats have to build the same kind of house, "A man can build any kind of house he can think of. So if his house don't keep out the weather, that's *his* look-out; he's free and independent" (13). Here the novel's lesson of moral independence is explicitly set in the context of American political independence.

Subsequent chapters test Laura's understanding of the challenges of independent choice. She has a first negative experience with exercising free choice when she and Carrie head off for an errand together in town, feeling "*free and independent* and comfortable together" (19, my emphasis). On the way home, they take a different route through the slough and get lost; Laura concludes, "We've learned a lesson. I guess we'll stay on the road after this" (26). Not all independent choices turn out well. But some do. When Ma tries making a green pumpkin pie, Laura comments, with surprise, "I never heard of such a thing"; Ma responds by telling her, "Neither did I. But we wouldn't do much if we didn't do things that nobody ever heard of before" (32). Most notably, when Laura's teacher leads the children home from school in a blizzard, Laura stays with the group though she fears they are going the wrong direction; it is Cap Garland, striking out on his own, who reaches town successfully and alerts the townsfolk to the danger faced by the obedient others.

In the novel's central story, Almanzo Wilder makes a moral choice to risk his life, with Cap Garland, to bring wheat to his near-starving neighbors. Almanzo's moral independence is emphasized from the start. He bends legal rules by lying about his age to claim his homestead at nineteen, telling the town clerk, "You can put me down as twenty-one" (100). Almanzo recognizes that many men follow the letter of the law but take advantage of legal loopholes to thwart its spirit—"Everywhere, men were stealing the land and doing it according to all the rules" (99); he violates the letter of the law but feels that he embodies the ideal of what the law intended a homesteader to be. In the chapter titled "Free and Independent," he makes his decision to set out across the barren, blizzard-ridden prairie to find wheat for the town, telling Royal, "This is a free country and I'm free and independent. I do as I please" (258–59). But it is made clear that this freedom is actually freedom to do not what one pleases but what one judges to be morally correct. Autonomy is equated with moral self-rule, not with moral anarchy. Nor does autonomy here indicate a disregard of community. Almanzo's independent choice is a choice to risk his life for others, to recognize and act on what he views as the plain moral necessity that "somebody's got to go get that wheat that was raised south of town" (257)—even though self-interest certainly plays a role, for part of Almanzo's motivation here is to justify to himself his refusal to sell his own precious seed wheat to his neighbors.

Almanzo's decision to risk his life to bring back the wheat is foreshadowed in two other discussions that raise questions of when and for what one should risk one's life. When Mr. Foster scares off Almanzo's horse, Lady, Almanzo comes to terms with the limits of what he will do to search out and rescue her: "The loss of Lady made him sick at heart, but he did not intend to risk his life for a horse" (205–06). In the following chapter, the Ingalls family engages in a lively moral critique of the railway engineer who refused what he viewed as a suicidal order to ram his locomotive into a formidable snowbank. Mary argues that the engineer should have simply done as he was told, on the grounds that the superintendent must know best; Laura disputes this claim of the superintendent's superior knowledge but disapproves of the engineer's refusal to find some independent solution to the problem.

The theme of freedom and independence is developed still further in the confrontation between the townspeople and Mr. Loftus, the shopkeeper who charges an exorbitant price for the wheat brought back by Almanzo and Cap. Pa tells Mr. Loftus that just as he is free to charge what he will for his wheat, so are the townspeople free to take their business elsewhere once the winter is over: "Don't forget every one of us is free and independent, Loftus" (305). Freedom and independence ground not only an individual's own moral autonomy; they also provide the foundation for the social contract, the regulatory framework for human community. This echoes the Lockean model of the state as based on a contract made by free individuals, each endowed by natural law with rights to life, liberty, and property, which so influenced the Founders in their shaping of our own political system.

Little Town on the Prairie prepares Laura's way for the freedom and independence she will exhibit in the final book of the series, *These Happy Golden Years*. When Laura attends her first Independence Day celebration, she articulates the lesson of *The Long Winter* for herself in its clearest statement in the series, and in a clearly American context, as she thinks to herself: "Americans won't obey any king on earth. Americans are free. That means they have to obey their own consciences. No king bosses Pa; he has to boss himself. Why (she thought), when I'm a little older, Pa and Ma will stop telling me what to do, and there isn't anyone who has a right to give me orders. I will have to make myself be good. . . . This is what it means to be free" (76–77). Note that freedom is not represented as a state of "boss-lessness" but as the state in which one bosses oneself. It is not the freedom to be whatever one might choose to be; it is the freedom to choose to make oneself be good. For Laura, this means the freedom to work as hard as she can to finance Mary's college education. Laura, who has always despised needlework, takes a job working six days a week as a seamstress, taking pleasure in giving her entire week's wages to Ma and Pa, refusing to keep anything for herself. Here we see a blending of Kohlberg's stress on autonomy with Gilligan's stress on interconnectness and care.

The novel's central story line shows Laura's encounter with an ostensible authority figure, her new teacher, Miss Wilder, who proves to be completely morally bankrupt. It is notable that Laura's climactic clash with Miss Wilder comes not in defense of any of her own interests but in her spirited protection of her helpless younger sister, Carrie, a target of the teacher's unfair punishment. Although Laura later chides herself for her thoughtless role in Miss Wilder's ultimate undoing, her real lesson here seems to be that there is no guarantee that adulthood carries with it moral superiority; the novel ends with Laura herself preparing to take on her first adult authority role as a young school teacher.

These Happy Golden Years brings to fruition the lessons of the previous two books, as Laura faces full-fledged adult responsibilities in her first teaching assignment. She must learn to deal with a difficult older student who challenges her authority at school, and she must endure the miserable and threatening atmosphere of the Brewster home where she boards.

In her encounter with rebellious Clarence, Laura learns that she must not only be free and independent herself but deal with the freedom and independence of others. Pa tells her that she must learn to manage Clarence rather than simply try to exert her authority over him: "Brute force can't do much. Everybody's born free, you know, like it says in the Declaration of Independence. . . . Good or bad, nobody but Clarence can ever boss Clarence" (54). As in Pa's encounter with Mr. Loftus in *The Long Winter,* the freedom and independence of one person in civil society must be reconciled with the freedom and independence of others.

In her encounter with bitter Mrs. Brewster, who stalks her house at night with a knife in her hand, Laura faces a possible risk to her life that parallels the risk Almanzo assumes in *The Long Winter:* Laura "was terribly frightened. She dared not sleep. Suppose she woke to see Mrs. Brewster standing over her with that knife? Mrs. Brewster did not like her" (66). Laura conceals the incident from Ma and Pa: "She was not exactly lying, but she could not tell them about Mrs. Brewster and the knife. If they knew, they would not let her go back, and she must finish her school" (82). As in *The Long Winter,* Laura's self-chosen values here are not self-directed but other-directed: more than her own life, Laura values the opportunity to provide financial assistance for her sister Mary. When she is finally paid her dearly won wages at the end of her assignment, she once again hands them over ungrudgingly to her parents: "Here, Pa. Take it and keep it for Mary. . . . I was only teaching school for Mary" (99).

The climactic moment of *These Happy Golden Years* comes not when Laura accepts Almanzo's proposal of marriage but when she tells him that she is unable to make the traditional vow of wifely obedience: "I can not make a promise that I will not keep, and, Almanzo, even if I tried, I do not think I could obey anybody against my better judgment" (269–70). This moment is the culmination of the moral development of all the earlier books in the series; Laura's hard-won moral independence must not end with her marriage to Almanzo but continue and deepen. In a linkage of this moment to the American historical context, Almanzo tells Laura that Reverend Brown does not believe in using the word "obey"; Brown is a cousin of the radical abolitionist John Brown "and a good deal like him" (270). Thus, the freedom and independence that is Laura's crowning moment of adulthood is tied to the moment in American history when America began truly to make good to all citizens the promise of freedom and independence that had so struck Laura on Independence Day. It is a freedom, however, that Laura will use not to pursue her self-interest in isolation from others but to build her new family in her own little house shared with Almanzo.

The series thus ends. Laura has grown from obedience to autonomy, from a rote follower of externally imposed moral rules to someone able to legislate her own internal care-based morality and to join in a life partnership on the basis of full equality with someone also capable of moral self-rule. Her development is an outgrowth of America's striving for self-governance—government of the people, by the people, and for the people—in the American Revolution, in the Civil War, and in the westward expansion. This is the enduring moral vision of the Little House books.

Works Cited

Abbott, Jacob. "The Reason Why." In *From Instruction to Delight: An Anthology of Children's Literature to 1850,* ed. Patricia Demers and Gordon Moyles. From *Rollo at School,* 1839. Reprint. Toronto: Oxford University Press, 1982. Pp. 167–72.

Fellman, Anita Clair. "Laura Ingalls Wilder and Rose Wilder Lane: The Politics of a Mother-Daughter Relationship." *Signs* 15, no. 3 (1990): 535–61.

Gilligan, Carol. *In a Different Voice: Psychological Theory and Women's Development.* Cambridge: Harvard University Press, 1982.

Kohlberg, Laurence. *Essays on Moral Development.* Vol. 1, *The Philosophy of Moral Development.* New York: Harper and Row, 1981.

Piaget, Jean. *The Moral Judgment of the Child.* New York: Free Press, 1932.

Segel, Elizabeth. "Laura Ingalls Wilder's America: An Unflinching Assessment." *Children's Literature in Education* 8, no. 2 (Summer 1977): 63–70.

Wilder, Laura Ingalls. *Little House in the Big Woods.* 1932. Reprint, with new illustrations by Garth Williams. New York: Harper and Row, 1953.

———. *Little House on the Prairie.* 1935. Reprint, with new illustrations by Garth Williams. New York: Harper and Row, 1953.

———. *Little Town on the Prairie.* 1941. Reprint, with new illustrations by Garth Williams. New York: Harper and Row, 1953.

———. *On the Banks of Plum Creek.* 1937. Reprint, with new illustrations by Garth Williams. New York: Harper and Row, 1953.

———. *On the Shores of Silver Lake.* 1939. Reprint, with new illustrations by Garth Williams. New York: Harper and Row, 1953.

———. *The Long Winter.* 1949. Reprint, with new illustrations by Garth Williams. New York: Harper and Row, 1953.

———. *These Happy Golden Years.* 1943. Reprint, with new illustrations by Garth Williams. New York: Harper and Row, 1953.

Mildred Taylor's Story of Cassie Logan: A Search for Law and Justice in a Racist Society

Hamida Bosmajian

Mildred Taylor's rich chronicle about an African American family in rural Mississippi during the years 1933–41 is narrated by the main character, Cassie Logan. The story she tells is not only about the adventures of her childhood and adolescence, not only about the deep bonds she has with her family, but also about the injustices a white, racist, and lawless society inflicts on the Logans and their neighbors. Although they are citizens in a nation that is framed by one of the most important legal documents in Western civilization, the Constitution of the United States, black Americans find themselves in Taylor's chronicle constituted in an unjust system of local laws and customs. It is not surprising, therefore, that as a child the intelligent and inquisitive Cassie is already quite aware of the binary injustice/justice. The first term of the binary is privileged in her life experience; it is the second, justice, that she yearns for.

The young reader of Mildred Taylor's *Roll of Thunder, Hear My Cry* (1976), *Let the Circle Be Unbroken* (1981), and *The Road to Memphis* (1990) will most likely focus on the adventures and relationships of Cassie Logan in rural Mississippi during the Depression and the years leading up to America's entry into World War II. It becomes quite clear, however, that these years also reveal Cassie's ongoing education in and growing consciousness of the liberating power of just laws. Moreover, Taylor treats law and justice and their opposites in a manner that is quite sophisticated, even technical on occasion. We can even say that her three narratives are novels of education in the need for law and justice. Although Taylor's story offers the literary critic a full range of interpretive opportunities, I shall limit my discussion to the significance of the theme of law and justice in Cassie's development.

It is a theme that is unusual in children's literature. Most often the law, especially in fairy tales, is expressed through irrational or tyrannical rules imposed upon the hero by persons in authority. The hero's

Children's Literature 24, ed. Francelia Butler, R. H. W. Dillard, and Elizabeth Lennox Keyser (Yale University Press, © 1996 Hollins College).

trial, then, consists often of impossible hardships and tasks to fulfill these rules. The mysteries of adult law and legal systems may also befuddle the child hero who, like Alice in Wonderland, finds herself or himself in an absurd world. We may well conclude that children's literature tends to depict law in a preconscious, even dreamlike sense. Taylor's chronicle, however, shows us characters who are conscious of the value of American law as a heritage of an age of reason. Although the titles *Roll of Thunder, Hear My Cry* and *Let the Circle Be Unbroken* are prayerful imperatives that reflect the religious heritage of African Americans—the first asking for vertical divine intervention, the second for the continued connectedness on the horizontal level of human experience—the novels do not invoke or appeal to divine law, but place the responsibility for justice on laws made by humans.

The relationship between law and literature is profound. The patterns of tragic narratives usually are generated by the violation of a law that must be righted; the patterns of comic narration begin most often with an unjust and irrational law that the comic hero transforms or transcends through liberation. The topic of law and literature also received much critical attention beginning in the 1980s, perhaps because so many former literature majors became lawyers. Not only do law journals frequently publish essays on the relevance of literature and literary theory to the law, but book-length studies have been devoted to this topic. James Boyd White's *Heracles' Bow: Essays on the Rhetoric and Poetics of the Law* (1985) and Richard Posner's *Law and Literature: A Misunderstood Relation* (1988) are two such representative studies. White argues that "the law is an art of persuasion that creates the objects of its persuasion, for it constitutes both the community and the culture it commends" (35). Thus law is a text made by humans, a narrative whose writer is a *maker* (comparable to the maker of literature) who creates meaning through words and speaks to a community (123). Posner sees the trial as a fundamental constituent of literature and finds that both the literary and the legal scholar are "centrally concerned with the meaning of texts" (8).

In these studies White and Posner comment extensively on literary and legal texts, ranging from Aeschylus to Shakespeare, from Franz Kafka to Albert Camus, from the United States Constitution to Supreme Court decisions. Both commentators perceive Aeschylus' *Oresteia* as a trilogy that traces the evolution of the law from the law of revenge to the law as the transcendent power in a civilized state. Although Mildred Taylor's trilogy does not end with Mississippi actualizing just laws, I was struck by the fact that Cassie Logan's emotional and rational need for justice moves from the satisfaction of a successfully executed revenge to the realization that just laws will have to become the agents for change in an unjust society. The threat that just laws can always be undermined by unjust actions is ever present, however, not only in Cassie's story but in the *Oresteia* itself.

Aeschylus intends to confirm the Athenian citizen in the rule of law, but his image of the apotheosis of the law is fragile: Athena's "inviolable court" stands upon the "Hill of Ares," the god of war lust, where the spirits of vengeance, the Erinyes, agree to become the kindly ones (Eumenides), who are housed in the hill's sacred cave. Civilization aspires to the temple of justice, but its foundation is human rage and anger, powerful emotions that constantly threaten the law that stays them.

As far as the values of law and justice are concerned, fictions such as the *Oresteia* or Taylor's trilogy are pedagogical in their rhetorical ethos. The Greek poet of antiquity instructs the polis through the mythic mode, where the gods are the authoritative teachers. Mildred Taylor, a writer in the psychologically and socially realistic mode, focuses on justice and law issues by recording the ordinary routines and events of human life, as with Cassie Logan, who grows from a pranksterish tomboy to an aspiring student of the law. In the Mississippi of her childhood and adolescence, custom and the unjust statutes of segregation have institutionalized racism, and those in power can vent their rage with impunity whenever they feel that "colored folk" are "forgetting their place." The victims of this willful power must constantly be vigilant and self-controlled, even if they are infuriated by the injustices inflicted upon them. To protect herself and her family, young Cassie has to learn that she cannot vent her anger. As she matures, she begins to place her hope for empowerment in the knowledge and interpretation of the law, particularly the law of the U.S. Constitution, which potentially can supersede the unjust law and custom of Mississippi.

At the conclusion of *The Road to Memphis,* Cassie is ready to go to college in preparation for law school. In the mode of realistic narration, this young Athena wants to realize and actualize the promise in the letter of the law. Like Athena, she is very much dependent on the male voice as definer of the law: the oral law of her father, David Logan, and the legal practice of the family's white lawyer, Wade Jamison. But because Cassie has strong role models in her mother and grandmother, she insists that she be treated as a peer of her brothers. Her alignment with her father's will seems less a submission to male authority than a subtextual acknowledgment on Taylor's part that African American men need to be authoritatively constituted in narratives for the young, because white racism constantly undermines the realization of such constructive authority. White men may abuse the values of American law as framed in the Constitution, but Cassie sees in Wade Jamison a model of how the law ought to be incarnated. In the course of the chronicle, she learns that "the Constitution has no force except to the extent that it is involved and used by individual Americans pursuing actual goals. Until it is used it is inert. Alone it can do nothing" (White, *When Words Lose Their Meaning* 244).

The first-person narration of the trilogy is from Cassie's point of view, though in age and education she is distant from the experiences she describes. Cassie's experiences in 1933 are not told in the language of a nine-year-old; rather, the narrator's mature voice reflects on the child she was in the Mississippi of 1933. In *The Road to Memphis* the language of the adolescent and intellectually precocious eighteen-year-old Cassie is closer to the fictional narrator's voice but must still not be identified with her. Because Taylor chose not to dramatize her narrator and tells us nothing of Cassie's present context, the reader never knows if Cassie did indeed finish law school and became a successful attorney. In her Newbery acceptance speech for *Roll of Thunder,* Taylor indicated that she planned two more books about the Logans, "which will chronicle the growth of the Logan children into adolescence and adulthood" (Taylor, "Newbery Award Acceptance" 407). Unless Taylor writes a fourth volume, there is a blank in the fictional narrator's story that makes Cassie's quest for law and justice ambiguous. The story ends with the third volume, and the reader can only surmise what will happen to Cassie. What has become subtextually clear, however, is that life in this racist society is far worse than the narrator-author admits to the young reader.

Mildred Taylor shows us Cassie's development not only in the context of growing up in a warm and nurturing family but also in the context of the middle-class values of life, liberty, and the pursuit of property (happiness). It is the Logan's landownership, threatened though it is by the difficulty of meeting tax payments, that is essential to their dignity, their life, and the liberty they claim. Her family's self-respect is based largely on the fact that they farm their own land, even though Mrs. Logan also teaches and Mr. Logan works on the railroad. This status helps Cassie avoid becoming the child Martin Luther King describes in his "Letter from Birmingham Jail": "The depressing clouds of inferiority begin to form in her little mental sky, and we see her begin to distort her little personality by unconsciously developing a bitterness toward white people" (King 81). Cassie gets angry at anyone who wants to designate her as inferior; she would agree with King's argument that "any law that uplifts the human personality is just. All segregation statutes are unjust because segregation distorts the soul and damages the personality" (82). Her childhood experiences and observations give her ample evidence to observe that effect.

Socially and politically, Mildred Taylor's chronicle is squarely within the context of the values of constitutionally guaranteed rights, no matter how these rights are violated in temporal local statutes. Such values give her story an affirmative narrative pattern that has the reader consistently root for Cassie Logan's struggle toward right and lawful actualization of herself and her community. Nevertheless, the narrative is filled with ambivalent countermemories and subtexts, for the building of the temple of justice is indefinitely deferred in the three novels and the furies have no intentions of becoming the "kindly ones." Taylor's storytelling skill manages to include all these ambivalences yet lets her young hero continue her struggle. *Roll of Thunder, Hear My Cry* depicts one year during the Great Depression (1933–34) and frames that year with the restrictive horizon of racist Mississippi; *Let the Circle Be Unbroken* focuses on 1935, a year when Cassie's knowledge of prejudice and its effects expands; *The Road to Memphis* opens the horizon to include the beginnings of the global conflict that follows the bombing of Pearl Harbor on December 7, 1941. Cassie's brother and friends will become soldiers to fight injustice and prejudice elsewhere, even as such flaws prevail in their own society. In examining Cassie's growth and education in awareness of justice and law, I shall limit the discussion to several key incidents.

The first example is the prank as a relatively harmless tactic of revenge against persistent abuse. *Roll of Thunder* begins with the Logan children's trek to school along the narrow road that "wound like a long red serpent dividing the high forest bank of quiet old trees on the left from the cotton field . . . on the right" (3). The school bus would come "roaring down the road spewing red dust over the children" while "laughing white faces pressed against the bus windows" (8). On a rainy day, "the bus driver would entertain his passengers

by sending us slipping along the road to the almost inaccessible forest banks . . . [and] we consequently found ourselves comic objects
to cruel eyes that gave no thought to our misery" (32).

Cassie's younger brother, Clayton Chester, or "Little Man," is enraged by this humiliation and eager for revenge. The children decide
to dig a ditch across the road that, filled with water, traps the school
bus whose passengers now get soaked in return: "Oh, how sweet was
well maneuvered revenge!" exclaims the narrator in retrospect. Their
prank is a playful retaliation, a momentary empowerment against
daily mistreatment, but it could easily become a more serious matter,
with disastrous consequences.

Revenge, argues Judge Posner, is the irresistible impulse to avenge
wrongful injuries, but it is also the underpinning of the corrective
justice of criminal punishment and the breakdown of law and order
when legal channels have become blocked (Posner 25–26). Revenge,
however, precludes the possibility of eventual cooperation (30). Taylor's characters feel repeatedly the upsurge of anger that could lead
them to revenge, but only in *The Road to Memphis* does that anger lead
to violence; usually Taylor depicts the black community as venting its
anger only in a prank or an attitude. An organized attempt at community action, such as the boycott of the Strawberry store organized by
the Logans and supported by Jamison, is bound to fail as whites react
by terrorizing blacks. Blacks experience the constant threat of violence, for anxiety makes the oppressor permanently vigilant against
the slightest signs of insubordination, signs that nearly always trigger
an excessive response. Shortly after the bus prank, therefore, when
"night riders" terrorize the neighborhood, the Logan children connect it with their prank and Cassie is overwhelmed by the terror she
will feel often during her childhood and adolescence: "Once inside
the house, I leaned against the hatch while waves of sick terror swept
over me. . . . I climbed into the softness of the bed. I lay very still for
a while, not allowing myself to think. But soon, against my will, the
vision of the ghostly headlights soaked into my mind and an uncon-
trollable trembling racked my body. And it remained until the dawn,
when I fell into a restless sleep" (*Roll of Thunder* 51).

The night riders in this case have another object for their revenge:
an adult black male. As Cassie gets older, she becomes aware that
the physical violence of whites against black men expresses itself as
a sexual threat against black women. The inciting moment for the
action in *The Road to Memphis* is, as we shall see, a combination of

both variables of violence. Taylor does keep within the conventions
of literature for young readers by preserving Cassie from witnessing
extreme acts of violence, but the threat of it permeates even the
most intimate "at home" moments. The Christmas chapter in *Roll
of Thunder* (106–24) is one such example. Here the narrator begins
by nostalgically evoking the smells, sounds, and sights of Christmas
in an almost Dickensian manner. Stories are told by the older folks
and, as the night deepens, Mr. Morrison, the helper and protector in
the Logan household, talks about how his ancestors were "bred" for
strength during slavery and how his family was killed on a Christmas
Day. Mrs. Logan tries to quiet him for the sake of the children, but
her husband admonishes her: " 'These are things they need to hear,
baby. It's their history' " (112).

How can a young person in such an environment still learn to
value the idea of law? The values of personhood and community
are instilled through the deep bonding among the members of the
Logan family and their ability to "talk things out." Mary Logan's
personal courage against injustice and David Logan's kind and disciplined nature provide the children with strong values. Moreover,
David teaches his children separateness from whites as a means of
survival. The family survives by finding strength in one another, for
all attempts to reach out and change the injustices in the community
fail, as the attempted boycott in *Roll of Thunder* or the thwarted labor
union in *Let the Circle Be Unbroken* demonstrate. Publicly, the importance of law is projected for Cassie through Wade Jamison.

Jamison, solicitous of the Logans' concerns and welfare throughout the three novels, is "Old South" and old money. He represents an
agent of social change who does not come from the disempowered
grass roots of the oppressed but whose education, property, and personal sense of justice have touched his conscience and enabled him
to publicly represent and advise the oppressed. Well aware that there
are as yet few of his kind, his effectiveness is limited to expressions
of attitude, for the context of his culture keeps him from turning the
gestures into effectual acts. Typically, Cassie aligns him with the positive expression of patriarchal values: "He was the only white man I
had ever heard address Mama and Big Ma as 'Missus,' and I liked him
for it. Besides that, in his way he was like Papa: Ask him a question
and he would give it to you straight with none of this pussy-footing-
around business. I like that" (*Roll of Thunder* 81). The Logans deal
with him because of their property but also receive his support when

they boycott an oppressive store owner. Most significantly, Jamison is a key figure when he tries to stop a lynching mob and defends fourteen-year-old T.J. Avery, on trial for his life.

T.J. and a white boy named Jeremy Simms function as complex scapegoat figures in the narratives. Typically, the scapegoat, ranging from the criminal to the sacred, manifests itself directly or subtextually in contexts where injustice generates an anger and rage that are vented on an individual defined as "the one." Both T.J. and Jeremy try to befriend the Logan children, and both want to cross the boundaries that separate blacks from whites. Both boys imperil themselves by their desire and eventually die because of it. Cassie feels ambivalence toward both, for she cannot really understand their motivations.

In a different context, T.J.'s character type could well be that of the trickster-boaster or the "signifying monkey," as Henry Louis Gates describes him (Gates 44–88). In Taylor's narratives, however, T.J.'s profound lack of self-esteem motivates both his ego inflation and his desperate need to be accepted. Such needs flaw his action morally: it is he who informs on Mary Logan and causes her to be dismissed from her teaching post. He takes up with R.W. and Melvin Simms, Jeremy's crude older brothers, who promise him a pearl-handled pistol if he helps them break into Barnett's store. T.J. does not realize that they are setting him up when they mask themselves with black stockings. When Barnett comes upon them, R. W. Simms kills him (188), but it is T.J., as a black, who will be tried for the murder. The incident is a variable of the stereotype René Girard identifies as "the mark," the victim who is "invited to a feast that ends with his lynching. Why? He has done something he should not have done; his behavior is perceived as fatal. One of his gestures was misinterpreted" (Girard, *Scapegoat* 33–32). T.J. is marked both as black and as a boundary crosser.

Cassie recognizes T.J.'s tragic isolation from both whites and blacks: "I had never seen him more desolately alone, and for a fleeting second I almost felt sorry for him" (*Roll of Thunder* 182). For whites, T.J. is a scapegoat of convenience who will be burdened with the blame for a criminal act, but his role as scapegoat for the black community is more complex. Cassie feels both anger and guilt toward him: anger because he has hurt her family and guilt because she cannot make him a friend in spite of his need. T.J. turns to the Simms brothers in part because he is unable to befriend the black children. T.J. is never liked, only tolerated by the Logan children, whose anger against him is very real after he informs on Mama. But T.J. also exemplifies the dangers of boundary crossing, a temptation especially acute for Stacey, Cassie's older brother, who is open to friendship with Jeremy. When the Simms brothers brutally beat T.J. after the break-in, he seeks out Stacey who, with his siblings, accompanies him home, for Stacey, surmises the narrator, "perhaps felt that even a person as despicable as T.J. needed someone he could call 'friend,' or perhaps he sensed T.J.'s vulnerability better than T.J. did himself" (189). As the Logan children are about to return home, they see night riders driving towards the Averys'. The lynching mob violently forces the Averys out of their house, including T.J., who is "dragged from the house on his knees. His face was bloody and when he tried to speak he cried with pain" (192). As the savage beating continues, Jamison drives up and says quietly: "Y'all decide to hold court here tonight?" (93). Jamison is unable to disperse the mob, whose rage now also begins to threaten Mr. Morrison, the Logans' live-in protector, and David Logan himself: "A welling affirmation arose from the men. 'I got me three new ropes!' exclaimed Kaleb" (194). The children gasp in terror and Stacey sends Cassie to inform Papa.

At this point a roll of thunder, the reply to the plea of the title, announces a storm that enables David Logan to diffuse the situation by setting fire to his crop, claiming that lightning struck a fence post. Everybody gets involved extinguishing the fire. When the truth of the situation dawns on Cassie, she realizes that "this was one of those known and unknown things, something never to be spoken, not even to each other" (208–09). Cassie intimates the awful consequences her father's act could have and internalizes that terror into her inmost silence. In Jamison's confrontation with the lynching mob, his appeal to the law has been ineffectual; instead, it is David Logan's lawless act of arson that disperses the lawless mob. Cassie, the witness-narrator, learns here both of the law's fragility and of the danger when lawlessness is used to deter lawlessness. In *The Road to Memphis,* Cassie herself will participate in a technically lawless act as she helps a fugitive escape from the "justice" of an unjustly constituted society.

Stacey's protectiveness towards T.J. asserts itself for the last time when he tells his parents that he intends to go to T.J.'s trial and perhaps tell the court how T.J. came to the Logan house. Mama tells him that no one would believe him and Papa agrees: "He is in the hands of the law now and that law like jus' 'bout everything else in this country is made for the white folks" (*Let the Circle Be Unbroken* 31). At the suggestion that the white folks may even get the idea that Stacey was part of the break-in, Cassie feels a "surging feeling of panic at the thought of Stacey facing the same order as T.J. . . . Stacey had been with T.J. the night Jim Lee Barnett had been killed, and he had helped him. We all had" (31).

How and for whom is T.J. a scapegoat? Northrop Frye chooses the Greek *pharmakos* to emphasize the scapegoat as poison and antidote, for the *pharmakos* "is neither innocent nor guilty. . . . He is innocent in the sense that what happens to him is far greater than anything he has done provokes. . . He is guilty in the sense that he is a member of a guilty society, or living in a world where such injustices are an inescapable part of existence" (Frye 41). Whites charge T.J. with committing the murder; he is innocent of the actual crime, and his punishment exceeds the wrongs he did. But T.J. also violates the unwritten law of the black community, a law articulated by David Logan as a lesson to Stacey, who wants to befriend Jeremy: "We Logans don't have much to do with white folks. You know why? 'Cause white folks mean trouble. Maybe some day whites and blacks can be real friends, but right now the country ain't built that way. Now you could be right 'bout Jeremy making a much finer friend than T.J. ever will be. The trouble is down here in Mississippi it cost too much to find out. . . . So I think you'd better not try" (*Roll of Thunder* 119–20).

In this society where whites insist on *difference,* blacks need to appropriate that difference in their own terms. T.J. becomes the victim-scapegoat who, as René Girard argues, is burdened with the role of surrogate victim, and he alone must assume the consequences of these ills (Girard, *Violence* 77). T.J.'s "crime" is that he has tried to deny *difference,* that he has confused the boundaries the black community must insist on for their survival. In a sense, then, he is the sacrifice for Stacey. Jeremy, too, will become, to a lesser extent, such a scapegoat when he is publicly and savagely beaten by his father for assisting in the escape of a black who had raised his hand violently against a white man. Ostracized from his family, Jeremy voluntarily joins the army to lose himself in the battlefields of World War II.

The children witness the ritual of the scapegoat, the subtext of T.J.'s trial, in the courtroom procedures where Jamison is the ideal defense attorney: he is completely in support of his client and is able to reconstruct the event so that the widow Barnett cannot swear "before God Almighty" that the men who attacked her husband were black. His efforts, however, are empty gestures before the foregone conclusion that T.J. is guilty. The prosecutor tells the sobbing fourteen-year-old T.J., "Whether or not you actually was the nigra who dealt the death blow, the blood on your hands is just as red and won't wash off" (*Let the Circle Be Unbroken* 65). In his summation, Jamison argues that T.J. followed two white men blindly: "We demand that they follow us docilely, and if they should dare disobey, we punish them for their disobedience. . . . T.J. murdered no one. His guilt lies more in his gullibility, in his belief that two white men cared about him" (70). Jamison has already lost ethos as a white man in this community and is now interrupted by the real criminal, R. W. Simms: "I knows what you tryin' to do, Wade Jamison! I knows it and everybody else here knows it. You're a nigger in white skin, that's what you are. Fact, you're worse than a nigger. . . . What kind of country is this when a white man's gotta defend himself 'gainst a nigger?" (69). Jamison, too, is defined as a boundary crosser, as a deconstructor of difference by means of the law. T.J. receives the death sentence. When he passes by the Logan children for the last time, Cassie's eyes dim with tears as she concludes, "We were never to see T.J. again" (74). In the final line of *The Road to Memphis,* in which Jeremy Simms is exiled from the hurtful community of his youth, the narrator commemorates Jeremy with a similar sentence: "We did not see Jeremy Simms again."

In spite of his ineffectualness, Jamison is a mentor to Cassie. It is he who gives her her favorite book, *The Law: Case Histories of a Free Society.* Not only is Cassie intrigued by the lines of argument, whose conclusions she likes to predict, but the case histories actualize the concepts of law through interpretation (*Road to Memphis* 141). Beginning with *Let the Circle Be Unbroken,* Cassie begins to be attracted to legal texts. Although the justice implicit in the texts prevails nowhere in the novels, Cassie increasingly sees in the texts the possibility for a just society.

However, Cassie's first book, presented to her as "new," is literally a "dirty book." The Board of Education pastes a grid in each primer to grade it from "new" to "very poor"; the last condition makes the texts suitable for "nigras" (17–18). Imprinted with this grid of institutionalized racism, the content of the reader insults further: "Girls with blond braids and boys with blue eyes stared up at me" (*Roll of Thunder* 15). Little Man, Cassie's fastidious younger brother, asks: "May I have another book please, ma'am. . . . That one is dirty." Little Man understands the Board of Education's grid of quality judgment: "His face clouded, changing from sulky acceptance to puzzlement. His brows furrowed. Then his eyes grew wide and suddenly he sucked in his breath and sprang from his chair like a wounded animal, flinging the book onto the floor and stomping madly upon it" (17). As the teacher is about to whip him, Cassie's sense of justice makes her shout: "See what they called us." The teacher, who is herself black, affirms "that's what you [nigra] are" and whips them. Both children refuse the book and the definition "poor-nigra." To ease their pain, Mrs. Logan pastes a piece of paper over the offensive grid, an act that is later interpreted as violating county property and contributes to her dismissal.

Cassie receives pride and confidence not from school but from the stories told by Big Ma (her grandmother) and her father; the oral tradition of black history provides the context for her identity (Harper 75). (Taylor herself acknowledged the value of her own father's stories ["Newbery" 403].) Papa also buys his children books for Christmas. Cassie receives Alexander Dumas's *The Three Musketeers*, because, Papa tells her, the author was a mulatto whose grandma was a slave in Martinique. The values of writing and reading are thus equally enhanced. Mama inscribes the books, " 'This book is the property of Miss Cassie Logan. Christmas 1933' " (116), thereby providing some healing for the harm done at the beginning of the school year.

In *Let the Circle Be Unbroken*, Cassie begins to be interested in the nature and argument of legal texts. The inciting moment occurs when the aged Mrs. Lee Annie decides to exercise her right to vote. In order to pass the literacy test, Mrs. Lee Annie needs to study her copy of the 1890 Mississippi Constitution, given to her by a judge. She wants Cassie to tutor her, but Cassie finds the print too small and the words too hard to understand, though Mrs. Lee Annie's decision interests her: "My papa votes. Back in the times of Reconstruction when black men got the vote—women didn't have no vote. Walked right up to the voting booth and made his X. Didn't have to take no test then. Then blacks were punished. Help me read the book" (99). As Mama tutors Mrs. Lee Annie, Cassie experiences a breakthrough in the thorny language of the text: "I suddenly found the dry words of the constitution beginning to take meaning. Mama explained that a number of the laws were quite good and in theory quite fair. The problem, however, was in the application, and if the judges and the courts really saw everyone as equal instead of as black or white, life would have been a lot pleasanter" (169–70).

Mrs. Lee Annie does not get to exercise her right to vote; she does not pass the test, but she knows the laws: "I knows it and can't nobody take away nothing I know. Nobody" (310). Like land, knowledge is property and can be acquired by anybody. With this philosophy, the aged woman is an important role model for Cassie; moreover, her decision to exercise her right to vote goes beyond what she intended: the racist society, threatened by her decision, perceives it as an act of rebellion. When the white landowner, Harlan Granger, represses the labor union, he sees Mrs. Lee Annie as a coconspirator in undermining the white power structure: "I ain't gonna have no niggers talkin' down to me and mine! Ain't gonna have no niggers votin' neither! I say any niggers gettin' beyond themselves oughta be taken care of, and we can begin right now with that ole woman up there" (320).

In *The Road to Memphis,* Cassie's reading focuses on her gift from Jamison, *The Law: Case Histories of a Free Society.* Her second mentor, Solomon Bradley, is impressed by her interest and knowledge, and with him Cassie can for the first time converse about the law. When he asks her if she has read *Plessy vs. Ferguson,* she is able to answer: "That's the one where the Supreme Court said that separate but equal was all right. It said that segregation was constitutional" (143). Interestingly enough, neither Cassie nor Solomon expound on the implications of the case. Authorial control leaves a textual blank in place of the anger that decision warrants. In contrast, a jurist such as Judge Leon Higginbotham described the 1898 decision as "the most wretched decision ever rendered against black people in the past century. . . . [It] established the separate but equal doctrine also known as Jim Crow, created the foundations of separate and unequal allocations of resources, and oppression of the human rights of Blacks" (Higginbotham 1009–10).

Solomon Bradley, who is no model of wisdom as was his biblical namesake, is at best an ambiguous mentor. He gives Cassie two detective stories, Dashiell Hammett's *Red Harvest* and a Sherlock Holmes mystery. After noting with admiration that so young a person reads *Case Histories of a Free Society,* he urges her to choose entertaining fictions over difficult texts: "*Case Histories of a Free Society* might be fine for bright young ladies boning up to become lawyers, but, believe me, Sherlock Holmes can be a lot more fun" (*Road to Memphis* 147–48). The text suggests that he is bothered by Cassie's choice of books— "And don't forget to check up on Sherlock Holmes and Dashiell Hammett" (149)—but whether it is because he feels threatened by her, is jealous of the influence of Jamison, or wants to keep her from the obstacles she would experience as a black attorney, Taylor does not make clear. Cassie does not interpret Solomon, nor does the authorial control of the narrative create an ironic distance between Cassie the mature narrator and Cassie the teenager infatuated with Solomon Bradley.

Nevertheless, Cassie clearly states her goals to Solomon. Having learned from Jamison the concepts of precedence and interpretation of the law, she confides: "I was thinking that if I got to know the law as well as they [white lawyers] do, then maybe I could get some different interpretation. If we know the law like they do, then we can use it like they do" (245). Solomon wonders, "Did you figure all that out yourself?" and then diverts attention from the discussion to the cut on Cassie's knee, displacing her from potential peer to subordinate. A shift occurs from Cassie as student to Cassie as romantic interest. Cassie herself feels the ambiguity.

She cannot understand how Solomon can edit a newspaper rather than use his legal education. His past remains somewhat a mystery, though the experienced reader senses that the obstacles he experienced as a black attorney were simply too great for him (244). He admits: "I also use my knowledge of the law to advise people who come to me on a personal basis, not as clients, but just people who want some advice from a knowledgeable source. I don't charge them for any advice I might give. So you see that's the extent of my law involvement and I don't consider that practicing law" (243). In a sense both he and Jamison are ineffectual in their *pro bono* advice and advocacy for blacks: Solomon Bradley lacks the official standing as a lawyer, and Wade Jamison, no matter how respected he is because of family and profession, loses ethos by the very fact that he is an advocate for blacks.

In *The Road to Memphis,* Cassie's inability to understand Solomon's ambivalent feelings could make her point of view an interesting study in narrative unreliability had Taylor intended to make this an issue in her narrative. In spite of their difference in age, she feels a strong attraction to him, a feeling he shares and manipulates as he tries to impress her with his education, knowledge, and flattery. As an older man, there is about him a fatherly solicitude displaced into a sexual attractiveness that is missing in the authority of the two other older males who influence her, her father and Jamison. Her tomboy self aligned itself with boys as peers and always rejected conventional socializations in femininity such as wearing a dress. She is, therefore, all the more readily receptive to a strong, attractive male figure who first approaches her as an intellectual equal but who really cannot tolerate a strong black woman who might ultimately achieve what he was unable to accomplish. As he admits to her in the end: "But there's a way about you, Cassie Logan. A way about you that's a cut between a sassie little girl and a most outspoken woman, and that's a dangerous combination for an old man like me, who ought to know better" (252). We see in her relationship with Solomon the beginning of a powerful ambiguity for Cassie, who is far more socialized as a potential student of the law than as a woman. The chronicle does not tell us how Cassie will resolve this conflict.

With *Let the Circle Be Unbroken,* law and sex-gender begin to inter-relate. This element is introduced when Cassie's northern cousin, Suzella, a teenage girl from a mixed marriage, visits the Logans for several months. Pretty and light-skinned, Suzella is constantly harassed by the rural white louts for whom she is visible evidence of the violation of the Mississippi constitutional law against miscegenation, though the violation of black women for passing sexual gratification is sanctioned by local custom. The terror of sexual assault by a gang of white males begins to emerge for Cassie in *Let the Circle Be Unbroken* and intensifies in *The Road to Memphis.* Both novels make it clear that black men who abandon their posture of subordination toward whites are "put in their place" with violence, but white men can make primary sexual claims on black women with impunity. The lynching mob makes black men impotent; rape or gang rape puts black women "in their place." Thus both novels complicate economic and social injustice with an ethnically defined agon of sexuality or gender. Again, Taylor keeps the issue within the borders of conventions defined as appropriate for young readers, but the tense reciprocity of racism and sexual dominance in both narratives provides the inciting moment for the main action in *The Road to Memphis.*

The last novel differs from the first two in that the young people are removed from the central image of the Logans' protective hearth; they are now "on the road," with all the dangers and adventures that this quest symbol implies. Moreover, in their quest they help a "fugitive from justice," Moe Turner. Moe, undeterred by Cassie's strength and ambition, is in love with her and has lashed out against Jeremy Simm's cousins, Statler and Troy, after they harass him. The incident begins when the two humiliate Clarence, an enlisted man, by rubbing his head for "good luck." Cassie realizes that protest is pointless: "We couldn't win, not against white folks. They did what they wanted, and there was no sense in starting up trouble just about a little ridicule," even if it "sliced like a knife" (118). Moe calls Clarence away from the situation, and just as Statler and Troy move in on Moe, Jamison disrupts the dangerous moment by calling both Moe and Clarence to his office. A short time later, while Moe is working on a car, the harassers catch up with him. Statler begins: "Ain't you the boy messed with our getting ourselves some luck with that soldier boy?" (122). Moe "eyeballs him"; Statler knocks Moe's hat off and commands: "Nigger, don't you eyeball me! Now, pick it up." Moe is about to do so when Statler insults him on a deeper level: "You must got a powerful lotta luck in you, boy, you courtin' a gal like Cassie Logan here. Put that head down, boy, let me get a good feel at it. Who knows . . . maybe I get lucky with Cassie myself" (123). The anger in Moe "burst forth like a thunderstorm. He knocked Statler's arm away with the tire iron, then smashed it full force into Statler's side" (123) and across Troy's head.

A shy, gentle youth, Moe has suddenly abandoned all caution needed for survival in the racist society. The "lucky" head becomes sexually associated with his "luck with Cassie," though he has "no luck" with her. Statler's "let me get a good feel at it" suggests a white man's attempt through sympathetic magic to acquire the legendary sexual prowess of black men and to lay claim to black women. Although Moe is inclined to accept the insult to himself, he will not tolerate dishonor to Cassie and explodes with an anger that resonates with the emotions the thunderstorm image expressed in *Roll of Thunder*.

Jeremy Simms hides Moe under a tarpaulin on his truck and drives him to the Logan siblings and Clarence; they in turn take Moe to Memphis, where he can board a train to Chicago. Significantly, it is Jamison who has indirectly provided the escape vehicle, the car that Stacey bought from him. Before they leave, Jamison makes them keenly aware of the legal and social situation Moe faces in Mississippi:

> What I'm telling you [Cassie] and Stacey now is some legal advice mixed with a good measure of common sense. If you are asking me strictly about the law concerning Moe's situation, I have to tell you what the law says. Any man who raises his hand against another man and injures him must be held accountable. If you're asking me what Moe should do, then I feel obliged to

tell you that the law is an imperfect piece of machinery and not
blind to color, not here in Mississippi. The law here is bound by
race. No matter what Moe's defense, his being a Negro will affect what happens to him. Yes, he could go to the police, but as
the law stands and as Mississippi justice stands, he could go to
prison. (157)

Jamison reluctantly admits that Moe would be better off if he went
north.

On the road, Cassie herself experiences serious humiliation. During the youths' stop at a gas station, she has to use the restroom designated for WHITE LADIES ONLY (177): "It made no sense to me that
I had to go stooping behind a bush when there was a perfectly good
toilet right behind the door." Although she knows what is in store for
her should she be discovered, she decides to enter the restroom. A
white woman finds her and screams for the gas station attendant, who
kicks Cassie "like somebody with no heart would kick a dog. His shoe
struck me sharply, but that's not what wounded me. It was my pride
that suffered" (179). Shocked at Cassie's torn stockings and muddy
coat, Stacey immediately suspects the worst: "What happened to you?
They touch you?" (180) Cassie brushes off his concern, but later that
night, after a nightmare about the incident, she wakes up and rushes
from the car into "the blackness, trying to find some shelter to take
my fear. I looked for a spot in the darkness, found some bushes, fell
to my knees and threw up . . . feeling so far from home and alone
in this world, even with the boys so near. On my knees, the vomit
all over my once beautiful clothes, I broke down and cried" (189).
She can no longer stomach a world that denies her even the most
natural urges; moreover, she cannot admit to her brothers that she
endangered the entire rescue mission by trying to use the segregated
restroom. In this existential moment of isolation, she relieves herself
from the pain in the depth of her being by vomiting near the bushes
in the darkness (the place designated to her by segregation) and thus
soils the beautiful and controlled appearance she has acquired for
her public persona. Cassie realizes here just how fragile her relatively
privileged persona is and how, like Moe, she can be subjected any
time to the humiliations that segregation can legally inflict on her.

The Road to Memphis opens up the context of racist Mississippi
within a much larger frame: the persecution of "the other" is aligned
with Hitler's Germany, as America, after Pearl Harbor, declares war

on the Axis powers. Solomon Bradley's assistant, Mort, declares patriotically to Cassie that he is going to join the army because "the Japs bombed us." Cassie objects that the Navy "didn't have all that many colored folks," but Mort argues that "negroes got to fight Hitler. . . . Haven't you heard about the master race? Why he figure, nobody is as good as folks of that so-called superior race." To which Cassie replies, "White folks the same here. . . . Here we can't even use a toilet in a gas station and they'll be wanting our boys to go fight" (231–32). After she tells Solomon about the gas station incident, she protests: "My brother is supposed to go fight? It's not right. It's not right" (234).

The goal of the journey to Memphis is completed when Moe boards the train to Chicago to join the Logans' Uncle Hammer, a World War I veteran. Another journey begins as Stacey and Cassie's young male friends accept the call to go to war. "There seemed to be no question now that Stacey would have to go to war" and Little Man hopes that the war will last long enough so that he, too, can join (282). Cassie is skeptical, for the condition of blacks had remained unchanged after the previous war, in which two of Big Ma's sons had died and another, Uncle Hammer, had lost a leg. Once again, the text suggests, blacks hope that life will get better if they "prove themselves," but there is also the suggestion that war, particularly war against Hitler, provides a legitimized structure of aggression against the universality of racism in Western civilization. Joining her friends is Jeremy Simms, who, after having assisted in Moe's escape, is expelled from the family as a "nigger lover." Unlike Cassie, whose direction is to transform society from within through the interpretation of the law, the young men accept the rallying call that glosses over how unacceptable they are to the society in which they grew up.

Thus, in spite of Moe's successful escape, the chronicle is left open-ended. The historical frame of the narrative suggests future possibilities, tragic or transformative. The personal lives of the young people reach toward the unknown future, yet there is the suggestion that the old problems remain unresolved. Jeremy and Stacey will be more effectually segregated in the U.S. Army than they were as children, for military integration does not come about until 1948, with an executive order of President Truman (Dalfiume 4); *Brown vs. The Board of Education* is more than a decade away; and the Civil Rights Movement of the 1960s will occur twenty years after Taylor's chronicle. By then Cassie will be in her late thirties. Will she be a lawyer and interpreter in that struggle, or will she send her children to the demonstrations in Mississippi or Alabama? The three volumes about her development in this place and time affirm that she will be a woman who struggles against injustice and yearns for justice, who makes clear and intelligent distinctions and advocates civic conduct supported by just laws.

Although Taylor does not appeal to the "higher law" of God that motivated Martin Luther King, Jr., so profoundly in his struggle for change through civil disobedience, she does accept the assumptions and enlightenment traditions that enabled King and the Civil Rights Movement to achieve major legal transformations. Without the framework of the Constitution as guarantor of the transcendent rights of individual equality, that struggle could not have led to the civil rights legislation of the 1960s. Taylor's faith can, of course, be problematized when we ask ourselves how the content and structures established by the Constitution institutionalize the privileges and differences a free and equal society seeks to avoid. The subtextual problematic of the Civil Rights Movement and of Taylor's novel, particularly in relation to Wade Jamison and Cassie, is the assumption that law is a sufficient means in the transformation of a racist society rather than a necessary first step. In the end Cassie begins to get in touch with this core problem as she senses that great historical struggles may not really eradicate the roots of prejudice. Young Cassie is on her way to becoming a rational and just individual who is aware that the temple of justice is always constructed on the Areopagus, the Hill of Ares, where the Furies are at best only tentatively persuaded to become the Eumenides, the kindly ones.

Works Cited

Aeschylus. *The Oresteian Trilogy.* Trans. Philip Vellacott. New York: Penguin, 1985.

Dalfiume, Richard M. *Desegregation of the U.S. Armed Forces.* Columbia: University of Missouri Press, 1969.

Frye, Northrop. *The Anatomy of Criticism.* Princeton: Princeton University Press, 1957.

Gates, Henry Louis, Jr. *The Signifying Monkey: A Theory of Afro-American Literary Criticism.* New York: Oxford University Press, 1988.

Girard, René. *Violence and the Sacred.* Baltimore: Johns Hopkins University Press, 1972.

———. *The Scapegoat.* Trans. Yvonne Freccero. Baltimore: Johns Hopkins University Press, 1986.

Harper, Mary Turner. "Merger and Metamorphosis in Mildred Taylor's Fiction." *Children's Literature Association Quarterly* 13 (Summer 1988): 75–80.

Higginbotham, Leon, Jr. "An Open Letter to Justice Clarence Thomas from a Federal Judicial Colleague." *University of Pennsylvania Law Review* 140 (January 1992): 1005–28.

King, Martin Luther. *Why We Can't Wait*. New York: Mentor/Penguin, 1964.

Posner, Richard. *Law and Literature. A Misunderstood Relation*. Cambridge: Harvard University Press, 1988.

Taylor, Mildred D. *Roll of Thunder, Hear My Cry*. 1976. Reprint. New York: Bantam, 1984.

———. *Let the Circle Be Unbroken*. 1981. Reprint. New York: Bantam, 1984.

———. *The Road to Memphis*. New York: Dial, 1990.

———. "Newbery Award Acceptance." *The Horn Book* 53 (August 1977): 401–09.

White, James Boyd. *Heracles' Bow: Essays on the Rhetoric and Poetics of the Law*. Madison: University of Wisconsin Press, 1985.

———. *When Words Lose Their Meaning*. Chicago: University of Chicago Press, 1984.

The Dreaming Picture Books of Chris Van Allsburg

Joseph Stanton

The picture shows us a darkly lovely rendering of a Venetian canal with two tight rows of buildings facing each other across a narrow waterway. A small arched footbridge delicately links the two sides. But in the background towers a gigantic ocean liner crashing its way into the far end of the canal. On a facing page is the title of the image, "Missing in Venice," and a caption: "Even with her mighty engines in reverse, the ocean liner was pulled further and further into the canal." Here indeed is a mystery—and a mystery that remains unsolved, because the single picture with its title and caption are all we have. Chris Van Allsburg's collection *The Mysteries of Harris Burdick* is, in fact, a collection of fourteen unsolvable, but intriguingly captioned, mystery pictures. According to the tongue-in-cheek introduction, these images, along with their titles and captions, were left by a man supposedly named Harris Burdick with a children's book editor supposedly named Peter Wenders. Harris Burdick and the manuscripts for which each of the images is just a sample were, of course, never seen again, leaving us with fourteen inscrutable fragments.

In interviews Van Allsburg has resisted attempts to pin down the origins and purposes of his picture-story ideas. He has indicated that he, too, finds his books mysterious and cannot offer simple explanations as to where and how they originate.

> A question I've been asked often is, "Where do your ideas come from?" I've given a variety of answers to this question, such as: "I steal them from the neighborhood kids," "I send away for them by mail order," and "They are beamed to me from outer space." It's not really my intention to be rude or smart-alecky. The fact is, I don't know where my ideas come from. Each story I've written starts out as a vague idea that seems to be going nowhere, then suddenly materializes as a completed concept. It almost seems like a discovery, as if the story was always there. The few elements I start out with are actually clues. If I figure out what they mean, I can discover the story that's waiting. (Ruello 169–70)

Children's Literature 24, ed. Francelia Butler, R. H. W. Dillard, and Elizabeth Lennox Keyser (Yale University Press, © 1996 Hollins College).

In this essay I do not promise to offer definitive solutions to the Harris Burdick mysteries or to any of the other bizarre fancies invented by the mind and art of Chris Van Allsburg. I shall, however, propose a theory concerning the traditions that lie behind his remarkable originality. Van Allsburg's work involves, it seems to me, the yoking together of two kinds of traditions that are almost never discussed together—a popular-culture tradition and an avant-garde, high-modernist tradition.[1] The popular culture tradition I have in mind will be referred to as the *strangely-enough tale*. The high-art, experimental tradition is, of course, *surrealism*. It too often happens that the popular arts are completely boxed off from the high arts—more often as a result of academic specialization than of overt snobbery— but some of the greatest innovations in the arts come from the surprising mixing of the contents of various boxes.

Furthermore, because surrealism is a high art with a proclivity for the low, it is of particular importance to understand the ways surrealism can and does connect with popular culture. Also, one should appreciate that, despite the "pastness" of surrealism as a movement of the early to mid-twentieth century, the transaction between surrealism and popular culture continues and flows in both directions: the surrealistically inclined have always appropriated images from popular culture, and popular culture in such forms as magazine advertisements, department-store display windows, and rock videos have often borrowed surrealist procedures and appropriated well-known images from classic surrealist works. As we turn our attention to the children's picture-book genre, we should also bear in mind that, although surrealism is not ordinarily thought of as being aimed at an audience of children, much was made in Breton's manifestos, and in other primary surrealist documents, of the value of a "childlike" outlook. It is not, therefore, surprising that Van Allsburg, a university-trained fine-arts practitioner working in the popular children's picture-book form should fuse surrealist and pop-culture motifs. What is remarkable, of course, is the wonderfulness of his results. If we can gain some sense of the cultural sources that underlie his work, we can better appreciate his success, even as we allow his mysteries to remain more or less unsolved.

I begin with a discussion of the several books in which the surrealistic element in Van Allsburg's work can be most clearly seen. I then discuss books that incorporate strangely-enough tales, with attention to how surrealistic and strangely-enough elements coexist in several of Van Allsburg's most distinctive books.

The three books that I discuss as primary examples of the surrealistic tendencies in Van Allsburg's work are *The Mysteries of Harris
Burdick, Ben's Dream,* and *The Z Was Zapped.* Because the term *surrealism* has been applied in so many ways, I must make clear that the
surrealism I have in mind is not primarily the surrealism of André
Breton and his closest associates. I am not thinking of automatic writing, found objects, random assortments, and frottages. The surrealism that embodies the irrational or unrational by relying upon the
accidental would seem to have little to do with the meticulously designed and arranged works of Van Allsburg. The surrealism I refer to
here is the secondary surrealism that derived sustenance, though not
methodology, from the liberations effected by Breton and company.
I have in mind Giorgio De Chirico,[2] Yves Tanguy, Salvador Dali, Max
Ernst and, most of all, René Magritte. It is, of course, terminologically
problematic that these artists did not always fly the surrealist banner.
What the works of these artists, as well as the works of Van Allsburg,
have in common is that they contain "highly detailed likenesses of
objects, straight or distorted, or three-dimensional abstractions, in a
fantastic and unexpected juxtaposition, or in a setting of a halluci-
natory kind" (Murray and Murray 402). This kind of surrealism constructs its dream images with a highly self-conscious sense of form
and style. The content of the images may arise from the tapping of
the subconscious, but the rendering of the work of art is realized with
conscious finesse. Van Allsburg's surrealism is quite deliberate, as he
himself has acknowledged: "If all artists were forced to wear a badge,
I'd probably wear the badge of surrealism. I don't mean something
as extreme as Salvador Dali's melting clocks, but a gentle surrealism
with certain unsettling provocative elements" (Ruello 169).

Passionate attention to selected likenesses and the employment of
unexpected juxtapositions are essential to my three examples of Van
Allsburg's surrealism. Perhaps the readiest way to recognize his affiliation with a certain kind of surrealism would be to compare the
humorous stage-set images of *The Z Was Zapped* to certain stage-set
images of René Magritte. Throughout his career Magritte employed
the stage curtain and the shallow space of a stage as a compositional
devise that gave a theatrical air to his images. The advantages of this
performance-evoking strategy include the compositional attractiveness of this mode of display, the basic wittiness of making a static
image into a dramatic action, and the effectiveness of this style of
presentation as a means of heightening audience attention. Magritte
works such as "Homage to Shakespeare" and "Wasted Effort" are

particularly amusing in their interplay of landscape and stage-set elements. The metamorphosis of the stage-curtain shape into the fragment of sky that we see in both of these works is typical of the transformative play Magritte develops in much of his work. Things often turn into sky or stone in Magritte's pictures. Or shoes become feet or bottles become carrots. A complete catalog of Magritte's warpings of one thing into another would be a very long list indeed. Similar transformations could be noted in the works of many other modern artists (and even in the works of some artists from earlier eras), but the clarity and fastidiousness of Magritte's likenesses make him the surrealistic forerunner most obviously comparable to Van Allsburg.

In *The Z Was Zapped* many of the letters of the alphabet undergo transformations in keeping with an alliterative phrase utilizing the sound of the letter. Thus, we have "The E was slowly Evaporating" as the caption for an onstage *E* that is fading away at the top as it gives off steam. "The G was starting to Grow" shows rootlike appendages bursting out of the edges of a *G* (fig. 1). Similarly, a *J* is shown to be jittery, an *M* is melting, a *V* is vanishing, and a *W* is warped. Other letters are under attack in a variety of ways. The *B* was bitten, the *C* was cut to ribbons, the *F* was flattened by a gigantic foot, the *K* was kidnapped by gloved hands, the *N* was nailed, the *P* was pecked by a nasty-looking bird, the *Q* was quartered by a knife that hangs in mid-air without the support of a hand, the *U* was uprooted, the *Y* was yanked, and, of course, the *Z* was zapped. The natural elements play a role in beating up on the hapless alphabet: lightning zaps the *Z*, an avalanche falls on the *A*, and water soaks the *S*. In addition to the emphasis on absurd transformations of objects, the use of stage settings, and meticulous attention to appearances, Van Allsburg shares with Magritte a knack for witty presentation of body parts (hands and feet in particular) separated from the rest of the body. (The illustrations for *F* and *K* are of interest in this regard.) It is even possible that Van Allsburg, perhaps unconsciously, derived the idea for this book directly from a work by Magritte. Some of the letters that Magritte did as chapter headings for an edition of Lautreamont's *Les chants de Maldoror* are interestingly similar to Van Allsburg's letters. Particularly pertinent is Magritte's drawing of an *R* with an eagle's clawed foot reaching out on one side and a human hand on the other (Hubert 194–205).

The violence of Van Allsburg's alphabet no doubt comes as a surprise to many readers. The brutal way that many of the letters are destroyed or threatened hardly fits with conventional ideas con-

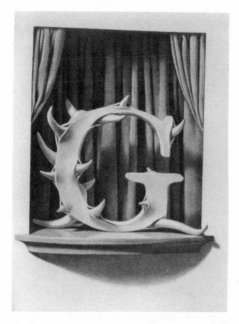

Figure 1. From *The Z Was Zapped.* Copyright © 1987 by Chris Van Allsburg. Reprinted by permission of Houghton Mifflin Co. All rights reserved.

cerning what is appropriate for small children; although superficially Van Allsburg's transformations may seem more ruthless than Magritte's, there is, however, an element of melodrama to Van Allsburg's staged destructions that makes them, ultimately, less unsettling than Magritte's. Although it seems odd that *The Z Was Zapped,* a book ostensibly to be shared with the youngest of children, is in several respects the least gentle of Van Allsburg's exercises in surrealism, it can be seen that Van Allsburg's "unsettling provocative elements" are held under control by our awareness that the artist-writer is having fun with his series of alphabetic horror shows.

Van Allsburg's *The Z Was Zapped* belongs to a genre of whimsical nonsense alphabets perhaps best represented by Walter Crane's *The Absurd ABC,* with its wonderful jumble of motifs from nursery rhymes and fairy tales, but it is the Magritte-like quality of Van Allsburg's ABCs that makes their absurdity distinctive.

Ben's Dream wears the badge of surrealism through the genuinely dreamlike nature of its narrative. Also suggestive of surrealism is its

Figure 2. From *The Mysteries of Harris Burdick*. Copyright © 1984 by Chris Van Allsburg. Reprinted by permission of Houghton Mifflin Company. All rights reserved.

humorous display of famous monuments and buildings. A specific connection to surrealism can be found in the obvious echo of an image from *Une semaine de bonté*, a surrealist montage picture book by Max Ernst.[3] Ernst's image of the Egyptian Sphinx seen through the window of a railroad car is reinvented by Van Allsburg in the image of the Sphinx seen from the front porch of Ben's floating house — in both images the head of the Sphinx is facing exactly the same way. It would not be surprising to hear that Van Allsburg was directly inspired by the example of Ernst's collage novel (Ernst 137). Beyond this specific reference, making famous buildings look ridiculous is entirely in the spirit of the surrealist project. It should be noted, however, that the punchline of *Ben's Dream*, which indicates that both the boy and the girl had dreamed the same dream, is suggestive of the strangely-enough motif. Also, although *Ben's Dream* can be seen to have derived from surrealism, it is too mild-mannered, too gentle in its dreaming to be fully in tune with the disturbing ferocity of the great surrealist masterpieces.

Surrealist qualities of a more unsettling sort are to be found, however, in *The Mysteries of Harris Burdick* (fig. 2). Van Allsburg's startling intrusion of an ocean liner into a canal that I referred to at the beginning of this essay bears a family resemblance to the startling emergence of a train engine from a fireplace in Magritte's *Time Transfixed* (fig. 3). The playful joining of the ordinary to the extraordinary are specialities of both Magritte and Van Allsburg. Van Allsburg gives us an unexceptional suburban street where we discover one of the houses to be blasting off like a rocketship, whereas Magritte gives us a fish washed up on the shore that just happens to have legs where its tail should be. The Magritte resemblance has been suggested by other commentators on Van Allsburg's books. For instance, John Russell, reviewing *The Wreck of the Zephyr,* noted that "some of the images of flight are worthy of Magritte himself."

The literary aspect of the *Harris Burdick* book also has a rough equivalence in Magritte. Magritte made the naming of his paintings into a game separate from the making of his pictures. Much could be said about how this practice helped Magritte put forth the fiction that his pictures were not self-revelatory. Magritte often solicited his literary friends to make up names for his pictures, thereby ensuring a mysterious disjunction between the picture and its label. In one sense Van Allsburg self-consciously cultivates mystery through the puzzling labels he forces us to connect to the *Harris Burdick* pictures, but the stronger effect of the labels is to demystify the pictures, at least to some extent. Each caption implies a particular kind of story. There would no doubt be much more agreement between stories generated from Van Allsburg's captions than there would be between stories generated from Magritte's often-baffling titles.

The fourteen inscrutable fragments that make up *The Mysteries of Harris Burdick* are deft excursions into the fantastic that demonstrate the potential of the picture-book form for combining literary and pictorial means to produce powerful literary-pictorial ends. Perhaps not everyone would agree with me that *The Mysteries of Harris Burdick* is the best of Van Allsburg's many excellent picture books, but I think it is the best place to look for an understanding of his profoundly whimsical art. Composed as it is of fragments, *Harris Burdick* shows us the artist-writer at play in his workshop.

In this strange workshop, the subgenre that I am calling the strangely-enough tale plays a prominent part. The term *strangely enough* is taken from the title of a popular book of tales published by C. B. Colby in 1959.[4] What made Colby's collection of strange

Figure 3. René Magritte, Belgian, 1898–1967, *Time Transfixed,* oil on canvas, 1938, 147 × 98.7 cm, Joseph Winterbotham Collection, 1970.426. Photograph © 1994, The Art Institute of Chicago. All rights reserved. © 1995 C. Herscovici, Brussels / Artists Rights Society (ARS), New York.

stories exciting for twelve-year-olds of all ages was the attitude he adopted toward the material and expressed in his title. Colby managed to present his brief retellings of startling tales in a manner that suggested they might be true, despite their strangeness. Colby's journalistic plain style of writing was one of the elements that seemed to attest to the truth of the tales. Paradoxically, if Colby had been a better writer, his tales would have seemed more literary and thereby less real.[5] The point is that Colby managed to make many of us want to believe that, strangely enough, something remarkable had *really* happened.

The only claim I am making here for Colby is that his work is typical of the genre and more enduring in its unpretentious appeal than many similar collections that have appeared over the years. *Strangely Enough* is primarily interesting as the most popular and widely distributed repackaging of contemporary oral tradition in the medium of print. Whether he knew it or not, Colby was a recorder of contemporary folk legends, primarily of the kind that Jan Harold Brunvand describes as "urban legends." Most of Colby's material appeared first in a newspaper column that he wrote for a number of years. His solicitation of tales for his column was his primary means of tale collection. The newspaper context has long been an important element in the spread and development of modern folk legends, because the inclusion of a tale in a publication dedicated to the reporting of fact tends to reinforce any assertion, however slight and whimsical, that the tale is possibly true.[6]

I have no idea whether Van Allsburg was directly influenced by Colby's book or by any of the numerous other books and comic books that have presented similar "strange tales," but it is apparent that several of Van Allsburg's books and all of the tales suggested in the fragments included in *The Mysteries of Harris Burdick* make use of the simple but powerful formula found in folk legends. In such tales there is an ordinary context out of which something extraordinary seems to develop. Journalistic versions of such tales tend to be brief and lacking in the histrionics common in oral presentations. Most such tales take no more than a page and a half to recount. The ordinary situation is explicated in a few paragraphs, then the extraordinary aspect is delivered as a kind of punchline. The understated manner of the telling in a newspaper context adds to the plausibility of the tales. Sometimes the situation seems to be falling short of the extraordinary until a chance remark by one of the characters betrays the almost dismissed extraordinariness.

Figure 4. From *The Garden of Abdul Gasazi*. Copyright © 1979 by Chris Van Allsburg.
Reprinted by permission of Houghton Mifflin Company. All rights reserved.

Recognizing the relatedness of Van Allsburg's tales to the journalistic retelling of strangely-enough tales, as exemplified by Colby's
Strangely Enough collection, provides a way of understanding the reason for Van Allsburg's peculiar flatness of delivery and brevity of exposition, which are among the most distinctive features of his storytelling style. In both Colby and Van Allsburg a flatness of tone and a
terseness of narration reinforce the surface plausibility of the tale and
stand in striking contrast to the bizarreness of what is taking place. Of
course, a critical difference between Van Allsburg's tales and Colby's
are the wonderful pictures that Van Allsburg employs to make us witnesses of the strange happenings. The startling contrast between Van
Allsburg's dull, though carefully crafted, prose and his extraordinary
images operates as a continuous irony. It is key to the tension between the ordinary and the marvelous that is his central subject.

    The Garden of Abdul Gasazi is an excellent example of the strangely-
enough plot and narrative strategy. In this tale, a little boy named
Alan is asked to take care of his neighbor's dog.[7] While Alan is walk-

Figure 5. From *Jumanji.* Copyright © 1981 by Chris Van Allsburg. Reprinted by permission of Houghton Mifflin Company. All rights reserved.

ing the dog, the disobedient animal breaks away and heads into the mysterious garden of the magician Abdul Gasazi (fig. 4). Gasazi's abhorrence of dogs is posted on a sign that declares: "ABSOLUTELY, POSITIVELY NO DOGS ALLOWED IN THIS GARDEN." When the dismayed boy reaches Gasazi's house in the center of the garden, the dog is nowhere in sight. It turns out that Gasazi has either used his magic to transform the dog into a duck or played a clever joke on Alan. The rediscovery at the end of the book that the dog was in possession of Alan's hat, which had been stolen by the duck, sets up a final remark by the neighbor ("Why you bad dog," she said. "What are you doing with Alan's hat?"), which suggests, in fine, understated, strangely-enough fashion, that the extraordinary explanation is probably the right one.[8]

In *Jumanji* (fig. 5), Van Allsburg turns away somewhat from the popular-culture tradition of Colby and his kind and draws on the more self-consciously literary tradition that derives from the nineteenth-century weird tales of Edgar Allan Poe and Nathaniel Hawthorne, among others. This tradition has continued to enjoy vigorous life in contemporary works of literary fiction and in films. Among the many writers and filmmakers whose stories fit the mold of the strangely-enough tale are Alfred Hitchcock, Roald Dahl, Ray Bradbur, and Stephen King. The question of interconnections between the weird tales of the literary tradition and the weird tales collected by journalists (such as Colby) and scholarly folklorists (such as Jan

Harold Brunvand) is a rich topic that has not been adequately addressed. For my purposes here it does not seem possible to cleanly separate the collected from the crafted with regard to influence on Van Allsburg; they are two sides of the same coin. Even the most carefully crafted of literary weird tales are aimed at popular audiences. Although the simplicity and blandness of Van Allsburg's narration of *Jumanji* suggest the collected tale, the twists of *Jumanji*'s little plot and the ironies it sets up recall, in certain respects, the tales of such popular modern storytellers as Dahl and Hitchcock. The grim little twist at the end, where the dangerous jungle game is found by two little boys who are well known for not following directions, is suggestive of one of Hitchcock's wittily gruesome, unhappy endings. But the somewhat more sophisticated feel of this tale does not conceal the strangely-enough mechanism.

Although I shall not discuss here all the varied graphic techniques Van Allsburg employed in his books, it should be observed that he has produced approximately one book a year since the appearance of his first book, *The Garden of Abdul Gasazi*, in 1979. For each of these yearly productions, his artistic procedures have changed. Each book is an experimental working out of design and material problems that Van Allsburg has set for himself. Underlying his structures and his choices of picture-making techniques is a sculptural sense that derives from his training and practice as a sculptor. Judging from remarks in recent interviews, Van Allsburg still seems to regard himself —even today, after all his years of success as a picture-book artist— as primarily a fine-arts sculptor who does picture books as something of a sideline. The scene in *The Garden of Abdul Gasazi* where Alan runs through the gate in the hedge to first enter the garden is one of many striking instances of sculptural form in Van Allsburg's work. In that scene, Alan and the two statues that border the gate seem to be three statuary variations on the theme "running boy" (fig. 4). The gateway itself seems palpably sculptural. Even the separate leaves and blades of grass possess a certain amount of what philosopher of art Susanne Langer would call "kinetic volume" (Langer, 90). Each of these figurations seems static yet uncannily capable of operating in the viewer's space as well as in the virtual scene. This picture subtly suggests to the viewer that he or she might walk into it. The sculptural palpableness of some of Van Allsburg's pictures offers powerful reinforcement to the strangely-enough element in his work. We are drawn into the spaces of the garden of Abdul Gasazi not simply because his style is realistic but because his sculptural effects break down the barrier between our space and the space of the picture. Van Allsburg's sculptural effects in *The Garden of Abdul Gasazi* evoke a twilight-zone mood and have, at the same time, affinities with the sculptural dimensions of works by Dali, Magritte, and other surrealist artists. Thus, the strange tale of popular culture and the dream image of surrealistic modernism are fused in a peculiarly powerful way.

The Wreck of the Zephyr is perhaps the work most completely conceived in the strangely-enough manner. Recounters of such legends add credibility to their accounts by using the framing device of casting the narrator in the role of a visitor to a scene of fantastic events; there he or she encounters a person residing in the place who tells the tale that the narrator presumably does no more than record.[9] There is a twist at the end of *The Wreck of the Zephyr* where we are left with the implication that the narrator was the boy protagonist of the tale he has just told. Van Allsburg sets up this turn of events well. Most readers are probably taken somewhat by surprise when the old man's limping walk and anxiousness to go sailing hint that he was once the boy who flew the Zephyr. As usual in the strangely-enough tale, the truth of the story rests on the presumed credibility of the speaker as an eyewitness.

The Wreck of the Zephyr represents a new direction in Van Allsburg's picture-book art, because it is his first venture into color. Later statements about his experiments with color indicate that he was dissatisfied with the technique he employed in this book. His efforts to blend pastels in ways that would create painted effects were apparently the source of some frustration for him. Whatever difficulties this book may have caused him seem to have been worth enduring; *The Wreck of the Zephyr* presents striking images that might not have been achievable in other ways. For instance, the luminescent greens of the ocean in the picture on the jacket of *The Wreck of the Zephyr* could not have been produced with the separate-strokes-of-color technique Van Allsburg used in *The Stranger.*

I have already cited John Russell's comment on the evident Magritte influence on *The Wreck of the Zephyr.* As with many Magritte images, several of Van Allsburg's pictures for this book present key elements as suspended or frozen within the scene. Thus, Van Allsburg's flying boats have an eerie silence and a seeming motionlessness that is reminiscent of the gigantic apples or rocks Magritte hangs over seascapes in such paintings as *The Beautiful Truths* or *The Castle in the Pyrenees.* Although we could also link the marine dreams of Van Allsburg with the dramatically lighted nineteenth-century luminist scenes of such artists as Fritz Hugh Lane and Martin Johnson Heade, the overall effect of these pictures is Magritte-like.

The best selling of Van Allsburg's picture books, *The Polar Express,* captures a strangely-enough motif that recurs in many forms in American popular culture. Van Allsburg's explanation of how this story came to him provides a fascinating glimpse into his way of imagining but provides little by way of interpretation.

> When I began thinking about what became *The Polar Express,* I had a single image in mind: a young boy sees a train standing still in front of his house one night. The boy and I took a few different trips on that train, but we did not, in a figurative sense, go anywhere. Then I headed north, and I got the feeling that this time I'd picked the right direction, because the train kept rolling all the way to the North Pole. At that point the story seemed literally to present itself. Who lives at the North Pole? Undoubtedly a ceremony of some kind, a ceremony requiring a child, delivered by a train and would have to be named the Polar Express. (Ruello 170)

An image that might have been one of the *Harris Burdick* fragments was developed into a story that resolves itself into a kind of seasonal legend. Although the polar rite of winter around which the story revolves is a product of Van Allsburg's knack for developing fantasy rather than a conscious manipulation of an archetypal motif, the archetypal motif of this strangely-enough tale is not hard to spot. The argument of this tale is the heart-warming contention that "Yes, Virginia there is a Santa Claus." The movie *Miracle on 34th Street* is, of course, relevant here. The popular-culture nature of this tale makes it no less important than it would be if it were tricked out in the trappings of classical myth. The truth-pretense of the reality of Santa is perhaps the most widely distributed of all American strangely-enough motifs. Santa is the "flying saucer" that parents profess to believe in as an important game of ritual affection, gift giving, and seasonal celebration.

We might expect to lose the dangerous edge of surrealism in Van Allsburg's embrace of Jolly Old Saint Nick, but when we consider the intrusion of a massive train into a quiet suburban street, the restrainedly demonic nature of Van Allsburg's North Pole with its bizarrely vast snow-covered urban appearance, and the quietly nightmarish hugeness of the crowd of identically dressed elves turned out to hear Santa's speech—when we consider all the elements of this late-night sojourn—we find the surrealist edge of danger subtly implicit. It might even be said that there is something about the visualization of Santa's speech to his army of elves that is reminiscent of the famous filmed sequences of Hitler addressing his storm troopers. Although Santa is treated as an unambiguously benign being in the context of the book, there is an unsettling quality to the North Pole scene that adds an aesthetically interesting element of disorientation to the miraculous presence of the godlike Santa figure.

An even more mysterious mythos figures in the strangely-enough notion that lies at the center of *The Stranger,* a work that resonates on a number of levels. Visits by gods among mortals are commonplace in mythic traditions. Not identified as a powerful immortal, the god appears on someone's doorstep. Often such tales are moral fables concerning the importance of offering hospitality to strangers. Van Allsburg's tale certainly follows this pattern but adds the twist that the stranger in his book suffers from amnesia owing to a collision with a car whose driver afterward takes him into his home. The stranger's exact identity remains unexplained, but he is suggestive of Jack Frost, a being responsible for changing the season from warm summer to cool autumn and cold winter. Because of the stranger's amnesia, autumn does not come to the place where he has stopped. The farm family he stays with benefits from the prolonged warm weather that produces a bountiful harvest. Eventually the truth dawns on the stranger, and he departs to return to his appointed rounds.

Of course, as with *Polar Express,* we can link the story in *The Stranger* to a variety of popular works that share its basic strangely-enough premise. In a number of recent films a godlike personage intrudes into ordinary lives. Most often these beings are presented as aliens from other worlds, but they are typically given Christ-like qualities of spirituality and innocence, as well as certain amazing powers, that mark them as something above and beyond. The cult classic science fiction novel *Stranger in a Strange Land,* by Robert Heinlein, fits this profile, as do the films *Starman, ET, Man Facing Southeast, Brother from Another Planet, Edward Scissorshands,* and *Wings of Desire.* Cocteau's *Beauty and the Beast* provides a largely surrealistic version of this motif. In fact, a surrealistic undercurrent could be claimed for all of the films mentioned above. As always, questions of influence are difficult, but it seems that Van Allsburg's stranger is descended from the godly visitors of ancient stories and has some kinship with the extraterrestrial visitors of recent urban legends and the many films and books those legends have inspired.[10]

It is in the undercurrent of danger and the irrationality of the premise that we sense the surrealist dream developing within *The Stranger.* The strange creatures that invade the ordinary lives in Ernst's *Une Semaine de bonté* are perhaps gently echoed by the kindly, but indisputably supernatural, presence of the stranger in Van Allsburg's book. The lovely and uncompromisingly ordinary depiction of a somewhat sentimentalized and gorgeously autumnal rural world serves, however, to de-emphasize the surrealistic aspect of this quiet fantasy.[11]

The two dimensions of Chris Van Allsburg's work that I have discussed here—surrealism and strangely-enough fantasy—can be found in all of his books to varying degrees. Because Van Allsburg's surrealism is largely manifested in his images and the strangely-enough fantasy is primarily evident in his narratives, these two aspects of his work are largely complementary and do not conflict. Both surrealism and the popular tradition of the strange tale provide opportunities to show that the extraordinary resides in the ordinary and vice versa. Surrealism and the weird tale constitute two different but related ways that dreams intrude on everyday life, and Van Allsburg has learned lessons from both of these living traditions.

Notes

1. It may seem odd to speak of the tradition established in the name of an avant-garde style of art whose founding practioners passionately declared themselves to be antitraditional, but it is undeniable that surrealism established stances and styles that have been continued and developed. By speaking of a tradition we are referring to the continuance of some of the ideas and forms of masters such as Magritte and Ernst in the contemporary works of artist-writers such as Van Allsburg.

2. Giorgio De Chirico could be considered a forerunner rather than a continuer of the surrealist movement. Some of his most surrealistic works predate Breton's founding of the movement. Chirico is one of those who did not like the term *surrealism* and did not consider himself a surrealist.

3. A large subject I cannot adequately address here is the important ways surrealist artists were themselves influenced by nineteenth-century children's picture books. It has been persuasively argued, for instance, that Max Ernst's *Une semaine de bonté* was influenced by Lewis Carroll's *Alice* books and their Tenniel illustrations (Wilson 364–71).

4. I wish to make clear that my adoption of Colby's title as the label for a genre of popular pseudo-nonfiction should not be taken as an unqualified tribute to the literary quality of his work. Certainly there was nothing particularly original about what he put together. Collections such as Colby's had been published before—notably R. DeWitt

Miller's *Impossible: Yet It Happened* (1947). Miller's book purported to be a study of the paranormal, a claim that was to be repeated by scores of authors who contributed to the paranormal publishing industry that mushroomed in the 1970s and still prospers. A recent series of such collections by Robert Ellis Cahill sells well at various "spooky" tourist spots in New England. The roots of all this can be traced back to the nineteenth century. Some of the early experiments in photography involved the use of multiple exposures to insert ghosts and faeries into "true" photographs. Such hoaxes and wishful musings have been rife in the flying-saucer and Loch Ness–monster subgenres as well. The superiority of Colby to DeWitt and many others, however, lies in the conciseness of his tale telling. Colby's *Strangely Enough* has maintained its popularity, I suspect, largely because its brief accounts spare the reader the often-pompous machinery of the typical paranormal author's explanation of his "field of research." Colby's stories, which have had numerous reprintings, are unencumbered folktales and provide the kind of pleasure any good story affords.

5. It could be argued that the more self-conscious storytelling style of Rod Serling, for instance, kept his published short stories from lingering in the mind with the peculiar aura of plausibility that inheres in Colby's tales. Serling did, of course, achieve a wide audience for his fictions, especially once he established his type of tale in the medium of television, but Serling's narratives seem to fill a different sort of niche in the popular imagination than do Colby's. With Serling we always knew that he was taking us into an artificial realm known as the "Twilight Zone," but with Colby the extraordinary events seemed to be things that had happened to genuine, though only sketchily characterized, ordinary people with whom Colby had talked.

6. It should be noted that journalistic accounts, even when they debunk the tales, serve to support the further spread of the legends. Published versions are disseminated informally through oral retellings. Tour-group leaders, for instance, often seize upon such anecdotes to entertain their customers. In Hawaii tour guides have gained wide audiences for their versions of such tales. On walking tours, the on-site nature of the tale telling enhances the strangely-enough effect of a story by adding the tangibility of observable buildings, streets, and landscape elements. Even when the conductors of these tours are academically trained scholars, the tales are seldom described as folk legends. It is much more fun for both teller and listener to subscribe to a strange-but-true approach to the material. Further, local tales are seldom related to larger archetypal motifs. For example, the reported tendency of Madame Pele, the volcano goddess, to hitchhike and then disappear from the car is never linked to the widespread legend of the "vanishing hitchhiker," which has been discussed by Jan Harold Brunvand in several of his books. The desire to consider the strange tale as possibly true tends to routinely overwhelm any attempt to debunk the tale. Brunvan claims, in fact, that debunkings merely serve to further the distribution of the tale (153).

7. The bull terrier that first appeared in *The Garden of Abdul Gasazi* developed into something of a game Van Allsburg plays with his loyal fans. This game involves the reappearance of the bull terrier in book after book; in many of the books the distinctive dog makes his appearance in an obscure corner of only one picture. This odd and amusing practice serves to link Van Allsburg's books to one another. The artist confesses to having enjoyed this find-me exercise. As he has pointed out, the dog is most difficult to find in *The Stranger* (Ruello 169). After *The Z Was Zapped* in 1987, however, this visual joke was dropped from his productions for the next three books; *Two Bad Ants* (1988), *Just a Dream* (1989), and *The Wretched Stone* (1991) are entirely dogless. The dog makes an amusing reappearance, however, in *The Widow's Broom* (1992) and can also be spotted in *The Sweetest Fig* (1993). It should be noted that his use of a repeated motif, which in popular culture would be called a "running gag," could be viewed as yet another resemblance to surrealist practice. Magritte, especially, is famed for the repeated appearances of his chess pieces, harness bells, men in bowler hats, and the like. Van

Allsburg's overall opus is a unity that allows a playful weaving in and out of a pointless but interesting signature motif; this same element of play in serious art is a hallmark of much modernist art influenced by surrealism. The inclination toward playfulness is a key element in Van Allsburg's embrace of both popular culture and surrealism.

8. The value of noticing the strangely-enough plot of *The Garden of Abdul Gasazi* is amply testified to by the misinterpretations of plot action that are fallen into by Peter Neumeyer in a recent article on Van Allsburg that appeared in the *Children's Literature Association Quarterly*. Neumeyer insists upon oversimplifying the story by making it into a case of the protagonist-fell-asleep-and-dreamed-an-adventure-and-then-woke-up ploy so common in the least imaginative children's books. It is, however, obviously the case that the boy wakes up and has the encounter with Gasazi in a waking state. After the adventure he returns to the house, missing the telltale hat. For the dream plot to be operative, the boy would have to be shown waking up at the end of the story. The strangely-enough plot provides a way of understanding the bizarreness of the tale without resorting to the unpersuasive leap to the it-was-just-a-dream explanation that Neumeyer felt he needed to give. In general, Neumeyer's article is flawed by his desire to render Van Allsburg's books as if they were coded messages rather than works of art. Because of Neumeyer's quest for "visual literacy," he fails to do justice to the magic and mystery of Van Allsburg's picture books.

9. This plot bears some resemblance to the plots of the many Japanese noh plays, in which a person from the particular place tells a tale of an earlier time. As in Van Allsburg's story, the teller is eventually discovered to be the character whose woes are being recounted. In noh plays this tale teller is usually a ghost.

10. The list of books and films cited here indicates a continuing theme in popular culture, in which Van Allsburg's *The Stranger* has played a part. Several of the films mentioned postdate Van Allsburg's book and are obviously not considered influences on Van Allsburg. Because the theme of the godlike stranger is so ancient and pervasive, it would be difficult to establish a sequence of influences.

11. The seasonal feeling of *The Stranger* is one of its especially attractive features. I can recall no other picture book more effective at rendering autumn and the harvest time. Van Allsburg's technique of painstakingly laying on tiny unblended lines using pastels provides him with excellent means to realize the bright subtleties of autumn colors. His attention to details—such as individual blades of grass in the foreground, separate dots for leaves in middle-ground trees, strokes suggestive of the grain of wooden floorboards, and attractively plausible stylizations to represent distant elements—results in a book that seems to love the look of its subject. Van Allsburg creates strong sculptural effects in several of the pictures in *The Stranger*, such as the soup-serving scene and the pumpkin-loading scene. For the most part, however, we are not compelled to enter the pictorial space as we are in *The Garden of Abdul Gasazi*. The images of *The Stranger* are separated from the audience by a haze of seasonal romance. The viewer is happy to step back and contemplate the seasonal display.

Works Cited

Breton, André. *Manifestoes of Surrealism.* Ann Arbor: University of Michigan Press, 1969.

Brunvand, Jan Harold. *The Vanishing Hitchhiker: American Urban Legends and Their Meanings.* New York: Norton, 1981. (Other Brunvand books include *The Baby Train, The Choking Doberman, Curses! Broiled Again,* and *The Mexican Pet.*)

Cahill, Robert Ellis. *New England's Things That Go Bump in the Night.* Peabody, Mass.: Chandler-Smith, 1989. (Other Cahill works include *New England's Visitors from Outer Space* and *New England's Witches and Wizards.*)

Colby, C. B. *Strangely Enough!* New York: Sterling, 1959.

Ernst, Max. *Une semaine de bonté.* 1934. Reprint. New York: Dover, 1976.

Heinlein, Robert. *Stranger in a Strange Land.* New York: Putnam, 1961.

Helprin, Mark. *Swan Lake.* Illus. by Chris Van Allsburg. Boston: Houghton Mifflin, 1989.

Hubert, Renée Riese. *Surrealism and the Book.* Berkeley: University of California Press, 1988.

Langer, Susanne K. *Feeling and Form.* New York: Scribner's, 1953.

Lautreamont. *Les chants de Maldoror.* Trans. Alexis Lykiard. New York: Thomas Y. Crowell, 1972.

Miller, R. DeWitt. *Impossible: Yet It Happened!* New York: Ace, 1947.

Murray, Peter, and Linda Murray. *A Dictionary of Art and Artists.* New York: Penguin, 1959.

Neumeyer, Peter. "How Picture Books Mean: The Case of Chris Van Allsburg." *Children's Literature Association Quarterly* 15, no. 1 (1990): 2–8.

Ruello, Catherine. "Chris Van Allsburg Interview." In *Something about the Author,* vol. 53, ed. by Anne Commire. Detroit: Gale Research, 1989. Pp. 160–72.

Russell, John. Review of *The Wreck of the Zephyr,* by Chris Van Allsburg. *New York Times Book Review,* June 5, 1983, 34.

Serling, Rod. *From the Twilight Zone.* Garden City, N.Y.: Doubleday, 1960.

Van Allsburg, Chris. *Ben's Dream.* Boston: Houghton Mifflin, 1982.

———. *The Garden of Abdul Gasazi.* Boston: Houghton Mifflin, 1979.

———. *Jumanji.* Boston: Houghton Mifflin, 1981.

———. *Just a Dream.* Boston: Houghton Mifflin, 1990.

———. *The Mysteries of Harris Burdick.* Boston: Houghton Mifflin, 1984.

———. *The Polar Express.* Boston: Houghton Mifflin, 1985.

———. *The Stranger.* Boston: Houghton Mifflin, 1986.

———. *Two Bad Ants.* Boston: Houghton Mifflin, 1988.

———. *The Widow's Broom.* Boston: Houghton Mifflin, 1992.

———. *The Wreck of the Zephyr.* Boston: Houghton Mifflin, 1983.

———. *The Wretched Stone.* Boston: Houghton Mifflin, 1991.

———. *The Z Was Zapped.* Boston: Houghton Mifflin, 1987.

Wilson, Sarah. "Max Ernst and England." In *Max Ernst: A Retrospective,* ed. Werner Spies. Munich: Prestel-Verlag, 1991. Pp. 363–72.

Other Works of Interest

Cummings, Pat, ed. *Talking with Artists.* New York: Macmillan, 1991. (Van Allsburg is one of the artists interviewed.)

Nodelman, Perry. *Words about Pictures: The Narrative Art of Children's Picture Books.* Athens: University of Georgia Press, 1988.

Reviews

When Criticism Comes Alive: Я Toys Us?

Mitzi Myers

When Toys Come Alive: Narratives of Animation, Metamorphosis, and Development, by Lois Rostow Kuznets. New Haven: Yale University Press, 1994.

> *Literature is a teddy bear.*
> Murray M. Schwartz

Expressing eighteenth-century notions of sociality, both Jonathan Swift and David Hume memorably describe their pleasure in embodied books, texts that come alive and speak personally to them or, if the subject is "curious and interesting" enough, carry the reader also into company, thus uniting the "two greatest and purest pleasures of human life, study and society." Because most academic critics sound like other academic critics, rather than possessing an idiosyncratic or authentically human speaking voice, they seldom deliver the sociable pleasures the Enlightenment valued, however much freight of learning or theory they carry. We may learn, but we're seldom pleased or enlivened. As readers of Lois Kuznets's other work might expect, this study is different. No doubt her style has been tempered to some degree, but one of the reasons that these tales of toys come alive are enjoyable is that they sound like a real person taking an individual stance on matters that she cares about, admitting freely that her choices are personal, not comprehensive. And the topic is surely "curious and interesting."

The preface begins with the author's early childhood discovery of the "secret lives of toys," and as this opening suggests, the book deals with this particular aspect of toys, although as it turns out, that secret

Children's Literature 24, ed. Francelia Butler, R. H. W. Dillard, and Elizabeth Lennox Keyser (Yale University Press, © 1996 Hollins College).

life is much more varied than a reader might predict. One value of good criticism is that it not only explores a field using a particular approach but also opens out other and different ways of thinking about the topic. Individual authors have elicited much attention, a great deal has been written on dolls and what used to be called "baby houses," and a flood of recent work on the current commodification of child culture, especially the hyping of toys as TV tie-ins, seems unceasing (and ever more disheartening). But toys and the narratives they generate, like many other areas in children's literature, have not been comprehensively explored. I'm sure that many readers will think of critical stories about toys they want to tell, and no doubt many teachers will also think of additions they might make to their syllabi. I can imagine, for example, some delicious seminars composed around toy stories, and this seems to be one area where students are wonderfully imaginative (or so I judge from those students I've had who tried the genre).

The first chapter, "An Introduction to My World of Literary Toys," offers a brief, personal overview of what the book covers and how the material will be approached. Animated toys as characters, we can expect, will transcend the real-world uses of toylike objects to become bearers of, and surrogates for, human subjectivity. First, when toys become "real," they embody our own anxiety about what being "real" means. I feel that current work on the construction of subjectivity might complexify this issue even further: "an independent subject or self" as opposed to an object polarizes the possibilities, when (as the book's own later discussions vividly show) toys and dolls may be constructed as subjects, just like people, in all kinds of disjunctive and sometimes contradictory ways. Second, toy characters are especially night beings, associated with sex, secrets, and the Freudian uncanny (itself a much richer concept than the original psychoanalytical explication of "The Sandman" allows—it's recently proved helpful in postcolonial political analysis, for example). Third, and most resonant for me, is the toy's embodiment of "all the temptations and responsibilities of power." Finally, especially for male creators, toys replicate divine creation. (There's rather more in the book about the divine than I expected, probably because I think of toy-origin stories mostly in relation to the exponential increase of playthings in late eighteenth-century England, when, as J. H. Plumb pointed out twenty years ago, the enormous number and variety of toys signaled a "new world" for children, a precursor to our own commercialization of the juvenile, as well as our own feminist, materialist, and ideological critiques thereof.)

Following this motif index, the rationale for choices is refreshingly frank. Critically eclectic, feminist, and personal, the agenda is not comprehensive, chronological, or demonstrative of a single theory. Most works are British and American, and although there's a nod toward history, the material is comparatively recent. Her approach is largely psychological, although she does touch on larger cultural issues, as in the polemic chapter on toy soldiers. No teddy bears except for the obligatory Pooh, no rocking horses, very little on the oddities of Carroll and Baum, because the author knows she writes best about what takes her fancy. She is engagingly upfront about the trajectory that informs her work, detailing among her toy journeys and quests her movement from nostalgia for doll houses to the mature critic's desire for toy narratives that would challenge, more subversively than most do, those forces of elitism, racism, sexism, and androcentrism that still delimit our polluted postmodern world—a desire that leads toward the rather unexpected final chapter, entitled "Life(size) Endowments: Monsters, Automata, Robots, Cyborgs." One thing I appreciated is the author's cross-references to specific topics, so that those in search of certain themes will know which chapter to investigate.

Chapter 2, "Toys: Their First Thousand Years," provides the book's historical grounding, with much reliance on Antonia Fraser's *A History of Toys* and other secondary sources. I'm sorry that what the eighteenth century had to say for itself came mediated through the familiar story of the "didactic," an off-putting term for what most of us devote our lives to and presumably value and certainly one that doesn't do justice to the extraordinary richness and diversity of eighteenth-century discourse on childhood, including toys and play. To enlist Plum (who can't be charged with my bias) again, Maria Edgeworth on toys "resonates with modernity," and for my money, what she has to say about the value of play in fostering creativity and problem solving beats all hollow much recent quantitative study. It's sad to reduce her contribution to the "rational toyshop" (which is a lot more exciting than the phrase sounds to us) and to find her criticized via the religious enthusiasm of Isaac Taylor and Charlotte Yonge. "Imagination" in this period is often a coded term for the religious and one that can be used to beat secular, rational, materialist (that is, "modern") thinking on toys, as in many other areas of discussion: it is also often antifeminist. Witness, for example, the debate on girls and dolls (unmentioned here) at the end of the eighteenth century. Rousseau insisted that girls were born doll crazy: writing and reading weren't for them, because they wanted and needed to learn only about babies and clothes and pleasing men. Dolls were vigorously attacked by Mary Wollstonecraft and Maria Edgeworth, among others, and as hotly defended by the High Anglican Sarah Trimmer; most reformers had things to say about war toys as well. Because Kuznets is especially interested in gender ideology as reflected in toys like dolls and soldiers, a bit more history would have been enriching, but then this chapter pretends to no more than a cursory overview. I especially liked the concluding section, an extended discussion of Rachel Field's *Hitty: Her First Hundred Years,* a story I also love for its adventure, its historical panorama, and its refreshing lack of sentimentality. I know I felt it was subversive, but I hadn't realized how many of Hitty's wild experiences come about through child disobedience. I should say here that I didn't know some of the tales discussed as well as this one, but one of the book's merits is its skillfully unobtrusive plot summary; the argument does not get mystifying even when the book analyzed isn't at hand.

"On the Couch with Calvin, Hobbes, and Winnie the Pooh," the third chapter, foregrounds the analysis with a summary of modern play theory, and I think, given the recent questioning of Piaget's godlike rank, it might have been even more skeptical than it already is (which is quite) about that founding father's contribution to child study. As Kuznets agreeably shows, there's far richer work to draw on. The analysis of both Watterson's and Milne's living toys is generous and alive to telling detail. It must have been tough to choose such good examples from the wealth of terrific cartoons we've watched for so many years; and it was perhaps still more difficult to strike the right note about the woman problem for these writers without being strident or unfair.

Chapter 4, "Coming Out in Flesh and Blood," deals with, among others, the work that an amazing number of my students wax lyrical over, rather to my puzzlement, *The Velveteen Rabbit,* by Margery Williams Bianco. Like all the chapters, this one opens with a theme-setting quote, and the one here—wherein the Rabbit tearfully proclaims his imaginatively bestowed Realness to a dubious rabbit, who's merely organically "real"—captures, I suppose, the fantasy of child power that my students are indulging. Following a commentary on

Steven Daniels's recent Kleinian reading, Kuznets amusingly observes that maybe "Rabbit himself needs a transitional object." More intellectually challenging works like Hoffmann's *Nutcracker* and Collodi's *The Adventures of Pinocchio* are attractively analyzed and compared. One of the book's many strengths is its teasing out of parallels in unexpected groupings of texts; I couldn't predict which works would be considered together or precisely where the argument would lead, a refreshing change from many books that mechanically belabor a single thesis throughout. Kuznets's method is always explorative, and she never claims to deliver the final truth; she always leaves the reader with something to think about, even when the text hadn't originally been a favorite.

"Where Have All the Young Men Gone?" builds on excellent previous work, with which many readers will be familiar, discussing *The Return of the Twelves,* along with Hans Christian Andersen's soldier and Lynne Reid Banks's series. Because these are delightful books that raise thorny ethical issues about war, this chapter is especially interesting. I have to say, though, in light of what's going on with TV and the toy industry these days, any lurking racism, patriarchy, or whatever between these book covers seems comparatively benign, although I was impressed with the searching attempt to come to grips with knotty issues.

Chapter 6, "The Doll Connection," might well have made a whole book. I've been much surprised lately by the numerous recent essays (one in this journal) on the diverse and not necessarily nurturing uses to which dolls are put, for example, among battered children. Doll abuse, sometimes violent and sometimes in the interest of storytelling, seems to be everywhere lately. I don't think parents always know what children are up to in doll play. Not at all interested in mothering my own dolls, I preferred doctoring them, especially giving them shots every time my baby sister got one; because I couldn't figure out how the eyes worked, I used to take them apart—sounds sadistic, but it wasn't. Certainly Frances Hodgson Burnett shocked everyone by violently lashing her doll, when she was imaginatively enacting *Uncle Tom's Cabin.* This chapter opens with two wonderful quotes on the opposing directions of child play, including Maggie's ritual doll abuse in *The Mill on the Floss,* and the lively analysis of the varied roles dolls take in a number of tales made me want to read the ones I didn't know. Closely related to the curative powers of dolls is the curative role of locale: "Magic Settings, Transitional Space" deals with the

evoked space of the dream and includes some interesting metafic-
tional as well as psychological examples of dollhouses and toy cities
as they impinge on child life.

Chapter 8, "The Animal-Toy League," makes a nice unit with the
next, "Beyond the Last Visible Toy," and there is much interplay
among themes here, as in the comparison between the rape of Miss
Hickory (when her head is bitten off by the squirrel) and Manny Rat's
rape of the genteel elephant. (I don't find the nonstop talking among
Hoban's motley crew so odd myself; after all, it is a book about trying
to make connection.) Kuznets is especially good on the disturbing
aspects of these tales. I forgive Hoban for the sexism that Kuznets
discovers, for I'm still seduced by the toys who keep on keeping on:
I don't think I've ever seen so neatly expressed what I take to be the
book's directive for postmodern living (middle paragraph on p. 176).
I've taught Hoban's toy tale a number of times and have always found
it a real polarizer, one much loved or detested because it's not comforting enough.

I confess that the last chapter's not my favorite: I can't warm up
to robots and am not sure that we have exhausted old literary forms
or that the new and the radical always arrive formally marked. As
Gayle Greene and Rita Felski have brilliantly demonstrated in regard
to modern women's fiction, old-fashioned realism and personnel are
still capable of changing their stories to invent new meanings. Unex-
pectedly, this chapter includes Marge Piercy's *He, She and It,* but not
Frankenstein, which still provokes interminable discussion. It would
have been interesting to discuss that tale, which is after all by a teenager, as a YAL creation story. The book thus concludes with a provocative and searching analysis of the animated object genre as we
approach a new century. Surprisingly, I did not find the coming-alive
motif I had expected to, although it's tantalizingly hinted at here and
there: that's the role of such moves as those the book describes in
founding representation itself. As Kendall Walton argues in *Mimesis
as Make-Believe,* "In order to understand paintings, plays, films, and
novels, we must look first at dolls, hobbyhorses, toy trucks, and teddy
bears. The activities in which representational works of art are embedded and which give them their point are best seen as continuous
with children's games of make-believe. Indeed, I advocate regarding these activities as games of make-believe themselves" (4). That is,
what Kuznets analyzes is foundational to art, period.

This book is nicely designed and most agreeably illustrated. I espe-

cially enjoyed the small pictures (reminiscent of many eighteenth-
and nineteenth-century books) with which each chapter begins, and
what a pity that libraries inevitably throw away book jackets, for this
one—illustrated from Margery Williams Bianco's *Poor Ceco*—is surely
one of the most attractive I've seen in a long while. It's tedious to detail errors, but there are the usual stubborn few: George Boas, who's
okay in text, turns into Samuel in the bibliography, and so on. But
I can't think of anyone who's at all interested in children's literature,
including readers who don't teach it, who wouldn't find something
"curious and interesting" here, even if they're not nutty for toys. Buy
the book: you'll enjoy it, and you'll get the jacket as a bonus.

Works Cited

Hume, David. *Dialogues Concerning Natural Religion*. In *Essential Works of David Hume*,
   ed. Ralph Cohen. New York: Bantam, 1965.
Schwartz, Murray M. "Where Is Literature?" In *Transitional Objects and Potential Spaces:
   Literary Uses of D. W. Winnicott*, ed. Peter L. Rudnytsky. New York: Columbia Univer-
   sity Press, 1993. Pp. 50–62.
Swift, Jonathan. "Thoughts on Various Subjects." In *The Prose Works of Jonathan Swift*,
   ed. Herbert Davis. Oxford: Basil Blackwell, 1957. Vol. 4, pp. 251–54.
Walton, Kendall L. *Mimesis as Make-Believe: On the Foundations of the Representational Arts*.
   Cambridge: Harvard University Press, 1990.

Inspired Lyric, Ponderous Prose, and the Promise of Salvation

Ruth B. Bottigheimer

Heaven upon Earth: The Form of Moral and Religious Children's Literature, to 1850, by Patricia Demers. Knoxville: University of Tennessee Press, 1993.

Patricia Demers is a pioneer in treating moral and religious children's literature on its own terms. In the small notice given religious texts in the past, collectors and historians of children's literature have usually scorned its often dreary substance and sympathized with its long-dead readers. When Charles Lamb railed at Mrs. Barbauld's moralizations, his criticism was, perhaps, less a literary evaluation than an oblique testimony to the fact that he himself had no children with jeopardized souls; that, more significantly, he wrote in a period during which child mortality had been greatly reduced, even among the poor; and that parental vigilance against early death and eternal damnation no longer craved the salvational promise held out by moral and religious literature.

In the early modern period, when moral and religious literature for children took on its lineaments, a grim infant and child mortality rate brought nearly 50 percent of the young to their day of judgment before adulthood, and an even grimmer theology engaged a vivid rhetoric to contrast the torments of hell with the bliss of heaven. Mortality and theology together persuaded parents to believe that it was a matter of desperate necessity to do everything possible to snatch children from the eternal flames to which their inborn iniquity condemned them. Once moral and religious literature for children had flowered in England, printer-publishers, preferring to copy rather than to compose anew, kept the genre alive well into the nineteenth century, by which time it had become epigonal to both the religious rhetoric and social conditions that had originally spawned it.

Demers's first chapter treats optimistic post-Reformation views that heaven could be achieved on earth by and for people who lived godly

Children's Literature 24, ed. Francelia Butler, R. H. W. Dillard, and Elizabeth Lennox Keyser (Yale University Press, © 1996 Hollins College).

lives and eschewed the ways of "a certayne kynde and sorte of chyl-
dren . . . which have smothe chynnes and toughe myndes" (13). But
between the 1500s and the 1800s, Demers concludes, "the concept
of a transformed, divinized earth [changed]. Although instructional,
reformative efforts hardly slackened, the prospects of this domain
of heavenly splendor became less global and more personal, individualized, and private" (154–55). That is, no longer a "heaven upon
earth," but a personal purging—or perhaps a purgatory?—on earth
in preparation for celestial reward.

Religious literature integrated children into a doubled family: the
domestic unit that rendered earthly life orderly and the family of
God that promised eventual entry into the mansions of the heavenly
father. It was the function of religious and devotional literature to
move children from home to heaven by training them to make moral
choices that would lead directly to a happy eternity.

This is an alien literature, Demers writes, "because the distance
between postmodern readers and these past spiritual mandates is
. . . very great, [and] we must admit that we read these neglected
works first with contemporary eyes and that their at times harrow-
ing righteousness triggers questions that emerge necessarily from the
present" (28). It is also a literature with many subgenres—general
education, catechisms, reading primers, poetry, emblems and allegories, stories, novels, and drama.

Schooling was required to produce Christian virtue, and success
in British charity schools meant effectively inculcating subjection,
meekness, and gratitude, habits useful to industrial employers. It was
a tutelege that William Godwin excoriated and that exerted so expel-
ling a force that at least one child needed fourteen-pound weights
tied to his legs to keep him from running away (30–31). Universal
elementary education would not be mandated until 1870, and until
then religious education took shape in class-specific and -distinct surroundings: in shabby Sunday schools for the poor or amid dancing
and drawing instruction for the children of the well-off.

In early modern England, Protestant and Catholic ideology con-
tended vigorously and often violently for the souls of English men,
women, and children. Demers, however, like many recent historians
of the early modern period, regularly emphasizes functional simi-
larity rather than doctrinal difference. Her discussion of catecheti-
cal variations (69–75), for example, addresses the catechisms of the
Catholic Recusant Laurence Vaux, the Puritan Nathaniel Vincent,

and the probably Anglican Dorothy Kilner to illustrate teaching and learning patterns common to all confessions in the sixteenth, seventeenth, and eighteenth centuries.

Most children learned to read from ABC books that were simultaneously moral primers carrying somber messages:

> Cry not: Be still;
> come, go, what will.
> Drink not when hot:
> death's in the pot.   (82)

Or more spiritually:

> Make me think vilely of my self
> Shew me my Want of Grace.
> Let not the love of any Sin,
> Within my Soul have place.
>
> Nothing's too hard for thee, O Lord,
> O therefore undertake,
> My strong Corruption to subdue,
> Ev'n for thy Mercies sake.   (82–83)

Little wonder that John Locke, the great theoretician of Enlightenment educational practices, reacted strongly and advocated making learning a sport.

Religious poetry for children seems little different from the primers' awkward attempts at versifying, but Demers has examined religious poetry for children in such quantity that she is able to detect directions in its development and to conclude that "as moral verse became more narrative and less abstract . . . it appears to have become more melodramatic and sanctimonious. In the field of poetry, spiritual writing for children moved from strength to weakness" (93). In her canon Isaac Watts, Christopher Smart, and Charles Wesley were "inspired lyricists"; emblematic versifiers, in her reading, began with John Bunyan and ended with such nineteenth-century jingles as

> Here in this body pent,
> Absent from Him I roam,
> Yet nightly pitch my moving tent,
> A day's march nearer home!   (101)

When narrated piety emerged in the eighteenth century, it was, in Demers's view, "the most cumbersome burdening of spiritual verse for the young" (107). One verse is worth repeating for its comic mix of jarring jingoism and pious reflection:

> I thank the goodness and the grace
> That on my birth have smiled;
> And made me, in these Christian days,
> A happy English child!
>
> I was not born, as thousands are,
> Where God was never known;
> And taught a useless Prayer
> To blocks of wood and stone.
>
> My God! I thank Thee, who has planned
> A better lot for me!
> And placed me in this Christian land,
> Where I can hear of Thee!   (112)

Demers delineates the scores of emblems and edifying religious stories (the best-known author of which is James Janeway), novels, and dramas (like those of the Comtesse de Genlis, Maria Edgeworth, and Hannah More), from which early modern children's booksellers profited so handsomely. Because so few literary historians have been able to read these books sympathetically, Demers's conclusion that Hannah More "concentrates on a dynamic that is at once faith-directed and psychologically complex" (144) has the unexpected effect of opening a door that reveals a well-furnished and curiously museumlike chamber.

Although some of the books discussed in this volume were written by women, the reader comes away with the impression that children's salvation was arranged by the fathers of the world, whether pater-nalistic employers, patriarchal heads of state, preacher-authors, or parental fathers. Indeed, on the handsome jacket a paterfamilias sits amid his assembled family, holding a book. But what do we observe? Illumined by two unshaded candles, the father's lips are closed. Since it is virtually impossible to read under the circumstances shown on the cover, perhaps that is why this father looks not at his book but over it at a preadolescent boy, one of a group encircling a round table at whose exact center the iconic book is held aloft. What do the father's unreading eyes and unspeaking mouth portend? Is it the book or the father the candles are meant to illuminate? If the book is not being read, what is its function at this family gathering? What book is it? If the Bible, then perhaps it radiates spiritual benefit by its mere presence. But it is surely one of the books discussed in Demers's study, mediated by a paterfamilias.

It is Demers's great achievement to have been able to assess the literary and psychological merit of a long-neglected literature that "refused to infantilize readers but treated them instead as sober, capable, eager pupils" (141). From Demers's sensitive analysis, devotional and moral literature emerges as a mother lode of telling cultural information where continued mining promises rich results.

The Poetics and Politics of Adaptation: Traditional Tales as Children's Literature

Jon C. Stott

Sitting at the Feet of the Past: Retelling the North American Folktale for Children, edited by Gary D. Schmidt and Donald R. Hettinga. Westport, Conn.: Greenwood Press, 1992.

To create for children of one culture written and sometimes illustrated versions of traditional oral tales from another culture is an activity fraught with difficulties. Must modern retellers remain faithful to the original contexts in which the stories were probably presented and received, or can they deviate widely? Are they successful in fulfilling the double requirements of accurately reflecting the culture of the narratives and meeting the needs, abilities, and expectations of modern child audiences? Have they the right to attempt the recreation of the stories, particularly when those come from cultures of which they are not members? These issues and problems underlie the twenty-three essays in *Sitting at the Feet of the Past: Retelling the North American Folktale for Children,* an extremely useful and interesting collection edited by Gary D. Schmidt and Donald R. Hettinga.

The book is divided into four sections, each containing essays by creators and critics examining four major categories of North American tales: the Native American folktale, the African-American folktale, the retold Western European folktale, and the American tall tale. Most of the authors re-create tales from cultures not their own; only one writes from within a minority culture. Although it might have been worthwhile to hear from more minority authors and from authors dealing with minority cultures other than African-American, Hispanic, and Native American, the selection here is no doubt appropriate. Most adaptations of traditional stories are by people of Anglo-European heritage, and stories about these three minority groups are most frequently published in children's versions. Thus, the limited range of the coverage also serves as a kind of implicit commentary on the state of this segment of children's book publishing. However, the

Children's Literature 24, ed. Francelia Butler, R. H. W. Dillard, and Elizabeth Lennox Keyser (Yale University Press, © 1996 Hollins College).

authors address the major issues surrounding the subject of adaptation, so that the inclusion of essays by, for example, individuals of Far Eastern backgrounds would probably have extended, but not radically altered, the nature of the discussion. The critics' articles reflect both the basic elements of academic debate and the types of ideas examined in university-level classes on children's literature.

Although the critical articles are placed at the conclusions of each of the sections, they provide, in a way, overviews of and contexts for the authors' statements that precede them. James Gellert surveys over a century of Canadian books presenting the history and tales of traditional Native peoples, from stereotyped portrayals of "good" and "bad" Indians, to non-Native adaptations that achieve degrees of success in embodying sympathy and accuracy, to the recent Native Renaissance, in which such authors as Maria Campbell, Basil Johnston, and George Clutesi have recaptured "the element of self-actualization, of developing through stories" (56), which was an essential component of the original oral tellings.

Two articles examine the history of written versions of the African-American tales of Br'er Rabbit. Working on the premise that "literary works can be copyrighted; oral tales cannot" (82), Hugh T. Keenan examines the role of retellers, both authors and narrators, especially Joel Chandler Harris and Uncle Remus. Harris himself shifted his attitude toward the nature of the stories, his role in their transmission, and his sense of audience; and scholars of folklore have been divided in their assessment of his achievement. Keenan emphasizes the importance of dialect in the narrative voice of the retellings, stating that the narrator's language is "grounded in classical rhetoric" (85), and traces the attitudes toward dialect in later African-American and white adaptors. For Tonny Manna, Harris's modern importance lies in his having left subsequent authors "a legacy to mine as they form their own new versions which . . . mirror their own values" (94). He praises the African-American author Julius Lester, who draws on Harris for basic events and then relates them in his retellings to "some timely, timeless, and controversial issues" (106).

Tall tales, those indigenous narratives referred to as "fakelore" by scholar Richard Dorson, are considered by Bette Bosma and Jan Susina, both of whom examine the relationship of the various tales to the cultures that produced and still reproduce them. Bosma suggests that the stories reflect the pioneers' need to make a vast and often terrifying landscape less intimidating by creating heroes who could control it with relative ease and that events were deliberately exaggerated to produce cathartic laughter. For Susina, the twentieth-century proliferation of books about the pioneers tells "us little of the values of the American frontier from which they supposedly emerged, [but] they do tell a great deal about twentieth century America's need to produce even imitation folk heroes who might exemplify the American spirit" (224). Interestingly, he notes, the majority of the tall tales celebrate white male heroes and their occupations, a fact that those who select children's books will certainly wish to consider.

Three essays examine the alteration of traditional European traditions and oral tales in books for American children (presumably white and middle-class). John Stewig studies eleven illustrated versions of "The Three Little Pigs," discussing the roles of medium, artistic style, and selection of details in each retelling. (Unfortunately, in considering two books, he refers to the villain as both a wolf and a fox.) Susan R. Gannon and Ruth Ann Thompson trace the sea change that the Saint Nicholas legends underwent in traveling from Europe to the eastern United States. In the nineteenth century, Mary Mapes Dodge used Saint Nicholas "as a model of virtue for children growing up in what the genteel tradition felt was a dangerous and difficult world" (181) and then reused her understanding of the traditions in her novel about Holland, *Hans Brinker.*

In perhaps the most interesting and important critical essay in the collection, Roderick McGillis analyzes the relationships among the traditional oral versions, the written adaptations, and the modern oral retellings of the Grimm Brothers' "The Fisherman and His Wife." He emphasizes the complexity of the subject by opening the essay with his written version of a story his grandmother told him and then reveals that it is really his own version, used in his storytelling sessions in Calgary, Canada, of a tale he heard presented by American storyteller Donald Davis. "Who," he asks, "is the author of this story?" (140). McGillis then analyzes the versions of the nineteenth-century German philologists Jacob and Wilhelm Grimm; a contemporary German novelist, Günter Grass; Americans of both genders and a variety of ages, including a ten-year-old boy; and two Canadians, one himself. The role of the audience is also emphasized: "We repeat the story first by reading [or hearing] it, then by talking about it, and perhaps even by writing about it" (150). Each retelling draws on unchanging elements but alters their significance, and that is why traditional stories continue to live. "To repeat the story is to renew it" (151).

This wish to renew a story, along with a desire to preserve in some form stories in danger of being forgotten, is the goal of most of the authors and illustrators. Noting that many younger Native Americans are either unaware of or care little about the traditional stories of their culture, Paul Goble attempts "to take these stories out of the dusty museum and folklore journals . . . and to use them as the closest glimpses we can have today of what Native American culture was like in the buffalo days" (7). In her written version of a Lenape tale from Pennsylvania, Nancy Van Laan considered it her task "to retell this legend in written form so that it sounded as though it was being told orally, for the first time" (15). Retelling Ojibway myths, Barbara Juster Esbensen tries "to make the words on the page come to life, using images and description the same way the oral storyteller might use gestures and facial expressions to enhance a story" (22).

In order to renew these stories, each author had to enter, as far as was possible, the cultural world of the original narrative. For Goble, an Englishman living near the sacred Black Hills, this involved immersing himself in the landscape; listening to his older Native friends who still knew of, and in some cases remembered, the times when the stories existed orally; and engaging in hours of research in museums and libraries. For Jane Louise Curry, a graduate student at Stanford doing research in England, her entry into retelling legends began with diversionary reading in London's British Museum. For others, it was a recovery of memories of their own childhoods. African-American author Patricia McKissack recalled the oral stories told by her Tennessee grandparents and her mother's recitation of the poems of Paul Laurence Dunbar before setting out to overcome the lack, for African-American children, of "a plentiful supply of good stories that reflect . . . [their] culture in various ways" (63). William Hook, a white writer, remembered his South Carolina childhood with his "immediate knowledge of swamps and southern plantations" (112), stories that had grown from those brought from Europe and those heard from African-Americans.

Renewing stories from other cultures presented the authors with some difficulties. Goble reports that "today I combat a certain amount of aggression on the reservations" (10). Nancy Van Laan is "allowed to listen to [some of the sacred stories] . . . being told, but cannot record them on tape" (18). All are aware of the current debate about the ethical rightness of presuming to tell another people's stories. Joe Hayes, who has retold Hispanic-American tales from New Mexico, takes a position found in many of the essays: "The tales . . . can't truly represent traditional Hispanic culture, but they shouldn't grossly misrepresent it—either by romanticizing or degrading it. I do feel an obligation to the original story and culture. I feel an even stronger obligation to the audience" (122).

For Hayes, as for several others, this obligation has two components: helping children to see the common elements of humanity underlying each story and writing in a form that relates to their expectations of what stories are. "Our enjoyment of tales from other cultures enables us to see how, despite the differences, we are like all other people. If we weren't we wouldn't be able to enjoy their stories" (125). Technically, this involves modifying the dialects in which the tales would have originally been spoken, rendering events and dialogue in language which, while it may attempt to recapture the "flavor" of what the authors take to be the original performances, is easily accessible to a wide variety of readers and listeners. Priscilla Jaquith, adapting the Gullah speech of the South Carolina coast, considers that dialect "is demeaning to the people you are writing about and difficult for readers to follow" (78). Some writers "tone down" (72), to use Steve Sanfield's phrase, or omit aspects they consider unsuitable for children. Jane Louise Curry leaves out scatological and sexual elements, so central to the originals, in her retelling of California Coyote tales. She even goes further, creating stories that amalgamate elements from the legends of different groups and then arranging stories so that each of her collections can become a unified book.

Their sense of audience and the adaptations they make in writing for this audience may leave authors and illustrators open to criticism. If there is such a thing as universality, which many people question, is the universality these authors and illustrators present at best a thinly disguised notion of what Anglo-Europeans think is universal? Does the toning down of the stories rob them of the elements that made them so significant for the original cultures? Does a story that draws on many sources selected and edited by the author really deserve to be called a written adaptation of a specific folktale or myth, or is it really the author's creation?

I would have preferred more emphasis on the political controversies surrounding the subject and more discussion about the uniqueness of each group's stories and the values they embody. It would also have been interesting to see a more detailed discussion of the tremendous differences between oral and written creation and reception of stories, as well as the difficulties of bridging these gaps in written children's books. Nonetheless, Schmidt and Hettinga have compiled a volume of essays that gives a clear idea of the poetics of adaptation for children as practiced by large numbers of authors and illustrators, along with a good overview of critical and theoretical perceptions of the process. As such, it is an essential resource for academics, students, and teachers, and it provides an excellent starting point for further analysis of the subject.

The Lost Foremother's Spell and Power

Jean Perrot

Whispers in the Dark: The Fiction of Louisa May Alcott, by Elizabeth Lennox Keyser. Knoxville: University of Tennessee Press, 1993.

The voicing of "Women's wrongs" and the vindication of women's rights have been a major feminist concern since Mary Wollstonecraft, but Louisa May Alcott is perhaps not the most qualified vindicator for the average English-speaking reader, so constantly has the author of *Little Women* been linked with the presentation of women's domestic virtues and of middle-class family life and its values. Elizabeth Lennox Keyser deals with this problem of authority in her recent book, reminding us of the related definitions of domestic and sentimental fictions as two consistent modes of writing in nineteenth-century American fiction, usually written by and intended for women and connected with home, which is represented as a model for society at large. Keyser also takes up Frances Cogan's considerations on the "Cult of True Womanhood" as opposed to that of the "Ideal of Real Womanhood": the conception of women as "fragile, sexless, dependent, and self-denying" in contrast with the quest for "intelligence, physical fitness and health, self-sufficiency, economic self-reliance and careful (combining love and prudence) marriage" (xiv), which is a more adequate attempt to qualify the accepted opinion of Alcott's work.

These contradictory ideas may help to explain the dissatisfaction felt by many readers with the fiction of a writer who may have been urged by circumstances and personal choice to express her most valued convictions in "a muted voice" (188). Alcott even got accustomed, Keyser argues, to "whispering her subversive messages" (145). This is Keyser's point, repeatedly stressed in her fine and passionate book: it is to bring into relief "the subversive power of Alcott's design" (81) principally expressed through "the subversive potentiality of domestic fiction" (57), which is but a disguise for the strategic interplay between woman's imagination and her principle of resistance to patriarchal oppression. Keyser's book is a hymn meant to

Children's Literature 24, ed. Francelia Butler, R. H. W. Dillard, and Elizabeth Lennox Keyser (Yale University Press, © 1996 Hollins College).

glorify "Woman's powers" (189), what she calls, after Nina Auerbach, woman's "disruptive capacity for boundless transformation" (189).

Keyser locates the paradoxical dimension of Alcott's achievement early in her book, when she notes: "Rather than abandoning a radical feminist critique for the creation of exemplary female characters, Alcott enables a critique of the exemplars themselves" (xiv). It is the duality of the picture given in her novels and short stories that fascinates us today, and Keyser wants us to share her enthusiasm and personal vision of the ambivalence of Alcott's secret critique of conventional values. She obviously delights in the way Alcott "camouflages the subversive implications of her sensation fiction, with its heroines conventionally subdued by love" and its " "Gothic paraphernalia" that "can convey to 'a sisterhood of readers' Alcott's indignation at their wrongs" (4).

Clearly, Keyser stands in defense of an artist whose "imagination" she credits with "ideological consistency and artistic control" (xiv), someone who engages in "dismantling the system of values that her more or less conventional plots . . . appear to support" (xv). This subversiveness may come, at least in part, from Alcott's practice of parlor theatricals from an early age, as is evidenced in the March family and in many of Alcott's fictions. Such practice, by admitting theatricality into the Victorian American home, acknowledged the artificiality of genteel life and its possible duplicity: the apparent idealization of the domestic realm screened a deep skepticism about the organization of conventions themselves.

Allowing a critique of the structure it exploits, Alcott's fiction leads Keyser to search for the keys one expects to find in the sensation fiction of the prolific A. M. Barnard, who was finally led to throw off the mask and write children's fiction under her real name. The second part of Alcott's career did not mean ideological recantation but, rather, a more sophisticated process of encoding, since she was addressing the more vulnerable audience of children. In both phases of her career, artistic coherence could be derived from the experience to which the novelist's mother subjected her. For, as Keyser writes, "we have in Louisa May Alcott's childhood journals the stuff of her children's stories: a record of anger and resistance to authority, a gloss that transforms the record into an exemplum, and a perspective, often conveyed by still another text, that undoes the transformation" (xvii).

This message of anger and rebellion, which is the gist of Keyser's book, Alcott received from her mother, Abba, who taught her daughter how to resist Bronson Alcott's tyrannical rule. As Bronson Alcott's journals show, the family home was not the paradise one might expect from a pedagogue who was influenced by Jean-Jacques Rousseau and Friedrich Froebel but more likely a place of conflicting influences, where the man looked upon his associates as devils: "Two devils, as yet, I am not quite divine enough to vanquish — the mother fiend and her daughter" (13).

Keyser's originality lies in the fact that she chose not to dissociate the analysis of Alcott's juvenile fiction from that of her more general production and to consider her achievement as a whole. For the conception of home as prison found expression soon enough in Alcott's "A Whisper in the Dark," first published anonymously in the June 1863 issue of *Frank Leslie's Illustrated Newspaper* and reprinted posthumously in 1889 together with *A Modern Mephistopheles*. It is the special stress put on this fiction that provides Keyser's book with its title, dominant metaphor, and ideological perspective. For in this story, Sybil, the young girl who is sequestered as a "madwoman in the attic" and then treated in Dr. Karnac's asylum (repudiated female patients in those days were treated by male doctors impersonating patriarchal domination), is eventually helped by her mother's spectral voice, which communicates through the closed door of her bedroom to her the advice that will save her. A cliché of Gothic melodramas, the dying companion Sybil discovers has been confined by her uncle in the asylum for eighteen years and is no other than her genetrix, in whose footsteps Sybil is unwittingly following. This melodramatic construction offers Alcott a means for placing her female characters on the stage of genteel society, where they can counterbalance and ultimately defeat the nefarious influence of male power, which alienated women to the point of real madness.

The pattern of matrilinear legacy is also to be found in two of Alcott's stories written for children in her six-volume collection *Aunt Jo's Scrap-Bag:* "Patty's Patchwork" (1872) and "Mamma's Plot" (1873). In the first, ten-year-old Patty "rebels against her socialization as a woman, represented by the tedious task of making patchwork," but her Aunt Pen shows her how the patches can, like a diary, become a means of self-expression (xv). In the second story, a mother's clever device helps her daughter Kitty "circumvent her headmistress's practice of reading and editing the student's letters home" (xix). Keyser suggests that the contemporary reader, too, is the recipient of edited texts and urges us to "occupy the position of Kitty's mother" in our reading of Alcott's novels. We can grasp the secret meaning of Alcott's messages "by unraveling her cover stories, by attending to what has been edited over or edited out" (xix). Keyser thus invites the contemporary reader to find in the nineteenth-century feminist "a lost foremother" (xix), someone "whose feminist voice would be barely audible to successive generations of readers" (4) but the discovery of whose "subversive meanings" is the implicit obligation of any critic truly respectful of the tenets of women's liberation.

And so Alcott's literary development can be considered as a continuous, natural building process from relative unpreparedness and dependence to maturity and balance. In the first chapters of her book, Keyser traces this evolution, beginning with the alienated heroines of early stories, such as "A Whisper in the Dark," showing that "patriarchy entraps women not only physically, but mentally" (10) and moving to Alcott's first admission of "the death of patriarchal order" (29) in *Moods*. This progression is supported by the growing psychological poise of the heroines: in *Moods*, Sylvia gets initiated into life but connects her initiation with patriarchal waste and brevity. As an object of man's desire, Sylvia fails to achieve the maturity of another female character, Faith Dane, the personification of independent Womanhood exemplifying perfect "androgynous development" (24). Sylvia's ordeal, in Keyser's opinion, indirectly reflects Alcott's transformation from the state of "overgrown child" (14) to the condition of real adulthood achieved while reading Margaret Fuller's main work, *Woman in the Nineteenth Century*, the feminists' Bible of the times.

The theme of androgyny is further enlarged and illustrated by *A Marble Woman or the Mysterious Model* (1865), which deals with a motherless adolescent girl involved with two much older men. Here the symbolic representation of woman's body is at stake, along with the social struggle involving the patriarchal preservation of political power, the true focus of the book. The image of the Marble Woman is but a rhetorical metaphor for female unawareness of men's unlawful aggressive desires.

Alcott's next story, *Behind a Mask or A Woman's Power*, published the following year—that is, two years before *Little Women*—leaves no doubt as to how these desires had to be thwarted: as with "A Whisper in the Dark" and other of Alcott's works, the story is indebted to *Jane Eyre*, and Keyser shows how Alcott uses stereotypes to demonstrate "the way in which the Victorian Cult of True Womanhood actually encouraged women to subvert it" (49). Jean Muir, a governess and the hero of *Behind a Mask or a Woman's Power,* is adept at playing little woman and sexual temptress simultaneously, thus heralding Alcott's own capacity, as the creator of *Little Women,* to be the consummate actress who can also play dual roles (56). Fittingly, Keyser, too, works through analogy in her analysis: "Just as Jean hides self-interest behind a mask of duty, lulls her audiences into complacency, and sustains an institution—the family—at which she looks askance, so Alcott seems to have catered to a reading public whose values she pretended to share or adopted under duress. Thus both Jean and her creator are accused of betraying their sex; but, whereas Edward would convict Jean of betraying the values of True Womanhood, some would convict Alcott, in *Little Women* and its sequels, of betraying her feminist values. . . . The removal of Jean's ironic mask, then, seems to predict Alcott's rejection of pseudonymity and the freedom it offered" (56–57).

As a governess, Jean has been able to infiltrate the patriarchal family, the "disruption of which has been her object from the outset" (59), and in Keyser's opinion, "Alcott's splendor" as a juvenile writer "derives from just such insurgency" (59). Keyser's examination of *Little Women* points out how the novel stages such a subversive coup through the "androgynous natures of Jo and Laurie," which suggest the possibility of a new order in which "divided selves" can be made "whole" (81), thus opening utopian perspectives heralded by the symbolic deaths of the male characters of *Moods* and *A Marble Woman.* It would take much more space than is possible here to fully explore Keyser's commentary on *Little Women,* and so perhaps it is best to stop here and leave the reader the pleasure of discovering the reasons that justify Jo's marriage to Professor Bhaer, a notable cause for the modern reader's disappointment with the "subversive power of Alcott's design" (81). One can just wonder whether the figure "early old," which lurks behind the charming model of little womanhood, has, as Keyser puts it, the "power to detonate that model" (82).

The last section of Keyser's book, "Beyond *Little Women,*" asks us to serve as witnesses to the difficulties of woman's aging; thus, *Little Men* leaves the "reader with a sense of sadness and loss" (96); for Jo, "by choosing the hearth as her base of operations . . . does not transcend the limitations of woman's traditional sphere, but becomes entrapped within it" (99). Still, aging does not deter Alcott in her "quest for identity," argues Keyser, who relentlessly pursues her analysis of all its twists and turns through *Work: A Story of Experience,* published two years after *Little Men.* In the chapter "An Identity 'Other' than Their Own: *A Modern Mephistopheles,*" Keyser examines the plot of Alcott's last sensation story, which indirectly refers to the writer's dealing with the problems of the artist, hinting at the disagreements she had with Thomas Niles, her editor. Keyser thinks that in this work, "by associating her artist hero, as well as her masculine and feminine alter egos, with Hawthorne's Dimmesdale, she [Alcott] confesses that she, like that pillar of the patriarchal community, is an accomplished actor" (141). The "Paradoxes of the Woman Artist" expressed in *Diana and Persis* finally lead to the triumph (177) of "A Voice of One's Own" in *Jo's Boys:* this triumph "is the dubious one conceded to woman—the triumph of influence" wielded "for the traditional purpose of curbing male passion and preserving female purity" (177). It has, Keyser argues, the "sad undertones of pathos" (179).

Keyser's epilogue is an examination of Alcott's last story in the sixth volume of her collection *Aunt Jo's Scrap-Bag,* "Fancy's Friend," first published in 1868, shortly before *Little Women.* This story, Keyser implies, was inspired by Nathaniel Hawthorne's *The Scarlet Letter* and, in particular, by the scene in which Pearl contrives a mermaid costume for herself. "Fancy's Friend" shows a young girl (Fancy) "and the creature of her imagination Lorelei," who, as typically feminine illustrations of the faculty of imagining, "confound the male power structure and contest its vision of reality" (182). This fantasy is a perfect representative of women's rhetorical nineteenth-century writing, which, according to Nina Auerbach, is "slithered with images of mermaids," emblematically showing the faculty women have to "submerge themselves, not to negate their power, but to conceal it" (189).

Keyser's book is clearly and meticulously written, with a wealth of detail, literary allusion, and quotation that bring into focus each story in the course of Alcott's affective and artistic development. One could wish that the bibliography of Alcott's works had been presented as a full list, giving the dates of first publication and showing the chronology of the stories that Keyser selected for analysis. Following Keyser's close investigation, however, is an intellectual adventure, a journey in which the reader is asked to take sides and risks in this convincing gender study and evaluation of one of the central figures of American children's literature.

Louisa May Alcott: Contradictions and Continuities

Elizabeth Lennox Keyser

Freaks of Genius: Unknown Thrillers by Louisa May Alcott, edited by Daniel Shealy. Associate editors Madeleine B. Stern and Joel Myerson. Contributions to the Study of Popular Culture, no. 28. Westport, Conn.: Greenwood Press, 1991.

Louisa May Alcott's Fairy Tales and Fantasy Stories, edited by Daniel Shealy. Knoxville: University of Tennessee Press, 1992.

From Jo March's Attic: Stories of Intrigue and Suspense, edited by Madeleine B. Stern and Daniel Shealy. Boston: Northeastern University Press, 1993.

In "A Curious Call," a story first published in *Merry's Museum* (Feb. 1869) and reprinted in *Fairy Tales and Fantasy Stories,* the narrator, "a literary woman," is visited one stormy night by "the great gilt eagle on the City-Hall dome" (176). On admitting the bird, the narrator likens herself to "Mr. Poe . . . when that unpleasant raven paid him a call" (177). But Louisa May Alcott's eagle proves a bird of a different feather. After describing his travels about the city of Boston, he concludes with an example of "practical Christianity," a Sunday school that welcomes the children of the poor. He then exhorts his auditor to "tell people about that place; write some stories for the children; go and help teach them; do something, and make others do what they can to increase the Sabbath sunshine that brightens one day in the week for the poor babies who live in the shady places" (179). The narrator promises to do her best, and thus Alcott points to her editorship of *Merry's Museum* and authorship of *Little Women* (part 1 appeared in 1868, part 2 in 1869, after "A Mysterious Call"). But the allusion to Poe is more slyly self-referential, for as many modern readers now know, Alcott wrote dozens of adult stories quite removed from the realm of Sabbath sunshine. Of the stories collected in these three new volumes, only those in *Fairy Tales and Fantasy Stories* were written under the aegis of the eagle, apt symbol of civic, national, and Vic-

Children's Literature 24, ed. Francelia Butler, R. H. W. Dillard, and Elizabeth Lennox Keyser (Yale University Press, © 1996 Hollins College).

torian (soon to be Gilded Age) ideals and values. *Freaks of Genius* and
From Jo March's Attic contain Gothic or sensation stories more akin to
Poe's unpleasant raven.

In *Fairy Tales and Fantasy Stories* editor Daniel Shealy reprints all
thirty-eight of Alcott's fantasy stories for children, using the text
of their first publication in book form. These stories, which Shealy
places squarely in the "didactic tradition of fantasy literature" and
"the long tradition of the moral tale in America" (xix), represent
three different stages in Alcott's career. In the first stage, Alcott
published two collections of fantasy stories, *Flower Fables* (1855) and
Morning-Glories and Other Stories (1868), as well as most of her anonymous and pseudonymous sensation stories. The immense popularity
of *Little Women's* domestic realism understandably diverted Alcott
from both fantasy and sensation writing, but although she seems to
have abandoned the latter genre, she continued to publish an occasional fantasy story during the 1870s, the decade in which most of
her children's classics were published. These fantasy pieces joined
more realistic short stories in a six-volume collection entitled *Aunt
Jo's Scrap-Bag*, which appeared between 1872 and 1882. Finally, in the
1880s, when Alcott's health was failing and she could no longer produce novels, she returned to the fantasy story, publishing a dozen or
so in the three volumes of *Lulu's Library*, which also reprinted stories
from her first book, *Flower Fables*. Thus *Fairy Tales and Fantasy Stories*
enables us to examine a little-known body of Alcott's work that serves
to frame her career.

Alcott's *Flower Fables* began as tales told by sixteen-year-old Louisa
to nine-year-old Ellen Emerson, to whom the volume was dedicated.
But it is hard to imagine any child, even a daughter of Emerson,
listening patiently to these tedious and overwritten tales. Although
Shealy rejects biographer Martha Saxton's psychoanalytic interpretation of the fables (see *Louisa May: A Modern Biography* [Boston:
Houghton Mifflin, 1977]), they do seem to represent dilemmas confronting the young author. Shealy sees the "power of love" as the
unifying theme of *Flower Fables* (xxv), but an even more obsessive one
is that of female self-sacrifice. In "The Frost-King; or, The Power of
Love," a fairy, Violet, undertakes a mission to the Frost-King, who is
ruthlessly killing all the flowers in the land. Confined by the king to a
dark dungeon, Violet exhausts herself working underground to nour-
ish the roots of the withered flowers. In "Lily-Bell and Thistledown"
Lily-Bell leaves "home and friends" (29) to follow wild Thistledown,

but in attempting to repair his ravages to birds, bees, and flowers, she too exhausts herself and succumbs to a Sleeping Beauty sleep. For all their cloying sweetness, however, *Flower Fables* contains nascent subversive elements. The Frost-King and Thistledown, beneficiaries of female selflessness, anticipate the coldly intellectual and the passionately rebellious heroes of the sensation fiction. Thistledown, especially, in his wanton destructiveness, suggests later Faustian heroes, who seek to deflower the virginal heroines, or wild boys, like Dan in *Little Men,* who rebel against efforts to tame them. For example, Thistle ruthlessly desecrates a rosebud while its mother looks on, crying "How could you harm the little helpless one?" (30). (She later forgives Thistle and takes him in, helping to effect the reformation that reunites him with the saintly Lily-Bell.) And Violet's underground activity of ministering to the flowers' roots anticipates later heroines' less literal efforts to undermine the male power structure.

Similar to *Flower Fables* but more interesting for its anticipation of *Little Women* is "The Rose Family," first published in 1863 and reprinted in *Morning-Glories and Other Stories.* In this tale three fairy sisters—Moss, Blush, and Brier Rose—overcome their character flaws with the help of a good fairy and "the memory of their loving mother" (xxvii). Each sister, in overcoming idleness, vanity, and temper, wears on her breast a talisman drop in which she sees her absent mother's face, much as the March sisters pin Marmee's notes inside their frocks as proof against temptation. Other tales in *Morning-Glories* develop formulas that Alcott would employ throughout her career as a writer of fantasy. In "The Shadow-Children" the children's shadows act as models that they are bound to emulate for a day and in so doing discover the rewards of good behavior. In "What Fanny Heard" a spoiled child is inspired to reform when she hears the flowers and the furnishings of her room gossiping about her. In "The Moss People" the creation of a miniature world enables Alcott to satirize society, and in "Fairy Pinafores" Cinderella's godmother establishes a home for poor children rather like Jo March's Plumfield. Here the children manufacture pinafores that magically transform the children of the rich into their generous benefactors.

But although one might be tempted to dismiss *Morning-Glories* as unequivocally didactic, "Fancy's Friend," later selected by Alcott to conclude the *Scrap-Bag* series, warns against limiting one's reading to the surface features of the text. In this story an imaginative child, Fancy, conjures up from the sea a mysterious playmate she believes to be a mermaid. Lorelei, as the stranger is called, charms Aunt Fiction, but she disturbs Uncle Fact, who is at a loss to account for her. Finally, Uncle Fact persuades Fancy to repudiate her friend, who immediately disappears from whence she came, leaving Fancy desolate. Interpreted by Angela Estes and Kathleen Lant (*Lion and the Unicorn*, Vol. 18, no. 2 [1994]) as a cautionary tale about the female child's loss of voice, a phenomenon documented in recent years by the research of Carol Gilligan, the story can also be viewed as a parable of the female imagination and the way a patriarchal culture forces it to submerge or disguise itself (see Keyser, *Whispers in the Dark*, 1993).

To modern readers, Alcott's most obvious disguise appears to have been her anonymous and pseudonymous sensation fiction. *Freaks of Genius* and *From Jo March's Attic* join four predecessors, *Behind a Mask* (1975), *Plots and Counterplots* (1976), *A Modern Mephistopheles and Taming a Tartar* (1987), and *The Double Life* (1988), all edited by the doyenne of Alcott studies, Madeleine Stern (the last with the help of Myerson and Shealy). Stern's introductions to stories in all these volumes recount the discovery of their authorship, their publishing histories, and their autobiographical sources. She concludes each volume with a bibliography of the now-known "unknown thrillers." How many more remain to be discovered is a tantalizing question. In her introduction to *Freaks of Genius*, Stern wrote: "It is certain that there are more such tales concealed in the now crumbling weeklies of the 1850s and the 1860s. It is equally certain that they will remain undiscovered" (21–22). *From Jo March's Attic*, as Stern admits in her introduction to that later volume, shows such certainty to be unwarranted.

The most substantial of the recently discovered thrillers appear in *Freaks of Genius* and, as Stern discusses in her introduction, have important connections with other major works of Alcott. "A Nurse's Story," first published in 1865–66 in *Frank Leslie's Chimney Corner*, is the first-person narrative of Kate Snow, a nurse-companion to a young woman suffering from bouts of hereditary madness. The story of Kate's growing relationship with her charge, Elinor Carruth, is virtually identical to the chapter of *Work* (1873), a highly regarded adult domestic novel, in which Christie Devon becomes a companion to Helen Carrol. The members of the Carruth family correspond to those of the Carrol family with one notable exception. In "A Nurse's Tale" Alcott adds a melodramatic subplot in which Robert Steele, Mr. Carruth's son by an earlier marriage, plots to rob his siblings of their inheritance. Kate's entanglement with Robert, who alternately repels and attracts her, makes for the dramatic tension and psychological complexity of the work. Even more fascinating is the relationship between "The Freak of a Genius" and *A Modern Mephistopheles* (1877), the one work of sensation fiction Alcott is known to have written after *Little Women* and which she published as a lark in Roberts Brothers' No Name Series. Both tales involve a pact between a brilliant older man and his handsome young protégé, who agrees to pass the older man's poetry off as his own in order to earn fame and fortune. Both also involve the older man's arrangement of his protégé's marriage to a childlike young woman whom the older man comes to love or is perceived as loving. In *A Modern Mephistopheles,* however, the older man is portrayed as a diabolic figure, coldly experimenting with the lives of the young people, who, when they escape, leave him the prisoner of a paralyzed body. In "The Freak of a Genius" the older man acts out of love for his protégé, who is nonetheless destroyed, while his mentor survives to marry the woman both men love and to establish himself as a writer. Central to both works are the complicated and ambiguous feelings between the two men and, especially interesting given Alcott's own double authorial identity, the idea of hidden authorship. The reprinting of these novellas provides further evidence for the view that Alcott's sensation fiction was intimately related to her domestic fiction and that gender and authorial identity were abiding preoccupations in both.

The remaining four stories in *Freaks of Genius,* as well as several in *From Jo March's Attic,* feature actresses and reveal Alcott's fascination with the theater. As the subtitle of "La Jeune: Actress and Woman" indicates, Alcott was especially intrigued by the problematical relationship between women and acting. On the one hand, many of her characters see a disjunction between the real woman and the actress. And her male characters, as in "La Jeune" or the more famous sensation story "Behind a Mask," attempt to dissuade one another or themselves from marrying an actress, however bewitching, because they believe the profession to be incompatible with true womanliness. On the other hand, the ubiquity of acting among Alcott's female characters almost suggests that to be a woman one must be an actress. As the cynical narrator of "La Jeune" discovers, the heroine is indeed something other than she seems—a light-hearted young prima donna whose reputation is above reproach. Rather than the scheming adventuress he suspects her of being, however, she is a dying woman, desperately struggling to provide for her senile guardian by affecting the glamorous life necessary to promote a brilliant but brief career. In "Fate in a Fan" and "Betrayed by a Buckle," both in *From Jo March's Attic,* two young women who are not professional actresses assume seductive masks: one is forced to drug her father's gambling associates; the other attempts to wrest from a male cousin the inheritance illegitimacy has denied her. Both meet tragic ends when, having fallen in love with their victims, they allow their masks to slip and reveal their vulnerability.

In their power struggles with women, men too are forced to become skillful actors, feigning emotions they do not feel and concealing those they do. One of the most amusing and provocative of Alcott's male actors appears in an *Attic* story, "My Mysterious Mademoiselle." In this tale, a traveler is persuaded to share his compartment with a young girl to whom he becomes increasingly attracted. The young girl appears shy and demure, but when her companion feigns sleep in order to observe her more closely, she helps herself to the contents of his flask as well as to his half-opened can of chocolate croquettes. Later, to evade a pursuer, the girl asks him to pose as her father, but he insists instead on playing her husband and taking certain liberties. The pair continues to flirt until, as the train emerges from a long tunnel, the older traveler finds his companion to be a mischievous boy who is running away from school, where he had learned to play female roles. Further, he proves to be the son of his companion's estranged sister, whom they are both traveling to see. "My Mysterious Mademoiselle" appeared the same year as part 2 of *Little Women,* though, as Madeleine Stern explains in her introduction, it was undoubtedly written earlier. The boy's prank is reminiscent of Laurie's penchant for mischief and intrigue, Jo's theatricality and cross-dressing, and the androgynous nature of both characters. Like the novel, the story points to the fluidity of gender and the arbitrariness of gender roles. The uncle's voyeuristic and predatory behavior, seemingly rendered harmless by the nephew's disclosure of his identity, suggests why girls such as Jo, who also desires to "run away . . . and have a capital time," have to be "proper, and stop at home" (chap. 21). "A Mysterious Mademoiselle," then, rather than being a mere freak of Alcott's genius, is a quintessential expression of it.

As Madeleine Stern writes in her introduction to *Freaks of Genius,*

"Alcott had many selves: she was feminist, delver into darkness, liter-ary professional. Like the actresses she loved to paint, she was pro-tean in nature" (14). Alcott's late fantasy stories, originally published in *Lulu's Library* and reprinted in *Fairy Tales and Fantasy Stories,* also offered her opportunities to indulge that protean nature. In one, "Queen Aster" (1887), a feminist fable masquerades as a children's story. Published a few months earlier in *The Woman's Journal* (Feb. 1887) under the title "A Flower Fable," it begins, "For many seasons the Golden-rods had reigned over the meadow, and no one thought of choosing a king from any other family, for they were strong and handsome, and loved to rule" (334). But the "unusually wise and energetic" Asters, some of whom "grew outside the wall beside the road," observe that the Golden-rods "care only for money and power, as their name shows" (334) and propose their cousin Violet Aster for Queen of the Meadow. Supported by Poetry and Philosophy, repre-sented by a venerable maple and substantial rock, Violet Aster wins the election only to be condemned by her rivals as a "Dreadful, un-feminine creature" (335). The smug Golden-rods predict that she will "soon be glad to give up" and restore them to their "proper place" (335), but Violet Aster persists, sustained by the Rock and inspired by the Maple. "The first thing she did was to banish the evil snakes from the kingdom." She then institutes temperance reform, prevents warring tribes from fighting, and purifies the press, to the chagrin of the Golden-rods, "who were so used to living in public that they missed the excitement, as well as the scandal of the magpies and the political and religious arguments and quarrels of the crows" (336). She establishes a "hospital for sick and homeless creatures," though "the rich and powerful flowers gave no help" (336–37). Gradually, however, the haughty flowers are won over. Clematis, who had felt "the palace was no longer a fit home for a delicate, high-born flower like herself" (335), concludes, "Since I must cling to something, I choose the noblest I can find, and look up, not down, forever more" (337). Prince Golden-rod acknowledges that "she has done more than ever we did to make the kingdom beautiful and safe and happy" and makes overtures, which the queen readily accepts, remembering that "both were born in the palace and grew up together very happily till coronation time came" (338). When Golden-rod confesses that "you are fitter to rule than I," Violet offers to share her power. The philoso-pher rock has the last word: "This is as it should be; love and strength going hand in hand, and justice making the earth glad" (338). This fable, slipped slyly into the volume that reprints her earliest tales of feminine humility and self-sacrifice ("The Frost-King," with its very different Violet, is the title story), does not so much repudiate as transmute those values, leaving us with a revolutionary vision of social reform extending far beyond the eagle's call.

Envisioning Mark Twain through J. D. Stahl

Carolyn Leutzinger Richey

Mark Twain, Culture and Gender: Envisioning America through Europe, by
J. D. Stahl. Athens: University of Georgia Press, 1994.

J. D. Stahl's intent in his recent study is, he declares, "to envision for
myself what nineteenth-century American culture looked like in the
writings of Samuel Clemens/Mark Twain. In particular, I have sought
to understand how Twain envisioned gender: masculinity, femininity,
and the social and emotional currents between men and women"
(180). The fairy tales of the Brothers Grimm, Hans Christian Andersen, and Charles Perrault possess a mythic quality that, for centuries,
has helped shape the constructs of the European child (that is, his
or her identity and expected social behavior). Similarly, Stahl argues, Mark Twain's writings, based upon the author's experiences and
roots in Europe and now ingrained in American consciousness, have
molded our perception of the nineteenth-century American child
and our subsequent American identity. This, says Stahl, "is how the
relativity of European values, customs, and beliefs in comparison with
Samuel Clemens's own American ideas, attitudes, and practices informed and permeated his envisioning of gender and vice versa" (1).

Pursuing this aspect of criticism, Stahl addresses a number of
Twain's works, analyzing how they serve the mythic purpose of explaining concepts of culture and gender. Stahl offers a study of
the progressive evolution of Twain's ideas and then systematically
examines his familiar and unfamiliar, youthful and adult, novels
and shorter pieces. Stahl's initial purpose is the discovery of "the
psychological inner workings of Mark Twain's characters, especially
with regard to sexuality and gender"—even including Twain among
these characters. The related second purpose—or "preoccupation,"
as Stahl labels it—is an investigation of "the archetypal son's search
for a symbolic father, a theme that unites many of his American
works with the works set in Europe" (xiii). The final aspect of Twain
that Stahl examines, and "one of the most significant and, until recently, relatively unexplored dimensions of Twain's writing, is his use

Children's Literature 24, ed. Francelia Butler, R. H. W. Dillard, and Elizabeth Lennox
Keyser (Yale University Press, © 1996 Hollins College).

of popular and stereotypical images of masculinity and femininity" (xiv). With these goals, Stahl embarks on what proves to be an enlightening and thought-provoking study.

Addressing the first of his stated purposes in "Privilege, Gender, and Self-definition: *The Innocents Abroad*," Stahl suggests that Twain offers a "new American voice" (31) to the world of literature that is "predominantly masculine" (31). Through the voice of his narrator, a male ingenue who is both confident and naive, Twain embarks on the definition of the gender roles representative of both the American travelers and the Europeans they encounter. Stahl claims that his "honest manliness is identified with the clarity of Victorian American gender roles and rituals, while sophistry, clerical hypocrisy, and sexual licentiousness are identified as European" (43).

Although Stahl points out that in *The Innocents Abroad* Twain begins to examine how his characters achieve these gender roles—particularly the masculine—in relation to culture, he continues the process of formalizing these roles in several of his shorter pieces. In "Mark Twain and Female Power: Public and Private," Stahl analyzes Twain's evolving ideas on gender in "A Memorable Midnight Experience" and "1601." In the former sketch, Twain "presents a dialectic between past and present; familiar and unfamiliar; living and dead; and, most subtly, between male and female modalities" (49). In the latter, he introduces the strong, sexual female, in the figure of royalty, who is able to overpower the male. Consequently, this juxtaposition of both gender and class displays Twain's "attempts to come to terms with the perceived cultural paradox of emblematic female power in European history" (65) and symbolizes the lifelong discourse that typifies Twain's writings.

In his third chapter, "Fathers and Sons in *The Prince and the Pauper*," Stahl discusses the manner in which this classic tale embodies American apprehensions regarding gender roles. He explains that Mark Twain's unfolding use and transposition of European history and culture depicts this anxiety through the expression of the class structure of Europe. Stahl effectively accounts for this theory as he expounds on Twain's treatment of the mythic search for a father figure by a number of sons. He claims that *The Prince and the Pauper* "abounds with symbolic father-son relationships" and, unlike *Huckleberry Finn* and *Tom Sawyer*, ends idealistically. He asserts that this tale offers the "dynamic possibility within society" (69) that new fathers will be found, despite the author's own disappointments.

In "Sexual Politics in *A Connecticut Yankee in King Arthur's Court*," Stahl continues with the topic of fathers and sons, pointing out that Hank Morgan embodies the downfall of the father figure. Relating this to Clemens's own traumatic loss of his father, Stahl maintains: "Hank's political failure is rooted in a psychological failure. His challenge to monarchy . . . leads him . . . to replace the role of king with that of boss, but technology and . . . Victorian family life cannot compensate for a deeper sense of lack that underlies the impermanence of Hank's and Twain's dream of fulfillment" (119–120). Stahl concludes that Clemens's rewriting of the legend of Arthur through his character-counterpart Hank Morgan authenticates, but does not tear down, the construct of the father figure.

Stahl concludes this mythic and cultural exploration by addressing Twain's uses of conventional images of gender. For Twain, Joan of Arc is the epitome of the legendary female and is "a figure in whom Clemens's American faith in political and sexual innocence is most completely embodied" (122). Stahl suggests, however, that the multiple assessments rendered to Mark Twain's Joan by the various critics provide "evidence not only of differences in theoretical approaches and national perspectives but also of the importance of Twain's *Joan of Arc* to the issues of gender as we are currently redefining them" (124–26). This, concludes Stahl, reduces Twain's preoccupation with the conflicts and issues of society and gender to "Twain's perpetual drive toward self-realization . . . [and] self-actualization through a male storyteller's quest" (150).

The three versions of Young Satan from *The Mysterious Stranger* manuscripts demonstrate a greater understanding of human nature regarding gender than does his idyllic *Joan of Arc*. These variant Satans also typify the author's move toward existential thinking during his later years. Analyzing these tales of the youthful Satan in "Culture, Desire and Gender in *The Mysterious Stranger* Manuscripts," Stahl demonstrates how Twain begins to blend the gender characteristics that typify the author's confusion and rejection of contemporary Victorian dictates of gender and culture. Stahl interprets the male characters in the various *Mysterious Stranger* renderings as "projections of the Twainian male self. . . . They exhibit a range of male responses to females that provides an index not only to Samuel Clemens's ways of thinking and feeling about the sexes but to the attitudes of his culture and time" (171). Thus, in both *Joan of Arc* and *The Mysterious Stranger* manuscripts, Stahl concludes that the female characters escape from the margins of otherness and develop more sexual identities, whereas the male characters' authority is placed in question.

If there is any problem with J. D. Stahl's study, it is a problem that critics have experienced over the years when dealing with the works of Mark Twain. No matter how many questions the critic answers, it seems that twice as many questions will invariably arise. Many of these, for this reader, come out of the Twain tales that are set in America. Although Stahl does deal with these questions to a degree, I would like to see further examination of the effect of Twain's European experiences on other works with an American setting, such as the unfinished "Hellfire Hotchkiss" and *Pudd'nhead Wilson*. Both of these tales focus on gender and cultural confusions, in addition to forming a link in Mark Twain's mythic cycle.

Ultimately, *Mark Twain, Culture and Gender* does address and acknowledge the dilemma regarding gender and cultural dictates that pervades the writings of Mark Twain. On the one hand, "Twain contributed to the glorification of female sexual innocence that was part of the denial of women's sexual nature in nineteenth-century American society" (151) and was integral to the myth of the Victorian woman. Paradoxically, however, Stahl affirms Twain as he appears to counter Victorian social biases regarding sexuality. Stahl concludes his study by saying that "for me, finally, the efforts to comprehend and critique Twain's cultural constructs is part of an effort to find and claim my own place and voice in the present dialogues about and between cultures and the sexes" (188). In essence, then, Stahl acknowledges that Twain has achieved the literary purpose of the storyteller when his readers envision the writer envisioning his world.

Works Cited

Lukens, Rebecca J. *A Critical Handbook of Children's Literature*. 4th ed. New York: Harper Collins, 1990.

Johnny We Hardly Knew Ya

William F. Touponce

Johnny Gruelle: Creator of Raggedy Ann and Andy, by Patricia Hall. Gretna, La: Pelican, 1993.

New Criticism, which held sway in this country until recently, de-emphasized the author by its assertion that the meaning of a literary work could not be discovered in its extratextual life or intentions. Fashionable rhetoric about the death of the author, which followed the New Criticism, also helped to discredit author-based studies. However, all this has done little to stem the longing of children—and adults, too, as Patricia Hall's book everywhere attests—to know the real person behind the books they have come to love. Literary biography continues to be a favorite category of childhood reading, and biographies of famous children's authors proliferate. In 1985, when I first started teaching children's literature in Indianapolis, I knew little about Johnny Gruelle and his creation. Since then, I have grown to love his stories. Largely through the efforts of students taking my courses, I have learned much about him, though a lot of that information has seemed contradictory and steeped in legend. For instance, an article in the *Indianapolis Star* (Sept. 8, 1985)—given to me by a student in my very first class—provides one version of the origins of Raggedy Ann, who was reportedly born in Indianapolis in 1914, while Gruelle was still working for the *Star.* Gruelle's only daughter, Marcella (then eight years old and suffering from tuberculosis), supposedly found this family doll in the attic, and the stories were Gruelle's way of making Marcella's long nights of coughing easier to bear. After her death, Gruelle was prompted by a *Star* staffer to write more of the stories; this led to their publication in 1918.

Most of the factual information provided in this version, however, is flatly contradicted or disproven by Patricia Hall's book. To begin, Hall's appendixes and narrative reveal that Gruelle had finished working for the *Star* by 1906. By 1910 he was living and working in Cleveland, and by 1914 he had moved to Silvermine, an artists'

Children's Literature 24, ed. Francelia Butler, R. H. W. Dillard, and Elizabeth Lennox Keyser (Yale University Press, © 1996 Hollins College).

colony in Connecticut, and was freelancing for New York newspapers. Gruelle probably discovered the doll himself while visiting his parents in Indianapolis, and named it after two poems ("The Raggedy Man" and "Little Orphan Annie") by James Whitcomb Riley, a friend of the elder Gruelle. Hall also records another account, that given by Myrtle, Gruelle's wife, in later years, which claims that when she and her husband and Marcella returned to Cleveland after that visit to Indianapolis, they took this family rag doll home with them, dressed in new clothes. Furthermore, Marcella was born in 1902, which would have made her twelve in the *Star* account, not eight. She did in fact die in 1915, at Silvermine, barely three months after her thirteenth birthday, but of complications arising from a bad vaccination (one of the most scathing documents that Hall reproduces is a bitter satirical cartoon about vaccination that Gruelle published in 1921), not from tuberculosis. The only point on which the two narratives converge is that Gruelle made up the stories, hoping to lift his little girl's spirits by incorporating her dolls and toys as characters.

Patricia Hall's book is so well researched that it will undoubtedly become the standard reference book on Gruelle. She takes great pleasure in presenting the true historical details of Gruelle's life and provides the reader with an extensive collection of pictures that document the major phases of Gruelle's career, from newspaper cartoonist to magazine illustrator and finally to book illustrator. One is surprised to discover how much the man accomplished during his thirty or so years of creative activity, which went far beyond creating perhaps the most beloved of all American folk-doll characters. Before rag dolls became popular, he designed several other characters and toys, including a humorous family of ducks. He was a respected political cartoonist and comic-strip artist as well, having created *Brutus,* a short cigar-chomping wise guy who managed to get himself into numerous scrapes (usually about lending or borrowing money) during the Depression. Hall relates many interesting facts about Gruelle's personal and public life, for example, his dabbling in spiritualism and his lengthy lawsuit to regain control of Raggedy Ann in the mid-1930s. She extensively researched the circumstances of publication surrounding almost everything Gruelle got into print (and in the process found some items that he did not).

I have only two complaints about this otherwise excellent book. The first is that like many books that attempt to set the historical record straight, or indeed to establish a record where none has been made before, the attention to minute historical details is sometimes overwhelming. For instance, do we really need to know that "funeral services for Marcella were held at the Gruelles' home in Silvermine at 3:30 P.M. on November 10, the Reverend Louis B. Howell officiating" (91)? Perhaps facts such as these will be of interest to Gruelle's fans, who are legion (at least in Indiana), but they fail to shed any light on how an author such as Gruelle could transform personal tragedy into literary triumph (I realize that not everybody thinks of these stories as literature, let alone a triumph, but I'm prepared to defend them, arguing that because of the indestructible core of pleasure so central to them, they helped, together with the Oz books of L. Frank Baum, to establish what children's literature in America is today—an unabashed literature of pleasure). In truth, Hall's book is made up of many thousands of such details, which, despite the seeming triviality of some, nonetheless gradually yield up her nuanced sense of this affectionate man's life and times.

Second, I had hoped that this book would be a literary biography, which it is not (nor did it set out to be). I therefore found the last chapter, which attempts to assess Gruelle's "literary" reputation and influence, to be a disappointment. Throughout the book Hall makes reference to Gruelle's use of "folk motifs," but spends a mere two paragraphs of analysis on his Americanization of these traditional storytelling devices (195). Although she notes that much of Gruelle's writing for children was produced under the commercial circumstances of newspaper publication, and later compiled for book publication—a fact that accounts for their deficiencies in style—she never manages to link the notion of Gruelle's popular style to any concept of aesthetic reception or response. As a historian she notes her frustration with Gruelle's preference for keeping the factual origins and inspirations for his rag dolls "shrouded in the romantic mists of his own fanciful prose" (107) but understandingly grants him a poetic license to do so. Although the main part of any biography is the separation of the mask from the man or woman who hid behind it, this is where Hall should have extended her analysis, incorporating the notion that the life of the author does include metaphorical or fictive elements. She seems quite aware of the fact that Gruelle played with the double audience of both children and adults, "using the simultaneous voices of the age-old sage and the wide-eyed child" (196), yet she offers her reader not a single paragraph of stylistic analysis showing us how Gruelle accomplished this feat, which, it could be argued,

every writer for children has to negotiate. And although she reproduces a letter from Dr. Seuss mentioning the influence of Gruelle's
"bird's-eye view" cartooning techniques on his own style, there is
no comparison of the two writers. In conclusion, even though the
book falls short of a literary biography, it does present the historical
Gruelle through an intricate juxtaposition of words and pictures that
in the end help us to know the author of the Raggedy Ann stories—
that gentle and loving man—as he probably was.

New Worlds for Children

Andrew Gordon

Science Fiction for Young Readers, edited by C. W. Sullivan III. Contributions to the Study of Science Fiction and Fantasy, no. 56. Westport, Conn.: Greenwood Press, 1993.

This volume for young readers is part of the growing series by Greenwood Press on specialized topics in the expanding field of science fiction and fantasy and serves as a useful introduction to this territory. As C. W. Sullivan notes, "Although both children's literature and science fiction have attained some stature as areas of legitimate literary inquiry, science fiction written especially for the young reader has been, by and large, ignored or treated only in passing" (xiv). He fills this gap with sixteen highly readable essays on a range of authors and subjects, from the Tom Swift books of the early part of this century through recent novels by Monica Hughes and Louise Lawrence.

In his introduction, Sullivan describes his excited discovery, during junior high school, of fantastic literature, which exposed him to a wide range of new ideas and new ways of thinking about the future. I, too, can testify to the seductive power of this literature, for I graduated from science fiction and fantasy comic books and started reading Isaac Asimov and Robert Heinlein when I was twelve. Unaware of marketing distinctions, I consumed both their juvenile and adult fiction during my adolescence. As they did for many other young readers, these novels helped to exercise my imagination, to pique my interest in science and technology, and to make me into a lifelong reader of science fiction.

Sullivan's anthology is divided into three sections that provide both a historical and a thematic perspective on the field: part 1, "The Shapers of Science Fiction for Young Readers"; part 2, essays on more recent authors; and part 3, "Science Fiction as a Vehicle for Ideas." One problem with this division is that there is some inevitable overlap and repetition. For example, some of the vintage or classic shapers of the field were still writing in the 1980s or 1990s: the Tom

Children's Literature 24, ed. Francelia Butler, R. H. W. Dillard, and Elizabeth Lennox Keyser (Yale University Press, © 1996 Hollins College).

Swift series continued until 1991; Asimov wrote the Norby series with his wife in the 1980s; Andre Norton's Magic series appeared in the 1960s and 1970s; and Madeleine L'Engle continued publishing into the 1980s. Similarly, one of the supposedly more recent books discussed, Alan E. Nourse's *Raiders from the Rings*, was published in 1962. Both Louise Lawrence and Monica Hughes get two chapters apiece, one in part 2 and another in part 3. They are both admirable novelists, but it would have been preferable to include more authors rather than to cover the same two twice.

The editorial prefaces to each section are brief, generally summarizing the contents of each essay. More by way of introduction would have been useful—in particular, an editorial overview of the field, summarizing the developments in science fiction and in children's literature in this century and relating them to the development of science fiction for young readers.

In the absence of such an overview, the opening essay by Francis J. Molson on the Tom Swift books helps as a survey of the changes in the field over time. The Tom Swift books, ascribed to the pseudonymous "Victor Appleton" (actually a series of house authors), appeared in four series—1910–41, 1954–71, 1981–84, and 1991—so that it covers the whole history of science fiction for young readers in this century. This formulaic series of technological action-adventures evolved out of late nineteenth- and early twentieth-century dime novels and pulp magazines, but the publishers hoped that the hardcover form would earn the genre respectability among young readers. The series signaled the decline of the literary fairy tale and the rise of a new kind of literature for children, one that emphasized the wonders of science and technology. The characters were flat, the situations stock, and the style pedestrian, yet the books sold by the millions over the years. "Tom Swift ranks, along with Nancy Drew, Frank and Joe Hardy, the Merriwell Boys, and the Bobbsey Twins, among the most read and admired of heroes in popular juvenile fiction" (4). I devoured Tom Swift adventures as a child, because he was a boy genius, a young Tom Edison who always triumphed with new inventions and astonished the adult world. Molson accounts for the popularity of the Swift series on the grounds that readers could identify with the young hero and that the books eased the transition from childhood to adulthood, offering career guidance to future scientists and engineers in the process.

The first series died after Tom grew up and got married. Subsequent revivals reflected changing times. The second series coincided with the post–World War II "resurgence of interest in children's and young adult science fiction that had been precipitated by the 1947 publication of Robert A. Heinlein's *Rocket Ship Galileo*" (10). Now young Tom begins to experiment with atomic energy and to blast off into outer space. The third series, of the 1980s, is "the most imaginative in conception and execution" (15). Set mostly in a colony in outer space, it introduces a teenage heroine, who is Tom's equal in intelligence and daring, and a Native American computer programmer. The brief fourth series (consisting of only two volumes in 1991) "fell victim, it would seem, to its competition in film, on television, and in print" (17).

If Molson's article is the best in part 1, Elizabeth Anne Hull's on Asimov's science fiction for young readers is the weakest, wasting too much time on lengthy plot summaries. Sullivan's essay on "Heinlein's Juveniles" is well researched and explains the popularity and influence of these novels: "Heinlein's juveniles set a standard for young adult science fiction by which subsequent works may be judged" (21), in terms of both writing well and taking science seriously. Andre Norton's Magic series is science fantasy; I would like to have seen Roger C. Schlobin's discussion of Norton's science fiction emphasize the science rather than the fantasy. The discussion of Madeleine L'Engle, by M. Sarah Smedman, considers her work for both children and adults—realistic fiction, historical romance, and fantasy—examining her preoccupation with the theme of human love.

Part 2 deals primarily with more recent works, not part of action-adventure series, in which there is "an increase in attention to details of setting and nuances of theme" (83). Howard V. Hendrix gives a sensitive political analysis of Alan E. Nourse's young adult novel *Raiders of the Rings* as a text that appeared around the time of the Cuban Missile Crisis and the Bay of Pigs invasion and yet is able to convey a pacifist message in the guise of science fiction.

K. V. Bailey analyzes in detail how the novels of John Christopher present "landmarks of the passage from childhood to adolescence . . . through powerful image and metaphor" (110). Christopher allows young readers "to recognize and vicariously to explore features of their own country or planet by 'distancing' these features, placing them at an imaginative remove" (107). These distancing effects of science fiction often make it a safe, ideal vehicle for young readers to explore difficult personal, social, and political issues.

Millicent Lenz compares three novels dealing with "post-nuclear-catastrophe settings and adolescent male protagonists" (113): *Danger Quotient,* by Annabel and Edgar Johnson; *Fiskadoro,* by Denis Johnson; and *Riddley Walker,* by Russell Hoban. She examines their relationship to the Campbellian monomyth, with *Danger Quotient* endorsing "paternalistic values" (112) but *Riddley Walker,* at the other end of the spectrum, critiquing the monomyth and opting instead for a new, nonviolent way of being human.

Thom Dunn and Karl Hiller praise the novels of H. M. Hoover for scientific accuracy and realistic portraits of alienated youth who nevertheless "manage to find the strength to snatch the reins of power and establish a newer, freer world for themselves" (122). Although Hoover is well known in the field of children's literature, he is as yet unknown to scholars of science fiction.

Marilyn Fain Apseloff analyzes the novels of Louise Lawrence, the British writer for young adults, emphasizing that "what Lawrence leaves the reader with in most of her books is hope for a better life, on this world or on some other" (143).

J. R. Wytenbroek discusses the novels of Monica Hughes, which she sees as arguing for a balance between nature and technology and stressing "the importance of preserving our own humanity by moving closer to a more natural life-style that will help protect and maintain our environment while utilizing the real benefits of humanized technology" (154).

Part 2 closes with Patricia Harkins's essay on the development of the character Menolly in Anne McCaffrey's Harper Hall books: "Readers identify with, and learn from, her protagonist—a female hero whose quest for self-realization within her society succeeds against all odds" (165). All the essays in part 2 are well written, clear, and balanced treatments of the authors, demonstrating in particular how these novels raise contemporary issues concerning science, technology, and human values in a way that appeals to young readers even as it helps to educate them.

Part 3 contains essays by Raymond E. Jones and Judith N. Mitchell that explore specific novels by Monica Hughes and Louise Lawrence. But the most interesting essay in the volume is Joseph O. Milner's, which divides science fiction novels into two broad categories, depending upon their utopian ("meliorist") or dystopian ("Spenglerian") views of the future of humanity, history, and technology: "Humanity ascends or is naturally ruined; civilization moves toward utopia or caves in upon itself; science and its offspring, technology, are means by which we enlarge and perfect ourselves or they turn, like Dr. Frankenstein's famous monster, upon us" (194). He demonstrates this dichotomy in two popular television series, *Star Trek* (meliorist) and *Dr. Who* (Spenglerian) and in a number of science fiction novels for young adults. Milner goes beyond the single-text or single-author analysis of most of the essays in the volume and provides a useful framework for comparing a broad range of texts.

The volume ends with another fine essay by Millicent Lenz (the only contributor with two articles), this one on Raymond Briggs's satiric cartoon treatment of nuclear holocaust, *When the Wind Blows* (1982), analyzing it as a book that helps teach youngsters "how to think" and how to recognize the consequences of bad belief systems: "We can, through informed critiques of texts such as *When the Wind Blows*, help young people realize that ignorance and unexamined premises can have fatal consequences" (203).

This training in thinking may be the most fundamental value of science fiction for young readers: besides helping youngsters to grow up and to orient themselves amid the rapid, bewildering changes of our scientific and technological society, it can, through the distancing device of writing about other worlds, future times, and alien beings, help to stretch young imaginations and to teach them how to think about the world around them in fruitful new ways.

Sullivan's volume will help acquaint teachers, librarians, and parents with the unexpected depth and range of quality science fiction for young readers. These fictions are truly tools for growth in an increasingly complex world.

New Communities from the Margins

Jack Zipes

Leon Garfield, by Roni Natov. New York: Twayne, 1994.

Although he is among the most gifted of contemporary British writers for adolescents, Leon Garfield has not received ample recognition for his achievements. Now, however, thanks to the comprehensive and insightful monograph by Roni Natov, we can see the great diversity and sophistication of his work produced between 1964 and 1991.

Instead of introducing Garfield through a traditional biographical sketch, Natov begins her book with an interview she conducted with him at his home in Highgate, North London, in June 1989. This is a unique but dangerous approach to an author, because Garfield more or less sets the tone for Natov's interpretation of his work, thus influencing the reader's views of Natov's study. Nevertheless, it is a worthwhile gambit, for in the interview Garfield openly reveals the difficulties he experienced as a Jew growing up in Brighton during the 1920s and 1930s and recounts with candor familial problems and his years as a war-crimes investigator in Germany during World War II. Moreover, Garfield discusses his social concerns, his great admiration for Shakespeare, and his reasons for writing various books. In all, Garfield provides abundant and fascinating biographical material that enriches Natov's approach, as well as providing other perspectives for readers who might want to view Garfield in a manner different from Natov's.

In the seven chapters that follow, Natov continues to draw on this interview for background material, but she is more interested in how Garfield takes a major theme and explores it in unique ways in such different genres as parody, myth, the historical novel, the fairy tale, and the biblical story. For Natov, Garfield's major protagonists are often fractured individuals, "functioning within or expelled from a dysfunctional family that in turn reflects the larger disjointed world" (x). Regardless of whether Garfield is writing a sea adventure like *Jack Holborn* (1966), a Dickensian novel of social realism such as *Smith* (1967), the historical novels *The Prisoners of September* (1975) and *The*

Children's Literature 24, ed. Francelia Butler, R. H. W. Dillard, and Elizabeth Lennox Keyser (Yale University Press, © 1996 Hollins College).

Blewcoat Boy (1988), or ghost stories such as *Mister Corbett's Ghost* (1968) and *The Ghost Downstairs* (1972), Natov demonstrates that throughout he seeks to expose the social and psychological forces that drive people to the margins in order to point to some possibility for salvation. She sees Garfield as a postmodern writer, disturbed by the fragments and fissures in contemporary society, but one whose major project is to use the range of his art to overcome social disparities, injustice, and fragmentation.

Natov explores Garfield's major works in detail, revealing how he creates bonds between such disparate characters as Harris and Bostock, in *The Strange Affair of Adelaide Davis* (1971) and *Bostock and Harris; or, the Night of the Comet* (1979), in order to suggest the need for community and the restoration of justice. Through these bonds one may hope to offset the cruel indifference of a materialistic society that often leads to the exploitation and abandonment of children. The theme of hope emerges strongly in his rewriting of Greek myths, as in *The Golden Shadow* (1973), and in his revisionings of Bible stories like *The King in the Garden* (1984), as well as in his uncanny fairy tales such as *Guilt and Gingerbread* (1984) and *The Wedding Ghost* (1985). In all these works, Natov maintains, reality is heightened to create an intensified representation of ordinary life that enables us to understand contemporary social problems in relation to the literary themes he has chosen.

Toward the end of her book Natov suggests that Garfield has his own mythic view of how to bring about the salvation of the individual and society. She argues that "in *The Apprentices* (1978) and *The House of Cards* (1982), more than in any of his earlier writing, Garfield works social realism into a moral allegory of a new order. . . . Both books involve a visionary regrouping of basic social units; both evoke a new moral order in which high, middle, and low class can come together to form an expansive community that collapses the old class distinctions" (86). Interestingly, the desire for a new community can also be connected to the search for the father, apparent in *The Empty Sleeve* (1988) and *The Blewcoat Boy* (1989), but it is not the traditional patriarchal order that Garfield wants to reinstate. Natov makes clear that the people who will decide how to reorder society and endow it with a new morality will have to come in from the margins. That is, the poor, the criminal, and the young will have to be heard from within the center of society if there is to be such a thing as a new moral order.

There is no doubt that Garfield's vision, expressed through his re-creation of history and manifested in marginal characters, is a compelling one in contemporary literature for young readers, and Natov's study is a splendid analysis that amplifies this vision and gives Garfield's works the resonance they deserve.

Limitless Wonder of Story

Susan P. Bloom and Cathryn M. Mercier

The Zena Sutherland Lectures, 1983–1992, edited by Betsy Hearne. New York: Clarion, 1993.

The Arbuthnot Lectures, 1980–1989, edited by the Association for Library Service to Children. Chicago: American Library Association, 1990.

When Katherine Paterson tells the listener that she "want[s] to talk about story" (49), she sounds a theme that resonates in almost every lecture in this celebratory collection. Maurice Sendak's lecture strings together powerful anecdotes, stories that serve to inspire him; Robert Cormier tells a story about himself as an eleven-year-old boy destined to wear blue neckties for eternity in exchange for his mother's recovered health; Paula Fox chooses to tell stories about some of the brave children she has met; Trina Schart Hyman shares a story about Leonardo da Vinci. Underlying, and central to all this tale telling, is a fundamental belief in the power of story to illuminate and transform lives.

In her warm, generous-spirited introduction, Betsy Hearne speaks no less movingly about story as "mind-saver" (ix). She credits the ten writers and artists whose words grace this volume with changing lives through their visionary ability to craft narrative and art that matters. In sharing the genesis of the lectureship, Hearne acknowledges the inestimable role of the talented, committed Zena Sutherland, whose cogent criticism and ready encouragement provided the bedrock for some of the best work in children's literature. Like the legendary *Celebrating Children's Books: Essays on Children's Literature in Honor of Zena Sutherland,* this collection commemorates her unparalleled leadership.

The opening essay by Maurice Sendak, filled with his characteristic passion and wit, reintroduces childhood not as a haven of security and happiness but as a "grand and terrifying and mostly uncivilized country" (3). Its province provided Sendak his originative encounters

Children's Literature 24, ed. Francelia Butler, R. H. W. Dillard, and Elizabeth Lennox Keyser (Yale University Press, © 1996 Hollins College).

with death and loss, twin obsessions that inform much of his work. The young, impressionable Sendak was inspired by pleasures seen as well as pain felt. Collisions between the real and the imaginary, between art and life, continue to be the stuff that fuels Sendak's genius and that receives wry and poignant expansion in this inaugural essay.

Lloyd Alexander calls on his young Geraint to speak about the real and the imaginary. Meaningful sorcery, says the hero of "The True Enchanter," helps us "imagine these things [the birds, the flowers, the stars] to be more than what they are" (42). Alexander reminds us of the obligation of literature to illumine through artifice, to create the lie through which truth shines brightly. Katherine Paterson echoes Alexander's commitment to the imperative of art. In "Tell All the Truth, but Tell It Slant," Paterson turns to story for amelioration and healing. Paterson's clear, humane, impassioned voice proves the strongest defender of story as releasing the imprisoned child caught between "silence and the scream."

Virginia Hamilton continues powerful considerations of reality and illusion as she searches to create in her art the "best unreal world" (77). She challenges herself to tell the truth by always addressing the black experience rooted in struggle, in becoming, in change. Unafraid of the challenge, Hamilton follows a story's path, even into often dangerous terrain, knowing, like Paterson, that therein lies accident and surprise—liberating discovery and the possibility of "growing consciousness" (92). Robert Cormier risks the emotional costs of traveling to his younger days and sharing the formative impact of both his mother's renunciation of movie going and of his father's life and death. In "I, Too, Am the Cheese," Cormier reveals his vulnerable boy self as counterbalance to all those readers who know him as the creator of *The Chocolate War.*

Paula Fox documents, with crystalline precision, the bittersweet memories of her encounters with children whose fragile lives bespeak profound courage. Their stories expose the lie that children invariably lead happy lives and want happy endings. Her lecture, "Unquestioned Answers," addresses the empowerment of literature to heal by speaking truthfully and honestly about the unanswerable, the mysterious, and the unknowable. It is life's mysteries that challenge David Macaulay. Attempting to pin down the meaning of nonfiction in his essay "The Truth About Nonfiction" results in a devilishly witty Macaulay conundrum. He turns deeply serious, however, when he talks about seeing, about our need to remain curious, about the demand for visual and intellectual alertness.

Jean Fritz follows Macaulay with her "The Known and the Unknown: An Exploration into Nonfiction." Here story is central again, and Fritz attests to the importance of mystery and surprise with no less fervor and excitement than the inquirer Macaulay, the fantasist Alexander, or the realist Paterson. She approaches her material as "unexplored territory" (172), permitting the unexpected to enter in and, with a jolt of recognition and delight, keep her young reader engaged and awake.

Trina Schart Hyman eschews those illustrations whose slickness and detachment "leave no room for the grand gesture, the excitement or mystery of just plain humanity" (194). Hyman holds to the primacy of story, not only as the safekeeper of excitement and mystery but also as the essence of truthful expression. Hyman espouses a commitment to the nature of human frailty inherent in all art that reaches—and touches—its child audience.

Ever aware of audience, the final lecturer, Betsy Byars, catalogues different kinds of humor, cautioning that "Taking Humor Seriously" serves not only to balance life's gravity but also to give the child reader a sense of control. She concludes by quoting Stephen Leacock, who parodies Shakespeare: "Here, tears and laughter are joined, and our little life, incongruous and vain, is rounded with a smile" (226).

Being privy to the creative process of such talented artists in the field of children's literature, through their revelations and challenging insights, provokes deep thought and wonder. The range and depth of these lectures, lovingly gathered and graciously introduced together here, testifies to the health of children's literature. Their commonality is equally comforting: in honoring the story, we honor the child reader.

Even as this book honors Zena Sutherland, she turns her pen to praise another formative influence in the study of literature for children and young adults. In the opening biographical tribute of *The Arbuthnot Lectures, 1980–1989,* Zena Sutherland defines the far-reaching contributions that established May Hill Arbuthnot (1884–1969) as "an authority on literature for children" (iii). Arbuthnot's preeminent textbook, *Children and Books,* not only served as an introduction for students from the varied disciplines drawn to children's literature but also offered demanding literary and critical standards through which to evaluate the literature itself. Even as the textbook, now in its eighth edition, survives its original editor, it continues to describe an evolving canon of children's literature and to hold firmly to its own canonical position in any serious study of children's literature.

This impressive volume marks the second decade of the annual lecture, sponsored by Scott, Foresman and Company and administered by the Association for Library Service to Children, a division of the American Library Association, to honor the educational legacy of May Hill Arbuthnot. Once readers get past the graphically boring book jacket, the tight typeface, and overall unimaginative design, they will encounter the kind of original thought, informed opinion, seasoned experience, and wordcraft that challenge them to read carefully, to learn avariciously. Some perspectives articulated by the Arbuthnot Lecturers will cut against readers' grain, but these disagreements can be the whetstones against which readers sharpen their own critical skills.

The internationally diverse array of speakers included in this set of lectures covers topics that traverse the landscape of literature for children and young adults. Australian reading and literature advocate Dorothy Butler and German expatriate Fritz Eichenberg invoke a wider historical perspective through which to view their independent journeys as educators and writers. James Houston, a Canadian, and John Bierhorst, scholar of North and South American Native literatures, both speak of ethnic authenticity in joining traditional literature and contemporary audiences. Horst J. Kunze, a German bibliographer, and Virginia Betancourt, a Venezuelan librarian, combine history and cultural individuality to discuss emerging literatures. The American educator Leland B. Jacobs addresses the multiple voices of author and reader, of critic, parent, and teacher, of fancy, and of realism that ring throughout children's literature. Turning to the individual resonance of Mark Twain, British author and critic Aidan Chambers discusses *Huckleberry Finn* as the touchstone novel for young adults that "first captures and then captivates" (96) readers with its form, its truth, and its vision. Australian author Patricia Wrightson ponders her individual call to story and New Zealand author Margaret Mahy deals a generous dose of humor as she entertains "the possible operations of truth in children's books and the lives of children" (127).

This offering presents an eclectic feast of serious fare, carefully prepared and generously dispensed to be sampled and savored. Like any buffet, all dishes will fill, some will call for a second helping, and a few will linger on the palette with their subtle, complex blending of unique flavors. Horst J. Kunze's lecture contains abundant information presented with comprehensive scholarship, yet it reads dryly. Fritz Eichenberg and James Houston share their biographies as a way of tracing the personal odyssey of the artist—a valuable, but somewhat limited, understanding of the particular concerns and methods of the artist emerges. John Bierhorst, Dorothy Butler, and Virginia Betancourt achieve greater success transcending their personal interests and the idiosyncrasies of individual aesthetics to reach "universal themes that bridge the gaps between literature and between cultures" (125). Bierhorst and Butler translate from the spoken lecture to the written word with particular ease, demonstrating this book's "capacity to give . . . wings, to lift . . . from the here-and-now to a place of wonder" (38). Leland B. Jacobs and Aidan Chambers meld the tools of the formalist and the reader response critic as they examine "such matters [which] directly affect the potential impact of the literary creation on the reader" (47). Although both discussions challenge the reader to think thoroughly—and even magically—about the interactions/transactions between literature, the intermediary reader, and the intended (child/young adult) reader, Chambers gains tremendous impact from his focus on individual text. In featuring his experience of *Huckleberry Finn,* he chronicles with perspicacity and wisdom the reasons why this novel succeeds (and fails) in critical realms even as it triumphs as an entangling work of art: "Sooner or later, you realize you don't want to be free of it, after all, that you love it and find it inexhaustible, a constant source of pleasure, of surprise, and of sustenance: a breeding place of energy and thought" (96).

Patricia Wrightson shares this limitless wonder at story. She claims that because "writers happen, some of the time, to be on the transmitting rather than the receiving end" (71) of the story, they have the opportunity, the obligation, and perhaps even the vision to communicate wonder. Margaret Mahy does just that with insight, spirit, and humor in the concluding piece. She agrees that "there should be room in reality for wonder" (77) as she follows the precarious and discrete path of story. Mahy's lecture also stands as the culminating piece of this collection. From a recounting of her first reading, then sharing, then discussion of *Ballet Shoes,* by Noel Streatfeild, Mahy reaches an essential question for a children's book writer: "How much truth should we tell children?" (131). She uses personal anecdotes to reach universal understandings throughout the essay in which she speaks as reader, writer, critic, and practitioner. Above all, she composes a lecture bound by intertextuality and resonant in sounding the joyful notes of stories.

One Was Maurice . . .

Elizabeth N. Goodenough

Angels and Wild Things: The Archetypal Poetics of Maurice Sendak, by John Cech. University Park: Pennsylvania State University Press, 1995.

Although the 1890s are often seen as a period of nostalgic escape, during which the cult of the child reached a pinnacle of sentiment, childhood in the 1990s has become a last frontier, as brutal and bucolic as mythologies of the American West. Neil Postman and other social critics lamented the disappearance of childhood in the 1980s, but the exploitation of the child as a cultural motif underscores today how eagerly adults seek their wholeness through this liminal figure. As our sense of endangered nature becomes acute, children embody freedom, possibility, and primitivism; they provide perspective on what Gaston Bachelard calls "antecedence of being." Shortly after the Academy Awards celebrated the trusting heroism of Forrest Gump, who never forgot what his mama told him, the full horror of the Oklahoma bombing was telescoped for Americans by the limp body of a bloody infant pulled from the inferno. In the televised aftermath of this tragedy, adult mourners clutched teddy bears and recalled Janet Reno's ironic rationale for the raid of Waco—"to save the children." As we slouch toward the year 2000, futuristic fantasies of the mid-century (now veering toward ecological apocalypse) are less empowering than travels taken inside and backward to that time before time of fairy tales—like Robert Bly's *Iron John* (1990) and Clarissa Pinkola Estes's *Women Who Run with the Wolves* (1992)—or to an elusive and enigmatic private beginning like David Mamet's off-Broadway "Cryptogram," which dramatizes the emotional abuse of a ten-year-old from his own perspective.

An important prototype for such journeys is the astonishing and extended "confrontation with the unconscious" recorded by Carl Jung at age eighty-one in *Memories, Dreams, Reflections* (1961). Although Harvard researcher Richard Noll, in a recent *New York Times* article, called the Swiss psychologist "the most influential liar of the 20th century," accusing him of falsifying data in order to advance

Children's Literature 24, ed. Francelia Butler, R. H. W. Dillard, and Elizabeth Lennox Keyser (Yale University Press, © 1996 Hollins College).

his belief in the collective unconscious, Jung's 1941 essay "The Psychology of the Child Archetype" is useful in explaining the urgency of the "wounded child" and the suspense of "earth in the balance" to New Age spirituality. His insights, as John Cech's *Angels and Wild Things* demonstrates, are also remarkably helpful in accounting for the career of Maurice Sendak, the world-renowned children's illustrator, author, creative designer for opera, ballet, theatre, and film, and the founder of the national Night Kitchen Theatre for children. Having remapped the "emotional and visionary terrain of childhood" (7), Sendak has, like his "masters" William Blake and George MacDonald, expanded the boundaries of children's books and recast the child as a symbol of transformative energy.

Centering his engaging study on Sendak's literary children—Rosie, Pierre, Max, Mickey, Ida, Mili, Jack, and Guy, "children of the streets and of the clouds"—Cech situates this illustrator of more than eighty books and winner of both the Caldecott and the Hans Christian Andersen Medals within the cultural climate of the past four decades. He indicates how the sudden changes that distinguish Sendak's work grew out of "a mosaic of influences" that range from Mozart to Mickey Mouse and include the English illustrators, the "crappy toys" and "tinsel movies" of his youth, advertising slogans, brand names, and the social and political upheavals of the post–World War II era. Thus one finds in Sendak's various styles and juxtapositions a fusion of "the refined and the commercial, the polite and the populist, the stuff of comics and glitzy movies and the black and white, pen-and-inklines of the serenely classical" (3).

Cech's book as a whole focuses on the "eight essential works" over which the artist exercised complete control and locates the genesis of these projects in Sendak's self-described obsession and "great curiosity about childhood as a state of being": "how all children manage to get through childhood from one day to the next, how they defeat boredom, fear, pain, and anxiety and find joy. It is a constant miracle to me that children manage to grow up" (19). *Angels and Wild Things* shows how the four features Jung identified with the child archetype—abandonment, invincibility, hermaphroditic qualities, and the child as beginning and end—permeate Sendak's books as they deal with such once-taboo subjects as "explosive anger, frustration, the polymorphous realm of dream and psychosexual fantasy, intense sibling rivalry, existential angst, death" (7).

Cech's book builds on the growing body of academic criticism as well as on Sendak's collected writings on children's books and popular culture, *Caldecott & Co.* (1988), to move beyond Selma Lanes's reverential retrospective, *The Art of Maurice Sendak* (1980), and Amy Sonheim's Twayne survey, *Maurice Sendak* (1991). Cech aims to define the "complex ecology" of Sendak's imagination, to get at the "unique energy" or "soul" of his art. Its synthesizing, multifaceted approach is well-attuned to an illustrator who composes his sketches to music. Linking inner and outer realities, it animates the artist's former studio in Greenwich Village, his current one in Ridgefield, Connecticut, and the multilayered world in which he grew up in the 1930s and 1940s as the son of Polish Jews in the "melting pot neighborhoods" of Brooklyn. Then in a wide-ranging narrative, which often demonstrates a "Proustian unfolding" like the instances from the past it opens to view, it traces the familial thread that Sendak draws between Ida and Mili to connect all the fictional infants and children into an Ur-story of the author himself. Cech uses Rosie's evolution into a public performer, for example, to mirror Sendak's own "steady rise to stardom" (43). Sketchbook drawings of this Dead End Kid (1948) and the bleak realism of early drafts of *The Sign on Rosie's Door,* along with unpublished notes from the 1950s, provide striking contrast to Rosie's appearance in the book, which was finally published in 1960. And comparing these earlier incarnations with the increasingly confident, open, take-charge Rosie of the 1975 animated film (initiated after the creator had earned international recognition) and the 1982 Broadway musical "Really Rosie" illuminates how this artistic career germinated from inside. Sendak's undiminished popularity, the critical interest he attracts in his sixth decade, and the fresh directions his work is now taking are thus integrated with the survival, even the flourishing, of the Brooklyn child fantasist/artist/shaman within. Asked about his qualifications to direct a new production of *Peter Pan* at Sundance Institute, Sendak joked: "I still have an unruly and tiresome 4-year-old in me" (25).

The rounded perceptions and dynamic balance Cech lends his subject are especially apparent in chapter 4, a tour de force on "Max, Wild Things, and the Shadows of Childhood," which rightfully occupies the heart of the book. Arguing that the prophetic energy embodied in Max was for picture books the "aesthetic equivalent" of Igor Stravinsky's *Rite of Spring,* which revolutionized modern music in 1913, Cech sketches a moment when "the spirit of the times and the creative spirit of the artist were in complete harmony" and

together produced "a work that challenged its readers and other creators of picture books to fundamentally change" (110). Quoting Jean
Cocteau, Ursula Le Guin, and Anthony Storr, he compares Max's
"wild rumpus" to films and rock songs of the 1960s and 1970s, Jim
Henson's Muppets, and contemporary works by Ezra Jack Keats and
Dr. Seuss. Formulating the status of *Where the Wild Things Are* on
mythic grounds, he casts the book as a "living mythology" that did
not invent the monster fantasy—now a subgenre of picture books—
but reconnected juvenile literature with its roots in the American
literary tradition of the good bad boy, the feral child in Rudyard
Kipling and Edgar Rice Burroughs, and such ancient myths as Romu-
lus and Remus. Tracing the fantasy sketch "Where the Wild Horses
Are" (1955) to the "outrageous rage" that led Sendak into psychoanalysis and memories of his Brooklyn aunts and uncles ("for the
monsters *are* our relatives") and to the rituals and "necessary games"
that children perform, this chapter effectively celebrates fantasy as
healing and the spirit of the child as a guide to the unconscious.

As persuasive as the argument is that the Sendakian Child is father
to the Man, those resistant to the idea that myths are universal
and precultural will question whether Sendak's characters—variously
described as European, ugly, "little greenhorns just off the boat,"
"hurdy-gurdy, fantasy plagued kids"—draw on an archetypal child
that gives "a universal shape" to their concerns (93). In returning
to his own childhood, does Sendak "inevitably" take "adults back to
theirs" or make it "possible for children to fully claim their own"?
In a country this diverse, does he "help give American culture, from
the mid-1960s on, a way to perceive its early childhood" (6) or touch
everyone with his "universal reach" (5)? Sendak himself allows for
the child who hates his book and throws it in the trash. Like the
overused term *archetypal* (by which Jung refers to "essentially unconscious" phenomena that elude rational analysis), such claims seem at
odds with the subtle texture of this learned book, with its sensitivity
to etymological roots and verbal precision.

Cech's taste for language and psychological nuance is finally what
makes this book rich and satisfying to read. Consistently well written, it is packed with arresting allusions and vignettes that cause us to
rethink our cultural assumptions about childhood. Cech effectively
guides the reader through the last half century of American juvenile literature, theories of child development, and the influence of
ancient mythologies on Western art, science and religion. His digres-

sions on such topics as the Wild Boy of Aveyron and the child artist Hermes, the emergent tradition of fantasy in American culture, and the ancestral roots of the nineteenth-century chapbook and miniature are detailed yet concise. The index and extensive bibliography make such unassuming erudition readily accessible for the student and researcher.

Beyond getting permission to reprint illustrations, obvious problems arise when a writer tries to capture a celebrated contemporary in print. As Sendak told an interviewer in 1970, "You'll find me quite verbal but I lie a lot." Although a darker side of Sendak and his wily, quirky genius come through in the objects he has collected and in moments when he speaks for himself, this complex man is portrayed at times as a mythic character who slips easily behind the mask of the romantic artist. One is left wondering about his isolated life, his insomnia, his early heart attack, and his self-description as "a notoriously unhappy young man." Yet Cech's readiness to take on a subject who is still in the process of becoming may account for the powerful appeal the idea of the child generates throughout this volume, dropping, as George MacDonald put it, "out of the everywhere, into the here" (20).

Even if a work like *Hector Protector* leaves one cold, this study makes it possible to revisit the entire Sendak corpus and to appreciate its unusual resonance and coherence. The airborne Mickey of *In the Night Kitchen,* like his female counterpart in MacDonald's *The Light Princess,* may seem distantly related to the less buoyant vision of childhood offered in *Outside Over There* and *Dear Mili.* Yet Cech's Blakean focus on how art makes "instants hold eternities" and his attention to "timeless conditions in the lives of children" provide a unifying context for this discussion of the "baby-crazed decade" of the 1930s and the Lindbergh case, angelic putti of Renaissance and Romantic imagery, the changeling child of folktales, attitudes toward toddler nudity in Europe and America, and the representation of infant waifs with AIDS or malnutrition.

Jung stated that the appearance of the child in myth or dream prefigures future developments; in an individual's or a society's consciousness. This archetype, he noted, is "a personification of vital forces quite outside the limited range of our conscious mind. . . . It represents the strongest, the most ineluctable urge in every being, namely the urge to realize itself." John Cech first encountered Sendak in Francelia Butler's class at the University of Connecticut, where, as a young graduate student and recent father, he found a spirit entirely different from his graduate seminars (5). The brief inclusion of Cech's own identity theme effectively evokes the late 1960s, when *Where the Wild Things Are* was new and, "with *In the Night Kitchen* ready to make its appearance, anticipation was in the air, the same kind that crackled whenever the Beatles were about to release a new album" (5). Cech's fascination with an irreverent and hilarious children's writer adds yeast to the unusual mix that makes *Angels and Wild Things* a testimony to how an artist's work takes on a life of its own and, as Jung says, "outgrows him, like a child its mother" (20).

Finally one has to appreciate the style and immense care with which this book has been put together. Images ranging from an eighteenth-century view of alchemists stirring in their kitchen to King Nebuchadnezzar as a fifteenth-century wild man and a Winsor McCay comic strip complement ten color plates by Sendak and scores of his figures. The inclusion of so many unpublished drawings and preliminary designs along with an explanatory text provides a virtual exhibition catalog for the Sendak holdings at the Rosenbach Museum and Library in Philadelphia. Illustrations, large and small, at chapter openings and endings, are, like the well-chosen epigraphs for each chapter, wonderfully congruent with narrative. Together they reflect a passion worthy of Sendak's for the physical properties and visual possibilities of the book as artifact.

Works Cited

Smith, Denitia. "Scholar Who Says Jung Lied Is at War with Descendants." *New York Times,* June 3, 1995, p. 1.

Dissertations of Note

Compiled by Rachel Fordyce

Ahl, Sally Webb. "A Framework for Textual Analysis: A Plan for Studying the Representation of People in Children's Books." Vols. 1 and 2. Ph.D. diss. University of Kansas, 1992. 534 pp. DAI 54:1265A.

Ahl believes that children's books can "contribute to [the] development of constructive ideas, world views, feelings, values, and prosocial activity" and that this should be relevant to educators who believe that we need to understand our culturally pluralistic society. She develops a model to answer the question "How can [teachers, librarians, and others] discern the image explicitly given in the written text of an individual book and then translate that information into a form allowing sound comparison of various books without damaging the text's essential integrity or the language used therein?"

Azeriah, Ali. "Translated Children's Literature into Arabic: A Case Study of Translational Norms." Ph.D. diss. State University of New York at Binghamton, 1994. 440 pp. DAI 54:3017A.

Using linguistic, cultural, and literary norms, Azeriah shows that although translated literature "has played a significant part in the emergence and development of Arabic children's literature . . . [it] has not been fully integrated" for a variety of reasons: Arabic children's literature is a recent phenomenon, teachers and parents have not realized its significance, and the teaching of Islam is not dependent on reading. He believes that this situation will change with the emergence of a secular education system and that "the need for translated children's books and the [further] emergence of Arabic children's literature" will become apparent.

Berger, Paula Silverman. "Peter Pan as a Mythical Figure." Ph.D. diss. University of Chicago, 1994. 262 pp. DAI 55:422A.

Berger examines how Barrie used "themes, motifs, and characters of Greek mythology to create a magical, imaginary world in which his contemporary counterparts of the gods reenact the Greek myths in contemporary guise" in his play *Peter Pan.* She believes that Barrie "idealized and glorified childhood," much as Kenneth Grahame and E. Nesbit did. She also compares the play to Spielberg's remake of *Peter Pan,* Shakespeare's *A Midsummer Night's Dream,* Tchaikovsky's *Nutcracker,* Mozart's *The Magic Flute,* and Strauss's *Die Frau ohne Schatten.*

Brand, Patricia Petrus. "The Modern French Fairy Tale: Aspects of 'Le Merveilleux' in Ayme, Supervielle, Saint-Exupéry and Sabatier." Ph.D. diss. University of Colorado at Boulder, 1983. 208 pp. DAI 44:1468A.

Brand believes that the modern French fairy tale is essentially unchanged from its late seventeenth-century model, although each author has a unique way of combining fantasy with reality. This is the first study on the subject of twentieth-century French fairy tales.

Bustard, Anne Stuart. "The Nature of Children's Book Selection: A Study of First and Fifth Graders in a Bookstore." Ph.D. diss. University of Texas at Austin. 1993. 241 pp. DAI 54:4378A.

Bustard analyzes the behavior of children in child-only bookstores and finds that they "displayed complex interpretive strategies in interacting with storybooks, strategies that challenge mainstream assumptions about the nature of storybook reading practices."

Children's Literature 24, ed. Francelia Butler, R. H. W. Dillard, and Elizabeth Lennox Keyser (Yale University Press, © 1996 Hollins College).

Cain, Melissa Augustine. "Children's Functioning in the Pictorial Symbol System as Determined by Responses to a Wordless Picture Book." Ph.D. diss. University of Toledo. 1985. 225 pp. DAI 47:450A.

Cain tests Stewig's and Sinatra's hypothesis that "non-verbal experience and oral language are the true basics of literacy rather than reading and writing [since] reading and writing are dependent upon schemata acquired through those prior levels of coding." Although her study suggests the need for further research, her work does tend to support the hypothesis.

Canepa, Nancy Lucia. "From Court to Forest: Giambattista Basile's Lo cunto de li cunti and the Baroque Fairy Tale." Ph.D. diss. Yale University, 1992. 241 pp. DAI 53:827A.

Lo cunto de li cunti, 1634–1636, the first published literary version of the fairy tale in Western Europe, is examined from a cultural, social, and rhetorical perspective. Canepa examines Basile's discontent with court life, as reflected in the tales, and sees the seventeenth century as "a grand laboratory of rhetorical experimentation [with] metaphor its prime project." She finds his stories about "erotic desire and exchange" and deviant sexuality thematically interesting as "allegories of the potency of language" and concludes that the fairy tale "tells the story of a search for wholeness in an era when the certainties of the past are felt to be lacking"; hence the need for the hero to triumph over trials.

Chase, Laura Doster-Holbrook. "Social and Educational Values Regarding Women in Selected Literature for Young Readers in Nineteenth-Century Georgia." Ed.D. diss. University of Georgia, 1994. 466 pp. DAI 55:892A.

Chase analyzes books written by women for women and finds that the writers (and, by extension, the readers) "had far greater expectations concerning social and educational values than may have been imagined and saw their gender difference within [a] patriarchal society."

Cheevakumjorn, Boonsri. "An Analysis of Prosocial and Aggressive Content in Thai Children's Literature and Its Relationship to Contemporary Societal Problems in Thailand." Ph.D. diss. University of Oregon, 1993. 198 pp. DAI 54:3669A.

Cheevakumjorn examined one hundred books for four- to eight-year-olds to determine the amount of "prosocial and aggressive content in Thai children's books and how this content relates to societal problems in contemporary Thailand." He found 4.3 incidents of prosocial and 1.8 incidents of antisocial behavior in the books that illustrated aggressive behavior, which was sometimes punished, sometimes glamorized. He also found most males aggressive who rarely participated in constructive solutions to problems. Moreover, most stories take place in rural settings, unlike the normal environment of Thai children, and characters and plots lack "the depth that can nurture the development of moral judgment and self-identity."

Coburn, Sarah Elizabeth. "The Invasion of the Comedy Snatchers: Fantasy Sitcoms and Cultural Criticism." Ph.D. diss. Bowling Green State University, 1992. 206 pp. DAI 52:3759A.

In her attempt to determine a relevant critical methodology, Coburn analyzes television fantasy comedies, such as The Addams Family, Topper, Bewitched, Gilligan's Island, and The Munsters "in relation to their use of figures of cultural 'others' to critique American society."

Cusick, Edmund. "George MacDonald and Victorian Fantasy." D.Phil. diss. University of Oxford, 1988. 400 pp. DAI 53:816A.

In a comparative, analytical, and historical manner, Cusick discusses both MacDonald's fantasy writing and his "neglected" realistic writing. He gives particular attention to contemporary, frequently conflicting, theories of fantasy and the place of the unconscious in intepretation, and he contends that "by adopting Jungian models, the imagery of literary fantasy can fruitfully be compared to the recurrent images that emerge in dream series and in visions." He applies this interpretation to fantasy as well as realistic literature, while offering a detailed analysis of three "fantasy complexes" in MacDonald's work: leopards, wolves, and angels. Appended is a fantasy index that tabulates the occurrence of these three images. He also deals with images of castles and "women linked with the stars," comparing MacDonald to Poe, Bram Stoker, D. G. Rosetti, and H. Rider Haggard.

Czarnik, Marian Ellen. "The Victorian Novel as Children's Literature." Ph.D. diss. Indiana University, 1993. 303 pp. DAI 54:3445A.

Czarnik notes that the Brontës, Dickens, and Thackeray are of the first generation to be raised on "children's literature" (Evangelical tracts and stories based in part on fairy tales and Puritan writers) written by women who "introduced a narrative style—part sermon, part confession, and part catechism." She believes this is also an aspect of the writing of the three authors cited above. Although they criticized the Evangelicals, they also used many of their elements of style and content, so perhaps it is not surprising that the work of the Brontës, Dickens and, to a lesser extent, Thackeray is now classified as children's literature.

Drennon, Ann Hendon. "A Descriptive Analysis of Children's Realistic Fiction about Chronically Ill Children, 1970–1990." Ph.D. diss. Georgia State University, 1993. 229pp. DAI 54:4017A.

Fifty-two realistic works of fiction for children and about chronically ill children is the subject of Drennon's disseration. She analyzes realism, authenticity, believability, accuracy of medical information, character, plot, and theme and concludes that most of the works were "good quality realistic fiction"; and that teachers, librarians, and health care professionals should tap this source as they attempt to heighten the awareness and understanding of illness and eliminate stigmatization.

D'Uva, Michele. "Barthelme's 'Snow White,' Calvino's 'The Castle of Crossed Destinies' and Contemporary Discourse on the Fairy Tale: Feminist and Foucauldian Approaches." Ph.D. diss. State University of New York at Binghamton, 1992. 238pp. DAI 53:1901A.

By applying feminist literary theory, Foucauldian theories on discourse, and the work of Propp, Irigaray, Chodorow, and others to fairy tales, D'Uva discusses mother-daughter relations, beauty, and the "mechanisms that objectify, idealize and universalize fairy tale female characters." She is concerned primarily with how authors transform a children's fairy tale into an adult one.

Foehr, Regina Paxton. "Using the Simple to Teach the Complex: Teaching College Students to Interpret Complex Literature and to Write Literary Analysis Essays through Fairy Tales and Children's Stories." D.A. diss. Illinois State University, 1989. 204pp. DAI 50:2885A.

Using seventy-nine freshmen and two teachers, Foehr investigates whether or not using "simple, familiar literature [to build] on college students' prior knowledge could be a more effective means to teach college students to analyze, to interpret, and to write about more complex literature than using common traditional literature." Interestingly, she found that this approach had both an immediate and a sustained effect: the experimental group improved in its ability to abstract "beyond a complex story [in order] to identify a theme or universal truth of the story and support it with examples"; this group also improved its overall ability to write, as compared to the control group. There was no marked difference in their reading ability, however.

Fouts, Elizabeth Sue. "Young Survivors: A Study of Gender and Social Roles in Contemporary Spanish Children's Literature (1940–1990)." Ph.D. diss. University of Texas at Austin, 1993. 253 pp. DAI 54:1387A.

Fouts finds that young, contemporary protagonists in Spanish literature for children are "increasingly critical of their environments and willing to question conventional ideals." She stresses the changes in tone and attitude of Spanish books for children created after 1980. "Traditional settings are still frequently employed [but] authors of Spanish literature address contemporary narrative with innovative perspectives." Authors seem to emphasize the need for young protagonists, particularly female characters, to "forge for themselves."

Fox, Lynn Ann. "Multiple Perspectives for Decision-Making: The Development of Scales for Identifying Literature Selection Decision Perspectives." Ph.D. diss. Claremont Graduate School, 1994. 243 pp. DAI 54:3385A.

In a dissertation that is critical of guidelines from the *Standards for Evaluation of Instructional Materials with Respect to Social Content,* Fox proposes different criteria for identifying "significant issues about children's literature selection" and also develops "scales for assessing adults' decision perspectives for selecting children's literature."

Fraser-Molina, Maria Juana. "*Stories from the Plains,* by Horacio Quiroga: Marginal Lectures." ("*Cuentos de la Selva* de Horacio Quiroga: Lecturas Marginadas.") Ph.D. diss. University of North Carolina at Chapel Hill, 1993. 187 pp. DAI 54:3051A.

This work analyzes eight short stories by the Argentinean writer of children's literature, Horacio Quiroga. Fraser-Molina discusses the stories from the perspective of the literary traditions of Quiroga's times to determine the effect of theme on a child reader. She is especially concerned with "what type of pleasure the child-reader might feel when reading stories that contain violence" as well as with the phenomenon of different interpretations that the stories produce for child and adult readers.

Galbraith, Gretchen Ruth. "Negotiating Class and Gender through Children's Literature and Reading in Britain, 1870–1914." Ph.D. diss. Rutgers, The State University of New Jersey—New Brunswick, 1992. 346 pp. DAI 54:1065A.

Galbraith links the history of children's literature in Great Britain between 1870 and 1914 to the social history of childhood and discovers that "children's books, and the reading process itself," because of adult authors' class consciousness and value judgments, "were being used to maintain class and gender boundaries at a time when these boundaries were under siege." She stresses "the tensions between attempts to forge an image of a universally innocent and pure childhood and the realities of childhood divided by race, class and gender." She also examines the nostalgia, "cultural pessimism," and common vocabulary of Andrew Lang, Frances Hodgson Burnett, E. Nesbit, and the working- and middle-class autobiographers whose use of their memories of children's literature is mere "talk about family, class, gender, politics, and the construction of identity." Essentially their narratives are an affirmation of the adult's understanding of the world and his or her place in it rather than a commentary on a child's experiences of childhood.

Hannon, Patricia Ann. "Away from the Story: A Textual Comparison of Men and Women Writers of the Fairy Tale in Seventeenth Century France." Ph.D. diss. New York University, 1990. 229 pp. DAI 51:2036A.

Noting the preponderance of women writers of early (1690–1700) French fairy tales (66 percent), she compares and contrasts the tales of D'Aulnoy, Bernard, L'Héritier, and Murat with the tales of the male writers Le Noble, Mailly, and Perrault. Although both female and male authors write "masculine and feminine versions of identical tale types," women's tales are marked by reflexivity while men's tales show the "antithetical structures and generalizing statements" that "work to articulate a series of successive actions, thus adhering to the conventions of the fairy tale genre." Conversely, the reflexive works of women authors contain "*mise en abyme* and metanarrative addresses to the reader which interrupt narrative line by highlighting the role of the narrator and reader in the production of the text." In essence, women narrators emphasize the "fictionality" of their texts.

Harvey, Brenda Sue. "Children's Use of Fiction and Nonfiction Literature in a Kindergarten Classroom." Ph.D. diss. Ohio State University, 1993. 402 pp. DAI 54:4048A.

"The purposes of this study were to investigate the role of the teacher for facilitating children's meaning-making with fiction and nonfiction literature and to investigate children's literacy behaviors as they interacted with fiction and non-fiction literature" in a kindergarten situation. She found that the teacher was a powerful influence on how children perceived and understood literature and that the children tended to incorporate what had been read to them in their writing.

Hendler, Glenn Stewart. "Women, Boys, and the American Novel: Figuring the Mass Audience, 1850–1900." Ph.D. diss. Northwestern University, 1991. 196 pp. DAI 52:4329A.

Hendler contends that "mass-cultural texts construct and draw on affective bonds between reader and character, commonalities and differences across race, gender, and class, conventions of narrative and character that are particular to their genre and cultural expectations." He focuses on Alcott's *Work* and Twain's *The Adventures of Tom Sawyer,* minimizes some of the distinctions between mass culture and "genteel culture," and concludes that "the mass audience is an ideological construct, and that canonical and non-canonical fiction contributed equally to its construction."

Hensley, Charlotta Cook. "Andre Norton's Science Fiction and Fantasy, 1950–1979: An Introduction to the Topics of Philosophical Reflection, Imaginary Voyages and Future Prediction in Selected Books for Young Readers." Ph.D. diss. University of Colorado at Boulder, 1980. 240 pp. DAI 41:3580A.

In an attempt to rejuvenate and enhance Norton's reputation, Hensley analyzes forty-five of the Norton full-length science fiction and fantasy works for young readers based on three topics: "Philosophical Reflection, Imagery Voyages, and Future Prediction." She appraises Norton's definition of the human condition (a constant struggle for survival against social subjugation), her use of telepathic links between humans and animals, traditional mythological patterns, fourth- and fifth-dimensional journeys, and her "powerful narrative control," as well as her uses of anthropology, natural history, archaeology, legend, folklore, mythology, and religion.

Hinson, Robert Wayne. "The Image of Blacks in Fiction for Children and Young Adults Written by Southern Writers, 1955–1985." Ph.D. diss. The Union Institute, 1993. 124 pp. DAI 54:923A.

Hinson studies "the everyday lives of American characters" in the works of Southern writers for children and young adults written between 1955 and 1985. His hypotheses are that black characters of various socioeconomic strata were portrayed, after 1965, as belligerent, unfriendly, or abusive toward nonblack characters and that male and young adults exhibited this behavior more than older people. His hypotheses were not confirmed. However, his dissertation does indicate a need for a wider variety of approaches to the study of Southern writers; "the potential advantage of the use of Southern-produced literature in values clarification"; and the need for research about readers' response to Southern writers.

Hoffman, Laura Okey. "The Incidence of Literacy Images in Notable Children's Literature Published in the United States from 1971–1990." Ph.D. diss. Kansas State University, 1993. 136 pp. DAI 54:3976A.

Hoffman read 243 books to determine the frequency of images of literacy in literature for children, based on her analysis of "performative, functional, informational and epistemic" images of reading as well as "illustrations, environmental print, numeracy, and technologically or graphically aided literacy acts." Her study shows a marked increase of literacy images from 1971 to 1990. She also notes that only the ethnicity of minor characters in the books showed much change in the period covered.

Horton, Nancy Spence. "Young Adult Literature and Censorship: A Content Analysis of Seventy-Eight Young Adult Books." Ph.D. diss. University of North Texas, 1986. 125 pp. DAI 47:4038A.

Horton examined seventy-eight current books for young adults to determine whether or not they contained "items which are objectionable to would-be censors," for example, profanity (5,616 occurrences), violence (1,849), sex (3,174), drugs (4,171), and bad behavior that is condoned (489). She argues, in effect, for minimal censorship based on clear guidelines, because young adults need a wide variety of reading experiences to broaden their learning environment.

Hunter, Linda Sue. "The Influence of the Medium on Children's Comprehension of Narrative." Ph.D. diss. University of Illinois at Urbana-Champaign, 1991. 253 pp. DAI 52:3759A.

Hunter compares the difference between second and fourth graders in their comprehension of print media and audiovisual media. She finds that children exposed to audiovisual media tested better on "image order" in media but that children who read a story to themselves "performed better on measures of inferential comprehension." She concludes that since children perceive television as a much "easier" medium than reading, they may put fewer demands on their intellect when they watch TV.

Jackson-Underwood, Penelope Joan. "Authority and Rebellion: The GDR Kinderhoerspiel (1981–1990): Its Role and Place in German Radio Drama." Ph.D. diss. University of Tennessee, 1993. 425 pp. DAI 54:3451A.

Using a small sample of East German children's radio programming, Jackson-Underwood hopes to open its discussion up to serious scholarly study. She finds that the radio dramas are of high quality, particularly those produced by the Department of Children's Radio Drama at the Rundfunk RDR, and that the dramas merit more study—particularly from their inception in 1923 to the present.

Johnson, Georgia. "The False Promise of Pluralism in Children's Books: 1965–1975." Ph.D. diss. University of Utah, 1993. 130 pp. DAI 54:4083A.

Noting that the expectation for children's literature, following the Civil Rights Era (1965–1975), was that it would be "one of the sites of multicultural emphasis within the educational system," Johnson examines prize-winning books from this period "from the point of view of minority writers and critics." She finds that children's literature "is ideological and serves to silence dissonant voices."

Kamberelis, George Alan. "Tropes Are for Kids: Young Children's Developing Understanding and Use of Narrative, Scientific, and Poetic Written Discourse Genres." Ph.D. diss. University of Michigan, 1993. 442 pp. DAI 54:4379A.

Kamberelis studied children in kindergarten and first and second grade and found that they were much more knowledgeable about stories than about poems or science reports—probably because that is what they read most frequently and that is what their teachers talk about. As children grew older, however, their level of sophistication in all genres increased appreciably.

Keeling, Kara Kay. "'A Glorious Host': The Appropriation of Adult Literature for Children in the Nineteenth Century." Ph.D. diss. Indiana University, 1993. 255 pp. DAI 54:3447A.

Keeling closely analyzes three works that inspired books specifically for children: Bunyan's *Pilgrim's Progress,* Defoe's *Robinson Crusoe,* and Scott's *Ivanhoe.* She finds that these authors "did not consciously aim to inculcate values particularly for child readers [but] their books contained themes or used forms that other authors saw as useful vehicles for conveying to children national, patriotic, psychological, religious, and ethical values." She also notes that these stories appeal to children because their protagonists confront crises and provide "a clear moral framework" based on a progression from sin to salvation or redemption.

Klassen, Kenneth Guy. "The School of Nature: An Annotated Index of Writings on Nature in *St. Nicholas Magazine* during the Editorship of Mary Mapes Dodge, 1873–1905," vols. 1 and 2. Ph.D. diss. University of Kansas, 1989. 815 pp. DAI 51:1229A.

Klassen contends that Mary Mapes Dodge and the nature writing in *St. Nicholas Magazine* were strongly influenced by the thinking of the Greek philosophers, the Transcendentalists, and the field-study movement promoted by Louis Agassiz: "This position maintains that the direct experience of the natural world (sometimes referred to as gymnastic) occasions the philosophical passion of wonder, which in turn leads to poetic celebration and subsequent consideration of the immutable principles of causation." Klassen's dissertation also contains an index of authors, illustrators, article titles, and typefaces that appeared during Dodge's editorship.

Larson, Meredith Ann. "Children's Literature and Resistance: Responses to Power." Ph.D. diss. Washington State University, 1993. 182 pp. DAI 54:4379A.

Larson questions why students in junior high school who have the ability and optimal opportunity to read don't. She finds that "the students' behavior was explained by a sociological theory of resistance. Individuals resist social control when they perceive that control as based on a manipulation of power not authority."

Lesnik-Oberstein, Karin Beate. "Principles and Practice in Critical Theory: Children's Literature." Ph.D. diss. University of Bristol (United Kingdom), 1990. 243 pp. DAI 52:2915C.

Criticism of children's literature, Lesnik-Oberstein contends, can be discussed "in terms of the idea . . . that 'childhood' and the 'child' are not stable ontological concepts" but changing and variable narratives that operate in conjunction with the hierarchically dominant narratives of "adulthood" re Foucault, Derrida, Phillipe Aries, and Jacqueline Rose. She centers her discussion of criticism on the concept of child as reader while giving a history of children's literature criticism and an analysis of what distinguishes it from criticism of adult literature.

Liu, Mei-Ying. "Portrayals of the Chinese in Fiction for Children, 1925–1991." Ph.D. diss. Ohio State University, 1993. 228 pp. DAI 54:3032A.

Liu's purpose is to analyze how Chinese people are portrayed in children's literature published in the United States from 1925 to 1991 and to determine if there is any significant change in the portrayal and whether or not it is linked to such historical events as World War II or the Civil Rights Movement. She finds the images of Chinese surprisingly positive, even during the Korean War. Yet American readers might conclude from reading a typical text that modern China is like the "China in the early twentieth century, particularly from the 1920s to the 1940s" and that the Chinese people are mainly "Mandarin-speaking, economically poor, Han farmers with two-syllable names, living mainly on rice and wheat."

Lolo, Eduardo Calixto. "Hispanic Modernism and Children's Literature." ("Modernismo Y Literatura Infantil.") Vols. 1 and 2. Ph.D. diss. City University of New York, 1994. 621 pp. DAI 55:275A.

Lolo studies the "convergence" of children's literature and Modernismo (Hispanic Modernism) as a literary movement, focusing on three masterpieces: *La Edad de Oro* (1889), by Jose Marti, *Platero Y Yo* (1914), by Juan Ramon Jimenez, and *Cuentos de la Selva Para Ninos* (1918), by Horacio Quiroga. He also makes reference to Romanticism, Symbolism, Parnassianism, Expressionism, the Pre-Raphaelites, "and other turn-of-the-century aesthetic or literary movements." He believes that what makes the three works masterpieces is that they appeal to both children and adults and that this probably occurs because of the convergence of Modernismo with the "categoric requirements of children's literature."

Mistele, Linda Mae Heddle. "In My Father's House Are Many Rooms: A Study of Father-Daughter Relations in French and English Fairy Tales." Ph.D. diss. University of Wisconsin-Madison, 1993. 356 pp. DAI 54:3738A.

Mistele compares the fairy tales of male and female writers—Mme. d'Aulnoy with Charles Perrault, Flora Annie Steel with Joseph Jacobs—while employing the assumption that "writers inscribe in fairy tales exemplary models of behavior to socialize children and adults into desired normative expectations, and that gender roles influence these expectations." Both pairs of writers substantiate her assumption if one allows for differences in historical situations, the class of the characters, origins of the tales, and other socioeconomic, cultural, and moral considerations.

Nickolajeva, Maria. "The Magic Code: The Use of Magical Patterns in Fantasy for Children." Fil.Dr. diss. Stockholms Universitet (Sweden), 1988. 162 pp. DAI 49:534C.

Using a morphological approach and defining fantasy as "a narrative where two worlds, a real one and a magic one, are described, and where the magical elements are used as literary devices to connect the two worlds," Nickolajeva attempts to create a "typology of magical elements" in fantasy literature loosely based on their function in a narrative.

Odoms, Lilly J. "A Content Analysis Approach to the Depiction of the Elderly in Literature Books for Children Published between 1950–1966 and 1970–1985 for Grades Five through Eight." Ed.D. diss. Temple University, 1992. 119 pp. DAI 53:1393A.

Although Odoms found few significant differences in depictions of the elderly in the two periods she studied, she does note that elderly characters who have major roles make decisions and are "independent thinkers"—contrary to earlier portrayals of the elderly.

Oswald, Lori Jo. "Environmental and Animal Rights Ethics in Children's Realistic Animal Novels of Twentieth-Century North America." Ph.D. diss. University of Oregon, 1994. 273 pp. DAI 55:271A.

Using realistic novels for children and focusing on authors who explore animal rights in their novels, Oswald investigates three themes: "animal consciousness, human and animal relationships, and predators and prey." She divides authors into three periods: founders, traditionalists, and animal-rights writers. Typical authors are Seton, London, Roberts, Kjelgaard, Rawlings, O'Hara, Henry, Roy, Thomas, and Adler. Although founders are often viewed as anthropomorphic "nature fakers," she finds this inaccurate. Traditionalists "promote hunting, land development, and the utilitarian value of animals" while portraying predators as evil and disavowing an animal consciousness. Animal-rights authors promote ethics, disavow hunting and development, and espouse a human-animal bond. Paradoxically, "while the rhetorical purpose of the animal rights novels is ostensibly the didactic one of promoting animal rights, the subtexts do not support this theme." The founders, in fact, through strong plot, characterization, and depiction of human-animal relations, more clearly represent an animal-rights ethic.

Peck, Elizabeth Greed. "Children in American Fiction, 1830–1920: A Cultural Perspective and Annotated Bibliography." Ph.D. diss. University of Rhode Island, 1986. 249 pp. DAI 47:3040A.

Peck's essay and bibliography emphasize "the emergence and development of the child character in fictional works written by American authors between 1830 and 1920." She includes novels, novella, short stories, fictionalized autobiographies, and comic sketches.

Phillips, Anne Kathryn. "Domestic Transcendentalism in the Novels of Louisa May Alcott, Gene Stratton-Porter, and Jean Webster." Ph.D. diss. University of Connecticut, 1993. 231 pp. DAI 54:3750A.

Phillips believes that Alcott, Stratton-Porter, and Webster were all influenced by the Transcendental movement. "While the novelists retain an Emersonian insistence on individualism and a respect for the relationship between God, Nature, and humanity, they affirm the necessity of community over solitude."

Rahn, Suzanne. "The Expression of Religious and Political Concepts in Fantasy for Children." Ph.D. diss. University of Washington, 1986. 672 pp. DAI 47:3050A.

Rahn believes that one reason fantasy dominates children's literature is its ability to make abstract concepts accessible to children. It is, therefore, a natural vehicle for conveying religious and political ideas. She explores the work of Andersen, Ruskin, Hawthorne, Kipling, Lucy Clifford, E. Nesbit, Grahame, Potter, C. S. Lewis, and Eleanor Farjeon.

Rhedin, Ulla. "Picture Books: Towards a Theory." ("Bilderboken: Paa Vag Mot En Theori.") Fil.Dr. diss. Göteborgs Universitet, Sweden, 1993. 276 pp. DAI 55:342C.

Starting with a historical examination of the theory and criticism of picture books through the work of Caldecott and William Nicholson, Rhedin proposes three ways of analyzing these books: through "the concept of the illustrated text, the concept of the expanded or 'staged' text and the concept of the genuine picture book . . . where text and picture cooperate within a narrative synthesis." She also compares picture books to other multimedia, such as film, theatre, and comics, and argues that the modern "poetic-expressive" picture book is a "genuine art form" appealing to children and adults alike.

Riley, Michael O'Neal. "Introductory Interiors: The Development of L. Frank Baum's Imaginary World." Ph.D. diss. Emory University, 1988. 397 pp. DAI 49:1458A.

In a critical biography Riley shows why Baum's *The Wonderful Wizard of Oz* is "the first unquestionably American fantasy" and why Baum was uniquely qualified to write it: Baum created "a native brand of fantasy" because he possessed "the necessary qualities of imagination and vision, [and] . . . had extensive, first-hand knowledge of most of this country."

Rousell, Laura Margaret. "A Comprehensive Examination of Grief Themes in Young Children's Books." Ph.D. diss. University of Oregon, 1992. 228 pp. DAI 54:77A.

Rousell compares and contrasts professional literature on how children deal with grief and death with eighteen picture books for young children on the same subject. The dissertation describes the similarities between the two genres, although the picture books rarely deal directly with the subject and do not focus "on complicated grief issues that result from suicide, homicide, natural disasters, or the death of an abusive parent." She also includes a list of children's books that deal with "grief from a death that is congruent with professional grief literature."

Sakrison, Dale L. "Self-Selecting Literature: A Qualitative Study in a Sixth-Grade Classroom." Ed.D. diss. University of North Dakota, 1992. 311 pp. DAI 54:877A.

Sakrison examines reading preferences among sixth graders who were allowed to self-select their reading material. Of the 286 books chosen by fourteen students, the majority overwhelmingly chose realistic fiction. She found that slow readers tended to read above their level if allowed self-selection; good readers below or at. She also found that selection was usually based on personal preference and interest first, on book blurbs, peer recommendations next, and on opinions of teachers, parents, and siblings last.

Saul, E. Wendy. "The School Story in America, 1900–1940: A Socio-Historical Analysis of the Genre." Ph.D. diss. University of Wisconsin-Madison, 1981. 302 pp. DAI 42:3481A.

Saul's history of the school story focuses on the years 1900–40 but extends to *Tom Brown's School Days* and work by Elijah Kellogg, Susan Coolidge, and Frances Burnett. Predominantly she is concerned with school sports stories for boys, school associations of the books (Brahmin, Mass-Market, and Religious), rhetorical features and marketing strategies, and the class distinctions and ideologies put forth in the books.

Shu, Hangli. "Sex Role Socialization in Chinese and American Children's Books: A Comparative Study." Ph.D. diss. State University of New York, Buffalo, 1992. 280 pp. DAI 53:3102A.

Shu compares two hundred Chinese and American books published between 1984 and 1989 to qualitatively and quantitatively analyze "sex role socialization." He finds that females, both women and girls, are underrepresented in contemporary books, although Chinese women fair worse; that men are still stereotyped in books of both cultures—never do housework and so on; that Chinese girls are especially clichéd; and that "the content of American children's books is much closer to reality and gender equality than that of Chinese children's books." He also discusses publishing in both countries.

Sierra, Judy. "What Makes a Tale Tellable? Narrative and Memory Process." Ph.D. diss. University of California, Los Angeles, 1993. 254 pp. DAI 54:1050A.

Sierra writes that "contemporary literate storytellers [observe] that some tales can be learned and told easily using a memory technique which is not verbatim, while other tales require painstaking word-for-word memorization in order to guarantee retrieval in a performance situation." She tests the work of Mandler and Johnson against this observation, using four tales: "Wiley and the Hairy Man," "Molly Whuppie," "The Elephant's Child," and "The Ugly Duckling." She then attempts to correct Mandler and Johnson.

Slaughter, Timothy Roy. "Performing Arts for Children in Hawai'i: A History of Dance, Puppetry, and Theatre for Children from 1900 to 1990." Ph.D. diss. University of Hawaii, 1992. 595 pp. DAI 53:1732A.

Slaughter discusses the role of individuals and, after 1965, the state government in arts and cultural programs for children—a phenomenon that is particular to the twentieth century in Hawaii. He focuses on state legislation, fine-arts projects, a state Curriculum Center, the Honolulu Theatre for Youth, Manoa's Theatre for Children, the Maui Academy of Performing Arts, the Artist-in-the Schools program, and the effect of cuts in federal spending on the arts.

Snyder, Nancy Karen. "A Cognitive Analysis of Concept Books." Ph.D. diss. University of North Carolina at Chapel Hill, 1993. 214 pp. DAI 54:4381A.

Snyder samples 197 children's books to determine the makeup of a concept book and finds that most do not meet any standard model for well-structured expository text; that they suffer from lack of cohesion and thoughtful content; and that "information included in almost three-quarters of the sample of concept books was as loosely connected as most shopping lists."

Speckels, Judith Marion. "Kiddy Lit. 995: A Linguistic Analysis of Selected Beginning Reading Texts." Ph.D. diss. University of Michigan, 1993. 134 pp. DAI 54:4078A.

"This dissertation proposes that text analysis be used as an alternative, and more substantive, method to study beginning reading books." Speckels concentrates on nursery rhymes, a fairy tale, a "See Dick Run"–type text, and "a story with a lot of grammatical words and embedded language" in it. She concludes with dos and don'ts for publishers of beginning reading material.

Su, I-Wen. "A Content Analysis of Cross-Cultural Interaction Patterns of Chinese-Americans in Selected Realistic Fiction for Children Ages 8 through 12." Ph.D. diss. University of Florida, 1991. 242 pp. DAI 53:429A.

Su analyzes six aspects of children's fiction that deal with Chinese Americans: frequency of crosscultural interaction; demographic information; basic stylistic attributes; values and behaviors of Chinese Americans and "problems they encounter in their interactions within their own culture and interactions with other ethnic characters"; and incidences of real and stereotyped portrayal. Analysis shows that integration was emphasized in the books and that "positive influences" affected both Chinese Americans and non-Chinese Americans, even though race and culture are still obstacles to the portrayal of sound realistic fiction. "While not all of the stereotypes were negative, their overpresentation might convey inaccurate messages about Chinese Americans."

Thomas, Jimmie Elaine. "The Once and Present King: A Study of the World View Revealed in Contemporary Arthurian Adaptations." Ph.D. diss. University of Arkansas, 1982. 200 pp. DAI 43:3316A.

Thomas discusses "the perennial fascination of the Arthurian Legend" and its manifestation after World War II. He deals primarily with T. H. White's *Once and Future King* and *The Book of Merlyn;* John Steinbeck's *The Acts of King Arthur and His Noble Knights;* and Mary Stewart's *The Crystal Cave, The Hollow Hills,* and *The Last Enchantment.*

Tucker, Brenda L. "A Content Analysis of the Black Experience and the African American Family in Children's Literature." Ed.D. diss. Temple University, 1994. 96 pp. DAI 55:958A.

Tucker examines thirty books in terms of demographics, personal relationships of characters, family values, community support, and the "Black experience" to see if attitudes toward African Americans have changed in the last decade. She does find changes that "seem to reflect the African American family."

Unterholzer, Carmen. "On the Phantom of Sexlessness: The Fixation of Traditional (Fatherly) Feminine Visions in Contemporary Children's Literature." (Vom Phantasma der Geschlechtslosigkeit: Zur Festschreibung her(r)kömmlicher Weiblichkeitsmuster in der modernen Kinderliteratur) Dr.Phil. diss. Innsbruck University, Austria, 1989. 282 pp. DAI 53:400C.

Using feminist theory Unterholzer examines twenty-three award-winning books "to identify four different images of femininity on a primarily semantic level." These images include women who lack authentic feelings; who espouse "patriarchal ideology"; who lack identity or sexuality; and "utopian women represented either by girls or by grandmothers." She is especially interested in how misogyny is an outcome of linguistic and literary devices. She attempts to show each image "as differentiated as possible by also presenting possible motivations behind the production of such patriarchal stereotypes of womanhood and by describing the implications of their meaning and operation within a larger social context."

Watson, Kathryn Danelle. "The Reviewing of Canadian Juvenile Trade Books as Listed in *Canadianna* 1988 through 1990 in Four Selected American Journals 1988 through 1992." Ph.D. diss. University of Alabama, 1992. 224 pp. DAI 55:1407A.

Watson finds that Canadian "juvenile trade books" were far more likely to get reviewed if they were published jointly in Canada and the United States and that American journals and other print media that publish reviews are not a good source of information about Canadian children's literature.

Weir, Marjorie N. "Inside the Ring: Victorian and Edwardian Fantasy for Children." Ph.D. diss. Simon Fraser University (Canada), 1989. 248 pp. DAI 53:165A.

Weir believes that many Victorian and Edwardian children's fantasies pose "a mythic universality which is as potent for the adult as for the child reader," possibly because the authors, such as George MacDonald, Beatrix Potter, Rudyard Kipling, James Barrie, and Charles Dodgson, used their work as a refuge to express "private realities": to communicate ideas and emotions subversive to the religious, intellectual, and social consensus" of their period. Because "the universal longing to remain in the golden world of childhood" is at the heart of the work of these five writers and because they grapple with "the impossibility of fulfillment of this desire [their work] imparts a sense of the tragic which renders the stories 'true for everyone.'"

Willhite, Gary Lynn. "Slaying Giants: Values, Morals and Fairy Tales at the Secondary Level." Ph.D. diss. Kansas State University, 1992. 251 pp. DAI 53:3164A.

Willhite attempts to determine whether or not teaching fairy tales at the secondary level inculcates moral and ethical learning. He recommends that "fairy tales can and should be used in teaching units at the secondary level as a means of teaching more complex reasoning concerning moral and ethical values."

Williams, Elizabeth Detering. "The Fairy Tales of Madame d'Aulnoy." Ph.D. diss. Rice University, 1982. 297 pp. DAI 43:465–66A.

In a detailed analysis of D'Aulnoy's *Contes des fées* and *Nouveaux Contes de fées,* Williams finds that "the popularity of the fairy tale genre was due to three factors: an existing belief in the *merveilleux,* popular literary tradition, and a number of historical, economic, and social factors." Williams also believes that d'Aulnoy's tales are more a product of contemporary prose fiction than the fairy tale genre; that love is a significant theme in the *contes*—an outgrowth of the nouvelle/roman tradition; and that travel, utopias, the character of animals, nature "as a courtier at Versailles would know it," magic, enchantment, and metamorphosis are significant themes. D'Aulnoy also employs a variety of literary techniques: "characterization through names, descriptions, and some psychology; humor and irony; a rapid and familiar style; realistic details," and structure are significant.

Williams, Helen Elizabeth. "The Image of Whites in Fiction for Children and Young Adults Written by Black Writers, 1945–1975." Ph.D. diss. University of Wisconsin–Madison, 1983. 139 pp. DAI 43:3915A.

Although Williams's study is not conclusive, she particularly notes in the books she analyzes the "12:1 representation of male to female characters in major roles" and that college-educated whites were more socially friendly with nonwhites than less educated whites.

Wilson, Anita Carol. "Literary Criticism of Children's Literature in Mid-Victorian England." Ph.D. diss. State University of New York at Stony Brook, 1981. 385 pp. DAI 42:4836A.

Using reviews from the *Examiner,* the *Spectator,* the *Quarterly Review, Fraser's Magazine,* the *Gentleman's Magazine, Household Words,* and *All the Year Round,* Wilson analyzes critical essays about children's literature from 1839 through 1865, the period when didacticism was being honed out of children's books. Criticism mirrored the books in that it became increasingly complex, because there was "the need to assess children's books simultaneously as literature, as entertainment, and as expressions of moral and religious beliefs." Critics and reviewers "did not encourage the smuggling in of moral messages under the guise of superficial entertainment, but sought a genuinely organic relationship between story and moral." Most criticism was a "protest against" typical literature for children.

Zobairi, Nillofur K. "Multicultural Literature in the Primary Curriculum: A Survey of Themes, Values and Goals." Ph.D. diss. Southern Illinois University at Carbondale, 1993. 413 pp. DAI 54:2879A.

Zobairi explores the effect of multicultural literature and a pluralistic approach to literature to determine their effect on young children's attitudes in terms of universal choices, change, the environment, human struggle, and intercultural-interreligious issues. The work contains an annotated bibliography that illustrates that "diversity and excellence are being promoted in multicultural literature."

Also of Note

Allen, Shelley Hooper. "Literature Group Discussions in Elementary Classrooms: Studies of Three Teachers and Their Students." Ph.D. diss. Ohio State University, 1994. 348 pp. DAI 55:1494A.

Anderson, Dianna Dillon. "The 1993 Basals Versus the 1987 Versions: Examining Four Reading Series for the Proportion of Literature-Based Stories, Adaptions, and Award-Winning Literature." Ph.D. diss. Texas A&M University, 1994. 83 pp. DAI 55:1886A.

 There were significant differences.

Anderson, Mary Ellen. "Young Audiences: The St. Louis Chapter, 1958–1988." Ed.D. diss. Saint Louis University, 1993. 283 pp. DAI 54:2500A.

Ballenger, Cynthia. "Language and Literacy in a Haitian Preschool: A Perspective from Teacher-Research." Ph.D. diss. Boston University, 1994. 181 pp. DAI 54:842A.

 An ethnographic study that attempts "to integrate sociolinguistic theory with contextualized accounts of classroom learning."

Battle, Jennifer Lee. "The Collaborative Nature of Language Learning and Meaning Making in Mexican American Bilingual Kindergartners' Storybook Discussions." Ph.D. diss. University of Texas at Austin, 1994. 318 pp. DAI 55:1511A.

Beger, Lois Lee Stewart. "John Donahue and the Children's Theatre Company and School of Minneapolis, 1961–1978." Ph.D. diss. Florida State University, 1985. 444 pp. DAI 47:21A.

Berger, Donald P. "*Shoka* and *Doyo:* Songs of an Educational Policy and Children's Song Movement of Japan, 1910–1926." Ph.D. diss. Kent State University, 1991. 632 pp. DAI 53:11A.

Berger, Paula Silverman. "Peter Pan as a Mythical Figure." Ph.D. diss. University of Chicago, 1994. 262 pp. DAI 55:422A.

Blenkinsop, Sandra Jean. "Children's Acquisition of Classroom Literacy Experience." Ph.D. diss. University of Oregon, 1993. 311 pp. DAI 54:3660A.

Brauner, Sigrid Maria. "Frightened Shrews and Fearless Wives: The Concept of the Witch in Early Modern German Texts (1487–1560)." Ph.D. diss. University of California, Berkeley, 1989. 441 pp. DAI 51:1625A.

Clifton, Nichole. "Kynde Innocence: Children in Old French and Middle English Romance." Ph.D. diss. Cornell University, 1993. 293 pp. DAI 54:4085A.

Connolly, Paula T. "Giving Testimony: Social Reform and the Politics of Voice in Nineteenth-Century American Texts." Ph.D. diss. University of Massachusetts, 1991. 278 pp. DAI 52:2142A.

 Connolly deals with Louisa May Alcott, particularly *Work.*

Cross, Linda Butcher. "Narrative Styles of African-American Children: The Effects of SES and Reading Stories to Children." Ph.D. diss. University of Maryland, College Park, 1993. 127 pp. DAI 54:3690A.

Detemple, Jeanne McLean. "Book Reading Styles of Low-Income Mothers with Preschoolers and Children's Later Literacy Skills." Ed.D. diss. Harvard University, 1994. 154 pp. DAI 55:1817A.

Flint-Ferguson, Janis Deane. "Putting the Pieces Together: Designing a Language Arts Curriculum That Meets the Needs of the Young Adolescent." D.A. diss. Illinois State University, 1993. 207 pp. DAI 55:38A.

Gardiner-Scott, Tanya Jane. "Mervyn Peake: The Evolution of a Dark Romantic." Ph.D. diss. University of Toronto (Canada), 1986. n.p. DAI 48:2879A.

Halpern, Pamela Ann Pandolfo. "The Effects of Enhancing the Mathematics in Children's Trade Books." Ph.D. diss. Boston College, 1993. 245 pp. DAI 55:235A.

Hare, Delmas Edwin. "In This Land There Be Dragons: Carl G. Jung, Ursula K. Le

Guin, and Narrative Prose Fantasy." Ph.D. diss. Emory University, 1982. 231 pp. DAI 43:165–66A.

The primary Le Guin text is *The Wizard of Earthsea.*

Labbo, Linda Day. "Negotiating the Path between Story Time and Young Children's Literacy Development." Ph.D. diss. University of Texas at Austin, 1993. 184 pp. DAI 54:2881A.

Lambert, Jane Gomillion. "How Children View Literacy." Ph.D. diss. University of Southern California, 1992. 183 pp. DAI 54:1217A.

Leith, Rena Margaret. "The Voice of the Book and the Voice of the Child: Whole Language as Poststructuralist Literary Theory." Ph.D. diss. University of Arizona, 1993. 186 pp. DAI 54:3691A.

"This dissertation explores the characteristics of a literary theory that recognizes the difference between children's and adult culture, the consequent youthism, and the need for ecological validity within the context of children's culture."

Leonard, Bonnie Herrmann. "Marie de France and the Poetics of Translation." Ph.D. diss. University of Pennsylvania, 1993. 214 pp. DAI 54:4436A.

Leonard deals with Marie de France's *Fables,* among other texts.

Libscomb, Luci Ann. "Recreational Reading and Its Effects on the Reading Achievement of First through Third Graders." Ph.D. diss. University of Texas at Austin, 1993. 158 pp. DAI 54:2966A.

McCollister, Deborah Hart. " 'Lords of (Her) Creation: Men in the Adult Bildungsromane of Louisa May Alcott." Ph.D. diss. University of Mississippi, 1992. 191 pp. DAI 54:178–79A.

Maragou, Helene. "Re-Defining an American Myth: Louisa May Alcott's Fiction for Adults." Ph.D. diss. University of North Carolina, Chapel Hill, 1993. 201 pp. DAI 54:1366A.

Martin-Smith, Alistair. "Drama as Transformation: A Conceptual Change in the Teaching of Drama in Education." Ph.D. diss. University of Toronto, 1993. 282 pp. DAI 54:3300A.

Mullarkey, Susan F. "The Adjunctive Use of the Developmental Role of Bibliotherapy in the Classroom: A Study of the Effectiveness of Selected Adolescent Novels in Facilitating Self-Discovery in Tenth Graders." Ed.D. diss. Ball State University, 1987. 280 pp. DAI 48:857A.

Nissel, Marva J. Goldstein. "The Oral Responses of Three Fourth Graders to Realistic Fiction and Fantasy." Ph.D. diss. Fordham University, 1987. 211 pp. DAI 48:857A.

Repka, Patricia Lee. "Search for Inner Peace: Louisa May Alcott and Duty." Ph.D. diss. Texas A&M University, 1991. 209 pp. DAI 53:153A.

Repka deals primarily with Alcott's fiction for adults.

Rigsby, Mary Bortnyk. "Margaret Fuller's Feminist Aesthetic: A Critique of Emersonian Idealism in the Works of Fuller, Alcott, Stowe, and Freeman." Ph.D. diss. Temple University, 1992. 352 pp. DAI 52:3285A.

Rohner, Janet Sue. "The One-to-One Read-Aloud Experiences and Literacy Development of Three Kindergarten Children At-Risk for Literacy Development." Ph.D. diss. University of Iowa, 1993. 493 pp. DAI 55:465A.

Rusch-Feja, Diann Dorothy. "The Portrayal of the Maturation Process of Girl Figures in Selected Tales of the Brothers Grimm." Ph.D. diss. State University of New York at Buffalo, 1986. 492 pp. DAI 47:4093A.

Rusch-Feja believes that one of the aspects of the Grimms' writing that makes it endure is its "importance as [a transmitter] of symbolic structures and content in the portrayal of female maturation."

Sampson, Mary Beth. "The Writing Behavior Portrayed by Selected Children's Books, Basal Readers, and Classroom Teachers." Ed.D. diss. East Texas State University, 1990. 149 pp. DAI 52:452A.

an anthology of imitations and parodies of *Alice's Adventures in Wonderland* and is currently completing a critical book about this phenomenon.

JOSEPH STANTON is director of the Center for Arts and Humanities at the University of Hawaii at Manoa. His essays on literature and the visual arts appear in such places as *Art Criticism, Journal of American Culture, Soundings,* and *The Lion and the Unicorn.* He has recent poems in *Poetry, Yankee, Poetry East,* and *Harvard Review.* He has published numerous textbooks and one volume of verse and is currently writing a book on Winslow Homer.

JON C. STOTT, professor of English at the University of Alberta and first president of the Children's Literature Association, is currently working on a book about the presentation of traditional Native cultures and myths in children's literature.

HILARY THOMPSON teaches courses in children's literature and children's theater at Acadia University, in Wolfville, Nova Scotia. She has written other articles on Thomas and John Bewick for the *ChLA Quarterly* (Winter 1995) and *Word and Image* (Oct.– Dec. 1994). Her work on Canadian children's literature includes articles on Elizabeth Cleaver and the poet Elizabeth Roberts MacDonald.

WILLIAM F. TOUPONCE is associate professor of English at Indiana University–Purdue University at Indianapolis. He has published critical studies of Frank Herbert and Ray Bradbury as well as articles on literary theory and criticism. His most recently published book was on Isaac Asimov (G. K. Hall, 1991). He is presently at work on a study of how children's books define the notion of literary pleasure.

JACK ZIPES is the author of numerous books about fairy tales, most recently of *Fairy Tale as Myth, Myth as Fairy Tale* and *The Outspoken Princess and the Gentle Knight.* He teaches German at the University of Minnesota in Minneapolis.

Award Applications

The article award committee of the Children's Literature Association publishes a bibliography of the year's work in children's literature in the *Children's Literature Association Quarterly* and selects the year's best critical articles. For pertinent articles that have appeared in a collection of essays or journal other than one devoted to children's literature, please send a photocopy or offprint with the correct citation and your address written on the first page to Gillian Adams, 5906 Fairlane Drive, Austin, Tex. 78731. Papers will be acknowledged and returned if return postage is enclosed. The annual deadline is May 1.

The Phoenix Award is given for a book first published twenty years earlier that did not win a major award but has passed the test of time and is deemed to be of high literary quality. Send nominations to Alethea Helbig, 3640 Eli Road, Ann Arbor, Mich. 48104.

The Children's Literature Association offers three annual research grants. The Margaret P. Esmonde Memorial Scholarship offers $500 for criticism and original works in the areas of fantasy or science fiction for children or adolescents by beginning scholars, including graduate students, instructors, and assistant professors. Research Fellowships are awards ranging from $250 to $1,000 (the number and amount of awards are based on the number and needs of winning applicants) for criticism or original scholarship leading to a significant publication. Recipients must have postdoctoral or equivalent professional standing. Awards may be used for transportation, living expenses, materials, and supplies but not for obtaining advanced degrees, for creative writing, textbook writing, or pedagogical purposes. The Weston Woods Media Scholarship awards $1,000 and free use of the Weston Woods studios to encourage investigation of the elements and techniques that contribute to successfully adapting children's literature to film or recording or to developing materials for television and video. For full application guidelines on all three grants, write the Children's Literature Association, c/o Marianne Gessner, 22 Harvest Lane, Battle Creek, Mich. 49015. The annual deadline for these awards is February 1.

Order Form   Yale University Press
P.O. Box 209040, New Haven, CT 06520-9040
Phone orders 1-800-YUP-READ (U.S. and Canada)

Customers in the United States and Canada may photocopy this form and use it for ordering all volumes of **Children's Literature** available from Yale University Press. Individuals are asked to pay in advance. We honor both MasterCard and VISA. Checks should be made payable to Yale University Press.

The prices given are 1996 list prices for the United States and are subject to change. A shipping charge of $3.50 for the U.S. and $5.00 for Canada is to be added to each order, and Connecticut residents must pay a sales tax of 6 percent.

Qty.	Volume	Price	Total amount	Qty.	Volume	Price	Total amount
___	10 (cloth)	$45.00	_____	___	19 (cloth)	$45.00	_____
___	11 (cloth)	$45.00	_____	___	19 (paper)	$16.00	_____
___	12 (cloth)	$45.00	_____	___	20 (cloth)	$45.00	_____
___	13 (cloth)	$45.00	_____	___	20 (paper)	$16.00	_____
___	14 (cloth)	$45.00	_____	___	21 (cloth)	$45.00	_____
___	15 (cloth)	$45.00	_____	___	21 (paper)	$16.00	_____
___	15 (paper)	$16.00	_____	___	22 (cloth)	$45.00	_____
___	16 (paper)	$16.00	_____	___	22 (paper)	$16.00	_____
___	17 (cloth)	$45.00	_____	___	23 (cloth)	$45.00	_____
___	17 (paper)	$16.00	_____	___	23 (paper)	$16.00	_____
___	18 (cloth)	$45.00	_____	___	24 (cloth)	$45.00	_____
___	18 (paper)	$16.00	_____	___	24 (paper)	$16.00	_____

Payment of $_____ is enclosed (including sales tax if applicable).

MasterCard no. _____

4-digit bank no. _____ Expiration date _____

VISA no. _____ Expiration date _____

Signature _____

SHIP TO: _____

See the next page for ordering issues from Yale University Press, London.

Volumes 1–7 of **Children's Literature** can be obtained directly from John C. Wandell, The Children's Literature Foundation, P.O. Box 370, Windham Center, Conn. 06280.

Order Form   Yale University Press, 23 Pond Street, Hampstead, London NW3 2PN, England

Customers in the United Kingdom, Europe, and the British Commonwealth may photocopy this form and use it for ordering all volumes of **Children's Literature** available from Yale University Press. Individuals are asked to pay in advance. We honour Access, VISA, and American Express accounts. Cheques should be made payable to Yale University Press.

The prices given are 1996 list prices for the United Kingdom and are subject to change. A post and packing charge of £1.95 is to be added to each order.

Qty.	Volume	Price	Total amount	Qty.	Volume	Price	Total amount
___	8 (cloth)	£40.00	_____	___	16 (paper)	£14.95	_____
___	8 (paper)	£14.95	_____	___	17 (cloth)	£40.00	_____
___	9 (cloth)	£40.00	_____	___	17 (paper)	£14.95	_____
___	9 (paper)	£14.95	_____	___	18 (cloth)	£40.00	_____
___	10 (cloth)	£40.00	_____	___	18 (paper)	£14.95	_____
___	11 (cloth)	£40.00	_____	___	19 (cloth)	£40.00	_____
___	11 (paper)	£14.95	_____	___	19 (paper)	£14.95	_____
___	12 (cloth)	£40.00	_____	___	20 (paper)	£14.95	_____
___	12 (paper)	£14.95	_____	___	21 (paper)	£14.95	_____
___	13 (cloth)	£40.00	_____	___	22 (cloth)	£40.00	_____
___	13 (paper)	£14.95	_____	___	22 (paper)	£14.95	_____
___	14 (cloth)	£40.00	_____	___	23 (cloth)	£40.00	_____
___	14 (paper)	£14.95	_____	___	23 (paper)	£14.95	_____
___	15 (cloth)	£40.00	_____	___	24 (cloth)	£40.00	_____
___	15 (paper)	£14.95	_____	___	24 (paper)	£14.95	_____

Payment of £_____ is enclosed.

Please debit my Access/VISA/American Express account no. _____

Expiry date _____

Signature _____ Name _____

Address _____

See the previous page for ordering issues from Yale University Press, New Haven.

Volumes 1–7 of **Children's Literature** can be obtained directly from John C. Wandell, The Children's Literature Foundation, Box 370, Windham Center, Conn. 06280.

Scapple, Sharon Marie. "The Child as Depicted in English Children's Literature from 1780–1820." Ph.D. diss. University of Minnesota, 1983. 383 pp. DAI 44:762A.

The purpose of Scapple's dissertation is "to discover the relationships between the portrayal of the child in literature and societal attitudes toward children."

Schroeter, Joan Gitzel. "The Canfield-Cleghorn Correspondence: Two Lives in Letters." Ph.D. diss. Northern Illinois University, 1993. 625 pp. DAI 54:1369A.

Seme, Phillipine Jane Nomathemba. "South African Teachers' Perspectives on Teaching Beginning Reading." Ed.D. diss. Harvard University, 1993. 282 pp. DAI 54:3357A.

Shannon, Donna M. "Children's Responses to Humor in Fiction." Ph.D. diss. University of North Carolina at Chapel Hill, 1993. 255 pp. DAI 54:4381A.

Noting that children do not read much, either at school or during leisure, Shannon makes a case for giving children humorous material to read.

Sheltag, Hussein Abdul-Azim. "The Influence of the *Arabian Nights* upon Nineteenth Century English Fiction." Ph.D. diss. University of Exeter (United Kingdom), 1989. 242 pp. DAI 51:868A.

Smith, Florence Mood. "The Effects of Story Structure Training upon First Graders' Memory and Comprehension of Wordless Picture Books." Ph.D. diss. University of Maryland, College Park, 1986. 148 pp. 47:3722A.

Stroinigg, Cordelia E. "A Reinterpretation of Sudermann's *Frau Sorge:* Jugendstil, Archetype, Fairy Tale." Ph.D. diss. University of Cincinnati, 1984. 283 pp. DAI 35:3A.

Sullivan, Patricia Rosalind. "Children's Literature as a Tool for Teaching Second Language to Adolescents." Ph.D. diss. Claremont Graduate School and San Diego State University, 1994. 159 pp. DAI 55:496A.

Sullivan uses picture books to teach French and finds that students' awareness of culture and language is greatly enhanced.

Swift, Gwendolyn Walker. "Effects of a Children's Book and a Traditional Textbook on Third-Grade Students' Achievement and Attitudes toward Social Studies." Ed.D. diss. Oklahoma State University, 1993. 82 pp. DAI 54:1752A.

Using four third-grade classes, Swift evaluates the effect of different texts on a child's ability to learn social studies. She found that knowledge acquisition did not differ much among groups but that children preferred children's books and preferred to be read to rather than read.

Thaden, Barbara Zembachs. "The Maternal Voice in Victorian Fiction: Rewriting the Patriarchal Family." Ph.D. diss. University of North Carolina at Chapel Hill, 1994. 226 pp. DAI 55:1571A.

Thaden discusses the representation of motherhood by women who were writers: Charlotte Brontë, Elizabeth Gaskell, and Margaret Oliphant.

Thompson, Barbara Clare. "Curriculum Theory in Action: A Case of Children's Literature in Teacher Education." Ph.D. diss. University of Arizona, 1993. 305 pp. DAI 55:937A.

Thompson attempts to create a "theory of content" for preservice teachers.

Wiedmer, Caroline Alice. "Reconstructing Sites: Representations of the Holocaust in Postwar Literary, Cinematic and Memorial Texts." Ph.D. diss. Princeton University, 1994. 245 pp. DAI 55:1554A.

Wiedmer studies postwar literary and film texts, particularly comic books.

Williams, Amelia Louise. "Venus' Hand: Laughter and the Language of Children's Culture in the Poetry of Christina Rossetti, Edith Sitwell, Edna St. Vincent Millay and Stevie Smith." Ph.D. diss. University of Virginia, 1993. 350 pp. DAI 54:3048A.

Withrington, John Kenneth Brookes. "The Death of King Arthur and the Legend of His Survival in Sir Thomas Malory's 'Le Morte d'Arthur' and other Late Medieval

Texts of the Fifteenth Century." D.Phil. diss. University of York (United Kingdom), 1991. 242 pp. DAI 52:3297A.

Zehr, Janet Susan. "Louisa May Alcott and the Female Fairy Tale." Ph.D. diss. University of Illinois at Urbana-Champaign, 1985. 221 pp. DAI 46:3355A.

Zehr concludes that because Alcott so often wrote "formulaic fiction 'to suit customers', as she put it, [her] real opinions about women and their roles elude the reader."

Zipper, Freya Johnson. "A Descriptive Study of Selected Fifth- and Eighth-Grade Students' Involvement with Futuristic Science Fiction." Ed.D. diss. University of Georgia, 1985. 179 pp. DAI 47:111A.

Zipper finds that students chose to read science fiction "because of its predictive nature and its images of the future" as well as the fact that it is more imaginative or dramatic than most literature for children.

Contributors and Editors

FRANCES ARMSTRONG is author of *Dickens and the Concept of Home* (Ann Arbor: UMI, 1989) and has published articles on Dickens, Louisa May Alcott, and Olive Schreiner. She has recently completed *Pocket Companions: Women, Girls, and Dolls* and is working on a study of the associations between women and littleness.

SUSAN P. BLOOM directs the Center for the Study of Children's Literature at Simmons College, the nation's first Master of Arts in Children's Literature degree program. With Cathryn M. Mercier she published a biocritical study titled *Presenting Zibby Oneal* (Twayne, 1991) and has contributed widely to children's literature journals.

HAMIDA BOSMAJIAN is professor of English and director of the Honors Program at Seattle University, where she teaches courses in children's literature and law and literature. Her publications usually focus on literature for young readers about Nazism and the Holocaust. What intrigued her in Taylor's trilogy was the possibility of legal and social transformation through the law. Unlike Nazism, which legalized and licensed murderous persecution, the constitutional frame in American society enables people to change and transform unjust state laws.

RUTH B. BOTTIGHEIMER, adjunct associate professor of comparative literature at the State University of New York at Stony Brook, has recently completed a study of change in Bible stories for young readers, *The Bible for Children from the Age of Gutenberg to the Present*.

FRANCELIA BUTLER, founding editor of *Children's Literature*, has published many books on children's literature, including *Skipping Around the World: The Ritual Nature of Folk Rhymes*.

JOHN CECH's most recent children's book is *The Southernmost Cat* (Simon and Schuster). His study of Maurice Sendak, *Angels and Wild Things*, is reviewed in this issue. He teaches in the English Department at the University of Florida in Gainesville.

R. H. W. DILLARD, editor-in-chief of *Children's Literature* and professor of English at Hollins College, is the longtime chair of the Hollins Creative Writing Program and is adviser to the director of the Hollins Graduate Program in Children's Literature. A novelist and poet, he is also the author of two critical monographs, *Horror Films* and *Understanding George Garrett*, as well as articles on Ellen Glasgow, Vladimir Nabokov, Federico Fellini, Robert Coover, Fred Chappell, and others.

ANITA CLAIR FELLMAN, who teaches women's studies and history at Old Dominion University, is completing a book on the place of the Laura Ingalls Wilder Little House books in American culture.

RACHEL FORDYCE, former executive secretary of the Children's Literature Association, has written five books, most recently *Semiotics and Linguistics in Alice's Worlds* with Carla Marello. She is a professor of English and the dean of humanities and social sciences at Montclair State University.

ELIZABETH N. GOODENOUGH has taught English at Harvard, Claremont McKenna College, and the University of Michigan. She coedited *Infant Tongues: The Voice of the Child in Literature* (1994) and has published articles on Nathaniel Hawthorne, Laura Ingalls Wilder, and Virginia Woolf.

ANDREW GORDON is associate professor of English at the University of Florida, where he teaches American literature and science fiction. He is the author of *An American Dreamer: A Psychoanalytic Study of the Fiction of Norman Mailer* and is completing a book on the films of Steven Spielberg. He has written on Le Guin's fiction for children in the *Dictionary of Literary Biography*, volume 52: *American Writers for Children since 1960: Fiction*, and is an editorial consultant for *Science-Fiction Studies*.

HOLLY KELLER, who lives in West Redding, Connecticut, is the author and illustrator of over thirty books for children. She has a strong interest in American intellectual history and is currently working on captivity stories in American children's literature.

ELIZABETH LENNOX KEYSER, editor of volumes 22–24, is an associate professor of English at Hollins College, where she teaches children's literature, American literature, and American studies. Her book *Whispers in the Dark: The Fiction of Louisa May Alcott* (University of Tennessee Press) won the 1993 Children's Literature Association Book Award. She is currently writing the volume on *Little Women* for the Twayne Masterwork Series.

CATHRYN M. MERCIER, an assistant professor at Simmons College, is associate director of the Center for the Study of Children's Literature. She is coauthor with Susan P. Bloom of *Presenting Zibby Oneal* (Twayne, 1991), chaired the 1993 Boston Globe-Horn Book Award Committee, served on the 1994 Caldecott Committee, and regularly reviews for *The Five Owls*.

CLAUDIA MILLS is an assistant professor of philosophy at the University of Colorado at Boulder and the author of many children's books, including *Dynamite Dinah, Dinah for President,* and *Hannah on Her Way*. In children's literature, she has written articles on books about orphans, books about young entrepreneurs, and the Twins series of Lucy Fitch Perkins.

MITZI MYERS teaches writing, children's literature, and adolescent literature at UCLA. She is finishing the first of two studies of Maria Edgeworth and is editing several volumes of Edgeworth. She's especially interested in historical children's literature and cultural studies (including theories of play) and feminist criticism.

JEAN PERROT is professor of comparative literature at Paris-Nord University. He is the author of *Henry James, une écriture énigmatique* (1982), *Du jeu, des enfants et des livres* (1987), and *Art baroque, art d'enfance* (1991), as well as articles in *Children's Literature* and the *ChLA Quarterly*.

SUZANNE RAHN is associate professor of English at Pacific Lutheran University and director of the Children's Literature Program. She is the author of *Children's Literature: An Annotated Bibliography of the History and Criticism* (Garland, 1981) and *Rediscoveries in Children's Literature* (Garland, 1995). She is currently editing an anthology of research and criticism on *St. Nicholas Magazine* with Susan Gannon and Ruth Anne Thompson as well as writing a book for the Twayne Masterwork Series on *The Wonderful Wizard of Oz*.

COLLEEN REARDON is assistant professor of music at the State University of New York at Binghamton. Professor Reardon's research interests center on musical culture in the Tuscan city of Siena during the Baroque. In 1993, Oxford University Press published her *Agostino Agazzari and Music at Siena Cathedral, 1597–1641*. Most recently, with the help of a stipend from the National Endowment for the Humanities, Reardon has been investigating musical performance in Sienese female monasteries of the Seicento.

CAROLYN LEUTZINGER RICHEY teaches at San Diego State University. Her essay "Doubles, Duality, and the Dilemma of Mark Twain's *Pudd'nhead Wilson*," presented at the 1993 Conference on the State of Mark Twain Studies, at Elmira, New York, will appear in a collection of essays on *Pudd'nhead Wilson* to be published by the University of Alabama Press. She recently edited a collection of essays written by year-round educators who participated in the San Diego State University and the National Endowment for the Humanities' Institute on Children's Literature entitled "Understanding Fantasy."

CAROLYN SIGLER is an assistant professor of English at Kansas State University, where she teaches children's literature, popular culture, and cultural studies. She has edited